GAMES WITH THE DEAD

James 'Jim' Nally began his reporting career at the Westmeath Independent in the Irish midlands before moving to London and working for National News Press Agency in the early 1990s.

As the agency's crime reporter, he covered Old Bailey trials and prepared in-depth 'backgrounders' for the national newspapers on all major cases in Southern England between '92 and '94.

His unfortunate expertise in the case of serial killer Rose West saw Nally recruited as a TV researcher by Channel 4's Dispatches. Since then he has directed documentaries on a gallery of rogues that include Kenneth Noye, Charles Bronson (the one from Luton), a set of unhinged Swedish twins who ran amok on the M1 (one of Louis Theroux's must-see docs), prison escapees, gem hunters and charity fundraising companies.

Nally has ghost written a number of books about yet more rogues, including IRA infiltrator 'Kevin Fulton' and the mercenary Simon Mann.

Although his official address is in Brighton, he spends most of his time at Southern Rail's pleasure, battling in and out of London. He has a partner Bridget and two children, James and Emma.

By the same author:

Alone with the Dead
Dance with the Dead

JAMES NALLY

Games with the Dead

This novel is entirely a work of fiction.
The names, characters and incidents portrayed in it are the work of the author's imagination. Any resemblance to actual persons, living or dead, events or localities is entirely coincidental.

AVON

A division of HarperCollins*Publishers*
1 London Bridge Street
London, SE1 9GF

www.harpercollins.co.uk

A Paperback Original 2017
1

A catalogue record for this book is available from the British Library

ISBN 978-0-00-814957-4

Typeset in Sabon LT Std by
Palimpsest Book Production Ltd, Falkirk, Stirlingshire

Printed and bound by CPI Group (UK) Ltd, Croydon CR0 4YY

Acknowledgments

First, to the people who so blessed this book with their patience and talent. Rachel Faulkner-Willcocks, the frankly brilliant editor at Avon. Razor-sharp copy editor Jade Craddock. PR whizz Sabah Khan, and Alison Groom, whose cover has so brilliantly evoked the essence of the book. Ed Wilson, literary agent at Johnson and Alcock and all-round rock of support and humour.

Thanks to Ben Mason, aptly-named literary agent and sculptor of rough talent, and Katy Loftus, whose verve and vision made this happen in the first place.

Thanks to those reviewers and writers who so kindly supported the previous two; Raven Crime Reads, Anne Cater, Liz Barnsley, John Sturgis and Tania 'Boo' Findlay of the *Sun*, Deirdre O'Brien and Nigel Atkins of the *Mirror*, Brook Cottage Books, Killing Time, Writing.ie, Books and Writers, Patricia Lenehan, Starry Marilyn, Crime Book Junkie, Bloomin' Brilliant Books, Claire Knight, Mairead Hearne, Short Book and Scribes.

Thanks to those TV stalwarts for their unwavering support and friendship; Bruce and Sam Goodison, Paul Crompton, Adam Wishart, Emma Shaw, Andy Wells, Kathryn Johnson,

Jeremy Hall, Duncan Moir, Laura Dunne, Peter Roemmele, Robert Gould, Paul and Max Williams, Hugh Williams and Andrew Mason.

Thanks to my good friends and endless sources of raw material; Ian and Zara Gallagher, Dennis Rice, Alison Clements, Frank and Elaine Roche, David and Sheila Hayes, Paul and Gaynor Morgan, Vincent Gribbin, the Bracken clan of Moate.

Thanks to my in-laws, the McGraths, for their Trojan support, especially Jim 'the Croc' and Anita. And to the Nally clan, especially my parents Jim and Bun, for always being there.

Special thanks to the three people who sacrifice so much so that I can get this done; my son James Nally, daughter Emma Nally and partner Bridget McGrath.

For Bridget, James and Emma.

Prologue

We all know Julie Draper now. Her twenty-four-year-old, shyly smiling face is everywhere. Can it really be just nine days since she rushed out of her estate agent's office in south London to show a client around a house, only to vanish into thin air? The hunt for Julie Draper goes on. Only two people know she's already dead. The man who killed her.

And me.

It's this cursed 'gift' of mine, you see. These Games with the Dead that I'm forced to play. Julie comes to me at night now, just like the others did before, haunting and tormenting me. And I know she won't quit. Not until I find her killer.

Don't judge me. *Please*. I'm not a dangler of wind chimes or a martyr to the Tarot. I'm a cop, for Christ's sake, a veritable tank of scepticism. That's why I'm so desperate to find a clinical explanation for these close encounters with the recently whacked.

Several shrinks on, I'm told its sleep paralysis, but with an inexplicable twist. Whereas sufferers typically hallucinate traditional 'bogeymen' figures, like demons, witches or aliens, I see people whose murders I'm investigating. More baffling still, these murder victims give me clues as to how they died.

There's nothing in their esteemed medical journals covering that . . .

Which is why I've never bought into this Sleep Paralysis quackery. Neither has my jaded girlfriend Zoe: 'More like Ambition Paralysis.' Or my hard-bitten hack brother: 'It's the DTs.' I didn't expect Mam to clear it all up for me like she did, on her deathbed. Presenting me the answer, wrapped in a family curse.

A curse I'm too scared to open.

Turns out mine is a 'gift' that just keeps taking. And taking. I'm twenty-five years old; trying to come to terms with an unthinkable new reality.

It's 50/50 I won't make it to thirty.

Chapter 1

New Scotland Yard, London
A few days earlier. Wednesday, June 15, 1994; 19.00

'It's not too late to pull out you know, Donal.' Commander Neil Crossley, Head of the Kidnap Unit, stares through my eyes into a future he barely dares to contemplate: 'If he's going to kill Julie Draper, there's no reason why he won't kill you. And we know he's killed before.'

But I know there can be no turning back now. I've got something to prove. To 'Croissant' Crossley. To my brother Fintan. To Zoe, my perennially disappointed partner. The kidnapper might be getting his ransom money, but the payback will be all mine.

Julie Draper's abductor has named his price. Crown Estates – her employer – must cough up £175,000 cash for her 'safe return'. He nominated Julie's estate agent colleague, Tom Reynolds, to deliver the cash. Any sign of police or media involvement during 'the drop', he'll kill both.

Crown Estates gambled on drafting in the police. Commander Crossley is gambling on a Tom Reynolds-lookalike to deliver the cash.

Me.

I'd never won a lookalike competition before.

Crossley remembered me from a previous attachment to the Kidnap Unit, thought me a ringer for Reynolds, rang me personally to ask if I 'felt up to becoming part of a top-secret operation'. Having spent the past eighteen months in a career Limbo – languishing in the Cold Case Unit as an 'Acting' Detective Constable – I agreed immediately.

My new status as hero-in-waiting has already propelled me into exalted company. Yesterday, I accompanied Crossley to New Scotland Yard's treasury, where we collected a Crown Estates cheque for 175k. Siren wailing, we floored it to a bullion centre in Chancery Lane, where we exchanged the cheque for equal numbers of £50, £20 and £10 used notes, just as the kidnapper had specified.

What a scene those 7,750 notes made! We then whisked the windfall back to technical support at the Yard, who spent the night painstakingly videotaping each note's serial number.

As if reading our every move, a second ransom note lands this morning with an additional demand: £5,000 in two bank accounts with cash cards and PIN numbers. Our nemesis knows that the serial numbers from cash machines can't be traced. He can use this 'clean' cash to travel anywhere in Europe to launder the dirty money. Our target is so smart, so well-informed, he reads our every move. Many of my colleagues are convinced he's done this before. Or that he's one of us, a serving or ex-cop, with a snout inside the investigation.

Today is our last chance to find out. To collect the ransom, he has to break cover. As in any extortion case, this represents our best and, possibly, only chance of catching the culprit.

We return to New Scotland Yard, take the lift to tech

support on the third floor and sign for receipt of a black Head sports bag with a transmitter sewn into the base. As per the ransom note instructions, we divide the cash into thirty-one equal units of 250 notes, wrapping each bundle in polythene no more than twelve microns thick. Crossley inserts the cash cards into one of the bricks, but trousers the piece of paper revealing their PIN codes.

'A little insurance,' he says. 'No matter what happens today, he'll have to get back to us for these.'

We stack the bundles together and gift-wrap them in brown paper. As per a diagram enclosed with the ransom note, Crossley uses nylon cord to secure the parcel, with a substantial loop on top. Why the kidnapper is insisting on certain specifics, we've yet to figure out. We place the loot carefully inside the sports bag so as not to disturb the transmitter, then head to the operational hub in East Croydon, just south of London.

As I get trussed up in a bulletproof vest, Crossley re-reads the kidnapper's delivery brief.

'At 9pm, the courier must await a call at the Mercury public phone in the foyer of East Croydon train station. He'll be given instructions and a trail to follow, which will take him from phone box to phone box over quiet roads so that the presence of police surveillance vehicles or aircraft will be detected. Any publicity or apparent police action will result in no further communication.' Crossley glances up: 'Which means he'll kill Julie Draper, and he'll probably kill you.'

As I refuse to let that sink in, he gets back to the kidnapper's instructions: 'Once the courier gets to the drop-off point, the money will not be collected by me, but by a young male who parks up in a nearby lovers' lane for a few hours every Wednesday night. His female companion will be held hostage while I direct the male to bring the cash to me via a two-way radio. Once I receive the cash, I will reveal Julie's location via an anonymous call to a media outlet, using the code phrase "Is Kipper a red herring?"'

Crossley folds the paper precisely, as if securing it for posterity, then searches my eyes deeply. For weakness? For reassurance? I can't tell, but it's a real ransacking of the irises.

'Okay Donal, in your car is a two-way radio linked to the controller here in the operations room. He, in turn, is in touch with surveillance teams in front and behind you. You know about the transmitter in the money bag, so keep it with you at all times.'

My mind lags behind, conducting a dry run, seeking out pitfalls. 'He mentioned quiet roads. How close will these surveillance teams be? I don't want them blowing my cover.'

'They're the best in the business, Donal, shadowed IRA terrorists, underworld hitmen, the lot. They'll be in constant contact with a stealth chopper who'll follow the suspect once he picks up the money. Look, if you remember just one instruction tonight, Donal, it's that these surveillance teams need to know the kidnapper's every move. Each time you get a fresh set of instructions, pass them on. You must get back into your car and repeat them over the radio, loud and clear, twice. You then wait five minutes before you drive on. Understood?'

I nod.

'I just can't wait to get it over with now, Guv,' I say brightly, diving into my car before his unflagging angst sucks the last bead of self-belief out of me. The door slams shut with a fatalistic thud.

'Actually, there is one last thing,' he says, passing me a note through the open window.

It's Met-police-headed paper; the word 'Disclaimer' screams out from the bold, underlined first sentence.

'They just handed this to me,' he says, leaning down to my level, eyes sizing mine for a reaction. 'It's to show we haven't put you under any undue duress if, well, anything goes awry.'

'Undue duress?'

'You know what it's like these days, Donal,' he smiles lamely. 'All about protecting the brand.'

By the second line of legal gymnastics, I'm sufficiently bamboozled to quit reading, get signing and hand it back.

'I expect this is going to be tortuous, Donal, but you must try to concentrate at all times. Be prepared for a last-second change. A sudden contact. You must be ready for anything and everything. But follow his instructions to the letter.

'Absolutely no heroics. Remember, he may have an accomplice ready to kill Julie if anything goes wrong. It doesn't matter if the money or the man slip away tonight. It's all about getting Julie back, alive.'

He passes the sports bag slowly, almost reverentially, through the car window, as if handing over her very fate.

'We're counting on you, Donal. Because one mistake, and we've all got Julie Draper's blood on our hands.'

Chapter 2

East Croydon, South London
Wednesday, June 15, 1994; 20.50

At 9.40am the previous Tuesday, Julie Draper left her office on Church Road, Croydon to show a client around a four-bedroom house. She didn't come back. Her colleague, Tom Reynolds, checked out the house, found her car on the driveway, her house keys on the landing. No Julie.

He checked out her client. John West's phone number doesn't exist. The address he'd provided doesn't exist. The kidnap squad baulks at the name.

Seven years ago, estate agent Suzy Fairclough vanished in West London. Neither her body nor her abductor have ever been found. Also aged twenty-four and a brunette, Suzy had arranged to meet a client called 'Mr Kipper'.

'John West Kippers' are a British supermarket staple.

Has he struck again? Or is it some sort of twisted copycat attack? The kidnapper's methodology has convinced senior officers that their fishiest nemesis is back.

The meticulous, almost obsessive attention to detail is the crowning Kipper hallmark. His demand, for example, that the ransom cash be wrapped in polythene twelve microns thick is a direct steal from the Fairclough abduction. Tech wizards have figured out why; through plastic that thin any bugs we might hide in the cash can be detected by a bog-standard, shop-bought metal detector.

Yesterday morning's proof-of-life phone call had also been classic Kipper. He rang Julie's office from a public phone box and played a tape recording of her reading headlines from that day's *Daily Mirror* newspaper. He made the call from a non-digital exchange, which takes longer to trace. But trace it we did, to Worthing on the south coast.

In another parallel with the Suzy Fairclough abductor, the ransom letter had been typed on generic WH Smith stationery using an old Olivetti, the typewriter equivalent of a Model T Ford – so, impossible to trace. Once again, he'd been careful not to lick the envelope or stamp, or to leave prints, fibres or hairs.

Without a solid lead, detectives agreed to pay the ransom. To my surprise, there is no secret police slush fund to meet this kind of shakedown. Crown Estates had to raise the cash. Now it's my job to hand it over.

East Croydon train station finally looms into view, just as Crossley's forlorn prophecies perform another club-footed cancan across my aching crown. *Change his plan at any second . . . ready for anything and everything . . . one mistake and we've got Julie Draper's blood on our hands.*

I park up and brace myself for the kidnapper's first instruction; stand by the open car boot for 30 seconds. Presumably, he or his associates want to ensure I'm not harbouring a crack team of SAS midgets between the golf clubs and the jerry can.

Getting out unleashes a Grand National of competing terrors. They're led at the first by the very real fear he'll realise I'm *not* Tom Reynolds. What then? I yank down my baseball cap's stiff peak until it fringes my vision. I take the holdall of cash and my identifying 'Crown Estates' clipboard from the back seat, walk to the car boot, open it and start to count. I feel exposed, helpless, JFK in Dealey Plaza. I make it all the way to seven before cracking. Boot still open, I set off pacing and weaving through people outside the station, taking sudden, wild turns like a coursed hare. If he's planning a head shot, he'll need to be Robin fucking Hood.

I rush to thirty, shut the boot and hotfoot into the station foyer. To my left, I spot the metallic-blue Mercury public phone he's selected for our cosy chat. It's framed by a glass hood, open at the front, New York-style. I wonder why he's selected such an exposed phone, and hover there twitchily, head scoping in case of ambush. Through the frosted glass of a nearby waiting room, a frowning man peers out. Kidnapper or cop? Who can tell? Opposite me, two scruffy men in their twenties loiter outside the ticket office. One of them clocks my clipboard and approaches. I stiffen.

'Are you doing a survey?' he asks brightly.

'No, I'm waiting for a phone call.'

He raises his arm. I flinch. Calmly, he reaches past me, lifts the receiver, checks for a dialling tone and replaces it. 'Well it's working,' he says chirpily and returns to his pal. Kidnapper? Undercover cop? Mercury Communications telephone angel? Who knows.

A thunderous rumble grows inside the station. I step out from my glass arch to see an army of knackered, dead-eyed commuters march up a walkway towards me, looking set to sack the city. As they storm the ticket barriers, I scan their addled, timetable-enslaved faces.

Ready for anything and everything . . .

He could be one of them, ready to pluck the bag from my grasp and sprint to a getaway car.

No one stops. No one even looks. All hopes of a swift exchange evaporate.

I sag and step back, my back raging hot against the phone's cold metal. The money bag's strap burns a timely reminder into my left shoulder blade; I'm standing here alone with everything he wants. What if he's watching me, planning to pounce? Who would save me?

I scan again. Those surveillance officers are either very good or very not here. The phone's shrill ring lifts me six inches off the floor. I pick up, killing the ring and every other sound in the world, as if it has ceased spinning. I picture birds tumbling out of the sky, landing with a thud on Croydon concrete.

Cold hard plastic cools my scorching right ear. 'Yes,' I croak.

'Tom Reynolds?'

'That's me.'

'What's your car reg?' demands the Geoff Boycott soundalike.

My addled mind empties like a toppled glass. I can't even remember my own licence plate!

I whimper. He barks: 'Make, model, colour?'

'Nissan Bluebird. Maroon.'

I hear a muffled rustle. 'Parked outside the station,' I hear him say, faintly, as if to someone else. *He's got watchers!*

'Get back into your car,' he demands, tetchily. 'Follow signs for the M23 and A23 to Brighton. When you see a sign saying Brighton 8 miles, look out for the next left, the A273. Take the exit. On the left after 200 yards you'll see a lay-by with two phone boxes. The first is a phone card kiosk. Taped beneath the shelf will be an envelope containing a new set of instructions.'

'My God,' I sigh into the dead phone. 'The world's grimmest treasure hunt.'

I almost run back to the car to parrot the details, then wait five agonising minutes before setting off south. Signs for Penge, Riddlesdown and Titsey flash past, making me wonder if every Croydon suburb is named after some squalid seventeenth-century disease. It would seem fitting. All I see are rows and rows of houses punctuated by identikit shopping parades, invariably featuring an estate agent, bookmaker, greasy spoon café, off-licence, post office, pharmacy and funeral parlour.

There's the futility and emptiness of modern life, right there, I think, in my fug of fatalistic gloom. Each cluster of shops tells our real-life story: you buy a house, spend your life paying for it, cheer yourself up gambling, drinking and eating shit, get ill, old and die.

Zap! The suburbs vanish to a vast, velvet night-sky being munched on by tiny, shiny, Pac-Men; on closer inspection, aircraft queueing to land at Gatwick airport.

'Sunset Boulevard,' Fintan calls the A23, leading as it invariably does to sun-kissed excess-by-sea. Not tonight. The prospect of messing up in the South Downs yanks my knotted guts to twanging.

Be prepared for a last-second change. A sudden contact.

Crossley's ceaseless advice drowns out all self-soothing inner monologues.

If he's going to kill Julie Draper, there's no reason why he won't kill you . . .

Christ, poor Matt. My sweet, adorable stepson. The single best thing ever to happen in my life. Why am I taking this risk?

None of this is *Matt's* fault. Stupid selfish grown-ups. I'm sure Zoe and I will be okay. We're just in bit of a rut right now. Living together but not really *living* at all. It's all work, childcare and sleep deprivation. I know I'm doing this for her. I'm just not sure why. To impress her? To prove myself? To make her worry about me? In place of an answer, I've coined a mantra: *If I get through this, everything will be better.* I'll have proven myself, to her, to me. We'll get back to how it was. She'll look at me in that way again, eyes soft and warm. Smile at my corny gags. Sleep facing me.

But doubt, like night, has swallowed the last of the half-light.

A ghostly white sign shimmers in the gusty, malcontent air. I squint it into focus: 'Brighton 8 miles'.

I slow to 40 and strain my eyes. The A273 slip road loops around so that I'm now heading north again; Brighton-bound A23 traffic pounds past to my left, headlights mercilessly fanning the lay-by like ravenous searchlights. The phone boxes command centre stage, spotlit by an amber streetlight. Good visibility brings mixed tidings; easier to see, harder to flee.

My car creeps into the lay-by, past the phone boxes. I perform a laboured three-point turn, helping myself to a 180-degree, headlight-illuminated view of the lay-by and the A273 beyond. I'm expecting the glint of hidden back-up cars, the outlines of poised police Ninjas. I see neither. Dread claws at my insides like a trapped rat. Surveillance are in front and behind. But they're not here. It's just me and him.

'Right, I've pulled up at the phone box,' I inform the dashboard's covert radio, squeezing into my baseball cap and forensic gloves. I leave the car engine idling, my headlights beaming so that at least my non-existent back-up can see me.

I lean back, grab the money bag and step out. The trees shiver like widows at the workhouse door. Gravel crunches beneath my feet, but I can't feel it. Halfway across, I spin 360. Nothing.

I jog to the phonebox, open it, the door squealing like

teeth down a violin. I palm the underside of the cold metal shelf, feel paper, yank it free. The small brown envelope has double-sided tape on each corner. I turn over to see a giant letter 'A' scrawled in black marker. *Christ*, I think, *how far through the alphabet is he planning to take me tonight?*

Sprinting back to the car, I throw the cash in the back, get in, lock the doors and rummage inside the envelope. I flick on my pencil torch and read the instructions, typed on a cut-down piece of A4 paper.

This route will show if you're being followed.
Continue on B273 for 75 yards.
Take Underhill Lane to right.
After 100 yards bear left (signposted public bridleway).
150 yards down is a small outbuilding on left.
Pick up black bag by red / white cone.
Further message in bag.
On reading the message, transfer money parcel from your holdall into this bag.
Take money and bag with you.

I repeat the instructions twice, then endure the longest five minutes of my life, at least since Matt's last car-based meltdown. God how he'd hate this; twenty minutes is the most he can take, almost to the second, before he kicks off against his car seat's straitjacket straps and sweat-sucking foam. I've found only one remedy to pacify us both; belting out nursery rhymes at full pelt.

Fuck it, I think, and launch into an impassioned version of *Wheels on the Bus*. Somehow, it works, banishing all terror so that by the time I take the right turn into Underhill Lane, I'm wondering what a bobbin is and lamenting the existential plight of Incy Wincy spider.

Hedges join hands above me, so it's a virtual tunnel. Potholes swallow individual wheels whole, rattling my teeth with such ferocity that I have to sing Postman Pat in scat.

I fork left onto the bridle path. My headlights pick out the unmistakeable metallic shape of a car buried deep in bushes. My heart throbs in my ears and behind my right eye.

'Donal?' crackles the two-way radio.

'Jesus,' I yelp; Crossley's urgent whisper just snapped my last functioning nerve.

Sounding like a snooker commentator, he husks: 'The bridle track is through open fields. He'll be able to see and hear surveillance vehicles.'

'Which means?'

'They can't risk following you.'

'Shit.'

'That's not all,' oozes Crossley. 'He's taking us so far out of range that our radio signals are getting weaker.'

'Spit it out for fuck's sake.'

'Listen carefully, Donal. Just because you can't hear us doesn't mean we can't hear you. Carry on as before. Repeat his instructions twice aloud and wait five minutes before proceeding. Just make sure we know his plans. Understood?'

'Great, so any second now, I'll be completely alone with this madman?'

Silence. Then a faint thwack dices the air; the reverberation of distant rotor blades.

'If I can hear a chopper then so can he. Call it off, for the love of God.'

'That may be our sole means of trailing you,' snaps Crossley, sounding posher now, under pressure.

'Then don't.'

The chopper's blades melt away to deathly silence, save for my juddering trundle.

'Have you at least got visuals on me sir?' I beg the silence.

The radio's dead. I'm on my own. My palpitating heart thrums against the seat belt, creating an unnerving sash of terror.

Four little ducks went swimming one day . . . I scat, sounding like Tom Waits strapped to a bucking bronco.

Sneering gargoyle vegetation melts away to something scarier; vast and empty night-sky nothingness.

I'm out in the wide open now, alone and exposed, completely at the mercy of this maniac. Of course, he knows that police radio signals don't work out here. He's been one step ahead of us all along.

The rutted track slows me to a bumpy walking pace. For all I know, he could be strolling alongside, gun trained at my temple. Maybe he's just waiting for me to pull up and get out, so he can soundlessly throttle me in the warm night breeze before spiriting away with the cash.

And no little duck came back quack, quack . . .

'I'm so sorry Matt, and Zoe,' I blurt, like some deathbed confessor. How I wish I was home with them right now, where I should be.

'We're picking you up again, Donal,' crackles Crossley's strangled whisper, jolting me back into cop mode.

'Thank Christ,' I mouth.

My feeble headlights suddenly pick out neat vertical lines. I squint, pulling into focus a wet corrugated tin roof weighing down a squat and long-forgotten outhouse. In this ocean of wet black, my eyes seize suddenly upon a luminous mini-lighthouse; a red and white traffic cone.

'Holy shit,' I whisper. 'It's the endgame. I'm approaching the traffic cone and, I presume, the bag. Sir?'

'Awaiting instructions.'

I pull up and look around. All black. I figure if he's here, my best hope of survival is to offer up the cash, the car and no resistance. I get out, headlights on, driver's door open, key in the ignition, cash on the back seat.

'Go ahead, Kipper, stitch me right up,' I cry.

I take a swift 360. Nothing. All I feel is night's balmy breath. All I hear is water slapping tin. I take another 360, my heart thrashing like a trapped bird.

'The money's in the car,' I shout.

Wind gasps, water splats.

I make out the black canvas ransom bag at the foot of the cone, empty, deflated, expectant. I palm it open, rummage until I feel a single sheet of paper in the base. I take both to the car. Sliding into the back seat next to the cash, I lock the doors, switch on my torch and, as instructed, transfer the daintily-wrapped parcel of cash into his bag. Somehow, he must have guessed that we'd plant some sort of a tracking device in ours. 'Ah well,' I soothe my pogoing heart. 'I should be dumping it soon and getting the hell out of here.' The note, stencilled in black capital letters, has other ideas. I read it aloud:

Go back to Underhill Lane.
Turn left towards Ditchling village.
Phone box 1.5 miles on left.
Message B taped under shelf.

My tired brain grapples with these latest commandments. To collect his money, the kidnapper needs to be at the end of this ransom trail. That means he can't be here. Adrenaline zaps off like a light. All life leaves me, clenched muscles melting to jelly.

'This is good news,' declares Crossley, sounding like a local radio DJ relinquishing his star prize. 'We should have no problems with radio signals at that end of Underhill Lane, so we can resume full surveillance. I've got an officer on standby briefed and ready to take over from you before then, Donal. You've had more than enough excitement for one night.'

'I'd like to see it through to the end, sir,' I say, solely because I expect that's what any decent cop *should* say.

'I admire your pluck. Give me ten minutes to get the lead surveillance team into position at the next phone box. Then I'll be en route with your replacement. Your night is nearly over, Lynch. Good work.'

'Thanks be to God,' I mouth, and set about turning the car on the narrow track.

I crawl back towards the overgrowth of Underhill Lane. As I slip into the hedgerow tunnel and radio silence, I help myself to a 'Thank fuck that's over.'

Out of nowhere, a red Stop sign appears, blocking the route.

'What the fuck?' I protest to no one.

I ease the car closer, spot a square of white card beneath the circular sign. I squint and recognise more stencilled instructions

'Sir. Sir can you hear me?'

I know he can't.

My heart revs hard, a pang of sickening realisation sending bile north. I swallow the burn and fight to breathe against that re-clamped chest. The kidnapper sent the cavalry east almost ten minutes ago, and stayed right here. For me. This is his sting-in-the-tail twist. He's got me precisely where he wants me now, all alone, no back-up, no comms, no hope of rescue, flush with 175 grand.

Shit.

My only way out of this is to do what he wants. I get out, read the instructions.

On wall by painted cross find wood tray.
Do not move tray, sensor attached.
Place money bag on tray.
If buzzer does not sound leave money there.
Remove Stop sign in front of car and go.

He's watching me. I know it. And he's killed before. Seven years ago, he kidnapped and murdered Suzy Fairclough. What's another life sentence to him? I'm totally dispensable.

I remember Crossley's request that I pick up anything on the trail that may prove evidential. Good little soldier to the end, I remove the cardboard bearing the instructions, take it to the car and read the contents aloud twice, hoping against all common sense that they can hear me.

They can't fucking hear me! He's selected this spot for that very reason. And I'm not hanging around for five minutes to confirm it; not with 175 thousand in hard cash! He might lose patience and whack me.

I grab the money bag, walk over to a four-foot wall. Above a white painted cross, a wooden tray sits on a bed of sand. About 30 feet below, I can make out some sort of lane, maybe a disused rail line. A few feet to my right, an oblong metal box must be somehow connected to the tray's sensor.

Good God, I am so out of my depth . . .

Somehow, I've got to lower this hefty bag of cash onto the tray without tripping the alarm. Face screwed into a tense ball of dread, I lift the bag and lower it slowly, painstakingly, ion-by-quivering-ion onto the tray. It sits, rests, no alarm.

I wonder why I'm standing here and turn to leave. As I remove the Stop sign from the middle of the lane, the tray scrapes the side of the bridge on its way down, courtesy of his improvised pulley system. He's below, collecting his winnings.

I'm just yards away from the most wanted man in Britain.

Fuck it, I think. I 've got to *do something*.

Chapter 3

Underhill Lane, East Sussex
Wednesday, June 15, 1994; 21.50

We know nothing about this bastard. I need to spirit over to that bridge, at least get a visual. I pad and wince in turn, Bambi on ice, gripping that metal Stop sign like a lollipop lady in a tornado. If I can bounce this hunk of rust off his bonce, he won't be going anywhere.

Oh my God!

There he is below, shovelling spilled bricks of cash into the bag. I raise the metal pole to my chest. If I press Go on this Stop sign, he ain't going anywhere . . .

He may have an accomplice ready to kill Julie if anything goes wrong . . .

If he's operating alone . . . we'll never get a better chance.

The money will not be collected by me, but by a young male who parks up in a nearby lovers' lane . . .

Damn it! I can't be sure that's our man. I need to find a way down there, grab whoever it is and hold him here until back-up arrives.

No heroics . . . It's all about getting Julie back, alive.

What do I do? How I crave a working radio, a direct order.

Below, I hear the splutter and tinny whine of a 50cc engine spurting into life. Good God, he's wheezing off into the night aboard a 'nifty 50' scooter with 175 grand. And I'm the only one who knows. I've got to find Crossley.

I dump the Stop sign, dive into the car, gun the engine and floor it east as fast as the lane's laddered surface will allow.

After a couple of bends, fast-approaching headlights ignite the hedgerows. I screech to a halt. Crossley and DI Mann spring out before their oncoming car even stops.

'Where the hell have you been?' demands Crossley.

As I jabber my story, they inspect me in wide-eyed disbelief.

'Why didn't you call back-up?' barks Crossley.

'The radios aren't working down here, Guv. You know that.'

'Dear God,' spits Crossley. 'You've let him get away.'

'You said no heroics . . .'

He turns to his number two. 'Peter, get back-up there, radio all units that he's travelling south from Underhill Lane on a scooter or in a vehicle large enough to carry a scooter. Lynch, take me to the bridge.'

Right on, right on, I manage to stop myself singing as I jump into my car and grab the seat belt.

'Just drive,' he snaps.

'Sir, I can't turn here . . .'

'Reverse for Christ's sake.'

Every male cop on the planet thinks he's Damon Hill. Some, like Crossley, even own special leather gloves for the task which, when they're not driving, they dangle on their belts like spare penises. Alas, I'm less Damon Hill, more Benny, especially going backwards.

'Swap!' cries Crossley and I'm out of that driver's seat before he's spat the 'p'.

Crossley throws himself in, flings one elbow over my passenger seat. Palm-steering, he roars off backwards, beaching my poor car into every coccyx-crunching pothole along the way. My anger rises in tandem with my rev counter.

Over mashing metal and screaming suspensions, I shout: 'Why are you pissed off with me? You specifically said no heroics.'

'And I specifically instructed you, over and over, that you have a surveillance team in front *and* behind you that needs to know his every instruction.'

I don't get it but why distract him now, when we're careering backwards towards a brick wall in my beloved old banger? After a totally unnecessary handbrake turn, I'm tempted to request his insurance details. Instead, under orders, I perform a walk-through of the drop. I show him the stencilled message and the sensor on the bridge, which he goes over to inspect.

'Sensor?' he scoffs. 'It's a concrete block painted silver.'

'Yeah, well I can see that now sir, with the headlights shining directly on it. They weren't when I was last here.'

We find a way down to the disused railway line where, mercifully, at least the pulley-driven wooden tray and scooter tyre marks are real. Overhead, cars pull up, resigned. Scapegoat grumblings. Yes, he's vanished into that great black rural night, but I did everything I'd been told to do.

I follow Crossley back up to the bridge, where they turn to face us as one.

'He's long gone,' spits DI Peter Mann, his eyes not leaving Crossley's. 'We should've put one of us up front as soon as we got out here,' he rants. 'It's pitch bloody black. Kipper was never going to identify the delivery man.'

'We didn't know that,' says Crossley, firmly. 'We didn't

know a lot of things, Pete. Like the fact he'd take us somewhere our radio signals don't work.'

DI Mann switches his glare to me, full-beam. 'Why the fuck didn't you run back to your rear surveillance team? You could've shouted at them, they were that close.'

'We were 100 yards behind you,' chimes in a moustachioed man I've never clapped eyes on before. 'You're supposed to brief us after every instruction. You could've walked to our car. What were you thinking?'

My brain's flailing. The radios were down. I didn't know how close the rear surveillance officers were. I couldn't *see* them. Anyway, what could they have done? Any attempt to pursue the suspect would've put Julie's life in danger. That was the deal, right?

DI Mann's head wobbles in contempt. 'Your fuck-up has cost us vital minutes. You'd best hope it hasn't cost Julie Draper her life.'

Involuntarily, my eyes clench shut. *Please, please no. What have I done?*

Crossley dry-coughs back control. 'Let's save the post-mortem for tomorrow,' he snaps, checking his watch. 'If you're quick, the Lamb in Pyecombe should still be open. Go get a drink and calm down. I'll wait here for forensics.'

Off they shuffle, muttering bitterly. I've never needed a pint so badly in my life, even if I have to toothlessly slurp it off the lino once they're done kicking the shit out of me, so I follow at a distance.

DI Mann spins around: 'Where do you think you're going?'

I slouch back to Crossley.

'Don't bother coming in for a couple of days Lynch, give me a chance to sort out this mess . . .'

'Hands up, Guv, I forgot about the vehicle behind me. But what would my alerting them have achieved? Their radios weren't working either. And it's not like they could risk chasing him.'

He rubs his face vigorously with his open palms, as if clearing it of live scorpions.

He sighs hard: 'I thought I'd spelled it out to you.'

His hands drop and his eyes look up to the heavens.

'All that space-age tech up there, and I've got the village idiot down here.'

'Now hang on just a minute there, Guv . . .'

'I told you about your number one priority, Lynch, keeping your surveillance teams informed of each fresh instruction. Above us is a chopper with state-of-the-art thermal imaging, infra-red, you name it. Seventy-five grand to scramble. Ten grand an hour to fly.' He turns to me. 'I redirected the lead surveillance team but the rear one was still behind you and in direct contact with that chopper via satellite phone. I told you they were constantly in touch. I told you, if nothing else, make sure your surveillance teams are privy to his latest instructions.'

'But my radio went down.'

'Had you gone to the rear surveillance team, on foot, that chopper would now be covertly following whoever picked up the money, and only we would know. Instead, we've lost the money and we've lost him.'

An icy snake of terror unfurls inside me. 'Shit. What have I done.'

'I tell you what you've done,' snaps Crossley, voice cracking, eyebrows arched to breaking. 'Whoever kidnapped Julie has got his money, so he has no further use for her now. He can't risk freeing her because of what she might be able to tell us about him.'

His upper lip stiffens, reining in his swelling emotions.

'He *has* to kill Julie now,' he states flatly, as if passing sentence himself.

Chapter 4

Green Lanes, North London
Thursday, June 16, 1994; 02.30

Had the shonky Shiraz bottles I'd unearthed from some dodgy all-night *spieler* in Haringey not required two fully engaged man-arms to uncork against a solid surface, I'd never have spotted Zoe's note on our kitchen table.

Written at some point yesterday, it reads: *Me and Matt gone to mum's. Thought you could use a night off, Zoe x*

What a selfless, thoughtful act, you may think. But you don't know a sleep-deprived mum. And you aren't competing in the Martyred Parent Olympics (so-called because it lasts four years and, unless you imbibe massive quantities of illicit pharmaceuticals, you've no chance of winning).

What the note really means is: 'It doesn't matter how late you've been working, this is going down officially as a night off for you.' I'll be made to pay, of course; she'll yawn pointedly all day tomorrow, slam anything slam-able and consistently ring friends and family to update them about the latest phase of her *tooootal exhaaaaustion*.

Aged twenty-two months, Matt still wakes five or six times

a night – every night. Having an insomniac stepdad helps. I'm always on hand to slurp drinks, binge Babybels and loop *Pingu*. Thrillingly, at least for me, Matt's taken to calling my name when he wakes, or at least his version of Donal. 'Dong, Dong, Dong,' he chants. Who he doesn't call for is mum, because mum minus sleep equals Crazed Harridan.

I'm 'Dong' because Matt isn't my biological son. His 'real' dad, Chris, is a fugitive from fatherhood somewhere south of the Equator. A posh, feckless surfer-raver type, he fled as soon as Zoe fell pregnant – leaving the way free for my uncharacteristic crime scene seduction.

Yes, we met over a dead body! Zoe is a rising star in forensics who, somehow, failed to spot the clues to my myriad flaws. She agreed to go out with me, and it soon became clear why; her morale had hit rock bottom. She'd convinced herself that 'no man would want me, not now I come with a baby.'

I wanted her with all that I had. When I got to know Matt, I wanted him too. For the first time in my life, ever, I let instinct override indecision, seized the moment, got the girl! A few months later, we bought this place and I'm still in utter shock, clinging onto the cliff-face of overnight fatherhood. But I wouldn't change a thing.

Being a dad is quite a responsibility, and not one I'm taking lightly. Not only have I reduced my nightly quaffing to two bottles of Shiraz, I only buy the stuff that's less than 14% proof. Well you do anything for your kids, don't you? And Matt's my son now.

A few weeks back, Zoe caught us partying at 3am and announced her 'gravest fear' – that Matt has inherited my insomnia. I had to remind her that this is impossible – we're not flesh and blood – then hated her for appearing so patently relieved. I let it go because we never row in front of Matt, which means we never row. She seems to spend every second of her child-free leisure time avoiding me. Seriously, she's either out with her girlfriends, at her mum's or collapsed like a capsized Alp in bed, clad in those massive off-white 'comfort' knickers, previously used to hoist the Mary Rose.

I know we'll get back to how it was. *Of course we will.* Once we get over the exhaustion. And the constant illness. And the lack of money.

No wonder Crossley's call last week had come as such a shot in the arm. How I'd craved the chance to get drafted onto a 'live' investigation squad, make a good impression, become a fully-fledged detective constable and prove all my doubters wrong.

All I had to do was not fuck up . . .

What a selfish prick, I scold myself. The only thing that matters right now, after my potentially fatal blunder, is that Julie's okay. My insides wince, cowering from those stabs of raw, primeval terror. My stressed temples buzz, as if planted against the window of a speeding train. A low electric hum grows louder in my ears, until it whines like the world's largest mosquito. My vision flickers, causing objects in the room to float in different directions, as if something telepathic is breaking through.

My God, Julie?

Somewhere close by, a church bell clangs, over and over, louder and louder. I can see it's driving those ravens wild. They smash into the sitting room window – *thump, thump, thump* – flinging themselves against the glass with all of their might.

They're inside now, flapping close to my face. I can't scream or turn away or raise my hands. I can't move a muscle! All I can do is scan their beady green eyes. I remember suddenly their collective term: An Unkindness of

Ravens. And this lot look especially unkind. One launches, pecking at my face savagely. The others join in; a greedy, feeding frenzy. I scream as they pick and pull and gouge at my eyes until all goes black.

I'm suspended in the air now, looking down. The ravens are yanking off bits of Julie's face and body, then flying off, tiny fish flapping in their mouths. I'm holding a metal crook. I should be beating the birds away. But I don't.

I'm lying down again. Julie appears above me, eyes wild with hate, face tattered and torn like bloodied tissue paper. She holds the silver block directly over my face, but I see another man's bearded face in the reflection. Who is he? *Please don't drop it,* I beg her. *Please.*

The reflection in the block is me. I smile just as the head of an axe plants itself into the left side of my face, slicing into my cheekbone, above my ear. Indescribable, ringing pain springs me to my feet. I'm screaming, clawing at the axe. But it's not there.

'Oh my God,' I hear myself scream. 'Julie Draper's dead.'

Chapter 5

Green Lanes, North London
Thursday, June 16, 1994; 11.00

'Morning has fucking broken,' warbles Fintan, my older brother, yanking open the sitting room curtains. Why did I ever give him a key?

I scrunch my dry eyes against the searing white, but the glare scores my sight, summoning splodges and a pulsing star-scape. My day of destiny is here. No doubt Commander Crossley's already in his office, knotting the rope and oiling the trapdoor. Well *someone* will have to pay for last night's cock-up. I'm low-ranking police plankton with an already sullied disciplinary record; he couldn't have hand-picked a more ideal scapegoat.

I suspect Fintan has already heard all about last night from his fathomless pool of 'police contacts'. That's why he's here, the diabolical cock, to get the inside story. It's this level of conscience-free cunning that has propelled him to the role of chief crime reporter at the *Sunday News*, the youngest in their history.

'Why can't you warn me before you turn up,' I croak. 'You know, like a normal person?'

'You could've done with some of that last night,' he beams, eyes alive with mischief. 'Warning, I mean.'

I groan instant and complete surrender, but my own personal Josef Mengele hasn't even got started.

'I hear you literally presented the cash to him, on a tray, like some silver-service waiter,' he mocks in fake shock, shaking his head out of the sheer orgasmic schadenfreude of it all.

'You've taken such a keen interest in this case, Fintan. Especially since they imposed a media blackout.'

'Good job you've got that to hide behind. I can see the headline now: "Bungling cops lose man, money and poor Julie". There'd be an outcry.'

'You and your journo pals would whip up an outcry, you mean. Who uses words like 'bungling' in real life anyway?'

He's off on one of his streams-of-tabloid-consciousness. 'We'd have to describe Julie as "pretty" of course, which is a bit of a stretch, wouldn't you say, Donal? She reminds me of Linda McCartney, if she hadn't married a Beatle or given up the sausages. But we can't call her "lumpen and pasty", can we? She is the victim, after all. I tell you what though, photos of her make me want to stand on my head while chewing a sack of raw vegetables . . .'

'Jesus, Fintan! Have some respect . . .' I stop myself, but not quickly enough for old Donkey Ears.

'You were gonna say "for the dead", weren't you?' he says, turning towards me, nostrils almost winking. 'What do you know? Have they found her body?'

'No. I mean we don't even know she's dead. I'm just assuming the worst, now he's had his money. What use is she to him now?'

My voice cracks, straining to contain that geyser of inner terror. What if my stupidity last night led to Julie's murder? How am I supposed to cope with that? Live with that? I screw the lid down tighter. I know she's dead because she came to me last night. That's how this cursed bloody condition works. But I don't know how or when she died. There's still a chance he killed her *before* the ransom drop. That would mean her death is *not my fault*. It makes no sense at all but, for now, I've got to cling to that flimsy hope . . .

I scold my emotions for running ahead of the facts. All I know for sure is I must have got close to her dead body at some point either before, during or after last night's ransom drop. That's the only time the dead play their games with me . . . when I've been physically close to their recently slain cadavers. Poor, poor Julie . . .

Fintan recognises my pain and changes tack. 'I heard you got a lot of stick. Don't feel bad. Crossley should never have put you in that situation, not with your lack of experience.'

'Gee thanks, Fint, for such a typically back-handed show of, er, support.'

'It's not just your fault, Donal. The kidnapper outsmarted you all.'

'The worst thing is, Crossley just stood there and let them slag me off. After I'd risked my neck for him. Then he told me not to bother turning up for work until he tells me otherwise.'

'That's the British upper classes for you, Donal. They see the rest of us as grateful Sherpas, bred to do the heavy lifting that carries them to glory. Now hose yourself down or something so I can take you out in public. Then I'm going to make you eat a solid before flies start circling your eyes.'

'Don't spend the day trying to wheedle info out of me, Fintan.'

'You affront me, Donal. You really do. I come here to offer nothing more than comfort and cheer after your latest dismal and abject humiliation, and this is the thanks I get. Why do you always assume there's an angle? Jeez. I'll be outside having a fag.'

With Fintan, there is *always* an angle. Having arrived here in London from the Irish Midlands a few years before me, he sees himself as my protector, especially now Mam is dead. But Fintan is always a journalist first, my brother second and would sell my arse for a scoop without even realising he's done wrong. Zoe thinks he's warped, manipulative and amoral, which, most of the time, is hard to dispute.

I shower, dress and catch up with him at the garden gate, where he wheels around theatrically to present a sporty black Porsche convertible, roof down.

'Where in the name of God did you get that?'

'There's a new rich kid on trial on the showbiz desk, son of an earl or a duke or something. Nice enough fella, but thick as pig shit, of course, and hopeless. But the editor thinks he'll get us into places we've never managed to penetrate before, and he's usually right about these things.

'Anyway, young *Jamie Benson-Smythe* finds it all *frightfully* exciting, especially crime and investigations. The fucker had the gall to march over and announce that he plans to get my job! Any other newbie would be thrown out on his ear for a stunt like that, but not Jamie.'

I've had my fair share of toffs at work and nod. 'They just have this unshakeable self-belief.'

'Wouldn't we all, if we never had to worry about paying the rent? Anyway, I don't blame them for making the most of their advantages. What really bugs me is the way the English middle classes unquestioningly defer to them, bowing and fucking scraping. It makes me almost like the French.

'So, yesterday morning, I bump into the jumped-up little fucker while he's parking this up at work. I tell him I need a smart motor for a big undercover job, and he just hands me the keys.'

'Poor guy. You commandeered his car.'

'Hey, Jamie's thrilled, feels like he's already contributing,' says Fintan, getting into the driver's seat.

'What if it rains?'

'*What if it rains?*' he whines, mimicking me. 'We put up the bloody roof.'

In heaving North London traffic, we barely make it above ten miles per hour. Each gossamer graze of pedal elicits a thunderous roar, earning us looks ranging from mild irritation to unabashed hatred.

'We need to get out of town,' I say, suddenly seeing an opportunity to act on last night's encounter with Julie. When the dead come to me, I can't just ignore them. Julie needs me. And, after my schoolboy error last night, I owe her. 'Why don't we head to the South Downs? I know some great pubs around there.'

Fintan grins. 'First we've got to pick up our smoking-hot dates.'

I groan.

'Models, Donal. And I'm not talking unemployed nail bar assistants here. Real models. I knew you wouldn't come if I told you.'

'In case you hadn't noticed, Fintan, I'm in a relationship.'

'Yeah I saw her note on the kitchen table this morning. Good old Zoe, if she can't dump Matt on you, she dumps him on her mum.'

'She doesn't dump him on anyone. It's a long day looking after a kid. She craves a bit of adult company in the evening. What's wrong with that? You'll see one day.'

'From what I see, Donal, you're in a job share. From what you sometimes let slip, I sense it's now a sexless, joyless job share at that. You told me yourself that even her mum labelled it a failed relationship.'

'That doesn't give me a licence to go running around with other women.'

'We're just having a bit of craic, Donal. To quote *Loaded* magazine, "life, liberty, the pursuit of sex, drinking, football and less serious matters". The thing is, bro, she's turning you into one of those lonely married men. You know, first you don't have time for friends, then you can't find time for hobbies. Next thing you know, you're a bonded slave reduced to work and childcare. The irony of it all is that your women end up hating you for it. And you're not even married.'

I turn to him, shaking my head in disbelief.

He grins: 'You can be my wingman then, okay?'

'I don't see that I've got any choice. So where did you meet two models?'

'Sandra's photo casebook. You must have seen it? Tania and Ellen are the paper's biggest stars now.'

'I must never have made it that far through your esteemed rag.'

'Every week, it features a letter from the problem page, but told as a picture story. It's always a raunchy storyline about threesomes and secret affairs so that Tania and Ellen can act their little hearts out in their undies. As Sandra herself puts it, something for the girls to read, and the boys to look at.'

'Never underestimate the intelligence of your readers eh? I can't believe any woman would actually read your newspaper.'

'Don't be such a snob, Donal. And a killjoy. What harm is it doing anyone?'

He pulls up at a smart art-deco block near Angel tube station and beeps the horn. Two skinny women dodder out, all big shades, fake tits and tan, and real attitude. Even from this distance, I can tell they are way out of our league.

'And I suppose these cardboard cut-outs are now eyeing Hollywood stardom?'

Fintan waves to them, muttering under his breath: 'Funny you should say that. They can't wait to meet a heavyweight TV drama producer. Like you.'

I groan loudly. 'There's no way I can pull that off . . .'

'It's the only way I could get them to come. Just use words like "rushes" and "the cutting room", you'll be fine.'

'Jesus.'

'What do you think of the wheels, ladies?' he bawls.

'Like, what if it rains?' says Ellen.

'Like, we put up the roof,' snaps Fintan. 'God that's exactly what my brother Donal here said. Talk about glass half-empty.'

'What you mean he's a pessimist?' says Tania.

'No,' says Fintan. 'I mean he's a roaring alcoholic.'

That gets a good laugh.

'Donal knows a nice pub near Brighton and he's going to treat us to lunch. You good with that, girls?'

'Yay,' they coo as I give Fintan the eyeball and mouth: 'You're fucking paying.'

We roar off for all of 50 yards before getting snarled up in yet more traffic. Fintan somehow manages to trump the awkward silence with a truly cringeworthy question. 'So, ladies, what do you look for in a man?'

'*Vingt-cinq*,' purrs Ellen and they cackle hard.

Schoolboy horrors come flooding back; the wink-and-elbow language of cruel-girl delight.

Ellen finally composes herself. 'We were at this party in Paris a few years back, this really sexy guy sidles up to me and whispers "*Vingt-cinq*" in my ear. I'm thinking twenty-five? Well he might be talking about his age . . .'

More cackling.

'Then he says in the sexiest French accent I've ever heard, *"Not ma age. My size. You don believe me?"* And I say, frankly, no. I mean a twenty-five inch penis would be some sort of world record. So, he gets his friend over . . .'

Tania butts in: 'Who's even sexier.'

'And he says: *"Oui, it is true. And I too am twenty-five."* He can tell we're not buying it, so he says, *"You wan me to pull down my pants and show you?"* and I say . . .'

They might now actually expire out of sheer mirth.

Tania finally comes up for air: 'Ellen says, "If you're twenty-five, you don't need to drop your trousers, just lift them up at the ankles!"'

We all laugh now.

'I'd forgotten about metric!' says Ellen. 'Mind you, once you've had twenty-five centimetres, you don't want less,' she adds quietly.

Fintan and I share glances of mild horror.

'Right, so physique is your thing, Ellen,' editorialises anchorman. 'What about you, Tania?'

'Money,' says Tania, refreshingly unashamed. 'The love peters out, the sex peters out, so you might as well be with someone who's loaded, make your life easier.'

'And you've found someone, haven't you darling?' says Ellen. 'Show 'em what he bought you yesterday?'

A spindly orange arm appears between the front seats. Perched on the tiny wrist, a green-faced vintage Rolex with a brown leather strap.

'Men who wear a certain brand of watch guide destinies,'

announces Fintan to confused looks all round. 'It's their slogan,' he adds impatiently.

'Very understated. Classy,' I say.

'That's exactly what I thought,' says Tania, holding my eye for a second, then smiling bashfully.

'Yeah and then you got it valued, you shallow bitch,' cackles Ellen. 'Eight grand. Can you believe it? Wear it? I wouldn't let it out of my house.'

As we speed along 'Sunset Boulevard', wind noise renders conversation mercifully impossible, so that I can turn my thoughts back to last night. If we retrace my journey from yesterday, maybe something will click and lead me to Julie's body. That must have been what last night's macabre, raven-based cabaret had been all about. I've just got to get down there and follow my gut.

It starts to rain just outside Croydon. Fintan pulls up at a lay-by but, of course, the convertible roof won't go up. Something is stuck or maybe he's pressing the wrong buttons. The girls moan, so Fintan guns it until we see a covered petrol station. As we shelter in eye-watering fumes, he sets to work on the roof mechanics until they're well and truly butchered.

'Like, what if it rains all day,' says Ellen.

'Like, we do something indoors,' snaps Fintan, and we sit in glum silence for twenty minutes.

The shower mercifully clears. Even with the girls along, I'm sticking to my plan and direct Fintan to Underhill Lane. As the track narrows and branches start scouring the paint-work, I call halt.

'Poor car,' I say. 'Shall we walk?'

'There's a pub down here?' squints Fintan.

'Just around the corner,' I say, setting off before anyone has time to object.

I lead the way towards the bridge, Fintan just behind. The girls are way back, heels floundering in mud.

'Is this where it went down last night?' says Fintan, his antenna as keen as ever.

I nod. The silver painted block still sits on the wall, above the white cross. After Julie's performance last night, I'm bringing that hunk of shiny concrete with me. Somehow, it must be significant.

I rewind the rest of Julie's pageant through my mind . . . the axe, the church bell, the birds, the shepherd's crook.

'There must be a church in the village,' I say, picking up the block. 'Let's take a quick look.'

'Why are we looking for a church? And what exactly are you planning to do with that block, Donal? Jeez, I know the girls can get a bit irritating . . .'

'I've just got a feeling about it,' I say.

'Hey girls,' I shout. 'My mistake, the pub's the other way.' They don't answer, just turn and totter with all they have back to the sludge-free sanctuary of the car.

I place the block in the boot.

'Is this pub far? I'm starving,' moans Ellen.

'Donal here has you down as a fan of Norman architecture,' says Fintan. 'He always takes his dates to a cemetery. I mean if you're going to corpse, you might as well do it somewhere appropriate.'

'Just drop us off at the pub,' sighs Ellen.

'Oh, come on, Ellen,' urges Tania. 'I love old churches and graveyards.'

'Wow,' says Fintan, 'you and my morbid brother here should get on like a funeral pyre.'

The car growls and Ellen yowls all the way through Pyecombe. I'm first out at the Church of the Transfiguration.

Fintan mumbles in my ear, 'You know Julie's dead, don't you? You've had one of your whacko dreams.'

'Oh come on, Fintan, you don't believe in any of that old codology, do you?'

'Jesus, don't find her now, Donal. We're well in here.'

'You think? Maybe if I find the 175 grand and you undergo some penile transfiguration of your own.'

'I know what you mean. Jesus, we'd struggle to make *vingt-cinq* between us.'

Built into the wooden gate, a metal hook identical to the one in Julie's post-mortem performance.

'I think she's here,' I say.

'This is creeping me out,' says Ellen.

'Why don't you two wait here and admire this lovely gate?' says Fintan.

'God, you're a patronising pig,' snaps Tania.

'Well said,' I nod.

My eyes are drawn to the far corner of the graveyard and a pair of all-business ravens. They're patrolling a candy-striped bundle under a creaking oak. As I get closer, I see it's a pink-and-white striped sheet trussed up with green cord. The sheet ends are tied together and stained dark. The rope winds about the package three times widthways and once lengthways.

'Expertly wrapped,' says Fintan.

'Got anything sharp?'

'Try these,' he says, handing me the car keys.

I tear a strip in the sheet. The stench knocks us backwards. A black cloud of flies descends.

'What is that?' screams Ellen.

'It's Julie,' I say, turning to her and, despite my best efforts, failing to suppress a smile. But what I've just smelled means I'm not responsible for her murder. 'Looks like she's been dead for at least twenty-four hours. Thank God,' I sigh, shaking my head out of sheer relief.

Fintan leans in close: 'I think we'd better make an anonymous call.'

We turn to see Ellen jabbing at her mobile phone.

'No wait,' I say, but she's already spilling to a 999 operator.

I look at Fintan. 'How the hell are we going to explain this?'

'We need to get away from here,' he mumbles. 'I'll suggest the pub. We let them walk ahead, as soon as they get around the corner, bolt for the car.'

Ellen ends the call: 'Don't worry, Tan, the police are on their way.'

Fintan pipes up: 'I don't know about you ladies, but I suddenly really fancy a steak. Why don't we wait for the plod in the pub?'

Ellen plants one hand inside her handbag, raising the other defensively. 'If you or your weirdo brother take one step closer, I swear to God I'll set off my rape alarm.'

'Understood, loud and clear,' says Fintan brightly. 'Can I just say though, Ellen, as a parting line to a double date, that may never be topped.'

Chapter 6

Pyecombe Cemetery, East Sussex
Thursday, June 16, 1994; 14.30

'Christ, check out the fourth horseman,' quips Fintan, nodding towards the cemetery gate.

'Croissant' Crossley – so-called, to quote an underling, 'because he's a fat, posh, perma-tanned poof' – has arrived, and looks set to smash through headstones rather than zigzag around them. He may even claw a few corpses out of the dirt with his bare hands and rent them asunder, just to underline his current feeling of profound irritation.

'Well, if it isn't Burke and O'Hare,' he snaps. 'More like Mulligan and O'Hare.'

I'm still swooning on the stench of Julie Draper's rotting flesh and shaking the hairy little hand of every passing bluebottle. It's all confirmation that my surrender of the ransom last night did not precipitate her murder.

'A perfectly innocent explanation, Commander,' Fintan pipes up. 'We were out for a drive with those delightful ladies. Donal loves an old cemetery, especially on a dreaded sunny day like today. Next thing he's calling us over to Julie Draper's body.'

'We don't know it's Julie Draper,' says Crossley.

Fintan smiles: 'I do know, Commander, and as soon as they confirm its Julie, the media blackout can no longer be enforced? Condition 11 of the code.'

I wince; his bitching isn't helping any bridge-building.

'I'll get a court order,' bawls Crossley. 'This maniac is still on the loose.'

'All the more reason to publicise it and warn the public,' says Fintan.

'All the more reason to starve him of the oxygen of publicity. This isn't a game, Lynch.'

For a verbal street-brawler like Fintan, Christmas has come early. 'Tell me, Commander, and just to warn you this is on-the-record for when they confirm its Julie, are you still convinced her kidnap is connected to Suzy Fairclough?'

Crossley eyes him warily: 'Suzy Fairclough was randomly targeted by a man called Mr Kipper. Julie Draper was randomly targeted by a man called John West. Now I know you only eat potatoes in Ireland but even you will have heard of John West Kippers. Draw your own conclusion, as you reporters always seem to do anyway.'

Fintan shakes his head. 'A crime of this magnitude, with this level of meticulous planning and forethought, and you're telling me it's another random kidnap and murder?'

Crossley sighs. 'Julie Draper had no enemies. She lived a very quiet life with her mum and dad, devoted to her pet dogs and fish. No ex-boyfriends to speak of. Why would anyone target her?'

'There's always something,' Fintan goads. 'Maybe you missed it. Maybe you weren't looking for it. Maybe you've been duped.'

I remember the fish from Julie Draper's deranged production last night. Before I can stop myself: 'She kept fish you say, Sir?'

Crossley turns to me slowly, wearing a look of flabbergasted contempt. 'Excuse me?'

'You say she kept fish, Sir. What kind?'

'Are you taking the piss?'

I shake my head.

'Goldfish.'

'Their names?'

'I don't know. Christ! Mutt and Jeff I think she called them in her proof-of-life call. Why in God's name do you ask?'

I don't answer.

Crossley stiffens. 'You know I can't help feeling it's fitting you found the body, Donal.'

'Sir?'

'As it was you who totally fucked up our chances of apprehending her abductor last night. And that's gone into my report.'

'Sir, less than an hour ago I was scared stiff that I may have caused Julie to be murdered. Now I know I haven't, I'll take anything that's coming my way on the chin.'

Fintan barely lets me finish. 'Did you also put in your report, Commander, that the kidnap must be the work of a former or current police officer?'

Crossley's startled reaction shocks me to the core. My God, he believes Julie's kidnap is an inside job, somehow. For Fintan, this is an open goal.

'I'm reliably informed that you wrote a memo to the Commissioner in which you stated that the expertise of Julie's captor has convinced you that it's an inside job.'

'Nonsense,' snarls Crossley, but way too animated.

'Is that why you're so keen to throw Donal under the bus, Commander, to cover up something that will embarrass the force?'

Crossley's rattled. 'I'd tread very carefully if I were you, Lynch. The only inside job I'm seeing here is an officer on my case bringing his reporter brother to the scene for an unofficial briefing. I've a good mind to arrest you both for obstructing the course of justice.'

Fintan smiles smugly. 'Oh, I know why you're so pissed off, Commander. Julie's body here dashes your hopes of making Assistant Commissioner. Losing her is a stain on your precious record.'

Crossley steps forward. 'Consider yourself and your rag banned from any further press briefings, Lynch. Understood?'

'We don't need your press briefings, Crossley. I've got the Prince of Darkness, Alex Pavlovic on the case.'

Crossley turns ashen, out of rage or shock I can't tell. All I know about Alex Pavlovic is he's Fintan's reporter-of-last-resort when dirt needs digging. Pavlovic, it seems, has dark and unspecified connections capable of delving deeper than any other Fleet Street reporter. The very mention of his name has sucked all life out of Crossley.

Fintan's fiendish smile signals a killer punchline. 'And, with respect, Commander, Alex Pavlovic would appear to command a lot more coppers than you do.'

Crossley explodes: 'Write whatever the fuck you like, Lynch. Just know one thing. As of this second, you no longer have a rat inside the investigation. Donal, give a statement to DI Mann about everything that happened here, then fuck off back to the cold case squad. At least there you can't bugger up any live investigations.'

Chapter 7

The Lamb, Pyecombe, East Sussex
Thursday, June 16, 1994; 16.00

Fintan whisks Sandra's Cherubs back to Angel Islington while I set about getting slaughtered in the Lamb where, mercifully, the hobbling, russet-faced locals leave me alone.

Before we'd left Pyecombe cemetery I'd run into Dr Edwina Milne, a forty-something, no-nonsense pathologist straight out of a mail order 'Tory Wives' catalogue.

'You're always finding bodies, Donal,' she'd bellowed across the headstones. 'Is there anything you need to tell us?'

'Yes, there is something I need to tell you, Edwina, or anyone else who'll listen, but I'm too scared,' I screamed internally, before scampering off through the headstones, like Michael Stone after he ran out of grenades.

Whiskey's peaty warmth soothes my nerves, melding all sparking thoughts and sizzling fears into a toasting glow of ambivalence. The burnt aftertaste spirits me back to Mam's funeral; my most recent and somewhat more controversial flit from a cemetery. Only I know what I was really running from. And that I won't be able to run from it for much longer.

It's almost time . . .

Those entire two days, Da couldn't bring himself to talk to me, or even look at me. When they finally lowered her into the dirt, Da earthed his grief by grabbing Fintan's arm. Why couldn't he have grabbed my arm too? Just for once?

I sling back the last of my Jameson and imagine the galvanising heat forging my iron will; I'll be a better father to Matt. A proper dad.

My mind drifts to the visions of Julie I'd experienced last night. The church bells and shepherd's crook have already paid off, leading me to her body. The silver block must be crucial in some way. What the axe, deranged ravens and tiny fish signify, I can't even begin to speculate.

Once again, I reassure myself that I don't possess some inexplicable telepathic hotline to the recently murdered. These performances can come from only one place – my subconscious – which has been obsessively gnawing away on this case for several long days now. My mind must process all the information, then present clues to me through my lurid, sleep-paralysis dream episodes. It's not that I soak up the spirit of the deceased so much as the essence of the case. That must be what's happening here . . . right?

Unless what Mam said is true . . . that it's all wrapped up in a family curse. But who could ever validate such a thing? I'll cross that bridge soon, when I'm good and ready.

Edwina's periscopic peer around the corner promptly torpedoes all thoughts. She's actively seeking me out; for what, my booze-fogged brain cannot even begin to fathom.

'Donal,' she hisses, as if secretly rousing me from deep slumber.

'Edwina, how are you?' I say, making to get to my feet but somehow failing.

'Er, stay where you are,' she laughs. 'I trust that's a double Scotch?'

'Jameson, thanks.'

Edwina and I go back to the very first murder scene I'd attended as a PC, the brutal stabbing of a girl aged twenty-one. I'd tried hard not to get upset, but failed, much to the glee of my emotionally stunted older colleagues. Edwina's regal upbraiding of them still makes me smile: 'You may be surprised to learn, gentlemen, that to the fairer sex, male vulnerability is a very sexy quality indeed.'

Since then, she's sought me out at murder scenes to check on my progress and educate me about her craft. I've even been teased about it by female colleagues, who rather cruelly dub her my 'Crime Scene Cougar'.

She stands at the bar with her back to me, her right boot perched on a foot rail running six or so inches off the ground. This uneven stance lifts one side of her white blouse to reveal a denim-clad buttock. On closer inspection, it's a textbook half-moon arse cheek that should belong to someone twenty years her junior. I'd never even considered Edwina as a sexual being before and blaze like a KKK cross.

Christ, Donal, I scold myself, *I know you're not getting any at home, but she's old enough to be your mother . . .*

Double Christ, Donal, is this some form of twisted Oedipal grief? Banish such thoughts at once!

'You look a little flushed,' she teases, and I notice her brandy snifter clasped classily between upturned fingers. I then notice perhaps one button too many undone on her cotton shirt, so shift my gaze swiftly up to her half-amused eyes.

'That'll be the old *uisce beatha*.'

'Ah, the one Gaelic phrase I know. The water of life, or whiskey as we inelegant Anglo Saxons call it. To poor Julie.'

'Julie,' I say and we clink solemnly.

She sits and sips reverentially. 'Watch this,' she says, tilting the balloon-shaped brandy glass. 'Don't worry,' she giggles, sensing my rising panic as she tips it all the way down onto its side. 'See how it comes right up to the rim but doesn't spill out? That's how you measure the perfect single shot of cognac. And that's the only thing I remember from my three-grand-a-term finishing school.'

'Sounds like the kind of school I should've gone to.'

'I heard about the kidnapper making off with the ransom money last night. The good news for you, Donal, is that Julie's been dead for longer than twenty-four hours.'

I'd already guessed, but now it's official, tension escapes me like air from a pricked balloon. 'Thank God,' I gasp. 'And thank you for letting me know, Edwina.'

She puts her hand on mine and I convulse violently, like a flatliner receiving an electric shock. It's all I can do not to bellow 'CLEAR'. My God, is she coming onto me?

'What else can I tell you?' she husks, the minx, giving my stunned, immobile hand a squeeze, then slowly withdrawing. Reluctantly perhaps? Has she got some sort of weird crime scene horn? 'The ground where she lay has no grass discoloration or flattened vegetation, so she hadn't been there very long. She was completely naked inside the blanket.

'There were two obvious fracture injuries to the back of her skull, both about a week-old and caused by a blunt instrument. I'll be suggesting these were inflicted nine days ago when she was first abducted.

'I found chain-like marks around her right ankle; she had been forced to wear some sort of restraint or leg iron. The redness of the injury shows it was caused before death. I found no chafing marks around her wrists though, which seems odd as this is universally the preferred method of restraint.

'I found another ligature mark running along the back of her neck. Her tongue was protruding through clenched teeth which you normally find in people who've hanged themselves. She must have been throttled very violently at the end.

'Her fingernails were undamaged and there were no marks on her forearms, the sort of defensive injuries that you'd expect if a victim had fought for her life. In other words, when the time came, she must have been restrained and strangled from behind, quickly and cleanly, which will provide some small comfort to her family.'

We both need a drink after that. But Edwina's not finished.

'Now here's an odd thing. The changes to Julie's flesh show she's been dead for about two days. That makes it impossible for me to determine if she'd been raped or sexually assaulted. But the insects in her body suggest she's been exposed to air for a lot less time, I'd say between twelve and twenty-four hours.

'There was also something really striking and bizarre about her appearance.'

She squints at her drink, as if still trying to make sense of it herself.

'She was completely bald.'

'How?'

She shuffles in her seat, theory still percolating. 'For several hours after she died, her body must have been stored in some sort of sealed container which kept the flies and insects out. If he wrapped her in a sheet or towels and this place got very hot, her hair must have stuck to the bloody sheets or towels. When he unwrapped her, it came away from her head.'

'Or he shaved her?'

'No. Its ripped out at the root.'

'God, her poor family, having to see that . . .'

She smiles. 'You're a sensitive old soul, Donal. I've instructed the mortuary to prepare a hairpiece.'

She takes a bigger swig than me this time.

'Other things of note, no food in her stomach, which suggests she hadn't eaten for at least eight hours prior to her death. And the sheet she came wrapped in today bears a laundry mark – MA 143 – so if you chaps can find the origin of that laundry mark, you may find her killer.'

She takes a final gulp as I consider how to even word my only question.

'We had a tip-off,' I lie, because the truth might get me sectioned. After all, I'm basing this on last night's bonkers visions of Julie. 'Look, I won't bore you with the details, Edwina, but there's been a suggestion that an axe is involved in Julie's murder, somehow.'

She frowns and I visualise my question grinding through her red-hot brain engines. She shakes her head finally. 'I've only ever known Triad gangsters to use an axe. Or Irish travellers, I'm sorry to say. How exactly is an axe involved in this?'

'Truthfully, I've no idea. I just thought I'd better mention it.'

She shakes her head some more. 'None of Julie Draper's injuries could've been inflicted with an axe.'

'Well, thanks so much for taking the trouble to find me, Edwina. I'm really touched,' I say. 'If I can ever buy you a drink back . . .'

'Well, I'm frequently alone in London on Sunday evenings,

when all my pals are doing family things. You can treat me to a convivial supper some time.'

'I'd love that,' I blurt, not giving myself time to fluster or dither or ruin the moment.

She gets to her feet, and I wonder what the hell I should do if she presents herself for an embrace. My finishing school didn't cover that.

'Well, it'll make a nice change from *Antiques Roadshow*,' I say, standing up.

'Not for you, it won't.'

She smiles and lingers there, eyes glinting. Is this some sort of cue for me to move in?

'See you soon then, Donal,' she smiles, searching my eyes.

What should I do?

She turns to leave, then, Columbo-style, spins at the door.

'There is one case you might want to check out, from five or six years back, still unsolved. A bailiff named Nathan Barry.'

She lifts her open palm to the left side of her face and starts karate-chopping her cheek. I try not to look alarmed or confused.

'Axed in the face. Really nasty. That's the only one I know of. Worth checking out.'

Chapter 8

Pyecombe, East Sussex
Thursday, June 16, 1994; 20.00

I set off home whiskey-bleak, intent on avoiding Zoe until the morning. At least I can count on the combined ineptitude of Southern Rail and London buses on that score. I'll be lucky to make it home by midnight.

The trouble is, I know exactly how it will play out. At first, she'll greet news of my dismissal from the Kidnap Squad with stoic, purse-lipped disappointment. She'll get busy with something to avoid me – ironing, sticking labels onto Matt's clothes, that damned dishwasher – humming in that way that makes me want to strangle her. Every now and then, she'll stop suddenly to stare sadly into space, and sigh.

All the while, her forensic brain will be feverishly constructing the case for the prosecution. She can't help herself. Soon the questions start. Did Crossley specifically say x? Did you consider all other options before you did y? She'll shift, gradually, until it becomes clear that she's entirely on Crossley's side, albeit in her infuriatingly factual, reasonable and logical way. Indeed, her devout commitment to be 'totally fair' to all parties involved is what makes me apoplectic.

'Why can't you just take my side and support me, for once?' I'll snap.

And then she'll launch her trusty cruise missile; the 'shock and awe' hate bomb that obliterates every penis over a radius of one square mile.

'I just thought we'd be living closer to Mum. *By now.*'

Her mother, Sylvia, takes care of Matthew while we work. That's his name when he's over there, after she declared Matt 'too communal garden'. For all her snobbery, Sylvia's ability to mangle common phrases is her unwitting Achilles heel. Just last week, she complained that her new spectacles were impairing her 'profiterole vision'.

Late last year, Zoe found 'the perfect flat' for the three of us in Crouch End, just two streets from her family home. Perfect, that is, if I'd been on a DC's salary. I pointed out that we couldn't afford it. Her parents offered 'to help' until I got my promotion. I refused – out of bullish, old-fashioned and foolish male pride, of course – forcing us to not so much downsize as capsize from cosy Crouch End to grungy Green Lanes, Haringey; home of the Turkish heroin trade, leering Albanian/Kosovan cigarette hawkers and heaving 24/7 traffic.

She's never got over it, especially now that each working day is bookended by the Matt drop-off/pick-up, a tedious forty-minute walk to where we *should* be living. It's as if I've failed in some fundamental, primeval, manly obligation that can never be reconciled. Postcode emasculation.

At least the grocers of Green Lanes never close. Hangover incoming, I snaffle two bottles of rancid Transylvanian Shiraz and shuffle home for my nightly 'couched grape' solo session.

I unlock the front door, quickly check on Zoe and Matt

– both out cold – then open bottle one. As the cork pops my mind snags on my mother-in-law Sylvia's cutting observation. 'Failed relationship' . . . why does that rankle so? Is it the non-attribution of responsibility – blame – as if our status as a couple is so doomed that Zoe and I are powerless to save it? Or is it the shock realisation that, were we to split up, our incompatibility will be judged by the world at large as a personal failing on both our parts?

As I wince through the first aquarium-scale glug, I decide it's time to pinpoint where this 'failing' began, and which of us is to blame. Top of my list: the chronic lack of sex.

By her own admission, Matt's birth marked the death of Zoe's sexual appetite. Of course, I wasn't there – I didn't even know Zoe then – but her oft-repeated, harrowing descriptions of the thirty-four-hour fanny-buster does little for either of our sex drives, in truth.

She lays the blame squarely on the National Childbirth Trust (NCT). It was the 'Nipple-Cracked Tyrants' – Zoe's term – who convinced her to undergo childbirth without drugs. As someone who won't clip a toenail without a tub of Savlon to hand, the notion of 'natural childbirth' boggles my mind. Ever since, she's suffered crippling bouts of thrush, so we just 'don't go there' any more, or even talk about it.

So imagine my surprise when I pick up her flashing mobile, on charge in the kitchen, click on a message from 'Charles', and read the words: Z, when can I see you again? Missing you every second!

My first reaction is disbelief. It's been sent to the wrong number. Or it's a prank. Or she's being stalked by some loon. We've had that before – a hazard of her job as a forensics officer. Crime scene weirdos find out her name, rank, place of work and won't stop calling her. But they'd never get hold of her mobile number . . .

I walk into our bedroom. She's a snoring bed hump. A human landslide. It is 11pm after all.

It can wait until morning. There has to be a simple explanation, surely. I tip toe into Matt's room. As usual, he's face down in the cot, bum-in-the-air. I touch his hot little back, my hand earthing the familiar beats of his busy little heart. We always joke how we never want that tiny heart to be broken. Whatever her feelings for me, Zoe wouldn't do it to him. Never.

I pad back into the sitting room, click off the TV and the lamp, pour a greedy red and fidget in the street-light orange gloom. For some reason, the Kübler-Ross model flashes into my mind. This is the Five Stages of Grief we'd been taught about – useful knowledge to any murder detective. DABDA – Denial, Anger, Bargaining, Depression. Then, finally, Acceptance. In a murder case, any close associate of the victim failing to adhere to the DABDA protocol becomes a suspect. It's not murder suspects I'm worried about here, but me. Am I in denial?

I've no idea how long it is before her phone flashes a second time. Charles again, still up, in more ways than one: Z, about to hit the hay. Won't be able to resist touching myself thinking of you x x x

Denial leaves town without packing. Anger stares at the number, wanting to call this fucker up, have it out. My forefinger quivers over the green button. Hang on, I tell myself, I need to be smarter than this. I jot down the number, cross-reference it with the contacts in my phone. Nothing. I check Zoe's calls and texts records, in and out. No sign of Charles. Then I notice how scant these records are. She's already been busy deleting.

Anger hatches a plan. I deposit her phone discreetly behind the empty flower vase, taking considerably more care to hide it than philandering Zoe. I don't want her to have any inkling that I know. I need to spring it on her in the morning, catch her cold, so that I can read her eyes.

I sit there stewing, unable to stop speculating: who is Charles? How long has this been going on? What have they done together? Who else knows about it? The thing that really bamboozles me; where has she found the time or the energy?

Hang on a minute, I remind myself, she goes out two nights a week. It was her childless former work colleagues who persuaded her to resume her pre-Matt social life.

'I want to get back to my old self,' she'd announced. Not as badly as me, so I agreed to babysit a couple of nights a week, hoping that 'the girls' could do something I clearly couldn't – make Zoe happy again.

I went out with them once, watched them guzzle bone-dry Chardonnay by the half-pint and become feral, so I fled. I now call them the WWF, the White Wine Fiends, and sit in quivering dread of her return, just like we used to with Da.

She always thunders in with the Chardonnay rage, ranting and raving about how shit her life is and the inherent injustices of motherhood.

The mornings are worse, when she's gripped by hungover paranoia about what she may or may not have said or done during those alarming blanks in her memory. But even this fails to poop her party lust; she wouldn't miss her 'girls' nights out' for the world. Now I'm beginning to suspect why.

Suddenly, another terrifying thought strikes – who else knows about this? Has she told her best friend? Could Sophie be trusted to keep her mouth shut? Of course not! What if everyone knows? How can I look them in the face again? How can she humiliate me like this?

Matt's even more unsettled than usual tonight. It's almost

like he *knows* something is wrong. Eight or nine times I fail to placate him. It's as if we're both being tormented by the same quandary: How can she do this to him?

By dawn, the anger has morphed into a sick sort of satisfaction. For months, she's been guilt-tripping me about my unsuitability for fatherhood. The *Bad Dada Intifada* always starts and ends with my drinking. In between that dual denunciation, she takes a tortuous route through my other myriad failings: working all the time; messiness; chronic insomnia. The irony of the latter complaint stings: guess who does the night feeds?

I'm stockpiling self-righteous claims as a Doomsday believer might tinned tuna. I can't wait to cut her down to size. I'll use my most patronising voice: *It's not about whether I can forgive you, Zoe, it's whether* Matt *can forgive you.* Dr Kübler-Ross is good. By the time Matt cries out at 6.10am, I've moved through Denial and Anger, and am well up for a good old Bargain.

You see, in the martyr barter that is our relationship, I'd rarely seized – let alone held – that key strategic piece of ground known as High Moral. I feel unassailable, statesman-like. Nobly, I elect to spare our confrontation until Matt goes down for his mid-morning sleep. I don't want him to hear us rowing and be traumatised in any way. To be fair, neither would she. Despite everything, we both love that boy with all we have.

'So,' I say breezily as she tackles the dishwasher, 'who is Charles?'

I'm expecting a smashed plate, a torrent of Data Protection Act-based indignation: *How dare you spy on me*. What I'm not expecting is a flat, emotionally detached weather report, as she focusses chiefly on installing the dishes in the right places.

The relationship has just started. Charles is no one I know. This, for reasons I don't fully understand, provides enormous relief. She then says the things I need her to say; the things I need to hear. It's all been a dreadful mistake. She'll finish it with Charles, in her own time. Her saying his name aloud staggers me – the gall. But, for some reason, I find myself believing every word coming out of her lying, cheating mouth. I need to believe every word. She will end it, for sure, I conclude – if only for Matt's sake.

I swallow hard on the gutful of questions I want to spew. Have they had sex? How many times? Where? When? Is he better than me? Bigger than me? Does she call out his name? Does she love him? In my heart, I know the one question I'm too scared to ask: Why?

'Please stop staring at me like that, Donal,' she says firmly. 'I've promised to end it. Can we just leave it at that?'

Later, while she's taking a shower, I get hold of her phone again to find out more. It's locked. I try both her email accounts; she's changed the passwords so, just like that, I'm frozen out of her life and powerless.

Chapter 9

Green Lanes, North London
Friday, June 17, 1994; 12.00

My eyes feel dryer than old grapes and my head thumps like Christmas afternoon. I make for our bedroom but can't feel the floor beneath my feet. I must still be in adrenalised shock at Zoe's admission of infidelity.

My temples buzz intermittently, my vision shuddering and dimming in time, obeying the sporadic white noise soundtrack. It's like I've just walked under the world's biggest electricity pylon. Something's interfering with transmission.

Then I remember. I'd been standing next to Julie Draper's dead body less than twenty-four hours ago and she's got my subconscious on repeat dial. She's desperate to connect to me. I must sleep so Julie can get through.

I lie down, eyes closed, exhausted brain agape; come on in, Ms Draper, the water's toasty.

Random phrases echo and overlap:

Failed relationship . . . the wink-and-elbow language of cruel-girl delight . . .

The love peters out, the sex peters out, so you might as well be with someone who's loaded . . .

Once you've had twenty-five, you don't want less . . .

There's Sinead O'Connor at the end of the bed, tears rolling down her porcelain white face. She's smiling at the same time, holding a photo close to her chest. I see it's Zoe, Matt and me on Brighton Beach last summer. Her mouth sneers and that photo rips right down the middle, as if by magic. Dolores O'Riordan of The Cranberries is beside her, drinking a pint of white wine and loving every second.

Jesus, ladies, what is your problem? Why do you hate men so much?

What's that they're singing?

Na na na na

Na na na na

Hey Hey

Goodbye

Oh and here's Julie Draper now, bald as a coot, singing her little heart out in that pink-striped blanket, giving it all Alison Moyet, thinking she's the bee's knees. *What is this, ladies, Fun Girl Three?*

Behind them, in black and white, Zoe is bowed and shuffling away at speed, dragging a reluctant little boy in shorts alongside her. Matt turns and smiles and waves. He's oblivious to the masked black figure in front of them, which, at that instant, spins and re-shapes into a perfectly ordinary shadow. They continue to march onwards and into that black shadow . . .

I follow and the black figure reconfigures between us. He starts to turn. I will him; turn . . . turn . . . make yourself known! A shape is forming. I know that profile from somewhere. I know this man. He wants to make himself known to me. He's turning to me . . . coming to me. Keep turning!

He freezes, spooked by a shrill, repetitive tone. I recognise that din. My brain clicks; it's my mobile. He flicks off like a puppet shadow. Damn! One more second and Julie's killer would have revealed himself.

What the hell was all that about? Why the cameo appearances by those self-styled Banshees of rage, Sinead and Dolores? And why was Julie Draper's killer stalking Zoe and Matt, then luring them into some sort of darkness? It's got to be cross-pollination of my current dual traumas – the death of Julie and the prospect of losing the people that I love. That can be the only explanation.

I'm stunned to see it's gone 4pm Why do I always sleep better after bad news? Maybe its pessimistic relief; the worst *has* happened, so you can quit your fretting now and relax.

I pick up. 'Fintan?'

'You still good for the Archway Tavern?'

'What?'

'What do you mean, what? It's Friday the 17th. The World Cup finals kick off in less than one hour! That's where we always watch the games. Is she letting you out? Because you know it's Ireland–Italy tomorrow night. If you've only got the one pink pass for the weekend . . .'

'I don't need her permission,' I announce, thinking if only he knew why.

'Good man. That's the spirit. Right so, I'll pick you up in twenty. Is she there?'

'Yeah.'

'I won't come in so.'

'Ah, come on, Fintan, Matt would love to see you.'

'I thought we had orders to address him only as Matthew. Anyway, I'm barred.'

'You're not barred.'

'Zoe made it very clear she thinks I'm a . . . how did she put it again?'

'A misogynistic menace. She didn't mean it. She just worries that every time I go out with you, we end up on a bender.'

'We end up on a bender because you're so pussy-whipped. She said the hangovers make you an unfit father. How can you put up with that shite? You do more for that kid than she does.'

'Come on, Fintan. Give her a break. She's under a lot of pressure lately and she hasn't been well,' I say, then realise I'm trying to justify her affair to myself.

'Damn right she's not well. She's a control freak. Every man needs to cut loose now and then. The day you roll over and let her control your social life, she'll end up hating you for it. I've seen it happen, Donal. You need to man the fuck up.'

'Why don't you man the fuck up and knock the door?'

'Listen, Donal, I'm dumping that silver concrete block on your doorstep. Then I'm off to watch the Americans fail to "get" soccer. My advice is: be ready, because I've sensational news.'

'Not like you to sensationalise news, Fintan.'

'Fine. If you don't want to know what Julie Draper's kidnapper is up to now, maybe you should stay in and watch *Friends*, like a proper dad.'

Ten minutes later, I find Fintan loitering on our front door step, awkwardly cradling the silver breeze-block so that it doesn't touch his suit.

'You should present this to Zoe,' he smiles. 'Tell her it's your first down payment on that house of her dreams.'

'Arsehole.'

'Remind me again why I've been ferrying it around southern England since yesterday?'

'I just have a feeling about it,' I say, taking the block and placing it in the boot of my car. He's still driving the flashy Porsche. 'I see you figured out how to get the roof up.'

'Not exactly. I took it to that grease monkey around the corner. He sorted it out for fifty quid.'

'Fifty quid? That's a miracle.'

'Let's hope the miracles continue, and it rains solidly for several months after I give it back to Jamie.'

'What do you mean?'

'Well let's just say, when they fixed it, they didn't bother too much with the electrics.'

He clocks my mounting horror and roars with laughter.

'They welded it shut.'

'Jesus, Fintan. Jamie will go apeshit.'

He throws his arms out in mock defence. 'I didn't know he'd set about it with a blowtorch. It kept raining!'

I get in to inspect. 'He's added lots of nasty-looking metal,' I say. 'It's now like being in one of those shark cages. Poor Jamie.'

Fintan's in fits now and takes several minutes to recover, giving me plenty of time to marvel at the crow-black cruelty of his humour.

I can't wait any longer. 'Commander Crossley hasn't been in touch. No one's been in touch. I presume that, as usual, you and your journo friends know more than me about what's really going on. Has John West or Kipper resurfaced?'

'Police got a typed note this morning, which they suspect is from him. He's threatening to abduct and murder again, unless he gets another pay-off. Except this time, he's going to target a child.'

'Bloody hell. Is it definitely the same guy?'

'Police think so. He explained in the note that Julie had to die because her mask slipped and she saw him.'

'She did know him then?'

'He said he couldn't risk her being able to identify him afterwards. Police think all this proves is that he has form and she could've picked him out of a photo album of ex-offenders. They're refusing to think anything except Kipper, Kipper, Kipper.'

'But you think differently?'

Fintan pulls that pained face, which revs his brain to max. I'd better pay attention.

'I think the kidnap of Julie Draper resembles the Fairclough case *too much*. It's like whoever kidnapped her is desperate for police to make that connection and not look elsewhere.'

'Maybe this Kipper character is taunting them. That's not uncommon.'

'Maybe, but I can't help thinking Crossley and co. have bought the Kipper/John West thing too easily. They're blinkered, which means they're not keeping an open mind or delving properly into Julie's personal life. If the kidnapper is someone else, he's done a great job of hoodwinking the police. Again, it smacks of the kidnapper getting help from the inside, and you saw Crossley's reaction when I said that. He knows there's something else going on here, a bigger play.'

'So, what now?'

'What now is we're doing your job for you, as usual. We're getting stuck into Julie's personal life, finding out who might have had a grudge against her or Crown Estates. I've got my ferret-like crime reporter Alex Pavlovic on it.'

'Has he got a source in the Kidnap Unit?'

'I don't ask, Donal. Though sometimes he tells me about his antics, if he's feeling especially proud of himself. So yesterday, Julie Draper's mum is under armed guard in hospital. Doctors, nurses and cops won't let anyone near her. Alex Pavlovic, aka The Prince of Blackness, sends her a massive bunch of flowers, hides a mobile phone in the stems with a note offering her £50k. She's agreed to meet him today.'

Fintan parks up, slaps his fake 'Doctor on Call' sign against the windscreen.

'You must lie awake at night, Fintan, worrying that he's more devious, underhand and amoral than even you?'

'And connected,' he sighs, oblivious to my dig. 'Ex-cops, private detectives, tech whizz-kids. He's got this one fella, Gerry Woods, on side, who used to work for the spooky wing of the Met. This guy can place a secret camera in a cigarette lighter. Amazing. That's how we've brought down all these cheating Tories.'

'Isn't secret filming and bugging illegal?'

'Using the material gathered is illegal. We don't use it. It's just insurance.'

'Insurance?'

'These people always deny it. You've got no idea how many politicians and people in power have got away with affairs because they denied it and we couldn't categorically prove it. We learned our lesson.'

'What does it matter that someone's had an affair? Maybe it was just sex. Or they made a mistake. Don't you worry about destroying families?'

I'm surprised at the raw emotion in my voice. The last thing I want is Fintan twigging about Zoe's affair. He might joyously choke from the satisfaction. Luckily, he's in full lecture mode so doesn't notice.

'Hang on, Donal. These are the same Tory politicians who launched moral crusades against single mothers and the press. David Mellor told us we were drinking in the last-chance saloon and threatened privacy laws; we catch him shagging a MAW.'

'A what?'

'Model-Actress-Whatever. John Major lectures the nation about morals and getting "Back to Basics" and we expose half his married Cabinet playing away. I wouldn't be surprised if he's at it.'

'And, of course, journalists never have affairs.'

'You know what, Donal? I think everyone has affairs. Monogamy is against our nature. Look at the closest relatives to humans, bonobos. They live in peaceful communes and shag like rabbits. That's what humans were like for millions of years until society evolved this idea of sexual incarceration.'

I hear my voice creak in emotional protest. 'Monogamy isn't always enforced. Some people like the security and the trust. What's wrong with that?'

'If we accepted that humans can't be monogamous, then there wouldn't be this sense of betrayal by the "wronged" party. That's what causes all the divorce and strife, someone playing the victim. Anyway, why the hell are we talking about this now? We've got to go and shout for whoever's playing Germany.'

For some reason, the only major international country without a professional soccer league has been awarded the 1994 World Cup. As Fintan puts it: 'Yanks just don't get soccer, the way I don't get fishing, unless I can catch a shark every five minutes.'

On the plus side, the Republic of Ireland has qualified. And the opening ceremony provides unexpected joy when Oprah Winfrey falls off stage and a lip-synching Diana Ross fails to kick a ball ten-feet into an empty goal. 'Are you watching, Tommy Coyne?' we chant in delight.

We shout for Bolivia as they lose to Germany. We roar on South Korea as they go 2-0 down to Spain. Then, out of nowhere, South Korea score two late goals and the pub erupts. 'I doubt they're this fucking ecstatic in Seoul,' shouts Fintan.

I can't face Zoe tonight. But I haven't got the energy to tell Fintan the truth.

'She'll be on the warpath if I come home like this. Can I kip at yours?'

'Any time,' says Fintan. 'You need to show her that you're still your own man.'

'God, you really are like something out of *The Quiet Man*.'

We stumble outside and head for the mini-cab office.

'Are you sure we should just abandon Jamie's eighty-grand Porsche outside a pub?' I ask.

'What Irish person would be caught dead in a sports car?' he says. 'We're just not like that. Anyway, I doubt if Houdini himself could get in through those welds.'

As we follow the cab driver across the car park, I think suddenly of Nathan Barry – the bailiff Edwina had mentioned to me who'd been axed to death behind a pub in East Croydon. I ask Fintan what he knows about the case.

'I know the guy who led the investigation.'

'Will he talk?'

Fintan laughs: 'Try to stop him! What's so interesting about the Barry case?'

'We got information that it might be connected to Julie Draper,' I say flatly, failing to add that the sole source is one of my rabid, booze-fuelled dreams.

'Really? How?'

'I don't know, but I said I'd check it out.'

'I'll text him in the morning. See if he's up for a meet.'

'What's your take on it?'

'My take? Donal everyone knows who murdered Nathan Barry. And so should you. The police just haven't been able to prove it.'

Chapter 10

Coombe Road, Croydon
Saturday, June 18, 1994; 11.00

Still not so much as a text from the Kidnap Unit, technically my current employer. I wish to God they'd get on with stitching me up over Julie Draper. There is truly no punishment worse than waiting for punishment.

DI Adrian Lambert insists on meeting us at the Nathan Barry murder scene, right away. Later today, Fintan has an errant Tory MP to 'front up' in that neck of the woods, so we bomb down together, spit-roasting in the welded Porsche.

'Inspector Lambert is somewhat obsessed,' warns Fintan. 'Failing to get a collar for this Nathan Barry murder stalled his career. It's now been investigated three times and they still can't make it stick.'

'Who do they think did it?'

'You're better off keeping an open mind. You'll be the only police officer who's done so since about day two.'

DI Lambert's pacing the car park as we pull in. He's slight, a little hunched with a long nose. 'Oh and he's Welsh, so he gets very animated,' warns Fintan. Lambert looks gaunt, nervous. His face seems too red, his hair too black, styled in a disturbing Hitler-Youth undercut, making him look like an emaciated Barry Humphries.

We race through formalities, then I explain my mission; to see if there's any connection between this case and the murder of Julie Draper. Lambert looks surprised. It's the first he's heard of it.

'It's the first anyone's heard of it, Guv,' I smile. 'And I'd like to keep it that way.'

'Understood. I hear Kipper sent a note yesterday threatening to take a child next time,' he says.

'You buy the whole Kipper theory then?' asks Fintan.

'I don't know squat about that case,' says Lambert, strolling over to a corner of the car park. 'But I know everything there is to know about this one. So, six years ago, April 3, 1988, about 9.30pm, a pub regular drove into the car park and saw Nathan Barry lying here, on his back, with an axe embedded in the left side of his face, right up to the hilt.

'The pathologist is in no doubt that he was effectively executed. He'd suffered three axe wounds to the head, each one would've been sufficient to kill him. The final blow was delivered by a backhand motion as he lay on his back, the axe penetrating four inches into his brain. The coroner had quite a job removing it. Whoever attacked him meant to kill him.

'The pathologist believes the attacker sneaked up on Nathan from behind, was less than five foot eight inches tall and left-handed.

'It was a common Taiwanese-made domestic axe, which could've been bought in any number of places and had no serial number. Elastoplast had been wrapped around the handle to ensure we couldn't take any prints off it. And it had been sharpened for the job. The paramedics who treated him found a few hundred quid in cash in his left-hand trouser pocket, so it wasn't a robbery.

'The first CID officer on the scene sealed off the car park and uniform officers took statements from everyone inside the pub.

'Forensics struggled to take prints off Nathan's car or any others in the car park. It was a cold, frosty night which is a nightmare for them. Last year, they found trace DNA on the axe but the sample is too minute to process.

'We got a lot of criticism for failing to seize glasses and ashtrays from inside the pub for prints or DNA analysis, to check if a known offender had been drinking here that evening. My argument is that whoever killed Nathan had been waiting outside in the car park and had never set foot in the pub. Why would he risk being seen?'

Fintan pipes up. 'Do you regret not seizing the glasses and ashtrays now, Adrian?'

'Every bloody day. But we didn't know much about DNA then. What we did know was how to spot a suspect. It's a known fact that ninety per cent of victims know their killer. This was clearly personal. At first, we speculated that it may have been someone he'd upset in the course of his work. But someone else kept cropping up, right from the outset.

'Nathan had been in the pub that evening with his business partner, John Delaney. In fact, Delaney had left the pub just moments before Nathan.

'I went personally to tell Delaney the news of Nathan's murder. He opened the door looking sweaty and agitated, as if he'd been expecting us. His first words to me were, "I'm not the mad axeman of Croydon". I asked him how he knew and he started dropping names of all his cop pals in Croydon CID. All this time, his wife's watching the TV, *Alfred Hitchcock Presents*, believe it or not. She doesn't look up even once.

'I take him in to make a statement. He tells us he and Nathan had agreed to meet an associate here in the White Horse that night called Tommy Buchan for a drink to discuss a loan to their company, BD Investigations.

'We track down Buchan who denies it flat out. Turns out Delaney called him *after* he left the White Horse that night and arranged to meet him at a wine bar a few miles away.'

Fintan editorialises. 'Trying to create an alibi after the event, perhaps?'

'Delaney's car phone records confirm this call to Buchan at 21.36. They also show a call from a public phone box to his car phone at 21.33. Now the system can't identify public phone numbers, but we believe that call was made from the public phone outside the White Horse.'

'The killer confirming job done,' says Fintan.

Lambert nods.

'Over the next few days, we discovered Delaney is a crook. Behind Nathan's back, he'd been up to all sorts, including hiring cops to guard Riley's car auctions in Bermondsey.

'Now, BD Investigations wasn't insured to do this kind of work, but Delaney signed the contract and employed serving cop friends, who he paid cash. One night last June Delaney decided to take the day's takings to the bank's night safe alone. According to him, the safe was glued shut so he'd no option but to take the cash home. Guess what? Outside his house, he's sprayed with ammonia and robbed of the fifteen grand.

'Riley, owner of the car auctions, doesn't believe a word, goes to see Delaney in hospital, where he's dabbing his eyes with tissue and joking with the nurses. Riley sues BD Investigations for the fifteen grand and that's how Nathan finds out about the entire racket. He goes mental, firstly because it'd been going on behind his back, secondly because Delaney had employed serving officers, which is against the rules, and thirdly because of the missing money. He refuses point-blank to stump up half.

'Anyway, we need to prove this, so we go looking for any paperwork concerning the Riley contract, but it's nowhere to be seen. Employees at BD Investigations tell us that the head of Croydon's murder squad, Detective Sergeant Phil Ware, attended the office the morning after the murder and seized it all, including the Riley's car auctions file.

'That same morning, Detective Sergeant Phil Ware took the first formal statement from Delaney, in which he makes no mention of his row with Nathan over the Riley auction.

'On Sunday, five days after Nathan's murder, DS Ware reveals to me that he and Delaney are old friends going back years. To make matters worse, Ware admitted that he'd been one of the officers moonlighting for Delaney at Riley's car auctions. Of course, we kick him off the case but by then he'd already buggered our investigation.

'Phil Ware retired on the sick and is now a partner with Delaney in BD Investigations.'

Fintan again: 'So you're convinced that Delaney and Phil Ware were co-conspirators in Nathan's murder?'

'Nathan had never drunk in here before that night. This pub is in Phil Ware's jurisdiction. None of Nathan's regular pubs were. Delaney lured him here for that reason, so that his murder would be investigated by his pal who heads the local murder squad. Of course, Delaney didn't swing the axe. Why get your hands dirty? But he had someone waiting outside that night who did.

'Now, how many people could've known Nathan was in here that night? Delaney's phone records show he made a call to Ware's direct line at Croydon police station on that evening at 5pm. I'm certain they were in cahoots.'

My brain is clinging on, just, and screaming one question: 'So Delaney is behind Nathan's murder, Ware helped derail the investigation. Who wielded the axe?'

'Delaney's brothers-in-law at that time were Chris and Gary Warner, major-league drugs importers with a history of extreme violence. Their alibis for the night are flimsy, to say the least. My information is that they even boasted about the murder in their local pub. We've arrested and questioned them but we haven't got any forensic evidence or witnesses willing to tell us what they know.'

Fintan starts pacing the car park. 'My old crime editor used to say there are only three motives for any murder. Dough, blow or a ho!'

Lambert frowns, confused.

'Money, drugs or a woman.'

He stops and turns to Lambert. 'Why don't you tell Donal here how there was more to Delaney having Nathan Barry wiped out than a fifteen-grand civil court action?'

Lambert hardly lets him finish. 'Nathan and Delaney were part of the West Croydon Lunch Club, a group of self-styled local high achievers who used to meet every other Friday and had gained legendary status for drunken shenanigans. Turns out Delaney and Nathan were romancing the same married woman, a local beautician called Karen Moore.

'In fact, before he went to the White Horse on the night of his murder, Nathan met Karen Moore at a local wine bar where they were seen in intimate conversation for well over an hour.'

'She must know something,' I say. 'Especially if things had come to a head between Nathan and Delaney.'

'I'm afraid Delaney has closed that line of enquiry on us,' he says, shaking his head. 'He left his wife and married Karen Moore a few months later.'

Chapter 11

Coombe Road, Croydon
Saturday, June 18, 1994; 15.00

Fintan and I remain astride the White Horse for a long liquid lunch.

'They'll never solve the Nathan Barry murder,' he declares. 'Not unless they get a walk-in confessor, a witness to the actual murder or some incontrovertible DNA.'

I sigh. 'I just can't see how there can be any connection to Julie Draper, except the fact they both worked in Croydon.'

'At least the Draper case is live. The Nathan Barry case looks dead and buried.'

'A bit like my career,' I grumble.

'There is another option, you know?' he says, surveying me archly like a disappointing art project. 'And this option would get you into CID tomorrow.'

'Like I've said before, I'm not joining the Freemasons.'

'Virtually every cop I know is in it. It's just a boys' club, Donal, you can use it purely for your own ends.'

'Virtually every criminal I've put away is in it too. It's rotten to the core. I'm having no part in any dodgy secret societies. Anyway, I thought you had some philandering Tory to front up for tomorrow's paper?'

'I do,' says Fintan, checking the time. 'We always leave it as late as possible, so he can't get hold of a lawyer or a judge or the Prime Minister or anyone else who might shoot the story down or leak it to a rival.'

'What about his right of reply?'

'That's what I'll be giving him at precisely 5pm. He wanted me to come to his home or constituency office, but I've insisted on a hotel lobby.'

'Why? In case he was planning on producing his Boer War Elephant gun?'

'Amongst other reasons.'

'And what is this man's grave crime?'

'He's a fifty-three-year-old married dad-of-two who had an affair with a rent boy about four years ago.'

'And how does this sexual peccadillo detract from his performance as an MP?'

'He's a "hang 'em and flog 'em", church-going Tory for one thing. And, last week, he defied the party whip to vote against reducing the gay age of consent to sixteen, in line with the heterosexual age of consent.'

'How old is his rent boy?'

'There's the rub, for want of a better word. When the Right Honourable George Field began relations with this man, he was a sixteen-year-old boy, which, under the law he himself championed, makes him a child sex offender and, even worse for a politician, a rampant hypocrite.'

'God his poor kids. And wife.'

'She must have known he swung both ways before she married him.'

‘How can you just assume that? And how can you square doing this to his kids?’

‘His sons are cocooned at some twenty-grand-a-year private school where buggery is virtually on the curriculum. I’m sure their wealthy friends will rally around and get them all massively paid numbers in the City.’

‘Is it a class thing with you really, Fintan? Are you the hunt sab who cares about foxes, or the one who just loves knocking over-privileged gits off their expensive horses?’

‘A bit of both,’ he grins, jumping to his feet. ‘Come on. Saturday is Take Down a Tory Day!’

Chapter 12

Lingfield, Surrey
Saturday, June 18, 1994; 17.00

Our Porsche turns not a single head outside the Lingfield Park Country Club.

'You watch, he'll sit there and lie through his teeth,' says Fintan.

'You can tell?'

'Jesus, don't they teach you anything at cop school? Two classic giveaways. If he glances low and left directly after the question, he's about to lie. If he keeps starting sentences with things like "truthfully" and "honestly", then he's in the act of lying. Look and learn.'

I recognise George Field MP as soon as we walk into reception. Tweedy, rotund, red-faced and hairy-eared, he's every inch the rugger-bugger buffoon who somehow defies evolution by earning the right to run the country.

Fintan introduces himself. Field wobbles to his feet, snorting like an addled rhino. He introduces us to Theresa Brunt, a Tory spin doctor dubbed 'Total' Brunt by *Private*

Eye magazine and a ringer for one of those cross-dressing brutes who frequented Mother Clap's in Victorian London.

We all sit and, like a magician flourishing a bunch of flowers, Fintan plucks a photo out of thin air and holds it beneath Field's purple, pockmarked nose.

'What is your relationship with this man?' he asks.

Field's nasal breathing grows so equine, it causes the photo clasped between Fintan's thumb and forefinger to flap. He takes a quick glance low to his left and blusters: 'I've never seen him before in my life.'

'He says he had a sexual relationship with you four years ago, when he was sixteen years old.'

'Absolute poppycock,' harrumphs Field. 'Honestly, are you really going to believe the word of some skanky drug-addict rent boy over mine?'

'How do you know he's a skanky drug-addict rent boy?' smiles Fintan.

George lists like a torpedoed old warship. Time to tag his prize-fighter mistress of spin.

'We know you were behind this ghastly man ringing George the other day and trying to trick him into admitting things over the phone,' she hisses. 'To resort to such desperate, underhand tactics clearly exhibits you lack any credible evidence to run this story. I dare say you've done your research into the Field family and are aware of their standing and influential friends?'

'I'm just trying to establish the facts, Theresa.'

'Well here's one undisputable fact for you, Mr Lynch,' she snaps. 'George's solicitor has Carter-Ruck on standby. If you print one word of this nonsense, we will sue. Do you understand?'

'Loud and clear, Theresa,' says Fintan, oozing humility. 'We'd best be on our way then.'

I can't believe he's giving up, just like that. At the exit, he turns back. 'By the way, George Field MP,' he bellows for the whole room to hear, 'our mutual friend Tommy wants to know if you still have those cigar-butt scars? You know, the ones he branded on your backside?'

Fintan scarpers, gesturing wildly to a fat man sat in a parked car. I recognise his trusty old snapper Ray 'Trundle' Taylor from previous capers.

'Raymondo, check out the wheezing tweed and his tranny Tory wench at the table nearest the fireplace. As soon as they step outside this door, hose them the fuck down.'

I follow Fintan's gravel-stomp back to the car.

'So, do you have evidence of this affair, or don't you?'

'Not yet,' he says. 'But we should have, very soon.'

'Why didn't you bring the rent boy here? That might have flushed him out.'

'Poor Tommy's already a nervous wreck. One death stare from Total Brunt and he'd have bottled it.'

'But you believe this Tommy character?'

'It's always the tiny details that make you realise someone is telling the truth. If George Field has got cigar butt scars on his arse, we're running this story.'

'Don't tell me, we're waiting for him to come out so we can rugby-tackle him to the ground and yank down his trousers?'

'Hopefully it won't come to that.'

'Hopefully? Jesus, Fintan. What are these cigar scars about anyway?'

'It's his thing. He made Tommy put cigars out on his arse.'

'My God! Why are the powerful and privileged almost universally into weird sex?'

'Powerful men have overactive libidos. And they just take what they want.'

Field and Brunt emerge grim-faced to a merciless 'monstering' from Ray.

'Right come on,' says Fintan, leaping out of the car.

'Just for the record, I'm taking no part in pulling this man's pants down.'

Flashgun-blind, the politicians stagger about the gravel like tasered apes. To my intense relief, we gallop past them, back into the hotel reception lounge.

Fintan strides urgently towards the table they just left, reaches under where he'd sat and says: 'Mmm, Juicy Fruit.'

He retrieves a matchbox-size metal box which he'd stuck to the table's underside with chewing gum.

'Let's hope I set this up okay.'

As we speed-walk back to the car, Fintan explains all.

'Alex Pavlovic, our venerable Prince of Darkness, came up with the idea. He calls it "our Inspector Goole" after that play, you know, *An Inspector Calls*. Basically, whenever we "front up" someone with an accusation, we leave this bug behind to catch what they say as soon as we leave. We've discovered that's when they always blab. He's such a good judge of human nature that man. He genuinely scares me.'

He pops out a tiny cassette, slips it into a Dictaphone.

'I call my version Dusko Popov, after the double agent, because it's 100 per cent reliable and you just pop it on and pop it off.' Fintan registers my confusion: 'Let me play you the tape.'

He presses rewind, then play. The moment the tape reaches Fintan's parting shot, we both lean forward.

BRUNT: Right, no more obfuscation George. Answer me honestly, did you fuck this chap?

GEORGE: Yes.

BRUNT: Did you know he was sixteen?

GEORGE: He was fifteen, the first time.

BRUNT: Christ. And what was all that about scarring on your bottom?

GEORGE: Those scars don't prove a thing. He could have seen my backside in any number of circumstances.

BRUNT: So, you do have these cigar scars on your bottom?

GEORGE: Well, strictly speaking yes.

BRUNT: That this male prostitute administered to you?

GEORGE: I, we . . . look he got totally carried away. It's not my thing at all.

BRUNT: Well that's just terrific, isn't it? If this does go to court, your arse cheeks are going to become the focus of national attention. Well done, George.

GEORGE: I think you're somewhat overreacting, Theresa, to a minor detail.

BRUNT: For God's sake, George, you're missing the point as usual. I'm trying to stop you, us, becoming a national laughing stock. I can see the cartoons now, some snotty-nosed rent boy picking out your butchered bum cheeks from an identity line-up of crinkled old arses.

GEORGE: Don't be unkind, Theresa.

BRUNT: Listen to me, George. We can't have this turning into a speculative national debate about the state of your arse. As your friend, I'm advising you to throw someone under the bus.

GEORGE: What?

BRUNT: You're a backbencher, George. Political plankton. You must know some lurid gossip about one of the big fishes that John Major despises.

GEORGE: I'm afraid I can't do that.

BRUNT: Is there anything at all we can throw at this sleazy bastard so he might leave you alone?

GEORGE: There might be something. I happen to know that a Scotland Yard Commander is up to his neck in corrupt activities. Though I'd have to break the confidence of my Lodge.

THERESA: We can't have you upsetting the Masons as well. Right, there's only one thing for it, I'll call the *Telegraph* now. You confess to having a brief relationship with this Tommy Allen character, only after he swore to you on his mother's grave he was twenty-one and they'll go easy on you.

GEORGE: If you think that would be for the best, Theresa.

BRUNT: I'll call the editor as soon as we get back to the car. It's the only way we can control this cigar-scarring business.

GEORGE: And what about the tabloid Mick?

BRUNT: We let him have the statement we give to the *Telegraph*, if – and only if – he drops any reference to cigars and scarred arse cheeks. You'd best get home and break the news to your family.

Chapter 13

Archway Tavern, North London
Saturday, June 18, 1994; 20.30

Fintan drops me off at the Archway Tavern, dictating that I find a prized perch for the big game. He paces outside, dictating his 'big game' prized scoop to a copy editor.

It's just 30 minutes until Ireland's World Cup clash against Italy. In Giants Stadium, New York. The game of all games. I'm already shaking. Somehow, Ireland's rise as a soccer force since 1988 seems inextricably linked to our renaissance as a nation. It's almost like we've been qualifying for major tournaments and shedding old Catholic shackles in tandem. Since '88, for example, we've legitimised divorce and homosexuality, elected a radical, liberal woman President and brokered peace in Northern Ireland. The Republic's role as poster boy for the EC has seen the introduction of free third-level education, the prosecution of kiddie-fiddler priests and the prospect of an economic boom.

Which is why I fear a hiding from the Italians tonight might bring it all crashing down around our ears. They knocked us out four years ago, and the British pundits talk of 'a grudge match' and 'Ireland's revenge mission'. But we're not really like that. We just want to make sure we don't make a show of ourselves. It's Ireland for God's sake; 0-0 will do grand.

I scope my phone for the umpteenth time. I notice it's what people do now, when they're alone. More texts from Zoe, checking that I'm okay. Childishly I refuse to reply, drawing perverse comfort from the idea she's beside herself with worry. My revenge mission.

Fintan slides onto the stool next to me, harassed.

'What's going on with you and Zoe?'

'What do you mean?'

'I had the deadline bends out there because she kept calling me, checking you're okay and asking why you're not coming home or getting back to her.'

His super-keen scoop-sensor is on high alert. I can almost see his nose twitching, so there's no point lying. I blurt it all out; about the texts, her confession of an affair with a man named 'Charles' and her admission that it had all been 'a terrible mistake' which she's anxious to remedy.

'I can't say I'm surprised,' he says.

'Well, all hail the mighty fucking prophet Fintan Lynch.'

'Bottom line is, she's never believed you're good enough for her, Donal. Neither has her insufferably snobby mother, for that matter.'

'Oh, thanks a bunch. What a shame OJ Simpson is otherwise preoccupied. I'm sure he could dispense some equally sage relationship advice.'

'I'm just telling you the truth. She's a uni-educated, *Guardian*-reading, middle-class liberal who loves the arts and is riven with ambition. You're a lumpen drunken cop whose sole ambition in life is to win some "dad-of-the-year award" for a kid that isn't even yours.'

‘Do not bring Matt into this, Fintan. I swear to God I’ll knock you out here and now.’

‘That’s more like it,’ he laughs. ‘Like the Oasis song says, you need to be yourself, Donal. You’re twenty-five and you’ve just spent the last six months sulking because she won’t have sex with you. Start living is my advice.’

‘Yeah well snorting coke every weekend and talking endless shite about yourself doesn’t work for all of us, Fintan. Unlike you, I don’t need to delude myself into thinking I’m living in some elusive fucking zeitgeist.’

‘That last line came straight out of Zoe’s mouth. I can actually hear her saying it. You need to leave her before you become completely brainwashed.’

‘I don’t want to leave her. Don’t you get it? I love Zoe and I love Matt. They’re my family now. At least I have a family.’

He recoils and I instantly regret delivering such a low blow. I know he’s missing Mam a lot more than he’s letting on. We both take an emotional standing count.

‘Look, Donal, if you want to win her back – and I can’t for the life of me imagine why now she’s betrayed you – then you need to earn her respect. That’s what has been lost here. You can’t have love without respect.’

‘How original. Maybe you should ring Sandra’s photo casebook, get Tania and Ellen along to act out our break-up?’

‘Your only hope is to move out right away. Show her you’re the boss and you’re not taking any shit. You’ve still got your room at ours. Me and Aidan would love to have you back at the Arsenal. Aidan was saying the other night he hasn’t seen you yet this year!’

I think back to our carefree, salad days living together. Aidan – psychiatric nurse and pothead – must rank as the most laid-back housemate of all time.

I smile for the first time in days. 'We were a happy crew, weren't we? The Hack, the Quack and the Insomniac.'

'It'll be like old times. You could do with the break. Give it a week or two and she'll be begging you to come back. Give it three and you'll be able to watch the entire World Cup tournament in the pub, guilt-free and still have the woman at the end.'

Someone cranks Jimmy Magee's foghorn to max, bringing Fintan's caveman relationship advice to a merciful end. Giants Stadium is rammed, at least ninety per cent of it green.

'They only gave us 3,000 tickets, amazing,' says Fintan.

Magee's rundown of the Italian team feels like a death sentence: Baggio, Maldini, Baresi, Donadoni, Costacurta, Signori, the other Baggio.

'Holy shit,' I say. 'The best players from the world's best league. Meanwhile we've got Terry Phelan and Eddie McGoldrick.'

'Hey, this team has beaten the best,' says Fintan. 'We can do this.'

He's right, of course. And not just about the football. But to make such a bold gesture as moving out, I need some sort of sign that it'll all work out okay. That she'll ask me back. An omen, to rubber-stamp my rubber spine.

Fuck it, if Ireland win, I'll ring her tonight and tell her I've moved back in with Fintan and Aidan, just until we sort things out. Of course, it won't come to that. Ireland can't possibly beat this lot.

Eleven minutes in, Baresi's weak defensive header bounces off the chest of Ray Houghton. He's thirty yards out, side-on to the Italian goal and their seven-foot keeper, Pagliuca. Once, twice, three times it bounces. Houghton swings his weaker left peg. The ball spins, floats, in slow motion, in silence, in a dream, over Pagliuca's flailing arms, under the crossbar, into the back of the net.

Mayhem! Colliding bodies. Spilt beers, spilt tears.

'Oh my Jesus,' screams Fintan, grabbing me in a headlock and running me skull-first into the wall.

For the next seventy-nine minutes, we cling on, and on, and on, every Italian attack an ulcer, every shot a full-on stroke.

The final whistle triggers my complete emotional collapse. Through a mask of tears, I watch our raggle-taggle band of Irish, English and Scottish-born players, some accomplished, more still journeymen, stagger over to the fans in delirious disbelief. I think of our aunts and uncles and cousins scattered across America and Australia, those generations of Irish cursed by forced exile and written out of our history, and how our 'blow-ins' like Coyne and Sheridan and Babb have done this for them. For us.

I then step outside to make that call, knowing that tonight, at least, there'll be no shame for an Irishman to be seen crying in public.

Chapter 14

Arsenal, North London
Sunday, June 19, 1994; 05.00

I'm walking through the front door of our flat. I can hear Matt wailing. I must get to him at once.

I look in the kitchen, then the sitting room, but he's nowhere to be seen. Then I realise where his crying is coming from; the cupboard below the stairs. How did he get in there?

The door opens only a fraction. There he is, his little wet face crumpled in despair, wailing my name over and over: 'Dong! Dong! Dong!'

But the door won't open. I grab the handle hard and pull with all my might. Still it won't budge. It's then I see the black hand reach around Matt's pale little throat. Frantic, I pull with everything I've got and roar blue murder at the figure in the shadows. But the door won't yield and the black swallows my screams.

That gloved hand closes in on Matt's little throat, turning off his sobs like a tap.

'Matt,' I wail from the very pit of my soul.

All flashes yellow. Fintan stands over me in bedraggled alarm.

I glance about, recognise his sitting room and flop back against the couch.

'Jeez, Dorothy, great to have you back,' he says.

Chapter 15

Arsenal, North London
Sunday, June 19, 1994; 10.00

The titanic emotional strain of watching Ireland win a football match *and* dumping the woman I love knock me out for five hours straight. If only I could endure the same emotional torment every day; there's the cure for insomnia right there.

As I lumber down the stairs, it's like I never moved out. Aidan's in his bedroom, taming his Sunday morning black dog anxiety with a fat spliff, noodling on his guitar and braying unrequited love for his latest bus-stop/supermarket crush. Aidan's an old friend from Ireland and an eejit, but a nice one. I say a hopeless romantic. Fintan says hopeless at romance and all its inherent politics.

Fintan's sat at the kitchen table, stacked ashtray and sacked newspapers telling their own story; he's been up for hours breaking down the news agenda. He pushes his rag my way.

'Our fat Tory friend made quite the splash,' he smiles. 'Alex Pavlovic won't be happy that I've trumped him yet again.'

Married MP Rent Boy Shame blares the front-page headline. *Happiness is . . . a Hamlet-scarred Butt!* teases the strapline.

'Isn't the cigar stuff a bit dark and twisted for your readers?'

'Sweet schadenfreude more like. It's a bit like David Mellor shagging that actress in his Chelsea kit. Our readers love seeing the powerful not just brought down but humiliated. Total Brunt was spot on. Debate about the precise condition of George Field's arse cheeks will run and run. And at least we know the "cigar butt" thing is true. The stuff about Mellor in the Chelsea kit was totally made up, icing on the cake if you like. But it's the image everyone remembers.'

'How do you know the football kit isn't true?'

'Our secret filming guy, Gerry Woods, showed me the footage. My God, talk about the albino walrus of love.'

'Don't you worry that, someday, one of these people you publicly humiliate might turn around and top themselves? Or that their innocent kids suffer?'

'I'm just the messenger, Donal. Besides, when you look at the family histories of these toffs, you discover Phillip Larkin was spot on, at least about one class of people. They're genetically doomed to emotionally fuck up their kids in every way imaginable, starting with boarding school aged five. You're going to like the next page even less.'

I open to the headline *Outfoxed!*

With unadulterated revelry in our failure, the sub-headline screams *Blundering Cops 'Sign Julie's Death Warrant', by Alex Pavlovic, Deputy Chief Crime Correspondent.*

I shake my head. 'Is there a default mode on your computer systems that ensures the word "cops" is always preceded by the word "blundering" or "bungling"?'

He smirks. 'You do tend to do both quite a lot.'

Hapless detectives who failed to save innocent kidnap victim Julie Draper were duped into handing over a £175,000 pay-off to her evil kidnapper, the Sunday News *can reveal.*

Pretty estate agent Julie, 24, had been dead for at least thirty-six hours when cops paid the ransom to her abductor, who calls himself Mr Kipper. Detectives remain convinced that Julie's killer also abducted and murdered Suzy Fairclough, also 24 and an estate agent, in 1988

Last night, the Draper family's MP condemned 'systematic police failures' in the investigation, and accused detectives of 'effectively signing Julie's death warrant'.

'They lost Julie, the kidnapper and the cash,' raged John Tilbrook MP. 'What's to stop this animal targeting another random victim now he's realised how easy it is to get away with it?'

Kipper sent a letter to police this week threatening to target a child unless he receives another pay-off. An insider on the investigation says they are anxiously waiting further contact.

Underneath, a shot of 'devastated Bill and Beryl Draper at their family home in South Norwood'. The accompanying caption plays tastelessly on the new National Lottery slogan: *It could be you!*

Said Bill: 'She never hurt a fly. We just don't understand why he targeted her.' Said Beryl: 'What scares me is anyone out there could be next. He's just plucking innocent people off the street.'

The article goes on to describe Julie as 'bright and independent . . . a gem collector and crossword fanatic . . . devoted to her beloved dogs, Rex and Dino, and her goldfish, Ben and Jerry.'

My mind snags on that final detail. I say to Fintan: 'I thought Crossley said her fish were called Mutt and Jeff?'

He smiles: 'He may have been treating your fishy question with the contempt it deserved.'

'So much for your theory that she knew her kidnapper,' I say. 'It's clear she didn't have an enemy in the world.'

'I just don't buy it,' he says.

I hope Fintan's right. Because if Julie had been randomly selected, then how could her kidnap be connected to the murder of Nathan Barry? My mind rewinds to those dreams. What had Julie been trying to tell me? I need her to come to me again, give me some more clues. For that to happen, I need to get close to her dead body. But how? As a mere acting DC, I'd need to get clearance from Crossley to visit her in the mortuary, which isn't going to happen. This is where my pathologist 'squeeze' Edwina Milne may come in handy. Though how the hell I broach the subject during a 'convivial supper' is another matter.

'It's not your brilliant brain or gratifyingly juvenile body I'm after, Edwina, it's your keys to the mortuary.'

I'll text her anyway, see if she's up for a bite tonight. How we proceed from there is anyone's guess. I just hope I'm not subconsciously engaging in some sort of Freudian 'mum substitute' thing.

'Oh God brace yourself,' Fintan sighs as I turn another page.

Massacre, says the headline. *Six shot dead in village pub.*

Six men were shot dead and five wounded when terrorists attacked a pub during Ireland's World Cup game against Italy.

'Jesus,' I hear myself say.

The Ulster Volunteer Force has claimed responsibility for the attack on the Heights Bar, a Catholic pub in the small village of Loughinisland, Co. Down.

'They murdered them for shouting for Ireland.'

All last night's unbridled joy now feels tainted, our wild celebrations shallow and spurious.

'Why is an atrocity like this stuck at the bottom of page 11?'

'We're under orders from on high, play down anything that might jeopardise the peace process.'

'Oh yeah, the peace process, punctuated by the occasional under-reported massacre of the innocent.'

My mind turns to our Da, a Sinn Fein councillor in the Irish Midlands and unashamed IRA supporter since the late 1960s. Only he knows how many people he helped slaughter in pursuit of the Provos' most nebulous of goals, 'The Cause'. Somewhat ironically, he's now risking his neck going against fellow 'volunteers' to support the peace process.

'Da says they were on the verge of announcing a total ceasefire,' says Fintan. 'Now they have to be seen to retaliate. Another round of tit-for-tat killings. I'm telling you, there are dark forces at work here, stirring this up, making sure peace can't happen.

'But he assures me it will, and soon, as impossible as that seems,' he says, standing and rubbing his palms together. 'So, what's the newly unattached, responsibility-free Donal up to today? I rather fancy a booze-fuelled, three-match World Cup marathon.'

'I'm seeing Matt today. Then I suppose I'd better show my face back at the Cold Case Squad tomorrow, though nobody's been in touch.'

'Oh, the joys of the lackadaisical public sector. What about tonight?'

'I may have a hot date!'

'Anyone I know?'

'Edwina Milne.'

I cringe in anticipation of a barrage of verbal abuse about false teeth and fallen arches.

'You hound,' he smiles. 'She is a silver vixen, in a sort of Susan George / Felicity Kendall way. When did all this come about?'

'I bumped into her in the Lamb in Pyecombe.'

'And now you're succulent lamb to her Wolverine slaughter. There's something a bit dominatrix about her, wouldn't you say?'

'You think that about all upper-class women,' I smile. Truth is, I don't really know if it'll lead anywhere. I'm just going along with it for now, no pressure, because I haven't the stomach for any more rejection.

'Well good for you,' he says, and I can tell he means it. 'A torrid affair might be just the thing to flush Zoe out of your system. Make sure you seize the moment if it arrives, Donal, and win the day.'

As I force down a coffee that could trigger a zombie apocalypse, my pounding head exhumes last night's drunken call to Zoe. Pumped by Ireland's fearless soccer heroics, I'd given it the full, unreconstructed, wall-thumping rhetoric.

First, I told her I was moving back in with Fintan and Aidan.

'I understand,' she'd said, 'but please don't disappear for days at a time again like you've just done. It really worries me.'

Second, I read her my rights. 'Regardless of what happens to us, I shall carry on being a dad to Matt, starting tomorrow.'

'Hang on, Donal, you can't just announce you're moving out and then start invoking rules about your role in his life.'

I was taking none of her lip. 'I'll be over at 1pm sharp, and you can expect me every Sunday at that time.'

'You charge on round at one then. You won't find us in.'

'What do you mean, you won't be in?'

'Matthew will be with his grandparents.'

I remember my mind cartwheeling through scenarios: She'll be out with Charles. No doubt catching a musical. Or gawping at some monstrous hunk of modern art.

'I'll pick him up from your parents so. As long as your mum doesn't make me tarmac the drive first.'

She sighed pointedly.

'All right, take him to the park tomorrow, but don't use Matthew as a way to control me, Donal. Not now you've announced you're leaving us. I won't stand for it.'

'I'm just thinking of him,' I said and hung up.

She's right of course. Since uncovering her affair, I've been using Matt's devotion to me as a way of punishing her and expediting her chucking of Chuck. But I've come to realise that our mutual, undying love for Matt won't be enough to save us. She has to still love me.

Those toxic Costa Rican caffeine dregs galvanise me. I grab my phone and psych myself with Fintan's rousing words: 'Seize the moment . . . win the day.'

I text Edwina: *I looked up convivial and would like to give it a go tonight!* I then press send before I have a chance to agonise/re-type endlessly/suck out every cheerful, carefree spark of spontaneity.

I refuse to let Edwina's lack of reply dent my new-found positivity, jump in the car and head up to Crouch End, for once not cringing at the prospect of meeting Zoe's mum and dad.

She's never believed you're good enough for her. Neither has her insufferably snobby mother . . .

Well look who's trundling up your fancy fucking hill now, the wronged man, so imbued with honour and decency that he eschews all personal grievance for the benefit of a twenty-two-month-old boy who isn't even his own. Look down on me now, Sylvia, with your wanton slut of a daughter.

Sylvia answers the door resignedly, as if I were the Gestapo and she'd been expecting me.

Matt runs for me like there's nothing else in the world, jumping and crashing face-first into my stomach. 'Dong!' cries his muffled voice and I feel myself go.

I bury my face in his hair and breathe deeply. I can't show weakness. Not in front of vinegar tits.

Zoe's dad appears, smiling meekly. Good old Arthur.

'We were surprised to hear you were coming, Donal, after all that's gone on.'

'Pleasantly surprised, I hope, Arthur.'

'Well I, or rather we're impressed actually, that you're handling it all so . . . maturely.'

I put Matt down in case I fall over from shock.

'Well I just want what's best for this little fellow. And for Zoe too,' I stammer.

'Matthew will thank you in years to come,' says Sylvia, nodding earnestly. 'You know, for swallowing your pride.'

'Sure, it's only a trip to the park, no big deal.'

'You know what we mean,' says Arthur, as Sylvia places her hand on my upper arm.

Jesus, I'm thinking, *zero to hero in a day. Moving out has proven a master stroke. Fintan's a fucking genius.*

I survey them both meaningfully, my newly proud parents-in-law.

'We'll find a way through this, I'm certain of that,' I say, cryptically but with conviction.

'It hasn't been easy for Zoe,' says Sylvia. 'But we know she'll always put Matthew's welfare first. And now we know you're doing the same, well, we're so relieved.'

'Well he's worth it,' I say, inexplicably mimicking the female American voiceover from that ghastly shampoo ad. Sylvia looks uneasy, Arthur aghast. Not for the first time, I wonder why I feel compelled to ruin genuine emotional moments.

'Make sure you're back here by four on the dot,' says Sylvia sternly. 'Or you can expect the Spanish degree.'

'Of course,' I say, fighting the urge to add: 'Don't you mean Spanish Inquisition?' But their kindness is just the emotional validation I need post Zoe's betrayal. *They'll never get my humour, but at least they're starting to get me.*

At Priory Park, we 'do the rounds' twice until Matt finally plants himself on his favourite ride: the see-saw. I straddle the other end and launch into a painfully slow and controlled 'Jane Fonda squat' so as not to send him into orbit. Undercarriage creaking and screaming for mercy, I check the time and realise we've killed a measly twenty minutes. I'd forgotten how tedious and knackering childcare is and ransack my brain for a plan B that might less strenuously pass the remaining 100. I'm then consumed with guilt. Is this all that parenthood has really meant to me; a relentless see-saw of duty versus guilt? Then I think of Zoe out on her hot date with Charles and feel instantly vindicated. How had she so effortlessly dismounted from the parenting see-saw? Even Sylvia is so obviously horrified by her daughter's selfish behaviour that she has finally identified some merit in me!

'Pelvis has left the building,' I tell Matt, heaving myself off and lowering his end with my hands. 'Dong's hips are a little rusty. A lot rustier than mummy's, as we now know.'

My phone pings a reply from Edwina. *Juan Gris, the Cut, 8pm?*

I've no idea what she means. Is that a restaurant, a bar or a man? Maybe it's some class of art house cinema, or Juan's a famous opera singer I should know about. I opt for a safe, *See you then Edwina,* until I can find out more, adding an 'x', then deleting it, then repeating that process countless times. *Seize the moment, win the day,* I tell myself, adding two kisses. I then remove the *Edwina* so that the kisses look more habitual than personal. Never mind seizing moments, I think to myself, let's just try to make sure she actually shows up. After all, I'm the only man I know with a track record of scaring women off *before* a date.

'I'm hungry,' whines Matt and I'm suddenly struck by a deliciously petty, small-minded way to hit back at Zoe and her folks.

'What about McDonald's?' I say, knowing that the recently opened branch in Hampstead village still has wax-jacketed local buffoons protesting outside. How I'll relish crossing that particular picket line. Of course, poor sheltered Matt has never heard of the ghastly American corporate behemoth and asks if we're going to Old McDonald's farm.

'In a way,' I say. 'It's like Old McDonald's organic farm shop, something I know you're far more familiar with.'

I'm one of several solo dads in there, hoping that a Happy Meal will provide at least some temporary emotional nourishment. I make sure he brings his box and toy back to Nanny's. *A message to you Zoe*, I hum, adapting the old Specials classic; *I'm not beholden to you, your parents or your parenting books any longer. I set my own rules now.*

We return to a welcoming committee of Sylvia and Arthur in their front garden. They seem in a real hurry to get Matt back inside and me gone, as if they'd earlier exhausted their annual allowance of 'niceness' towards me.

Back in the car, I suddenly remember the breeze block I'd retrieved from the Julie Draper ransom drop. I haul it out of the boot, carry it to the front door, ring the bell and wait. After an eternity, I ring again. Finally, Arthur's voice warbles from above.

'Now look here, Donal, we don't want any unpleasantness,' he says. I take a reverse step and look up. He flinches from a barely open upstairs window.

'What are you talking about, Arthur?'

'Leave now, without using that, and we won't call the police.'

I laugh. 'What? You mean this block? What do you think I'm going to do, Arthur? Smash your lead-glass windows?'

'I've got the phone in my hand.'

'Arthur, for God's sake, it's an exhibit from a case. I was hoping Zoe could use her forensic skills to check it out for me. Why would I suddenly want to smash your windows?'

'Very well then. Leave it right there and go, at once.'

'Jesus, Arthur, what the hell is going on?'

The window slams shut, the aftershock shattering my heart into a thousand stabbing little shards. Because, at that very moment, I realise; something's changed and they're plotting to take Matt away from me.

Chapter 16

Waterloo, Central London
Sunday, June 19, 1994; 19.30

It worries me that Time Out's London Guide rates the Juan Gris tapas restaurant 'one of London's cosiest and most authentic Balearic experiences'. My only previous 'authentic Balearic experience' involved heat stroke and an emergency stomach pump.

By 'cosy' they clearly mean overcrowded, over-hot and underlit, with tables rammed so close together that salsa splashback is a genuine peril.

To top it all, perched upon what appears to be an oversized Ikea shelf above the mayhem, some moustachioed wannabe Gipsy King wails 'Bamboleo' as if it were a Mexican ten-second bomb warning. I'd anticipated an intimate evening getting to know each other; not a front seat at Los Lobos.

It doesn't help that the horseshoe-shaped bar dominating the centre of the restaurant is rammed, shoulder-to-shoulder. I could really use a few sharpeners, but there isn't even a tiny gap to 'motor boat' through. I notice with thinly disguised contempt that most of these barflies aren't even drinking. They're eating meals. At the bar! They'd never stand for that in Ireland. It's all I can do not to reclaim some ancient bar rights for the liquid-only species by yanking one of them off a stool.

I finally manage to demand three bottles of their strongest beer, hurriedly plucking the alien green fruit from the spouts before they pollute the contents. I stand there drinking at the very spot every single waiter needs to repeatedly pass through. But I ignore the chorus of Iberian harrumphing because I need this pre-emptive alcohol hit. Booze is the antidote to my crippling twin social shortcomings: lack of confidence and lack of energy. But I've got to get the balance just right; anaesthetise and energise without straying into morose or mental. And by Christ, the margins are slim, as I've discovered to my cost.

For some reason, I turn towards the entrance just as Edwina makes hers, oozing the right amount of confidence and well-bred poise; summer-school muscle memory. She looks elegant but foxy in a high-collared white blouse, short black jacket and pencil skirt. I've never seen her in a skirt before; the notion that this is a component part of her overall seduction strategy sends a lightning bolt of glorious anticipation zinging through me. It's followed by heaving great black thunderclouds of guilt; I still love Zoe.

Waiting staff almost collide in their rush to greet a favoured regular. The pieces click together. A Home Office pathologist must earn a packet. Edwina leaves her country pile every Sunday evening, taking the train to Waterloo and a short walk to her bijou flat overlooking the Thames. She hasn't time to shop or cook so joins the barfly diners here where she can eat alone unnoticed.

She glances about, sees me and smiles. She points to the

only empty table in the joint, buried deep in a corner, mercifully the furthest from El Throat Cancer's dismembering of Spanish culture and his own guitar. Maybe we're going to have that intimate evening after all.

'Your usual, Edwina?' says the waiter as we sit.

'Yes, please Marco. This is Donal, a friend from work.'

He frowns at me in confused disapproval.

'Hi Marco. What is her usual, if you don't mind me asking?'

'Dirty Martini.'

'Shaken not stirred?'

He scowls at me. 'Shaking a Martini is the sure-fire way to spoil it.'

'And it should be stirred with a wooden spoon, not a metal one, isn't that right, Marco?' teases Edwina.

Marco smiles, his eyes misting bashfully like some loved-up Lab Beagle. Time to remind El Horno that she's my date tonight.

I hand him back the drinks list. 'Make that two.' *Why am I feeling so possessive? Has what little confidence I possessed been so obliterated by Zoe's betrayal?*

I watch her weighing up the menu. Her lustrously constructed Anne Bancroft hairstyle could render a less classically beautiful woman severe. It would make Zoe look like De Niro in *Cape Fear*.

I'm mildly terrorised by the menu; no English translations or helpful photos.

'You know it might be best if you order for both of us, Edwina,' I say casually.

'Well I have had everything here at least ten times.'

'Oh it's not that,' I say. 'The only words I know in Spanish are *cerveza* and *cigarillo*.'

She smiles. 'How refreshing. You're not a veggie, are you?'

'God no! If I'd been a veggie in 1980s Ireland, I'd have starved.'

'Good. You'll like it here then.'

Marco brings the drinks and takes her order.

'To our trusty source of income, the dead,' she says, raising her glass.

'The dead,' I smile and we clink.

I manage not to wince, just, at the bitter, salty onslaught, and wonder if love rival Marco further muddied my Dirty with a lace of vinegar. He has that malevolent look; like a camper version of Angel Eyes in *The Good, the Bad and the Ugly*.

'Do you know what I love about this place,' she says, second-guessing my first question. 'It makes me feel like I'm on holiday, without a care in the world.'

'If I was exposed to so much gore, I'd need a regular dose of cheerful release.'

She laughs kindly. 'The gore doesn't bother me remotely. I've never been squeamish. I started out in vascular surgery where we sometimes found ourselves working in geysers of blood. I remember after one operation, I removed my boots to find each filled with a pint or so of blood clot. I suddenly understood why everyone else had worn their scrub trousers on the outside!'

She giggles at the memory while I grip a table leg and will my light-headed swoon to pass.

'At medical school, I remember my excitement at the prospect of cutting a real human body and dissecting it with my bare hands. Of course, it was all a bit of an anticlimax. They prepare bodies for dissection by embalming them with formaldehyde solution. Embalming leaches blood from the body, and formalin stiffens the tissues and fades them dull grey. It felt more like cutting up alien dummies. After the first couple of incisions, I knew I'd be okay. In fact, the worst part was my hands getting all greasy and slippery from the fatty tissue.'

Right on cue, bowls of assorted meats land on our table.

'I strongly recommend this,' she says, pushing one my way. 'The Spanish have a way with pork.'

I force a smile and swallow hard at the shiny white meat, trying not to think of her elbow-deep in porcine human flesh.

'Are you okay?' she asks.

'I am a little squeamish to be honest, Edwina.'

'How bad?'

'Put it this way, last Christmas morning I fainted while stuffing the turkey.'

'I thought you'd be inured to it all by now,' she says, her voice steeling. 'You do keep finding young women's bodies, after all.'

'I know! I'm like the Grim Reaper,' I say brightly, guiltily, giving myself away. I tag on an unconvincing: 'Just one of those strange things, I guess.'

A single eyebrow pump prompts a Marco pitcher invasion; some sort of cocktail by the jug. 'I think we're going to need this,' she announces gravely. 'Marco here introduced it to me as the world's most underrated cocktail. Gin and honey. Might be more to your taste, Donal.'

'All alcohol is to my taste, Edwina.'

As Marco pours two kamikaze measures, I think: *Forget soulmate, I've finally found a female drinking partner who can hold her liquor*.

She takes a decidedly unladylike glug and I imagine the honey gin taste on her lips.

'Last year, when you were probing the deaths of those street girls, you found two bodies, isn't that right?'

I nod. 'One of them in your mortuary.'

'A year before that, you were the first officer at two more murder scenes, again young females?'

She knows something's going on; that I can't be stumbling across all these murder victims by chance.

'And this week you found Julie Draper.'

'What are you implying, Edwina?' I laugh weakly.

She stops blinking, tilts her chin down to inspect my eyes.

'I've been doing this job for almost twenty years. In all that time, you're the only officer I know that keeps stumbling across all these freshly murdered young women. At least five that I know of. How many more has there been, Donal? Is there something you need to tell me?'

Her tone has turned accusatory, toxic. I freeze in disbelief. It's only when I try to say 'what?' that I realise my mouth is hanging limply open.

'Well?' she snaps.

I refill my tumbler. She clocks my shaking hand. I hear the gin mix pouring, the ice clinking off the inside of the glass. Nothing else. I've been amazed that none of my police colleagues had spotted my frankly alarming run of stiffs. Fintan knows I get these visions, but it's all too whacky and 'out there' for him to handle. Zoe's scientific mind is even less forgiving, so I tell her as little as possible.

I take a long hard draw on my cocktail.

'I really like this drink, Edwina. Does it have a slang name, you know, like John Collins or Margarita?'

'It's called Honey Trap,' she says, deadpan as hell.

I suck up some more, realising with a certain sweet satisfaction that she's got me. For once, the truth might be more palatable than her competing theories. I might be a bona fide unstable nutter, but at least I'm not a killer.

'Okay, you're going to think I'm bonkers, Edwina, but something keeps happening and I don't understand how or why.'

She sits forward, stirring her cocktail absently.

'Every time I've been physically close to a murder victim . . . they've come to me that night, in really vivid visions. I can't say dreams because they're not. They're too real and they happen when I'm awake.'

She nods greedily, demanding more.

Gin-trapped, I run her through every incidence; the visions, the clues, how it helped me find bodies and even crack some tricky investigations. She hangs on every word, a rapt audience of one, growing increasingly uneasy with each revelation.

To assuage her mounting horror, I tell her about my sleep paralysis diagnosis, and how this might explain what's happening to me. I then hit her with my own pragmatic theory; that my subconscious mind is presenting clues to me in an unorthodox, visual way.

'I really can't listen to much more of this,' she declares suddenly, standing and flapping about for her belongings.

'Look, I know as a scientist you don't buy a word of it. Trust me, I wish it wasn't happening to me.'

'I really must be off.'

'But there's half a pitcher left . . . why don't we take it with us down to the South Bank?'

'Have it,' she snaps.

'I feel like I've angered you, Edwina.'

'Not at all,' she says. 'It's just this place can get so noisy and stuffy. I need some air, okay? I'll call you.'

She casts me an apologetic, closed-mouth smile before vanishing into the throng. She's right. It is noisy and hot, but I know few things bring a date more swiftly and decisively to an end than declaring you receive regular one-on-one briefings from the recently murdered.

Then it hits me. Mam made it clear on her deathbed why this thing is happening to me. It's time I dealt with it, once and for all. Otherwise I'll never be able to hold down a proper relationship, or live an ordinary life. I need to book that appointment tomorrow.

Chapter 17

Croydon, South London
Monday, June 20, 1994; 10.00

When London banned skyscrapers in the 1960s, Croydon's town planners stepped in and invited every phallic-worshipping developer down to Surrey for a good old high-rise orgy. They duly delivered an inferno of towering vanities, throwing up forty-nine thundering concrete blocks in a kamikaze act of self-destruction so breathtaking that it even gained its own neologism, *Croydonisation*. Aiming for mini-Manhattan, they wound up with a brutalist Benidorm, minus beach and sunshine, plus flyovers, feral youth and fried chicken.

As I negotiate the endless, blood-knotting one-way systems, I recall how David Bowie once said Croydon represents 'everything I want to get away from'. BD Investigations, owned by John Delaney, one-time business partner of murdered bailiff Nathan Barry, is everything I need to get *to* right now, but I can't. During her visit to me, Julie led me to a murder victim who died with an axe in his face. There is only one; Nathan Barry. Julie came to me five nights ago to tell me his murder is connected to hers. The only connection I can see so far is geographical. Their workplaces are just over a mile apart. Her home is two miles from here, in South Norwood. Now I need to speak to the prime suspect in Nathan's murder, but I'm struggling to even get to him.

Dizzy and distressed, I park up near East Croydon train station to tackle the tangling tarmac on foot.

As I walk, I re-examine the text message that kept me awake all night.

If you want to know the truth about Nathan Barry's murder, be at BD Investigations HQ tomorrow, 10am, JD.

There can only be one JD. How does John Delaney, Nathan Barry's erstwhile business partner and the prime suspect in his murder, know I've been investigating the case? And how has he got hold of my phone number?

Along the way, I'm accosted by religious maniacs, screamed at by a regular maniac and treated to 'evils' by a succession of brooding hoodies lashed to pumped and pink-eyed pugs. Reaching the infamous lair of an alleged axe murderer comes almost as a relief.

BD Investigations conducts its joyless work in a fittingly low-rent drab brick terrace house that sits between a bunting-festooned car sales yard and one of those fried chicken shops ingeniously named after a US State that isn't Kentucky. I press the nose of a grey metal intercom. A nasal female voice instructs me to push the buzzing door and go upstairs.

Delaney is waiting for me on the landing, wearing a cream shirt, densely patterned blue tie, beige suit trousers and incongruous blue suede slip-on shoes. Everything about him is meringue-shaped; from his bouffant mousey hair and jowly face to his equator of a waist. Hail fellow well-fed, he smiles and offers me his hand: 'DC Lynch. John. I had a feeling you'd come.'

'Please, call me Donal.'

He directs me past a timid, tightly permed and heavily goggled secretary whose head bobs like a woodpecker as she types. Delaney performs a hilarious imitation and, despite myself, I warm to him.

Inside the office, behind one of two desks, sits the Tory minister Ken Clarke, if someone had ironed his hair into a comedy fringe and fed him pie and ale for two decades.

'Phil Ware,' he declares, wobbling to his feet in a straining all-grey ensemble. 'Why don't we sit over there.'

I lead the rhinos to our watering hole, a glass table next to the bay window. Phil brings an ashtray, a box of Players and a Zippo lighter, determined to clog his last good artery. With their hangdog faces and crinkled necks, they look about as murderous as a pair of St Bernard rescue dogs.

'I hear you've met our old friend DI Lambert? Let me guess what he told you,' says Delaney in his no-nonsense Geordie brogue. 'I lured Nathan to the White Horse that night to set him up to be whacked because he was about to blow the whistle on the fact I hired a few serving police officers to help me at Riley's car auction. Am I warm?'

'Red hot.'

'DI Lambert seemed surprised that I knew about Nathan's murder when he knocked on my door at 1 o'clock that morning. Funnily enough, knowing most of the officers on the Croydon murder squad, I got several calls about it. And the reason my ex-wife didn't react to the news is because I'd already told her, and she'd just taken a sleeping pill.

'As for the auction, there is no record that I paid any of those officers and, even if I had, the most they'd get for moonlighting is a slap on the wrist. Do you really think I'd have my business partner murdered for that?'

I meet his stare head-on. 'But you had more than one

motive, John. You and Nathan were both married, and you were both seeing the same mistress.'

'We both liked Karen. She and Nathan had dated, briefly, months earlier. Me and Karen didn't become an item until about a year after Nathan's death.'

'That still seems soon to me,' I say.

John smiles, his eyes twinkling. 'When you realise you want to spend the rest of your life with somebody, you want the rest of your life to start as soon as possible.'

I'm not about to get suckered by his schmaltz. 'Apart from you, Karen was the last person to see Nathan alive that evening. They had a cosy little date in that wine bar. Why did she need to see him, John? What was she trying to persuade him to do? Or not to do?'

'They bumped into each other outside her work. Look, Donal, if Karen thought for one second I'd anything to do with Nathan's murder, she'd go straight to you lot. Nathan Barry was worth more to me alive, and there isn't a shred of evidence to prove any of this nonsense.'

Poor Mr Karen Moore, I suddenly think, empathising with a fellow cuckold. Then I wonder if he's been properly examined as a suspect.

'What about Karen's husband in all this?'

'Their girls had grown up. She and Walter had been living separate lives for years, so it's not like Karen did a midnight flit.'

I move onto the other damning evidence against Delaney, alleged commissioner of the murder, and Ware who, at the very least, covered it up. 'What shocks me is that you two didn't declare your close friendship for several days at the start of the investigation. And the fact that in your first statement, John, which you, Phil, took the morning after Nathan's murder, you both decided to make no mention of the Riley car auctions business. Oh, and the small fact that the Riley auctions file vanished.'

'What auction file?' says John. 'It was a cash deal that I didn't want to declare to the taxman. Why would I have kept a file?'

Phil lights up and pipes up: 'I didn't think the arrangement with Riley's auctions was worth mentioning.'

I let him know I'm not buying that. 'You didn't think that an ongoing row about fifteen grand that had gone missing was worth mentioning?'

'It wasn't worth killing for, was it?' says Ware. 'Look, we're both cops, Donal, albeit I'm retired now, and we both know that the standard rate for a hit in south London is twenty grand. Whacking Nathan over fifteen grand makes no sense.'

I don't take my eyes off Phil. 'Why didn't you declare your friendship with John right away?'

'I did. I told DI Lambert's boss, DCI Frank Vaughan, the day after the murder and he told me to stay tight with John over the next few days to see if he'd let anything slip. He denied this later, but it's the truth. By the Sunday, it was causing a lot of friction between us, wasn't it John? I realised my position was untenable and stood down.'

'With respect Phil, DI Lambert believes five days was enough time for you to, in his words, bugger the investigation.'

Phil bristles. 'Come on, think about it? We had twenty-five cops on this case from day one. How much damage could one officer do to a murder investigation over a few days? Even a senior officer? It's not like I was some puppetmaster pulling all the strings. That was Lambert's job, and if anyone buggered the investigation, he did.'

'And how did he do that?'

Ware takes a long drag of his cigarette. 'He'd just been on one of those bloody courses at the FBI headquarters in Quantico. He loves all the forensic psychology stuff and thinks its bible. One of the mantras he brought back is that the last person to see someone before they're murdered is almost always involved. He kept quoting the rate of eighty-five per cent and, of course, some of the lads were taking the piss. He didn't like that one bit. He's very puffed up, Lambert. From that moment on, he became totally blinkered and fixated on John. He wouldn't listen to or consider anything that didn't point to his guilt. He became obsessed.'

I feel my engines revving. 'DI Lambert had been a detective for over twenty years. I dare say he knew a collar when he saw one. It's always money, drugs or a woman, isn't that what they say? I've seen people murdered for fifteen quid, never mind fifteen grand. To top that, John, your macho code couldn't countenance losing Karen to this man you'd clearly grown to hate. You just had to click your fingers to get it done, didn't you, John, at mate's rates too. Your psychopathic brothers-in-law, the Warners, were desperate for money at the time and happy to do your dirty work for you.'

John picks up his mobile, taps a few times and puts it to his ear. 'Can you meet me and Phil at the Harp in half an hour? Yeah, put him right on a couple of things. See you then.' John hangs up and looks at me: 'I'll let Gary Warner answer that charge himself. In the meantime, let me tell you about all the suspects DI Lambert didn't bother to check out. You know he sent me to break the news to Nathan's wife, Emma, that night? He must have been testing his Quantico theory already. We rang the doorbell, she answered and led us to the kitchen. As soon as she sat, DC Rooney said: "I'm afraid John has bad news". She stared at me. I said: “Sorry Emma, Nathan’s dead.” She said: “How?” I said: “He’s been hit over the head”, and she said: “I thought they might hurt him, but I never thought they’d kill him.” I looked at DC Rooney as if to say: “Aren’t you going to press her on this?” He just blanked me.

‘I had a hip flask of Scotch. She took a swig. She then told us that Nathan had left an envelope with someone important containing the details of someone who wanted him dead, as insurance. DC Rooney asked her what she meant and she just went into hysterics. They had to send for a medical team to sedate her.’

I know nothing of this; at a stroke, he’s turned me from interrogator to pupil.

‘Did they ever track down this envelope?’

‘They tried all the usual suspects: his solicitor, his closest friends, the local vicar. Nothing.’

‘And who might these enemies have been?’

They share a glance and a grim, knowing laugh.

John chooses his words carefully. ‘Nathan was a small man with a large chip on his shoulder.’

‘A sack of King Edwards, more like,’ says Phil.

‘When you’re a bailiff and you go to repossess a car or shut down a business, you’re going to get a lot of verbal. You can’t blame people for becoming emotional. I hated that side of the job and would always try to placate people and explain that I was just the messenger. Nathan would rub their noses in it. He couldn’t help himself and the stories are legion.’

Phil picks up the thread. ‘Once he went to seize assets from a builder and brought Dave along, one of the biggest guys on our books. As Nathan’s seizing stuff, Dave starts kicking a ball about with the guy’s little kid outside, you know, keeping it all civilised. When they drove off, Dave turns to see what Nathan managed to get his hands on and there, in the back of the van amongst the tools, is the kid's football.'

John shakes his head. 'He would've found that hilarious. He pissed people off and sometimes they came after him. He was always getting threatening phone calls, there were always psychos turning up at the office wanting to hurt him because of what he'd said to their partners or kids or parents. And then there were the women.'

They blow out their cheeks and shake their heads like a couple of gossiping fishwives.

'One of his jobs was serving court papers to violent husbands,' says John. 'Barring orders, injunctions, that type of thing. Nathan would always read the case paperwork, find out all he could about the battered wife. He'd then approach her, knight in shining armour, give her his phone number and tell her to call if there was any trouble. Later, he'd be round there smashing a window or slashing a car tyre to make sure she called.

'He'd use the knowledge he gained from the case papers, which were always massively detailed, to bring round her favourite takeaway or video or wine. For him it was just a leg-over, but these women were vulnerable and would fall for him head over heels. I think nowadays they call it grooming.'

Phil takes up the slack. 'And then violent husband gets wind. A lot of these men were obsessives, you know, spying on their partners, planting bugs. Needless to say, they didn't take kindly to the man who barred them from their own homes now getting his feet under the table.

'We had a couple of husbands turn up here threatening to kill him. And I know one followed him for a few days. We had several complaints from solicitors.'

'Can you give me names, addresses?'

'We stayed well out of it,' says John. 'To be honest, Donal, I didn't agree with that kind of carry-on at all. Nathan had a wife and young kids at home. I had words with him about it. He was damaging the business, so he started keeping it all low-key.'

'There must be records somewhere?'

'He used to do a lot of the bailiff work with a young freelance guy called Danny Bremner. He lives with his mum near Oval; I think her name is Doris or Dorothy. He can give you chapter and verse.'

John leans forward, plants his elbows meaningfully on the table. 'The thing is, Donal, I don't have a violent bone in my body. Yet I've been repeatedly arrested, interrogated and publicly accused of Nathan's murder for the past six years. Yet you've got all these bad men out there, gangsters, drug dealers, wife beaters, who've never even been looked at properly. If you want to become famous as the detective who cracked the Nathan Barry case, get after them. Now let's go and see Gary Warner.'

Chapter 18

The Harp Bar, Croydon, South London
Monday, June 20, 1994; 12.00

The musical instrument the harp dates back 5,500 years to the first urban civilisation of Southern Mesopotamia. Judging by its exterior, the Harp Bar in West Croydon couldn't have been far behind.

Scary, condemned and covered in bad graffiti, and that's just the Monday midday clientele. Holding court amid the tattoo soup at the bar, two oafish crew cuts stop dead at the sight of me and my affable-but-possibly-murderous Oompa Loompas.

They exchange some curious code of nods and grunts, then Delaney escorts me to a table in the most remote corner.

'What are you drinking, Donal?'

'Cooking lager, thanks.'

'I wouldn't if I were you. Not here. You'll be shitting through the eye of a needle for a week. Try a cask ale. They can't poison that.'

'Thanks for the tip.'

Phil Ware seems to know everyone at the bar, but that's

no surprise. Until recently, Met detectives received a booze allowance to frequent dives like this, where they'd bilk underworld intelligence from pissed wannabe villains. Older colleagues describe local 'faces' queueing up to spill in return for a top-up. So much for 'honour among thieves'.

The crew cuts look too old and podgy for their 'swiped' designer brands, favoured by football hooligan 'casuals'. The older one nods a lot, eases himself off his stool and strides towards me. I work hard not to flinch. Delaney trots behind him urgently with an armful of pints, as if warm ale is the only thing that might stop this guy ripping my head off.

'John tells me you need putting straight,' he squeaks in a surprisingly high-pitched, almost tearful voice, reminding me of Steve Coogan's pool supervisor in *The Day Today*. It's all I can do not to say: 'In 1988, someone died . . .'

Delaney drops the pints on the table and squeezes in beside me. Phil backs his arse into a chair on the other side. It's as if they're buffering me from any sudden violent outbursts. I take a long draw of the warm, soapy liquid and wonder what single quality qualifies it as refreshment.

'I'm just doing my job. Gary, isn't it?'

'I haven't carried out any hits myself, you understand,' he says sarcastically. 'But I know blokes who do and they'd never take a local job. Never. I mean that'd be stupid.'

I nod. 'Of course. So, if you wanted someone whacked, here in Croydon say, how would you go about it?'

'I'd hire one of your lot from Northern Ireland. Plenty of them going freelance right now. He'd want me to carefully select the job site. Despite what the media said at the time, a pub car park is ideal, especially if it's dark.

'The hitman would wait for the target to bring his car there. As soon as the target goes inside the pub, he'd slash the tyre that's least exposed to view. When the target comes out and sees the tyre, he'll bend down to inspect. That's when the target would get his OBE.'

'His what?'

'One behind the ear,' explains Delaney.

'What if someone witnesses it, or hears the shot?'

Gary Warner shrugs nonchalantly. 'He'd use a .22 or .32 revolver, stolen specifically for the job. It doesn't spit out casings and it makes less noise than a cap gun. It doesn't matter if he gets seen. Eye witnesses never get the description right. Shock I suppose.'

'What then?'

'For a job like this, he'd have flown into Gatwick, rented a car and booked a hotel room at least half an hour from the job site. He'd head back there, stopping on the way to buy a hacksaw and a takeaway.'

'Makes you peckish, does it, knocking someone off?'

He glares at me with bored contempt. 'Back in his hotel room, he'd put on his cheap, cotton work gloves and saw his tool into pieces. He'd wrap these pieces in the fast food packaging and chuck each one into a different bin all the way back to the airport. Same with the gloves and hacksaw. By the time hitman returns the rental car, there's nothing to connect him to the murder. If I ordered a crime like that, to make sure I didn't get nicked for it, I'd be abroad on holiday at the time getting photographed a lot, know what I mean?'

A whispering chill flickers the back of my neck like a blowing veil.

'Only a muppet uses an axe,' declares Gary. 'Or someone who has lost it, you know, heat-of-the-moment thing and he just grabbed the closest thing at hand. Nathan was a shagger. My bet is Nathan had been followed for a few days by the husband of some tart. He waited in the car park and took his chances.'

I nod. 'That's my bet too. But now you're all here, we've received information that Nathan's murder is connected to Julie Draper. Any thoughts?'

'First I've heard of it,' says John. Those had been DI Lambert's exact words.

Gary leans forward, planting both hands on the table so we're eye-to-eye.

'You've had your time here, copper. If I was you, I'd walk out while your legs still work. And don't think about coming back, because you won't be walking out next time. You get me?'

'I get you,' I say.

But I'll have to show my face in here again. I've just stuck Fintan's magic bug, Dusko Pavlov, to the underside of the table.

Chapter 19

Vauxhall, South London
Monday, June 20, 1994; 13.00

No one at the Cold Case Unit, my regular employer, seems to know I've been booted off the Julie Draper investigation, which suits me fine. I can use the unofficial gardening leave to seek out connections between her and Nathan Barry.

I order up the Nathan case files only to be told I can't have them.

'The paperwork on that case could fill several rooms,' explains the records clerk. 'You'll have to go into deep storage and find what you need there.'

'Where's deep storage?'

'Behind Boots on Camden High Street. There's an underground storage facility there. Just show your warrant card and they'll provide an index.'

I squeeze my eyes shut and rack my brains; how could the axe murder of a bailiff outside a sketchy South London pub six years ago be connected to the kidnap and murder of a twenty-four-year-old female estate agent? Apart from the fact they both worked in Croydon, it makes no sense.

All we know about Julie Draper's kidnapper is that he selected her at random and exhibited the expertise of someone with inside information, just as the enigmatic Kipper did when he abducted Suzy Fairclough seven years ago. Same *modus operandi* suggests same offender, which is why the police are convinced it's Kipper.

As for Nathan Barry, I now feel much less certain about his killers. John Delaney clearly had the connections to commission a textbook 'clean hit' while he could have been abroad with his sun-kissed alibi. I do believe Delaney and DS Phil Ware cooked up a conspiracy the morning after Nathan's murder; but one designed to protect 'moonlighting' cops, not derail the murder investigation.

For me, the most compelling motive for Delaney to have had Nathan Berry wiped out was the men's competing affections for Karen Moore. The question is, had she really finished with Nathan Barry, as Delaney claims? If not, did this make Delaney so deranged with jealousy and desire that he carried out the ultimate romantic gesture?

When you realise you want to spend the rest of your life with somebody, you want the rest of your life to start as soon as possible.

It sounds like Karen wouldn't be the type to appreciate it. But as I've learned lately, you never know with women.

My thoughts turn to Karen's cuckolded husband, Walter. Did he know his wife had been road-testing two potential replacements? No matter how amicable their split, he must have felt humiliated by her sudden status as West Croydon Lunch Club's dish-of-the-day. Maybe he resented how flattered she'd felt by the cock-jousting japes of Nathan Barry and John Delaney. Maybe he grew to hate her for encouraging them. He's got to be a suspect.

Deep down, part of me hopes Walter did it. Seize the day

and slay the bastard who stole your missus. The emasculated part of me constantly fantasises about confronting Charles. I feel a primeval shudder at even the thought of it, and realise with alarm that my wounded, overweening male rage would use whatever might be at hand to hurt the bastard. Moments don't get any hotter than those. I feel certain, suddenly, that the killer of Nathan Barry must have been an enraged love rival. Somehow, six years later, the same man abducted and murdered Julie Draper. Maybe Fintan is right; her kidnap had been personal. But why? Let's hope his satanic crime reporter, Alex Pavlovic, is busy unearthing secret enemies and murderous motives in Julie Draper's personal life. Without that, we've got nothing.

Those bloody fish. That silver block. Why doesn't Zoe call? What is going on? Has she finished with Charles yet? If not, why not? Does she miss me ever . . . think of me at all? Surely Matt has noticed I'm gone, after all we've been through. How is he coping? Why doesn't she call?

The block! The silver-painted block I took from the Julie Draper ransom drop and delivered to her parents; I can call her about that! Purely professional, of course. Fintan would hit the roof but I need to know how that might be evidential, if at all.

My finger shakes as I dial our home number. I set myself some ground rules: remain business-like, unemotional, in control. I'm perfectly within my rights to ask about Matt's welfare, but not about 'nookie with Chucky'.

She answers, reciting the number; something I used to tease her about.

'Hi.'

'Hi,' she says cautiously, nothing more.

'Don't worry, it's a work call. I was wondering if you had a chance to check out that concrete block?'

'Oh yes, actually I've spent all day on it,' she gasps, embracing the professional diversion as a drowning woman might a lifebuoy. 'It is a highly unusual industrial brick, blue-coloured beneath its white coating and the silver paint. The three channels or flutes are a very rare feature so it was most likely designed for something specific, probably connected to drainage. I've sent images to all the major masonry associations and no one's recognised it.'

'You make that sound like good news.'

'The rarer it is, the more useful it might prove evidentially, if we can just pinpoint its manufacturer. I've persuaded a local college to carry out thermoluminescence on it, which should date the china clay. That'll narrow it down, hopefully.'

'There's an electrician in Dublin who'll do that for a pint, yeah, Dermo Luminescence.'

Nothing.

'Great, well I really appreciate it, Zoe, and be sure to invoice for every hour.'

'I noticed you deposited some money into my account at the weekend.'

'Yeah, well I called the CSA and they were able to tell me, pretty much to the penny, what I'm legally obliged to pay.'

'You're not obliged to pay anything, Donal, legally or otherwise.'

'I want to.'

'Please, I'd really rather you didn't. It doesn't feel right.'

My mind winds back to that night she told me she'd quit her job at the Forensic Science Service; some embittered, barren female manager had been making her life hell. Why do women do that to each other? I hugged her, told her she did the right thing, promised to win whatever bread needed winning while she established herself as a freelance. That warm glow of satisfaction flickers briefly in my chest. As painfully old-fashioned and patronising as it sounds, becoming the sole breadwinner made me feel like a real man. Somehow it legitimised me as a father to Matt. The money I earned clothed him, fed him, kept him warm and dry. It must be a primeval instinct. Paying now keeps my foot firmly in the door. Which is why I don't want to stop.

'It feels right to me, Zoe.'

'Thanks, but I don't need it, Donal. Mum and dad are already helping. They really want to and they can afford it.'

I don't get this generation, who so willingly enslave themselves to their parents' bumper mortgage equity. Don't they realise the consequences; that their mum and dad will try to control them for the rest of their lives?

'I'm still his dad, aren't I? As his dad, I pay. Unless there's something you're not telling me?'

'That night you call, pissed, and announced you were moving out, you agreed to give me time to sort things out. It's only been a couple of days. I knew you'd do this. I knew you couldn't just trust me to do it my way, in my own time.'

'Trust?' I say, shivering in disbelief, screwing the lid down on that volcano.

'All I ask is that you give me some space and time, Donal. Okay?'

My mind spins back to her parents' odd behaviour yesterday when I dropped Matt off.

'I'm still picking Matt up on Sunday?'

She sighs. 'Yes.'

'Is he missing me?'

The ice queen's voice cracks. 'Please don't guilt trip me.'

'I need to know, Zoe.'

'Yes. He doesn't stop talking about you, okay? Happy now?'

She breaks down. So do I.

'I really miss him so much,' I cry, but she's gone.

Chapter 20

Oval, South London
Tuesday, June 21, 1994; 10.00

I figure that if Nathan Barry's ruthless grooming and inveterate shagging of the wives of violent men did lead to his murder, one man would know.

'He was my best mate,' confirms former colleague Danny Bremner. 'We worked together pretty much every day for six months before he got killed.'

Bremner is slight, fair and fidgety. Although in his late twenties, he shares a flat with his mum in a classic four-storey, red-brick council block, one of dozens between Brixton and Oval in South London.

'I want to take you for a drive,' he says. 'Show you something that might be of interest.'

He leads me to one of those small, white panel vans favoured by London's most committed tailgaters. Stencilled along the side in red vinyl; *Dan the Van Couriers . . . Faster, Safer, Cheaper* and an 0800 number.

'Your own business?'

He nods.

'Impressive. How long have you been in operation?'

'Since not long after Nathan died. I couldn't work for Delaney anymore.'

'Why not?'

We jump in, he wheel-spins and the van takes off as if catapulted. I'm beginning to wonder about the coexistence of his dual boasts; 'faster' *and* 'safer'.

'He hated Nathan and, as I had been his best mate, he let me know he didn't want me around. I'd had enough of Delaney anyway, constantly bad-mouthing him.'

'What sort of stuff?'

'He had a real thing about Nathan being red-haired and of Scottish descent. He used to call him the bitter little Jock, or agent orange or the ginger minge nut. Even after his death. I couldn't listen to it. He might have been smaller than them but he was a hell of a lot braver.'

'In what way?'

'Nathan took on the stuff no else dared to. John did the investigations side of the business which, as far as I could tell, mostly involved boozing in pubs with coppers.'

'Delaney says Nathan was too gung-ho and provocative.'

He smiles: 'The situations he was sent into, he had to have front. But he loved it too. And he only got nasty if provoked. If someone was giving him lip, he'd tell them they'd just been "Nathanised" to wind them up.

'In January that year, he brought me down to Brighton to repossess a Range Rover from some Maltese drugs dealer. We turn up at the address and its proper Eldorado, the souped-up Range Rover sitting on the cobbled drive behind big metal gates. We try the intercom three times, no answer. Nathan reverses his van up to the gates, climbs out, hops up onto the roof and over, gets in the Range Rover, finds the fob for the gates and drives off. He got threatening calls for weeks after that.'

'Did you tell the police about this?'

'They dismissed it, said real gangsters wouldn't bother calling up on the phone first.'

'If I may be blunt, Danny, Nathan sounded like a liability to me: his aggressive attitude and gloating, his flings with married women?'

'I don't know anything about any flings.'

'Yes, you do Danny. You said yourself you were with him virtually every day for six months. I've got witnesses who say you know.'

'Honestly, I don't know what you're talking about,' he says, taking a glance at his left-hand wing mirror for the first time on this drive, unwittingly tripping the second of Fintan's infallible 'lie wires'. Time to administer the blow torch.

'Okay well if that's your stance, Danny, then it's you versus several witnesses who insist you do know about Nathan's affairs. Oh, and unlike you, these conflicting witnesses don't have criminal records.'

He throws his head back like a footballer whose penalty kick has just been saved. 'For God's sake, that was a few ounces of grass. I was nineteen.'

'If you end up in court charged with obstructing the course of justice, it'll be all over the South London Press. Your clients might then decide that *faster* and *cheaper* isn't enough without *safer*. And your poor old mum will be mortified.'

I hate myself, but he left me no option.

'If you tell me the truth right now, Danny, I'll keep it unofficial, off-the-record; you won't have to make a statement.'

He shakes his head, whether in refusal or disbelief I can't tell. I keep the verbal going, just in case.

'I trust that a well-informed man such as yourself will have read and heard about all these amazing developments in DNA and forensics. Let's just say all the pointers are now facing away from Delaney and towards a man with a grudge. This man then went on to kill someone else, a woman, but I can't tell you any more about that right now. Bottom line is, you're our best hope of identifying this suspect.'

He sniffs and sighs, his resistance crumbling.

'The thing is, I was friends with Nathan and Emma, his missus. I don't want to make things worse for her and the kids, especially when the police seem so convinced that Delaney did it.'

'Like I said, not any longer.'

He takes a self-psyching deep breath. 'One woman he mentioned was Yvonne Morris or Morrison. She lived in a cul-de-sac in South Norwood, I don't know which one. Her husband is the CEO of some tech company. Apparently, she was convinced her husband had been bugging the house and the phone, trying to prove she was having an affair. Nathan told me how he'd found a tiny device under the marital bed which, judging by his expression, he may have planted there himself. Next thing he's having it away with Yvonne. A few weeks later, he's knocking off some other bird and he wants rid of Yvonne, so he plants his business card under Yvonne's marital bed, right next to her husband's copy of *Moby Dick*, which he seemed to think hilarious. Sure enough, Mr M finds the card, kicks out Yvonne, gets his solicitor to make a formal complaint to the Association of PIs, whatever that's called. Nathan tells Yvonne he has to ditch her or he'll get struck off.'

'Didn't Nathan's wife ever suspect anything?'

'I think Emma knew, but they stuck it out for the kids. That's what decent people do, isn't it?'

'Decent people,' I nod, and my guts twinge. Even if Zoe gives me the chance, will I be able to swallow my pride and forgive her, for Matt's sake? It's been several days since I discovered her deceit, yet my feelings of wounded betrayal have actually intensified. *Decent people?* Zoe has always regarded herself as the more decent of us: she's smarter, better educated, more cultured. But it wasn't her bit of Irish rough who had sex with someone else.

'He mentioned another married woman, Joan something, who he seemed really keen on, but she went back to her husband in the end, despite the fact he was violent to her. I've never understood that.'

'Do you remember Joan's surname?'

'Carter, I think. It's been, what, six or seven years . . .'

'Did he ever mention Karen Moore?'

He inhales slowly, measuring his words.

'You never knew if Nathan was gilding the lily. He didn't tell outright porkies, but he had a sort of image of himself which he liked to reinforce, as much to himself as to anyone else. Overweening pride, I suppose you'd call it.'

I nod impatiently. Everyone thinks they're Freud these days. I blame Oprah, Springer, Kilroy-Silk and their TV ilk, who've elevated bad behaviour to some sort of emotional pseudo-science. In this new touchy-feely world, nobody is ever responsible for their actions. You know the kind of stuff: *I shoplift not for the nice clothes but to fulfil an emotional void . . .*

'Can you just tell me what he told you about Karen and I'll find out which parts of it are true.'

'Yeah alright,' he sniffs defensively. 'Nathan and Delaney were in this lunch club. They used to get pissed every second

Friday. By all accounts, no one went back to work and it sometimes got pretty out of hand. Nathan and Delaney were very taken with Karen and her friend Stacey. He didn't tell me either of their surnames but they were both married.'

Fucking hell, I think, *is the whole world engaged in illicit sex, except me?*

'According to Nathan, the girls joined them at a hotel bar and they ended up in some presidential suite with a jacuzzi. Cut a long story short, they have a foursome. Nathan, at least in his own mind, proved the superior swordsman. Well, he was in better condition, so I believe it. Delaney wasn't happy. Male pride and all that. According to Nathan, that was the beginning of the end.'

'You believe that?'

'It doesn't matter what I believe, does it? It's your job to find out which parts of it are true.'

Touché!

He swings right off the South Circular onto Baring Road, towards Bromley. After about a quarter of a mile, he slows down to a crawl, leans forward and peers about.

'I remember we were approaching that pub, the Summerfield, when he pointed down one of these roads on the right.'

'What did he say exactly?'

'I can't give you verbatim, but something like, "if something bad happens to me, and I end up in hospital, it'll be down to the man who lives at that house." We were just past the pub and he pointed back.'

I'm finding this all a bit convenient, and wonder what his game is.

'Where did he point exactly?'

'It was more of a general . . .' he mimics the action; an irritatingly vague thumb jab towards Ronver Road.

'I'll have to make you do that again. Go much slower this time.'

He swings the van around, repeats the drive-by. I make a mental note.

'Did he say whether it was a jealous husband, a criminal or just someone he'd upset?'

'He didn't elaborate. Like I say, he was always quite melodramatic about his own activities. A bit of a fantasist, I suppose.'

'You told DI Lambert all this?'

'Not about the affairs, but I showed him this address. He was sat in the van, just like you.'

'Did he follow it up?'

'I don't know. They never got back to me.'

'Are there any other sexual conquests I need to know about?'

He shakes his head.

'You sure?'

'Why would I hold back now I've spilled the beans? But I'm glad I have, to be honest. I always thought it must've been Delaney. But if one of those jealous husbands killed Nathan, I want you to catch the bastard.'

Chapter 21

Camden, North London
Tuesday, June 21 to Friday, June 24, 1994

An old-school birdcage lift lowers me deep below Camden Town.

As Northern Line tube trains rumble fifty feet above, helpful Geoff explains how this bunker had been carved out during World War Two to act as a bomb shelter for 8,000 people, one of several across the city.

By the time they completed the bunkers, the Blitz had ended. Since then, these vast spaces have been used for military exercises, farming, accommodation for the first 'Windrush' immigrants from the Caribbean and, more recently, as film sets for *Doctor Who* and *Blake's 7*.

Geoff leads me down one of countless, seemingly infinite fluorescent-strip tunnels, revealing each to be a quarter of a mile long. Flanked by modern Dexion shelves packed with cardboard boxes, I can't help thinking we're headed towards ground zero of the world's largest fire hazard.

'The Nathan Barry paperwork starts here,' he says,

pointing at box one. 'It ends . . . oh my goodness . . . here,' he bellows, some forty odd feet away.

'On all levels?'

'I'm afraid so. Rather you than me.'

His clerical hell is my punctilious paradise. Only by ploughing through every sheet of this paperwork can I sift fact from fiction; find out every single action those Nathan Barry detectives have taken since 1988 . . . and what they've missed. I may even unearth Nathan Barry's killer and connect that crime to the murder of Julie Draper.

Besides, methodical, brain-numbing labour proves the perfect emotional decoy. In between subterranean days spent at the bunker in subconscious mourning – Jonah in the stomach of the whale – I'm safe from all those everyday reminders of Zoe and Matt and my enigmatic romantic nemesis, Charles. Not for the first time, work saves me. Work saves many men.

All life outside this black hole represents a Trojan emotional challenge. The most banal everyday events can set me off; a family merrily gambolling along a pavement; knocking over my coffee in a Wimpy; passing the pub where we first smooched.

Radio-friendly songs I normally despise start to speak to me. I'm talking real aural arse gravy here: 'I Wanna Know What Love Is' by Foreigner, for fuck's sake. Neil Diamond's 'Love on the Rocks' is almost laughably 'on the nose' and about as emotionally subtle as a Hispanic daytime soap opera; it had me sobbing out loud at the traffic lights. I realise for the first time that the entire middle-of-the-road pop canon is devoted to either the joys of illicit sex or the pain of infidelity. I can't turn it off.

Suddenly I have evenings free: something I'd fantasised about ever since I moved in with Zoe and Matt. 'Me Time' had been the thing I'd missed most. Except now I can't find anything to do with it. How did I use to fill my evenings? When did I forget how to enjoy doing nothing?

Fintan is always out drinking with 'contacts' or chasing some scoop, and Aidan on 'nights', so I find myself alone in empty pubs, watching obscure first round World Cup games between nations I couldn't pick out on a globe. I usually get so pissed that I need to check the score next morning. I start playing the slots. Or I sit near the machines and spy on other players, marking the pattern of cherries and lemons, the nearest I get to fruit these days. I learn the signals: I know just when the burbling box is ready to spew. I wake up on the sofa, pockets leaking greasy pound coins that smell vaguely of piss, oblivious to how much I've won or lost.

I don't call any friends or colleagues. Nobody calls me. Where is even a basic level of concern? 'Are you okay, Donal, it's just that no one's heard from you for nearly a week?'

Where *are* they? Fuck them all.

But I can't stand the uncertainty. Craving some sort of sign; any sort of sign, I cave in and call Luke, boyfriend of Sophie, Zoe's best friend. We know girls tell their best friends everything. Sophie, in turn, tells Luke everything and Luke is a man refreshingly incapable of a) lying and b) keeping a secret.

He seems his normal self, even asking after Zoe. Relief flushes through me. Clearly the news hasn't broken in our circle yet. There's still a chance. Zoe hasn't told Sophie, because she's going to dump Charles.

Of course . . .

Charles is a mistake she doesn't even want her friends to know about. A blip. That's all. Why else wouldn't she tell her best friend? I know in my heart she'll finish it. She just needs time and space to do the deed, like she said. I need to trust her, as ironic as that might seem.

The woes of the outside world evaporate as soon as I climb back into that caged lift. Like Clark Kent in his phone box, that thirty-second descent below ground transforms me from hobo to Robocop.

I discover boxes of alternative evidence that officers deemed irrelevant to the CPS or Delaney's defence team. Of course, these days they'd have to disclose it but, just six years ago, police could rig the game any way they liked.

Happily, the entire felled rainforest has been indexed with clerical zeal. I riffle through until I find what I need to check out; Danny Bremner's statements and the resulting police 'actions'.

Angry husband number one – Moby Dick Morrison – had a watertight alibi that checked out.

I find no reference to Nathan's next married conquest – Joan Carter – so move onto the third, Karen Moore; Nathan's ex and Delaney's current wife.

In her statement, she describes having a 'brief fling' with Nathan just after Christmas '86, four months before his murder.

'I didn't consider it a serious relationship,' she says. 'I think perhaps he thought it was more serious. I had to be quite firm with him about the fact I didn't want it to develop into anything more.'

DI LAMBERT: 'How many times did you sleep with Nathan?'

KAREN: 'On two, maybe three occasions.'

DI LAMBERT: 'Where did these liaisons take place?'

KAREN: 'Do I really have to answer that?'

DI LAMBERT: 'Yes you do.'

KAREN: 'I remember the first time was at the Croydon Park Hotel.'

I wonder if this had been the gruesome foursome, as relayed to Danny Bremner. If so, then clearly Nathan's self-proclaimed 'expert swordsmanship' hadn't proven enough to slay either woman. Come to think of it, any man who refers to his cock as a sword is, by definition, deluded. I suppose 'pink penknife' just doesn't quite cut it.

DI LAMBERT: 'And after that?'

KAREN: 'One night we met in his office at BD.'

DI LAMBERT: 'You had full intercourse in his office?'

KAREN: 'Yes.'

DI LAMBERT: 'When was the last time you had sex with Nathan Barry?'

KAREN: 'It would've been sometime during that Christmas holiday, before the New Year. He popped round to my home one evening. My husband, Walter, works nights as a chauffeur.'

DI LAMBERT: 'We'll come to Walter later. And how did you end it with Nathan?'

KAREN: 'Early in the New Year, I told him I didn't want anything serious. I was just coming out of a twenty-one-year-marriage and needed some freedom and space.'

DI LAMBERT: 'How did he respond to this?'

KAREN: 'He seemed quite hurt. He asked me several times to reconsider, but I said no each time.'

Those swordsmen and their feelings! I'm struggling to work out if Nathan had been a heartless philandering hound or some perennially lovelorn fool. Can you be both?

Karen insists she and John Delaney 'didn't become an item' until 'several months after Nathan's death'. Her interrogator, DI Lambert, clearly believes otherwise, reciting the vast number of calls Delaney had made to her and the frequent sightings of them together in the days and weeks after Nathan's murder. She refuses to budge.

My mind turns again to her husband Walter; if she was taking calls on their home phone at weekends from Delaney and Nathan, he must have known. I make a note to track down his statement.

Back to Karen; next comes her insistence that meeting Nathan just after 6pm on the evening of his murder had been 'purely by chance'.

KAREN: 'I was locking up my office when he came out of his across the road. I waved and he came over. He said he had an appointment later, did I fancy a drink. We went to Silvers wine bar and shared a bottle of white wine.'

DI LAMBERT: 'Did John Delaney know you were meeting him?'

KAREN: 'No. Like I said, it was a spur-of-the-moment thing. It hadn't been planned.'

She insists Nathan seemed his normal self and made no mention of any concerns or problems. Statements from employees at DB Investigations paint a different picture; relations between the business partners had hit an all-time low. Nathan complained that Delaney wasn't pulling his weight; Delaney complained that Nathan was pulling all of their vulnerable female clients.

One document lists all 'known' disgruntled men who'd complained about Nathan's behaviour. Their alibis for the night had all checked out, but I can't help wondering how rigorously they'd been examined, especially once DI Lambert donned his Delaney goggles.

Three months after the murder, BBC's flagship *Crimewatch* programme featured a hammy reconstruction of the murder and appeal for information. I run through the 416 calls that came in, aware from experience that at least 400 of them will be useless.

The first name to catch my eye is DC Neil Rooney;

intelligence from current or former officers tends to be the most useful. The female officer who took his call wrote the following: *DC Rooney explained that he was the first CID on the scene on the night of Mr Barry's murder and still serves in East Croydon. He complained that senior officers on the murder squad are not running it properly, accusing them of ignoring good suspects put forward by junior officers and other sources.*

I'd never known a call like this before and add Rooney to my urgent 'people to see' list.

One other call catches my eye. The officer who took it wrote: *'IC1 female called in, saying she believed her husband had carried out the murder but refusing to reveal her identity. When I pressed her, she said she feared that he'd kill her next if he found out she'd made this call. I explained that we can't follow up a lead unless we have at least some basic information. She said her name was Joan, got distressed and hung up. We were able to trace her number to a public phone box on Baring Road, SE9.'*

My mind races. The caller had said her name was Joan; Danny Bremner had named Joan Carter as one of the married women Nathan had been having an affair with. The address Nathan had warned Bremner about – 'if something bad happens to me, check out the man at that address' – had been just off Baring Road. But back in '87, cops knew nothing of Nathan's affair with Joan Carter.

'Holy shit,' I yelp, my voice echoing through the bunker. 'I've just found our prime suspect.'

Chapter 22

Camden, North London
Friday, June 24, 1994; 13.00

As the archaic birdcage lift hoists me noisily back to civilisation, my mobile pings. It's a text from Zoe: *Breakthrough re block, call asap.*

I still cringe at mistaking that silver-painted concrete block for some sort of sensor at the Julie Draper ransom drop-off. In my defence, it had been pitch black, and the kidnapper had clearly set out to make it look like part of some hi-tech, ransom-securing contraption. It would still be sitting on that bridge had Julie not come to me that night and dangled it in my face. I can't even imagine why it might be significant, but if anyone can determine its provenance, it'll be Zoe. When that girl gets the bit between her teeth . . .

She launches straight into it. 'I managed to trace retired mould-maker David Baskin who's now in his eighties. He recalls designing this block back in the 1960s to be used in road gutters. It was produced by a brick-making firm called Metallic & Masonry near Stoke-on-Trent but, get this, they only made 40,000. And it was manufactured for Wettern

Brothers, who were a Croydon-based builders' merchants.

'Now, 40,000 is a comparatively tiny volume, so this brick is rare, and so is the silver paint covering it. It's cellulose paint, petroleum-based, full of isocyanides and likely to be banned soon. Car enthusiasts use it to restore the paintwork on vintage cars, so it's pretty specialist. The bottom line is, if you've got a suspect and you find these blocks and this paint at his home, you've found your kidnapper.'

I'm stoked. 'This is so impressive, Zoe. Well done.'

'I'm glad that's put you in a good mood,' she says. 'Because I don't think what else I've got to tell you will.'

I can't even speak.

'Don't freak out okay, Donal, and don't start parroting everything Fintan says or thinks . . .'

'What do you mean by that?'

'Oh come on. He's never liked me and he's been poisoning your mind against me since we first met.'

'I love the way you always make me sound like some gullible, impressionable halfwit incapable of forming my own opinions, Zoe.'

I wait for her to dispute this. She doesn't.

'Er, what? That's what you think of me? Jesus . . .'

'I think Fintan's a misogynist and when you've spent time with him, it rubs off on you.'

'Can I just have the headline please.'

'Remember when you went to Ireland last time? After you called, Matt was really upset for a few days. I asked you not to call again, and you understood?'

'Er, yeah.'

'After you dropped him off on Sunday, he's been impossible. Constant tantrums, waking all the time. It's just too unsettling and confusing for him.'

'What are you suggesting, Zoe?'

'For the sake of his emotional stability, can you not see him this Sunday?'

'What, so you can get more sleep?'

'No, Donal, come on. You know I'm only thinking of Matt here. I don't want him to wind up emotionally damaged by all of this. Once we sort things out, then we can make proper arrangements, but right now we can't expect him to understand what's going on.'

'He's not the only one.'

'I know you hate me right now, and I get that. But can you please do it for Matt. I know you want what's best for him too.'

'I'll think about it,' I say, and hang up. But I know what's going on here. She's weaning Matt off his surrogate dad. I'm as good as dumped.

Chapter 23

Holdernesse Road, South London
Friday, June 24, 1994; 15.30

God knows what any watching neighbours must be thinking as I stalk Joan Carter and her two kids through the front gate of their terraced home.

Earlier, I'd searched all the 'Joan Carters' in the police computer and found one whose address in 1987 had been Summerfield Street, SE12. A London A to Z confirmed that Summerfield Street is joined to Ronver Road, the one Bremner pointed out to me as home to someone who wanted to do Nathan Barry real harm.

Joan had been married at the time to Steve Carter, a wife-beating scumbag whom Nathan Barry had presented a barring order early in 1987.

As I shadow Joan and the kids towards their front door, I realise in horror how easily I could be her psychotic ex, doing the same. Judging by the amount of times she and the kids have moved since 1987, Joan's clearly trying to stay one step ahead of deviant Steve. For the victim of an obsessive, violent partner, there really is no hiding place.

I remind myself that I'm shadowing them for more noble reasons. I've got to catch Joan before she gets inside that front door. I don't have a warrant or any official mandate to be here. If she makes it inside, she'll be well within her rights to slam that door in my face and refuse to re-open it. How then will I find out the truth about that call she made to *Crimewatch* six years ago?

At the same time, I don't want to alarm her young kids, who've already suffered enough. I'm gambling that they'll tear inside as soon as that front door opens, giving me a precious few seconds to Get Carter before she can barricade me out. I don't have a plan B.

Thankfully, Joan's kids have read the script and sprint straight towards the kitchen snack cupboard.

'Excuse me, Joan?'

She turns, startled and on guard, so I rattle off my follow-up line like a voiceover artist racing through terms and conditions.

'Detective Constable Donal Lynch. Please don't worry, Joan, it's not bad news,' I gabble, flashing my badge and most innocuous smile.

'Oh God, what's this about?' she grumbles, in the fatigued, world-weary tone of someone who's spent her life answering doors to prying coppers. 'It's nothing to do with the kids, is it?'

'No, no. I'm looking into the murder of Nathan Barry.'

Joan's body sags as if suddenly deflated. Her right hand still clutches the key anchored in the front door's top lock; it might be the only thing keeping her upright.

'Are you okay, Joan?'

She nods absently, as if preoccupied by a past life flashing before her eyes.

'You'd better come in,' she sighs resignedly, pushing the

door open and trudging through. I realise I'm the knock she's been dreading for six long years.

I follow her through a jaded, woodchipped hallway that's doubling as a bike workshop, into a messy kitchen full of ill-fitting white goods and mismatched furniture.

'Go and watch TV in the other room,' she orders her monster-munching kids.

They leave reluctantly, and only after relating their feelings towards me through a series of well-rehearsed 'evils'. I comfort myself that at least deviant Steve appears to be off the scene. That's what the intelligence report had said, and Joan is sporting no facial signs of his handiwork.

She takes her time filling an electric kettle and switching it on; then opens a cupboard to four chipped mugs.

'Tea?'

'I'm fine thanks. This will only take a few minutes.'

'Well I'm parched, so you may as well take a seat.'

I know she's buying time to get her head and tale together. Colleagues would seize upon this as a sign of guilt, use it to 'get into her'. But I can't bring myself to bully an already brutalised woman. Maybe that's why I'm still an acting DC, not a fully blooded detective on a murder squad.

Instead, I look for signs that might help me prise her open later, when I hit her with my own particular brand of interrogation . . . you know, the one that makes Terry Wogan look like Klaus Barbie.

There are no photos or family mementoes, no fruit, flowers or pot plants. The place screams barrel-scraping short-term rental; the latest temporary bolthole in Joan's constant race to keep them one step ahead of that controlling, out-of-control creep, Steve Carter.

It's bereft of feminine touches, as is Joan. She's wearing grey sweats, a stained, shapeless white T-shirt and shoes you wouldn't put on your feet to escape a fire. I've seen it before with women who've been abused long-term; their entire body language and dress speaks 'sexless and worthless'.

Then I recall how Zoe had 'let herself go' earlier this year, spending days in the same tatty pyjamas and jumper and, to my mounting horror, not bothering to shower or brush her teeth. No one had been battering her around, so I really shouldn't judge. What I should have paid far more attention to, in hindsight, was when she'd started sprucing herself up again, no doubt for Charles.

Joan sits opposite me, stirring her steaming, milkless tea in a cracked and stained old mug and I wonder how starved her life has been of kindness or comforts.

'Thanks for agreeing to talk to me, Joan.'

She sneers and I suddenly see her as a surly teen rebel who didn't so much 'fall in with the wrong crowd' as joyously embrace them. For status. For belonging. For any kind of love.

Steve gave her that love, then hollowed out all her humanity to feed his own worthlessness. I've no doubt he did what all these bastards do; isolate her from family, friends; hitting her so she couldn't go to work out of shame or social workers out of fear of losing the kids. Slowly, methodically, he broke her until she became utterly dependent upon just him. Today, I'm going to show her that we're not all bastards.

'Look, Joan, I'm not going to take a formal statement or even write down what you tell me today. I just need to establish some facts and you're the only person who can help me.'

Her head nods but the eyes aren't buying it.

'Honestly, whatever you tell me won't come back on you. You have my word on that. I appreciate the risk you're taking even talking to me.'

Now she looks confused.

'How did you first meet Nathan?'

'It was two days before Christmas '87. I'll always remember it because I had no money to get anything for the kids. I was in a right state.

'Stephen had walked out on us a few months earlier and left me with all the bills. I couldn't cope. They sent Nathan round that afternoon to cut off the electricity, gas, phone.'

Her face softens. She's right back there. 'He saw how desperate I was, rang them all and negotiated a deal.'

Her eyes well up. 'He then handed me a fifty pound note and told me to buy a turkey and the kids something for Christmas. He said I could pay him back later.

'He popped round on Christmas night wearing a Santa hat with a gift for me, a bottle of perfume, and told me to arrange a babysitter for the evening of the 30th. That night he told me how he felt trapped in a loveless marriage and was only sticking with it for the kids. I really admired his honesty and it felt so nice to be . . . I don't know, fancied I suppose. We got together but neither of us had any real expectations. We just thought we'd see how it went for a few months.'

'Four months later, you're calling *Crimewatch* telling them your ex, Stephen Carter, murdered Nathan.'

She shakes her head: 'It wasn't me. Why would he hurt Nathan? He didn't know anything about us.'

'Okay, so the three occasions Stephen turned up and battered you between January and March that year, which gave Nathan grounds to present a barring order . . . what had that been about exactly?'

Her eyes darken and mouth stiffens.

I've got one card left to play, and it's a blatant lie. 'Look, Joan, *Crimewatch* traces every call it receives, and records them, despite their claims to the contrary.'

Her mouth opens a fraction and I visualise her insides collapsing like cliffs into a raging sea. Now I've got her on the ropes, I land my second tactical fib.

'I've listened to that recording, Joan. It's clearly your voice.'

She gazes down into her untouched black tea; it's no longer spinning or steaming.

She sighs. 'I thought Stephen had gone for good. And I'd no intentions of taking him back. Of course, someone told him I was seeing another bloke. They couldn't just let me enjoy a bit of happiness.

'He must have started spying on me and following us. He turned up begging me to finish it with Nathan and take him back. When I said no, he lost it.'

'And then, when he couldn't batter you into dumping Nathan, he took matters into his own hands. You know he killed Nathan and that's why you phoned *Crimewatch*.'

'No, no,' she protests. 'I called *Crimewatch* because I wanted to get back at him for ruining what I had with Nathan. Then I couldn't go through with it.'

'Oh come on, Joan. Stephen had the motive. He has a dangerous, violent streak. He couldn't stand the idea of another man having you, so he followed Nathan and took his chances in the pub car park.'

'He wouldn't have killed Nathan,' she states, challenging me with a glare. 'He would've killed me.' For the first time, she's looking directly into my eyes. 'Don't you get it? He would've taken it out on me and the kids. So I ended it with Nathan.'

'When was that?'

'End of March. Two weeks before Nathan was killed. Stephen didn't need to get him out of the way, as you put it, because we were already finished.'

I try a new tack. 'You provided an alibi for Stephen on the night of Nathan's murder. Now's your chance to retract that statement, Joan.'

She folds her arms and stares right through me.

'If you have any suspicions, Joan, you must state them now, or you'll be the one landing in prison.'

'Why don't you ask him yourself?' she says.

'I plan to.'

'He'll be back at five.'

I feel like my jaw has landed on the battle-scarred table.

'You're still . . . together?'

She nods. 'Of course. Love drives people crazy sometimes, but it's still love. As a mum, I've got to think about the kids, do what's best for them. Kids need to be with their mum and dad.'

Chapter 24

Clerkenwell, Central London
Friday, June 24, 1994; 17.00

Fintan insists we watch Ireland versus Mexico in an English pub.

The Three Kings in Clerkenwell don't just share a fictional throne, they also share one stingy 16-inch TV set; a fact we establish only after it's too late to go anywhere else.

'Great call Fint, I can't make out the players or hear the commentary and I'd wager there's more atmosphere in the crypt across the road.'

'Yeah, great isn't it?' says Fintan. 'No George Hamilton wittering on or pissed people singing or women screaming. I know the Archway has always been our sports pub, but the mob in there just don't understand soccer. There's a good chance we'll get hammered today but they'll still party like we've won the bloody tournament. I don't know about you, but I'm sick of all this "just happy to be here" underdog shite.'

'We beat Italy. Why do you think we'll get hammered?'

'FIFA are desperate to get us knocked out. That's why

they've sent us on this 2,000-mile round trip to play a game in Orlando at lunchtime. It's 104 degrees. Irish people aren't even supposed to lie out in that!'

'Steve Staunton may die!'

'Don't laugh, six of our players are well over thirty. Remember what happened to poor old Barry McGuigan in Vegas? And he was a fit, non-drinker.'

'Paul McGrath will definitely die.'

Sure enough, Los Mexicanos appear to be made of Los Asbestos; fresh featherweights bobbing and weaving around our lumbering George Foreman tribute act. Every time there's a break in play, the Irish backroom staff throws on bags of water. Sadly, for our sun-drunk albinos, the bags split on opening so that the precious water splats comedically onto the parched sward.

'It's like watching a troop of baboons trying to break into a Capri Sun,' quips Fintan.

Moments before half-time, the Irish players are deliriously helpless to prevent Mexico scoring. Fintan rants and rails but I can't shake Joan Carter's words out of my head.

As a mum, I've got to think about the kids, do what's best for them. Kids need to be with their mum and dad.

This is a woman savagely beaten by her husband on at least three occasions. My worst crimes have been to leave unfinished bowls of cornflakes on the sideboard, or used towels on the bathroom floor. Yet I'm the one getting kicked out. Matt's losing the only real dad he's ever had in the world. How can Zoe behave so selfishly?

Fintan seems even keener than me to avoid the inane half-time analysis, so I tell him about my trip to see durable Joan, the human punchbag and devoted wife of Carter the Unstoppable Slug Machine.

'It wasn't Carter or any other jealous husband who killed Nathan,' he laughs. 'It just doesn't fit.'

'Yes, it does.'

'The pathologist described the attack as an assassination, it was so savage and clinical. The man who wielded the axe wound tape around the handle knowing this would eliminate his prints. We're talking a professional enforcer here, not some irate suburban cuckold.'

I bristle. Is this how he sees me now? Of course, Fintan will never be a cuckold; he always ensures he gets his infidelity in first. I can't think of a girlfriend he hasn't cheated on. It's almost like a compulsion. He justifies it by claiming that as soon as he finds a woman who wants sex as often as he does, he'll commit.

I try again: 'People have murdered out of sexual jealousy, Fint, you know that.'

'Okay then, suppose you want to get back at this Charles fella who's been messing around with Zoe.'

'Don't even . . .'

'I'm serious, Donal. I know manly confrontations aren't your thing, but I'm sure you've fantasised about it. How would you do it?'

My arched eyebrows let him know I'm only fleetingly participating in this twisted little parlour game.

'I'd find out where he lives or works, wait for him to come out one morning or evening, let him know how I feel and scare the shit out of him.'

'Exactly. Even if he was Marvin Hagler, you'd confront him. No matter how violent any of these jealous husbands might be, they'd make sure they confronted Nathan first and had their say. No jealous husband is going to wait in a dark corner with an axe, attack him from behind, whack him repeatedly in the skull, then, after he falls, bury the hatchet into the side of his face with a backhand worthy of Roscoe Tanner. That's too efficient, too decisive and too personal. Whoever used Nathan's skull as a chopping board was sending out a very clear message to lots of other people. Mess with us and this is what you'll get.'

I hate him for being so certain; isn't that what scuppered all previous investigations? I'm keeping an open mind.

'Unless he was shagging the wife of a violent criminal,' I say. 'Maybe the guy had already warned him off. He ignored the threat and paid the price.'

Fintan screws up his face in mild disgust. 'You want it to be a jealous husband who killed Nathan, don't you Donal? You're so desperate to prove that a shagger like Nathan got his comeuppance because of what's happened to you, it's almost biblical. That's what this is all about, isn't it?'

I recoil in disbelief.

'For you, putting away a jealous husband who did this to Nathan is really about getting even with Charles by proxy. You're living vicariously through Nathan's killer because you're too spineless to front up Charles yourself.'

'I'm not scared of confronting Charles. I just don't see how it's going to help. If it was Joan Carter at the centre of this love triangle, I dare say she'd have an orgasm seeing me knock him out. But this is Zoe. God forbid there should be any unpleasantness.'

'Maybe some unpleasantness is exactly what she wants! Maybe she wants you to make a statement, be decisive, win the day? If you really want her, why don't you stop whingeing and moaning and go and get her? Show her what you're made of.'

'I know her better than you, Fintan, and, trust me, she's not Scarlett O bloody Hara okay? If I confront Charles, she'll finish with me for good. And, don't forget, I'm one disciplinary offence away from getting booted out of the force. One rumble in the car park shrubbery with Chuck and they'll throw the book at me.'

Fintan shakes his head. 'You're like some fucking Poundland Hamlet. Honestly, stop thinking and follow your gut or you'll never get anywhere.'

'Hang on a second! Your last manly pep talk convinced me to move out, and look how rosy that's turned out for me. No offence, Fintan, but relationships are a bit too complex for your rousing rhetoric.'

The teams emerge for the second half in the nick of time. The old hippie barman cranks up the volume to barely audible and we settle in for more heatstroke humiliation.

Mexico score again, Fintan spews expletives then spots a group of sneering English observers and tells them to fuck off. Luckily, they're beanie-hatted graphic designer types who promptly flee. But there is a raw, unashamed, unapologetic honesty to Fintan that I've somehow lost over the years. Maybe he's right. Maybe I need to man up, knock out Charles with my fists and Zoe with my unfettered, primal passion.

Back in the steaming Florida Glades, all seems lost when our striker Tommy Coyne staggers off the pitch and some flabby FIFA official refuses to let substitute John Aldridge on. Aldridge goes batshit. Manager Jack Charlton goes batshit. Fintan's way beyond batshit, and I fear for the fate of the sixteen-inch TV.

'I'm telling you, they want us out,' he screams.

Aldridge has to be forcibly restrained as he unleashes every obscenity known to mankind before a global audience of half a billion people.

'That's what I'm talking about,' roars Fintan, jabbing his finger at me. 'Don't let any fucker walk all over you.'

A possessed, demonic Aldridge is finally released into the fray and scores almost immediately; not with his left foot, or his right foot or his head, but out of sheer bloody-minded apoplectic rage.

Fintan erupts as if exorcised.

'I don't get it,' I shout. 'We're still losing.'

'Goal difference. That goal means we only need a draw against Norway to get through to the knock-out stages,' he bellows in frothing disbelief, as if he's just cracked relativity.

I'd promised myself never to let events on a football pitch dictate my private life again. But Fintan's assertion that I lack backbone followed by his Aldridge-inspired war cry has ignited that long-dormant fire in my belly.

'Fuck it,' I say to him. 'She's had almost a week. If she hasn't finished it with this Charles fella by now, then we're through.'

'That's the stuff,' says Fintan, giving my shoulder a manly thrashing. 'Now go get her.'

I march out of there pumped, stoked, fists beating metaphorical chest. *Poundland Hamlet my arse.*

The low evening sun burns holes through my squinting vision and squiffy resolve.

'I'd better ring first, just in case *he*'s there,' I instruct myself.

A surly young female voice answers. It's Lily, the posh goth, who Zoe insists is qualified to take care of Matt despite her stapled face, neck and unspecified nether regions.

Zoe must be out, gorging on culture with Chuck, making up for those famine years with philistine me. I visualise pallid Lily in our sitting room, cowering from the sun, picking at her scabs, and recognise a glorious opportunity. I need to know if Zoe's still seeing Charles, and how serious it is. With no leads, clues or anyone to ask, I decide to do what any desperate detective does in such circumstances: resort to forensics.

I take a mini-cab to Haringey, making him stop up the street a little from our flat. I'm not sure why. Squeezing the key in my hand, I feel giddy, excited. I know exactly what I need to do.

The key turns satisfyingly in the lock. At least Zoe hasn't changed it. See, she is planning on having me back, one day. I walk in and tremble at the familiar smell. I next get a whiff of Zoe's perfume and work hard to quell a full-scale palpitation.

Goth horror is gassing on the landline. I squeeze the pips and press twenty quid into her protesting paw.

'Now run along before I set some magnets on you, or a nice soapy flannel,' I say, and she bolts.

I stalk silently into Matt's little room. He's upside down in his cot, as usual, arse in the air, face scrunched into the mattress. Something's different, but I just can't put my finger on it. Then I realise; she's had his hair cut for the first time. My God! This was something we'd planned to do together, at that place in Crouch End where they take a photo and charge by the hair. How could she just press on ahead and do this without me?

I place my hand on his hot little back; how I miss the feel of him, his honeyed smell and sing-song chatter. But she's left us both floating in a sort of emotional Limbo.

No more. Decision-time is nigh.

'Don't worry, Matty,' I whisper. 'Daddy's coming home soon.'

I head into our old bedroom high on a sort of fatalistic glee. There's no turning back now. Time for Acting DC Lynch to find out the truth.

I switch on the bedroom light, head for her knicker drawer.

I know it will take real bottle for me to give her an ultimatum about us, bottle I just don't possess. That kind of steel can only be forged from more hurt. I want to hurt. Bring on the hurt.

I riffle gently through some familiar, workaday panties. Then my hand and heart stop at a black, raunchy, see-through thong. I hold the box-fresh garment in the palm of my shaking hand. She never wears stuff like this for me. I rummage some more and find a white lace baby-doll nightie, see-through save for tiny little pink flowers. That Pixies' lyric blazes through my mind: 'You're so pretty when you're unfaithful to me.' I marvel at the pretty feminine gloss on such an ugly, black betrayal. But it clears things up. It empowers me. I want more.

Heart pumping in my ears, I turn my attention to the laundry basket. Not far from the top, a pair of black lacy knickers, one of Zoe's raunchier numbers I used to peel off myself. 'Weekend pants', as we jokingly called them. Except, judging by the state of them, they're now getting a good work-out on Thursday nights too.

It's then that I spot the boxer shorts. His boxer shorts. In our laundry basket. I stagger a little, my heart flapping like a trapped bird. He was in our bed. Last night. The sheer scale of the violation shatters me. I need to sit down, but I can't bring myself to sit on the bed – our bed – not now they've been in it.

My God has Matt seen them? Does he jump in between them in the mornings like he used to with us? A base, primeval, intolerable hurt scorches through me. I put a hand against the wardrobe to steady myself, taking long, deep breaths. Everything inside me pulses out of time.

Well, at least her fanny's better, I console myself as I wobble down the stairs. I grab a bottle of red from the top of the fridge. I down it fast. It fails to numb the shock. I go in search of more. All I can find is a bottle of rosé in the fridge, a quarter down. 'Oh Zoe, you're sooo restrained,' I mumble as I fill a pint glass. 'Well, I've fucking paid for it. And I'm still paying for you,' I remind the house.

I'm busy mentally listing all the gross injustices she's brought down upon me when the key rattles in the front door. I meet her in the hallway. Thank Christ he isn't with her, or one of us would be up on a murder charge tonight. She stops dead. I wave an accusatory rosé bottle under her nose. 'You said you'd finish it, and you haven't!'

She eyes the bottle warily.

'Not the rosé! Your affair!'

She barges past me towards the kitchen. I turn to follow.

I feel ribs crack, bend open, hatred spewing out. My turn to administer some home truths; I want her to hurt badly.

'Why have you done this to me? To Matt? Why are you so unhappy? What the fuck do you want, Zoe? Explain it to me. Right here, right now.'

She spins around, eyes wild.

'Maybe I'd prefer to be with someone who doesn't drink themselves into a stupor every single night, you know, someone with plans and ambitions?'

'I have plans and ambitions. I can quit drinking.'

'Maybe it'd be better for Matt not to be around someone who keeps getting fired and who thinks he speaks to the dead. And maybe it'd be better for Matt to have a dad who's not going to drop dead suddenly when he's a teenager, because both you and I know there's a very real chance that might happen.'

She's gone straight for the jugular, the one thing I've been too scared to confront. My heart's banging like a couple of dustbin lids. I can't breathe.

Zoe's gasket has blown. 'That thing that killed your mum in the end, you haven't even gone to get it checked out. Well, have you? How unfair is that on me? On Matt? I keep asking you to go and you just ignore me.'

'Well funnily enough, Zoe, I've been fairly preoccupied dealing with Mam's death. I'm not sure I'm quite ready to start coping with my own possibly imminent passing yet. Now had I known you were going to use it as a reason to cheat on me . . .'

'It's not like that.'

I snort, in a slightly more demented way than I'd planned.

I fix her with my meanest Clint squint: 'If you really loved me, a thing like that wouldn't matter. You don't see the husbands and wives of cancer victims swinging in the hospital car park, do you?'

'God you make it sound so . . . sordid. It really isn't like that at all.'

'What is it like then, Zoe? I'm clearly a bit slow on the uptake here. Explain to me what it's really like?'

'I told you when we first met that I'd always put Matt first, and you accepted that. I'm trying to work out what's best for him right now, because frankly I think he deserves better.'

'Better than me, you mean? You say this now because presumably you think you've found someone better than me. Is that it? I seemed to fit the bill fine when no one else would take on a single mum and a child that wasn't theirs. You think that was easy for me? And yet from day one I've treated Matt like my own. This is the thanks I get for it, you running about with this fucking Charles character.'

'His name's Chris.'

'Jesus that was quick. What happened to Charles?'

'There never was any Charles. It was an in-joke. We went

to see that film *Four Weddings and a Funeral*. He reminds me of the main character Charles.'

'Well whatever his name is, Matty doesn't need a third dad in fourteen months. If you were really putting him first, you'd realise that.'

'It won't be his third dad,' she says quietly, avoiding my eyes now and staring at some faraway floor. 'It's his first dad.'

Her head doesn't move but her frightened eyeballs peer up to find mine.

'Matthew's dad, Chris, is back.'

I lose all feeling. Life loses all meaning. I'm falling off the planet and there's no one to save me.

'You can't just take Matt away from me like that. You can't . . .'

My bloodless head swoons. In the eerie strangled silence, her face morphs in and out of focus.

'You can't,' I hear my last breath hiss, before my body sheds all of its feeling. Not now, cataplexy. Not now.

Too late. I turn to liquid and pour to the floor. Any extreme emotion can trigger it, even a joke. My neurological fuse box short-circuits and, pop, everything stops functioning. I've had it since my teens, a side-effect of the insomnia and sleep paralysis.

A firework explodes inside my head. My eyes pop open to the tiled floor and the sound of her snivelling. I'm a useless puddle of bones and flesh, but I manage to look up, see her cry and it feels good.

She stalks off and I collect my limbs.

I grab my pint of rosé off the sideboard and take a long sour mouthful.

All hope is lost now. I know that.

Yet I feel strangely elated. Released. I realise something

– it's the hope that kills you. The hope that the horse you've just plunged all your money on will be first past the post. Ask any serious punter and they'll tell you – when that horse loses, their gut reaction is relief. Once the money has gone, the hope has gone. You're free.

I've seen it in the job. People waiting for a missing loved one to walk through the door, when we all know in our hearts that they're dead. It's not the tragedy that destroys these people, it's the futile hope.

Zoe could never understand why finding the body means so much to relatives in a murder case. I tried to make her see – it's so they can bury their child, and their futile hopes with it. It's a release. Acceptance. The last part of DABDA.

I raise my pint of rosé to the fridge magnet photo of our family trip to Brighton, toast the woman who just trampled my heart into so many pieces that it can never be repaired, and bury our relationship.

Chapter 25

Arsenal, North London
Saturday, June 25, 1994; 09.00

'I'm not letting you mope about in here all day,' says Fintan, yanking open my bedroom curtains. 'And, don't forget, you've an appointment with *Crimewatch*'s most unlikely tipster, DC Neil Rooney.'

I'd completely forgotten about calling Rooney yesterday. He's the officer who, six years ago, complained to *Crimewatch* that the Nathan Barry murder squad was so focussed on John Delaney that they were ignoring other 'good' suspects.

I sit up, hunt around for my mobile. 'I'll call him up and cancel.'

'No you won't,' says Fintan, waving my phone in his hand. 'You need to keep busy and I'm coming with you.'

'What are you doing with my phone?'

He sniggers and frowns at the same time.

'She's got back with Matt's dad. Can you believe it?'

'I know,' says Fintan. 'Forget about her. She wasn't your type anyway.'

'What do you mean, you know?'

'You came crashing into my room last night. Remember? It was all very dramatic. I had to take your phone off you because you kept trying to call her, then her parents. You kept asking me to look into this Chris St. John Green guy, find any skeletons in his cupboard, which I thought was ironic, bearing in mind the disdain you usually reserve for such scurrilous antics.'

'Oh yeah. Sorry,' I say but I don't remember much after slamming her front door behind me. The last thing I heard was Matt crying out for me, almost as if he knew. 'Dong! Dong!' he called and I wailed along with him, all the way back to the Arsenal.

'By the way, have you seen Dusko Popov anywhere?' he asks, referring to his tiny bugging device.

'No,' I lie and he can tell.

'You didn't use it on Zoe did you?'

'It's under a table at the Harp bar in Croydon. At least that's where I left it on Monday. '

'What?'

'John Delaney and Phil Ware took me there for a drink.'

'Five days ago? Why the hell haven't you gone back to get it?'

'Gary Warner said he'd break my legs if he ever saw me again. Don't worry it'll still be there. They haven't cleaned that place in centuries.'

'Right,' he says, shaking his head and checking his watch. 'Let's go see DC Rooney first. I'll pop into the Harp on the way back and retrieve it. If it's still there.'

'It'll be there. And you don't have to babysit me, Fintan. I'm okay, honestly.'

'I know,' he says. 'But this Rooney character sounds fascinating. You don't get many cops breaking rank like that.'

Like DI Lambert last week, Rooney insists on meeting us at the murder scene.

'I've checked Rooney out,' says Fintan. 'He's a bit of a maverick. Not afraid to take on bosses or kick up a fuss. He's paid the price though. He's still a DC despite being a very good detective.'

'Don't you think it's bizarre, him calling up *Crimewatch* like that?'

'I've never heard anything like it before. He wasn't even on the Nathan Barry murder squad, he just attended the scene on the night, so I'm not sure how seriously we can take it.'

We park behind the pub, right where Nathan did six years ago. Before we go in through the rear entrance, we take a look through a window. Rooney's inside, half a Guinness down and it's not yet 11.15am.

'Amazing how many mavericks are alkies,' says Fintan. 'Nothing like a permanent banging hangover to make you bolshie.'

I introduce myself, then Fintan as a mature student shadowing me on work experience, which makes both of them bristle. Rooney's a Dubliner, so we connect immediately over Ireland's World Cup exploits and the furore at home about new, stricter drink-drive laws.

'What people don't understand is that drinking and driving to the rural Irish is like guns to the Americans,' says Rooney. 'Despite the odd tragedy, they see it as a sort of birth right. Now, phones on the table please, gents, and batteries out.'

We obey. 'Why the secrecy?'

'I get a police pension. I don't want anything changing that. And this case is riddled with snakes.'

'So, you were first on the scene here, on the night of Nathan's murder?'

'I was first CID on the scene. There were a couple of uniforms flapping about panicking. One of them had never seen a dead body before.'

'Anything unusual that I haven't read in the paperwork?'

'Well the Senior Investigating Officer, Detective Chief Inspector Frank Vaughan, turned up at about 11pm pissed out of his mind. It wasn't unusual for him to be pissed, but not at a murder scene. First thing he does is order a bottle of whiskey and glasses for his team. You can imagine how that went down with the locals.

'I suggested he should hand over to DI Lambert, who was too miserable to ever touch a drop. Vaughan went mental. He sent me and my partner back to the station.'

'Do you think his drunkenness affected the investigation that night?' I ask, wincing at such an obvious opening question.

'Absolutely. Clearly things weren't done properly because Nathan's Rolex watch went missing.'

'I didn't know this.'

'Oh yeah. His family confirmed he owned one and it hasn't been seen since. Forensics officers say they saw it on his wrist in the car park. By the time they got him to the morgue, it was gone. I tried everything to track it down. Every Rolex watch has a unique serial number and a recorded service history, but it never showed up again. God knows what else vanished that night, or got contaminated. It sounded like chaos.'

'What was your next involvement in the case, Neil?' I ask.

'I was back at the station later when DI Lambert brought John Delaney in. It must have been about one in the morning. Even at that stage, Lambert seemed convinced Delaney did it. He came up with the bright idea that I should bring

Delaney to Nathan's house to break the news to his wife, Emma. Lambert felt certain this would crack Delaney and told me to report back.

'How did Delaney seem?'

'Scared, nervous, how anyone would be in that situation.'

'Did Emma say words to the effect of, "I thought they'd hurt him, I didn't think they'd kill him"?'

'No. Any cop would seize upon something like that and make it the first line of enquiry. Why?'

'Delaney claims she said that.'

'Delaney acted strangely during the entire investigation. I always got the sense he was undermining it, any chance he got, and that he knew a hell of a lot more than he was letting on.'

I'm beginning to wonder how much else Delaney has spun in his determination to create alternative suspects. First, I ask about Neil's call to *Crimewatch*.

He takes a long draw of Guinness, blinking slowly like a wily old crocodile. 'I'd planned to make it anonymous, but sure everyone on the team knew my voice. Besides, by giving my name, I knew they wouldn't be able to dismiss me as some crank.'

'You accused the senior officers of tunnel vision and rejecting other viable suspects.'

'Lambert had a hard-on for Delaney, no two ways about it. I even put up a suspect myself, but I know it was never checked out.

'My son Paul had a friend who worked for BD Investigations at the time. Three or four weeks after the murder, he came around to pick Paul up. They were going on a surveillance job and were both kitted out in combats and camo gear.

'When this guy opened his van, I saw an axe in the back

identical to the one used to kill Nathan. It even had the same coloured masking tape wrapped around the handle.

'I told the incident room. When I heard nothing back, I did some checking myself. Turns out Nathan's widow, Emma Barry, invested some of the life insurance money she'd received into this guy's new business. A couple of days after the murder, they were seen together in a wine bar by someone who worked at BD Investigations, looking very cosy. I tracked down a builder who did some work at Nathan Barry's home a few months before the murder, and he said this fellow was always round there and he'd once caught them in a romantic clinch.'

'And the name of this man?'

'Bremner. Daniel Bremner.'

'He now owns a courier company?'

'That's him.'

I work hard not to react. Bremner had been so keen to point out potential suspects to me. Now it turns out he may have been the killer all along.

Rooney continues: 'I had a couple of pals on the Nathan Barry murder squad who confided in me that DI Lambert wouldn't consider any suspect other than Delaney.

'One of them found out that Nathan had been in the process of selling a story to one of the newspapers for big money. I think sixty grand was mentioned and it was something to do with bent cops.

'According to the information, Nathan had been peddling this story with a friend of his, a serving police officer called Duncan McCall. When my cops pals handed this information to DI Lambert, he ripped it up in front of them and told them to focus on Delaney.'

Fintan can't contain himself: 'Who was their source?'

'Williams. Peter Williams. A bailiff at BD Investigations.

He later got employed full-time by Delaney and refused to make another statement. I presume he'd been paid off. Delaney's paid everyone off, even the ex-husband of his current wife. Anyway, Pete Williams is dead now. He had a very serious drink problem.'

'And Duncan McCall?'

'Dead too. A few months after Nathan's murder he topped himself. Shotgun at home. There was an inquest and quite a lot of publicity. Bad drinking problem too, apparently.'

Fintan's well ahead and takes control. 'Will we be able to find Peter Williams' statement anywhere?'

Rooney laughs: 'No. And the officers who got this information out of him won't speak. They're too scared of crossing the scoundrels.'

'The scoundrels?'

'There's a group of senior officers who, how can I put it, seem to do things their own way and enjoy a lot of protection from on high. They're Freemasons, of course, and I'm pretty certain they're all bent.'

I lean forward: 'How on earth can we prove any of this?'

'Well, the first thing you need to do is find the journalist who offered Nathan and Duncan McCall sixty grand for their story. He must know who and what they were about to expose. He may even have an idea about who killed Nathan.'

'Why didn't you do that, Neil?'

'I already stuck my neck out, making that call to *Crimewatch*. I didn't fancy winding up with an axe in the face too. I suggest you two should think very carefully before upsetting whoever Nathan Barry upset.'

Chapter 26

Croydon, South London
Saturday, June 25, 1994; 13.00

As soon as Fintan revives his phone, it buzzes and pings like he's won a jackpot. 'Oh God,' he groans at the violent volley of thwarted correspondence.

He calls 'the desk', endures a maniacal tirade about his whereabouts, then soaks up the skeletal details of a breaking story.

'I'm on it,' he declares, and I chase him back to the car.

We roar off before I get my door closed. 'What's happened?'

'A nineteen-year-old girl is in a coma. She took ecstasy at some rave club in Windsor.'

'Hasn't this happened quite a few times in the last few years?'

'Yeah, but this one is a daughter of Middle England. Her mum's a police officer stationed at Windsor Castle, so there's a royal angle. And her dad's a tutor at Eton College, so there's a toff angle.'

'Does your news desk tell you what to do now, or do you just know from experience?'

'Bit of both really. The parents are holding a press conference at 2pm. The boss will want tears and an "if it can happen to our Molly, it can happen to any of your children" quote. They'll want dirt on the club owner and the club itself, so I'll have to get one of my specialists onto that.'

'Specialists?'

'A private investigator. Find out if the owner has form and what big juicy profits he makes from peddling death.'

'Maybe he has no idea they deal drugs at his club. What if she bought the pill somewhere else?'

'He's hardly in a position to sue, is he?'

His phone rings. He puts it on speaker.

'His Royal Lowness, the Prince of Darkness. How are you?'

'I've got the desk chewing my arse about this Molly girl. How are we going to manage the slaughter on this one then?' says Alex Pavlovic.

'You must have snouts in Windsor nick, Alex, for royal stuff?'

'No. I get it all from a royal protection guy.'

'Know anything about this Oasis nightclub?'

'No, but I'm pulling all that. Leave it to me,' rasps the Prince.

'What about the hospital in Slough, Wexham Park? Any insiders there?'

'No.'

'Right, well you need to get your arse over there now. Send your usual bouquet of flowers to the mum and dad, with a note and phone tucked inside. Don't make them an offer. These people are too classy for that. Just say that the proprietor of our newspaper has personally agreed to fund the best possible private medical care for Molly in return for their full co-operation okay? Then you need to blag your way into Molly's room and get a photo.'

'She's in intensive care. I'll only get so far carrying a bunch of flowers. Even if I turn up dressed as Nurse fucking Ratched, they won't let me in there.'

'Okay, well you'd better get the old invisibility cloak on then.'

'I'll give it a go.'

Fintan kills the call and I almost die of curiosity.

'Okay, I have to ask, what do you mean by invisibility cloak?'

'Hi-vis, ironically,' he smiles.

I don't get it.

'Our old friend the Prince discovered it years ago. You put hi-vis working clothes on and no one even looks at you. You literally become part of the furniture. The city is full of these hi-vis ghosts. Take a look next time. You pass hundreds every day but you don't even look at their faces. So, if we need to get in somewhere, that's what we use. Everyone just assumes you're either maintenance or contractors.'

'I'd never have thought of that.'

'All part of the Prince's diabolical genius. Right,' he says, skidding to a halt outside East Croydon station. 'You're on your own from here. I'll try and check out that Duncan McCall suicide later, see what him and Nathan Barry were trying to flog. I've got to race over to Slough. Are you back to London?'

'Yes,' I lie, climbing out.

But I'm staying in Croydon and heading straight to the pub. Not to drink, but to find out, once and for all, who killed Nathan Barry.

Chapter 27

The Harp Bar, Croydon, South London
Saturday, June 25, 1994; 13.30

The first people to spot me as I walk into the Harp Bar are the Warner brothers, Gary and Chris – the psychotic ex in-laws of John Delaney. According to the police theory, one of these brothers swung the axe that killed Nathan Barry. Delaney paid for the hit and their pal Phil Ware – head of the local murder squad – derailed the police investigation.

Perched upon the same stools as five days ago, their glares follow me all the way to the bar. I lay down my *Sun* newspaper and pretend to read the back page. Seconds grind past as I stand there basking in terror, trying to stop the trembling. After what seems an age, they lose interest and turn back to the football highlights on TV – cue for the Irish barman to come over.

'Fosters,' I growl, thinking *I've made it*. Fintan's tip about hi-vis had been inspired; they haven't recognised me, though I'd never have risked it without this baseball cap.

'What part are you from?' smiles the barman and I almost gasp in disbelief. How could he tell from a single word?

'Offaly. And you?' I mumble, feeling guilty for being so hostile.

'Cork,' he says. 'Didn't I see you in here a few days back?'

I shake my head way too quickly and vigorously.

'I never forget a face,' he says. 'You were dressed smart like.'

I cock my left ear; they've stopped talking. I'm dead. My eyes beg him to stop.

'Not me,' I say, my voice high and cracking, my chest closing in on itself.

'It was you,' he laughs, placing the pint down in front of me. 'I can spot another Paddy from 300 yards.'

The glares of both brothers slice through me like cop-seeking lasers. I hand Cork's most observant barman a fiver but avoid his eyes, staring instead at the pint's internal geysers. Every fibre of my being is braced for explosive violence.

Gary Warner's plaintive voice lifts me six inches off the carpet: 'My old mum says it's rude to wear a hat indoors.'

I pretend to be so enthralled by the *Sun*'s back-page exclusive that I don't hear. I pick up my pint and paper and wheel away from them, feeling their stares all the way down to the furthest table.

'Your change?' shouts the barman.

Part of me wants to grab Dusko and make a run for it. But what if they chase after me? I'm on foot. This is their manor. One roar and the whole of West Croydon would be out, hunting me down.

I pull my cap down to my eyebrows, sit and stare at the newspaper. As I count to 100, the gobshite barman just won't let it lie.

'I've your change here,' he says.

I glance up and, horror, he's walking over. The brothers watch on, dangerously curious.

'Here,' he says, counting the change out on the table.

'Thanks,' I say quietly, sliding my warrant card across the table's surface so only he can see. 'Now shut the fuck up and leave me alone,' I mutter.

He freezes for a second; then turns slowly around. I can't believe my life is in the hands of this nosy gobshite.

My insides clench and grind. One word from the Corkman and I'm fucked. I've no mandate to be here. No one in the world knows I'm here. If this barman exposes me now, they're bound to find Dusko. They'll listen to the tape, make me tell them who I am and what I'm doing. Then, I'm in no doubt, the Warner brothers will kill me. *That's All Folks!*

'My mistake,' the barman declares loudly, and I breathe for what feels like the first time in several minutes. I sink half the pint, grab Dusko, polish off the rest and slip out. As soon as I turn the first corner, I sprint.

Earlier, I'd splashed out on hi-vis clothing and a lo-fi Dictaphone. I see a Wetherspoons pub, lock myself in the disabled toilet, slip the tiny cassette in and press play.

Chapter 28

Mayfair, Central London
Saturday, June 25, 1994; 17.00

The only words I'd planned to utter for the rest of that Saturday were 'beer', 'wine' and 'thank you'. Alas, the pathologist Dr Edwina Milne has other ideas. Her text apologises for the 'hasty' exit last Sunday and requests a chance to explain all this evening. How could I say no?

The bar of Dukes Hotel in Mayfair looks like a gentleman's club redecorated by your nan; all swirling carpets, garish velvet seats and gold picture frames. Edwina had warned me to dress smartly, so I did, but staff at places like this can see right through you and duly treat me with an almost exquisite degree of contempt.

Eventually, a disapproving waiter leads me to a table out in the foyer.

'Fine by me,' I tell him. 'The chintz was making me delirious.'

I survey the Martini bar menu and smirk at its rather desperate boast that Bond creator Ian Fleming had once been a regular here. Everything about this glorified Cumbrian tea room screams the Great British Bond Delusion: other nations might have all the money and power, but we still have the class and history. And we'll charge you handsomely to envy us. So many upper-class British generations have internalised the Bond myth – we might be outnumbered and outgunned, but we still do it better – that their entire political outlook seems stuck in a post-war time warp.

You see it during Royal events. Or how excited they get when buccaneering sporting eccentrics like Ian Botham or Nigel Mansell 'stick it to Johnny Foreigner' in the most bombastic, cavalier fashion imaginable. I can't help thinking that the Harp bar's contingent of slumped, overweight, apathetically violent petty criminals provides a more accurate snapshot of modern England.

'What are you doing out here?' laughs Edwina. 'I thought daylight was your sworn enemy?' I'm so relieved to see she's back to her old ebullient, piss-taking self. She's clearly decided I'm not a nutter after all.

'I didn't realise I'd need a cravat and a cane to get inside.'

'It is a bit snooty, but the Martinis are worth it.'

'That's what I say about you, Edwina.'

Of course, the staff fall at Edwina's feet. We're fast-tracked directly to the front of the Martini bar queue and forced to marvel at the barman mixing our drinks. I've yet to encounter a cocktail barman who doesn't consider himself a fruit-flinging, tumbler-juggling sex god. Quite why the filling, shaking and emptying of liquid vessels has been elevated into an art form is beyond me. Judging by the pompous head on this pot shaker, you'd think he was rustling up a cure for Multiple Sclerosis.

If they could carry Edwina to a table in a ceremonial litter, they surely would. The professional fawners finally disperse and Edwina gets straight down to business.

'How's the Julie Draper case going?'

I tell her about possible links to the murder of Nathan Barry and the suicide of Duncan McCall.

'I can cast an eye over the Nathan Barry and Duncan McCall pathology reports, if that might help?'

'That'd be priceless, Edwina. Thanks.'

'Look, the real reason I asked you here is to apologise for the other night,' she says.

I start to protest but she cuts me dead.

'I've done a lot of soul-searching and I think you deserve an explanation for my somewhat brusque exit.'

She wants to lead this dance, so, Martini-numb, I fall in.

'For a long, long time, the job didn't feel real to me. Cops and crime scenes and court cases . . . I felt like I was in a film. I've always believed that people watch violent films to see their nightmares play out, so that they can then walk away from their worst fears unscathed. Seeing dead people made me feel immune to death. It was something that happened to other people. That was part of the bargain.

'I spent five years at Hornsey Mortuary and it honestly felt like a corpse conveyor belt. It wasn't until this year I finally realised I'd been mistaken all along. Death isn't an abstraction and no one in our line of work gets left unscathed.'

She looks at me anxiously, clearly unused to unburdening.

'What happened, Edwina?'

'The Home Office gave me this new role, which I was terribly excited about, a sort of roving pathologist-for-hire in major cases. I was enjoying it too. Until February.'

She gets down and dirty with the Martini, slinging a third in a single, wincing swig. *Anaesthetise and energise . . .*

The bitter taste sends a whip-crack command to her composure. 'They sent me to 25 Cromwell Street.'

'Oh Jesus,' I mumble, those grim news bulletin images flickering in my mind. They'd dug up eight young women and an unborn baby in Fred West's home and garden. They found more of his unspeakable handiwork elsewhere.

'They sexually abused them, tortured them, hung them from beams in their basement. I found drill holes in some of their shoulder blades. They were violated in every way imaginable as they hung there, helplessly.'

She shakes her head, her eyes looking beyond me, into that abyss.

'There were even signs that they'd been cannibalised.' She laughs bitterly. 'Why not? It was the only thing left to do to them.

'Just one of those girls had been reported missing. The rest hadn't been missed at all. By anyone. They'd been turfed out of care homes aged sixteen and left to fend for themselves. Nobody in the world gave a shit about them, leaving Fred and Rose West free to devour them like wolves.

'I just can't stop thinking about their final hours, left for dead in that basement, knowing no one could hear their cries for help, no one was out there looking for them, or missing them or even thinking about them. They already didn't exist.'

She looks at me startled, the shock of her upcoming revelation still box-fresh in her mind.

'I'm going to tell you something about the West case I haven't told another soul. And I'm only telling you because of what you told me last time. I think we may both be reluctant witnesses to the inexplicable.'

With a build-up like that, it feels only right that I order another brace of Martinis.

'Most of West's victims had been buried with gags in their mouths, and with these ghastly torture masks over their faces. One of them, Carol Ann, had been buried next to an underground drainpipe that had several slow leaks. The waterlogged soil had preserved her body surprisingly well. When I removed the mask, her face was almost completely intact. The thing is, Donal . . .'

Her eyes widen, pleadingly.

'She had this big beaming smile on her face. It was almost beatific, as if, at the very point of death, she'd seen the most wonderful spectacle ever. It seemed so utterly incongruous, and was so utterly unexpected . . . it floored me.'

She shuffles in her seat, taking a new tack. 'Of course, it could've been caused by a cadaverous spasm at the point of death. It's a sort of reflex action, usually connected to the cause of death. I've seen suicides clutching the gun they'd used to shoot themselves. That's how they found Kurt Cobain. It's eerie but logical. That's what a pathologist would say happened here.'

'What do you say?'

She shakes her head. 'This was more than an upturned mouth. Her whole face looked overjoyed, ecstatic. Scientifically, it makes no sense whatsoever. So, for the first time in my career, I allowed myself to think that maybe, just maybe, there's something more to death than simply expiring.'

She takes another slurp, then helps herself to a long, controlled, almost yogic intake of air, summoning some uncomfortable truths.

'You see, Donal, I've come across all sorts of things during my career that can't be explained by science. Near-death experiences, people being pronounced dead, then reviving, a woman who spoke to transport police after she'd been sliced in two by a train. Everyone in my line of work has stories like this that defy science, but we're actively discouraged from exploring them, reporting them or even acknowledging them. Our job is to explain it all away neatly, sign the form and move on.

'Carol Ann's smile made me realise that I'd amputated my own spirituality to cope with my work. Like that blues singer, Robert Johnson, I'd sold my soul to be the best at my job. I'd conditioned myself to reject anything that didn't adhere to science and logic and cold fact. It made me very good at my job. But at what cost?

'I did what the vast majority of us do in life. I traded in my spirit, curiosity, honesty, my soul really, in return for security, prosperity, respect, status. We all do. We all end up climbing onto this career rock face and clinging on no matter what, don't we?'

She takes stock with another mournful mouthful.

'I stopped looking at the stars, Donal. Do you know what I mean?'

'I think so.'

'It's like we've decided we know enough so we don't need spirituality any more. It just distracts us from the climb. Yet we don't know anything, do we? Not really. The universe, where humans came from, or where we go after we die, the essence of who we are, why we're here. Why do we ignore these things?

'I stopped thinking about the bigger questions. The important stuff. Because I thought it would make me weak, less professional, less able to cope. But after Carol Ann, I can't ignore it anymore.'

She sips and momentarily closes her eyes, as if silently acknowledging the completion of some dreaded ordeal. I realise how much it took for her to tell me this, and wonder why she has.

'Anyway, I'd planned to keep all this to myself. Then you told me about your episodes. The scientist in me felt a desperate urge to shoo you away or mock you. Then I thought; why am I so scared of what you told me? Why are we so afraid to admit there's loads we can't explain? Why can't we just open our narrow little minds and accept what you've experienced on face value?

'Just because it's illogical, unusual and inexplicable, doesn't mean it isn't worth treating seriously and exploring properly. As I often say, I don't believe in sceptics. So, I've been giving it some proper thought.'

I'm staggered, flattered, almost overcome. At last, someone far more intelligent and worldly than me is taking my encounters with the dead seriously. It's all I can do not to get up and hug her.

'What do you think is going on, Edwina?' I squeak, my throat quelling a volcano of emotions.

'I'd say your episodes are definitely linked to sleep paralysis. But you should be seeing a ghost or an alien, whatever your bogeyman is, not murder victims. Unless . . . are you afraid of death, Donal?'

'Aren't we all?'

'Indeed, but we don't keep the prospect of death at the forefront of our minds. Did you witness a violent death in your youth perhaps?'

I shake my head.

'How old do you think you'll be when you die?'

'Seventy-five or so,' I lie.

She frowns, sensing I'm holding back. 'It sounds to me like you're suffering some sort of post-traumatic stress disorder. There's a fear buried deep in your psyche that the sight of a murder victim triggers and your sleep paralysis brings to life. Maybe it's so deeply buried that your conscious mind isn't aware of it. But I'd wager that sudden, agonising, violent death is your bogeyman. You just don't know why.'

You're good, Edwina, bloody good. Maybe even a genius. You've bared your soul today, now it's time for me to come clean . . .

A fresh brace of Martinis land, as if on cue. I help myself to a sterling swig and let loose.

'My mother died on New Year's Eve from a very rare condition called Fatal Familial Insomnia. She couldn't sleep at all for the last three months, developed dementia and wasted away to a skeleton.'

'I'm so sorry, Donal, I know how close you were.'

'I keep suddenly remembering she's gone, you know, several times a day, almost like my brain refuses to let it sink in. I know it sounds stupid, but I'd just love to know she's okay.'

I swallow hard again, my chest set to burst.

'Anyway, it's a very rare disease, just a few hundred known cases in the world. We had academics fly in from Iran and the US to observe her treatment. Before she lost her marbles, the doctors and nurses back home made her feel so exotic and special. She loved the attention, bless her. God knows, she didn't get much of it during her life.

'She was lucky, in a way. It can strike any time from eighteen to sixty. She was fifty-two, so at least she saw us grow up.'

Edwina tilts her head and smiles sadly. 'She must've been delighted you'd found someone, and turned her into an instant grandmother.'

'You can't imagine what it meant to her, being able to see a photo of her first grandchild. I never told her he isn't biologically mine. I didn't want to spoil it for her, you know?'

She nods, eyes twinkling. She's about to go too.

Now the part I've never uttered aloud before, so I gallop through it. 'Anyway, this thing is genetic and if one parent has the gene, there's a 50/50 chance the offspring will inherit it and develop the disease.'

Edwina mumbles 'Oh my gosh' and blinks dementedly.

'Mam was losing her marbles when she grabbed hold of my hand one night and said: "This is why you keep seeing those spirits, Donal. Part of you has always known you might have this damned thing. Every time you see a body that's died in agony, you see yourself. I'm so sorry." That's the last comprehensible thing she ever said to me.'

Edwina looks upset, alarmed, then stern as the scientist in her sucks up the blows. 'I genuinely don't know what to say, Donal. There must be a way they can test you for this.'

'Fintan's had the all-clear.'

She nods impatiently.

'I haven't been able to face it. Please don't lecture me, Edwina. Not unless you've played Russian roulette with three bullets in the chamber . . .'

'I bet you've had enough lectures from your other half. But surely she deserves to know, Donal, and sooner rather than later.'

Jesus, I might be dying, but all the women in my life care about is whether or not I can confirm it, so that Zoe can crack on with alternative plans!

'Why? So she'll have an excuse to leave me?'

'Good God, Donal, how can you think like that? I mean she needs to know so she doesn't worry herself to death. And what if she wants children with you? If you love her, you'll do the right thing . . .'

Children with me? She doesn't even want sex with me.

I focus on a spot on the table top. 'Okay, okay, I'm booking it any day now.'

'Good,' says Edwina. 'I always knew there was something different about you, Donal. Something special. I just couldn't put my finger on it. Sadly, I think there really could be something in what your dear mother said. She was clearly a very astute woman.'

'I just hated the fact she felt so guilty about passing it onto me. I told her not to, over and over.'

Edwina puts her hand on mine. 'As you now know, Donal, guilt is the main qualification for the job of parent.'

She pats kindly, then withdraws. Emotional circuit broken, she resumes as a scientist tackling a particularly stubborn equation.

'So your subconscious terror of inheriting this genetic condition explains the post-traumatic stress and why your sleep paralysis conjures up dead people you've recently encountered. What it fails to explain is why and how you glean clues from these encounters, pertinent to that victim's murder.

'It's tempting to attribute it to your subconscious beavering away and coming up with answers out of the blue, as if engaged in a cryptic crossword. But to do so, I'd just be repeating what I did as a pathologist. It's a square peg and a round hole, don't you think?'

'That's exactly what I've always thought. The desperation of people to rationalise it has never done justice to the experiences.'

'Right, that's settled,' she barks. 'I'm going to explore this exotic condition of yours with a renewed, open mind. Are you okay with that?'

'I'd be honoured,' I say, thinking, if nothing else, it'll earn me a gallon or two of top-grade Martini.

Chapter 29

Arsenal, North London
Sunday, June 26, 1994; 10.00

That afternoon of overpriced Martinis provided a gloriously steep slipway into a night of drunken self-indulgence.

As ever, the CD cases scattered across the living room floor this morning reflect my now nightly DABDA routine. It always starts with the stuff Zoe and me used to listen to; Pavement, The Lemonheads, The Breeders, ending some seven hours later with that Holy Trinity of delicious despair: Scott Walker, Radiohead and Tom Waits.

The final song I always wallow in looped misery to is 'I Know It's Over' by The Smiths because, like Morrissey, *still I cling, I don't know where else I can go*. Despite everything, I refuse to accept me and Zoe and Matt are finished, and I won't be engaging with DABDA's final 'A for Acceptance' until I'm shown our relationship's cold dead body.

I wander down the hall to find Fintan attending to his usual Sunday service; filleting the days' newspapers. Every front page is emblazoned with the same image; the bright eyes and coy smile of nineteen-year-old Molly Parker-Rae.

'Sorted!' blazes *The Sunday News*. 'Evil E claims another victim', by Alex Pavlovic.

'Please tell me the Prince didn't manage to inveigle his way into her intensive care unit?'

'He did, and he got the shot, but the editor decided it was a bit tasteless.'

'Wow, makes you wonder what would qualify as just plain tasteless? When did your editor sprout a conscience?'

'Oh it's not that. The Parker-Raes are middle-class, church-going pillars of the community.'

'Right, so their grief deserves more respect than, say, that of an unemployed single mum?'

'Don't start, Donal. It just makes it more relatable to the average person, which sells more papers, so we need to keep the Parker-Raes on side. Like we do with Princess Di. Every time she's on the front page, sales spike. Whose fault is that? You get the government you deserve and you get the press you deserve.'

A double-page spread inside warns of a 'lethal batch of corrupt tablets'. 'How many more will die?' screams the headline.

'Wow, toxicology reports back already?'

'Nah it's just speculation.'

'Right, so you're scaring the living daylights out of anyone who took an E in Southern England last night?'

'Well if anyone has a funny turn, they won't hesitate to seek help now, will they? The police were all for running with that angle. It might save lives.'

Another piece reports that 'a crack team of thirty-five officers are hunting down the drug dealer who put Molly in a coma'. Meanwhile, the notoriously ill-considered Home

Secretary Michael Howard – sworn enemy of fun and under-forties – announces: 'Every drug dealer is a murderer and should be sentenced to life.'

He rails on: 'I am declaring war on dance clubs and the druggie rave culture that has spawned these tragedies'. A sidebar helpfully summarises the 'six high-profile ecstasy deaths' since 1988.

'My God, more people have died from eating bay leaves,' I point out.

'I know. But it shifts units. Every parent with a teenage kid will be freaking out this morning.'

'You mean it's outrageous scare-mongering, Fintan.'

'It's what Molly's parents want, to scare young people so no one else dies. They're planning to launch a massive publicity campaign and we're getting behind it.'

'What, you and your fellow coke-snorting journos are supporting the Parker-Rae "Just Say No" campaign?'

'Oh come on, you're not averse to the odd doobie yourself, Donal. And you couldn't face another day without your legal drugs crutch, booze, so spare me. Besides, do you agree with everything your police force advocates? Like stopping and searching black people with no grounds other than their colour?'

Edwina's words from last night chime.

I traded in my spirit, curiosity, honesty, my soul really, in return for security, prosperity, respect, status. We all do.

We're all forced to sell out. In the end. I'm just as bad as he is. Only this week, I illegally tape-recorded murder suspects in a dodgy Croydon boozer to gather evidence. My God how would that sound in court?

'By the way, Dusko's delivered again!'

I set off up the stairs, Fintan in hot pursuit. He watches in horrified fascination as I press the play button.

First, we listen to what was said while I was there, including Gary Warner's chillingly deadpan account of how he'd arrange a 'hit'. In between his rasping menace, my squeaky questions sound inane and ingratiating.

'You'll hear his threat in a second,' I say, talking over one of my particularly cringe-worthy saccharine moments.

'Christ,' yelps Fintan in response. 'I can't believe you had the bottle to go back in there after that.'

'I borrowed your hi-vis technique.'

'Jesus, you've turned into a luminous Bad Lieutenant.'

As I exit stage right, we instinctively shuffle in closer to the blue plastic Dictaphone.

JOHN DELANEY: Someone's talking, because no one's been connecting Draper to any of this.

PHIL WARE: This lad hasn't come up with the idea all by himself. Who the hell put him onto it?

DELANEY: He's cold case squad. It must've come from someone connected to Nathan Barry. I know Walter's boozing again.

WARE: Walter knows fuck all. Why don't I get the Prince to sort this copper out?

DELANEY: Get him to check him out first. Then we'll decide how to deal with him.

Fintan turns to me. 'Right, this proves they know Julie Draper is connected to Nathan Barry. This means her kidnap had nothing to do with Kipper. But whoever kidnapped Julie had the inside track on Kipper, because they've completely hoodwinked the police.'

'It's got to be someone on the inside of the Suzy Fairclough/Kipper investigation six years ago.'

Fintan's revving that brain and adopting his constipated face. 'How the hell are Julie Draper and Nathan Barry connected? Who's Walter?'

'The only Walter I can think of is Walter Moore, husband of Karen Moore. Remember, she was sleeping with both Nathan and Delaney when Nathan was murdered.'

'Did you check out Walter's early statements, you know, before Delaney bought him and everyone else off?'

'No.'

'Why not?'

I'm kicking myself that I didn't, but I'm not going to let him know that.

'The paperwork for the Nathan Barry case would fill this house. That's why not. I'll check it out tomorrow.'

'Go in today.'

'I'm hoping to see Matt today, although I haven't cleared it with Zoe yet. Anyway, shouldn't you be more concerned about how Delaney and Ware know your crime reporter. I presume that's the Prince they're referring to?'

Fintan only chews his lip when he's rattled. 'Delaney and Ware must be his snouts. Alex must be using them, you know, to pull records and stuff.'

The full magnitude of this is only hitting us now. 'That means your newspaper, through your crime reporter, pays a company ran by a suspected killer and a bent cop to break the law?'

'Who says they break the law?'

'Oh come on, Fintan. I've seen you pull people's medical and financial records. That can't be legal. And now your paper is paying a couple of killers to do your dirty work. My God, this is a police matter surely?'

Fintan harrumphs in derision. 'No senior police officer would dare take us on. Look what happened to any politician that tried. David Mellor threatened press privacy laws. We destroyed his career. We can pretty much do what the hell we like.'

I let that fly over me. I'm struggling to keep up as it is. 'What did ex-police officer and Nathan Barry murder suspect Phil Ware mean about getting the Prince to "sort me out" exactly?'

'I don't know. Dig up some dirt on you, threaten to run it if you don't back off.'

'Can he do that?'

'My God, it's all clicking into place,' says Fintan, a celestial glint drifting across his eyes. 'The Prince was chief crime reporter on our rival paper back in '88. I bet Nathan and Duncan McCall approached the Prince with their scoop about police corruption. Instead of running with the story, the Prince tipped off Delaney, Ware and the other people this scoop was about to expose. That must be what first connected the Prince to Delaney and Ware; he must have told them what Nathan and McCall were trying to sell. That's why Delaney, Ware and the Prince are so tight, they must be all in this together. My God, the Prince is key to this whole thing.'

'If that's true, then how in hell do we get the Prince to talk?'

Fintan shakes his head. 'I don't know, but I'll think of something.'

Chapter 30

Arsenal, North London
Sunday, June 26, 1994; 12.30

Zoe's name beams out from the phone's screen, causing me to almost drop it into my lunchtime recovery pint. I haven't spoken to her since Friday night, when news that Matt's dad, Chris, is back on the scene triggered my complete emotional and physical collapse.

I answer and she launches straight in, all psyched up. 'I explained how much seeing you unsettles Matt. He's just about on an even keel again, so I trust you've canned any plans to come around today?'

'I've done no such thing Zoe. I never agreed to not see him again. I mean, come on, that's not fair to him or me. I don't know how he feels, for one, and I do have rights you know.'

'You're clearly not in a fit state to look after yourself, let alone a toddler. You're in a pub now, for God sake.'

'No, I'm not,' I lie, scampering towards the door, wondering how she can tell. 'I'm in a café. Not that it's any of your business.'

'You're in a café that has Smashing Pumpkins on the jukebox?'

'It's a smashing café. They play it every time someone orders pumpkin soup.'

Nothing.

'You scared me the other night, Donal, wielding that wine bottle and screaming. You've become . . . unhinged. How can I let you take my son away from me in your state of mind? It'd be irresponsible.'

'Oh, he's your son now, is he? I'm coming around to see him, as we agreed originally. You can't stop me.'

'I can stop you. I can call the police. Tomorrow I can go to a solicitor and apply for a court order. And don't think I won't. Is that what you want?'

'Why are you being like this, Zoe? I'd never harm Matt in any way. You know that. Your parents know it too. They might not rate me as a breadwinner but they were delighted to let me take Matt out last Sunday.'

I decide not to mention the tense drop off later, when they virtually snatched Matt from my grasp and scuttled inside.

'I lied to them okay?' she screeches. 'I told them that you'd accepted Chris's return maturely and you were giving me time to work things out. Wishful thinking on my part. While you were out with Matt, Mum called me and I told her the truth, that you'd no idea Chris was back on the scene. I told her that I couldn't tell you in case you freaked out and did something stupid. Of course, all they care about it Matt's welfare, so she flipped. I had to stop her calling the police to go and find you both.'

'Jesus, Zoe. I'm still me. I thought you loved me? Now you're all treating me like some Fathers for Justice nut job. This is so unfair. I've done nothing wrong.'

She sobs and I can't help enjoying it. 'You thought about hitting me with that bottle. I could see it in your eyes. Don't deny it.'

'You'd love that, wouldn't you, Zoe? That would get rid of all your guilt at a stroke. Truth is, the thought never crossed my mind. I am not that type, and you know it. Look, I'm planning to take Matt to the boating lake up at Alexandra Palace. Why don't you come too? Then nothing bad can happen to anyone.'

She sobs some more: 'I said no, Donal. We won't be at home, so don't even think about turning up and making a scene.'

She's cutting me out of Matt's life and there's not a thing I can do about it. I have to make her realise how much I love Matt . . . how much I love her.

'I'm sorry I've been a bit crazy, Zoe,' I blurt. 'Love does that sometimes, but it's still love.'

'If you really loved me and Matt, you'd have gone to a specialist and taken that test by now. And you'd have quit drinking and found a job you can handle. You're always playing the victim, Donal, but when it comes to the crunch, you always let me down.'

Chapter 31

Arsenal, North London
Sunday, June 26, 1994; 12.45

I march back into the Plimsoll pub, vowing to stay there until I'm unable to walk back out again. For once, I manage to keep a promise. It's one of my few fragmented memories of the day. The others are:

* Upsetting some Americans by shouting very loudly for Romania.
* Dropping a full plate of Sunday roast, food-side down.
* Getting called by Fintan repeatedly, demanding to know where I am.
* Refusing, repeatedly, to tell Fintan where I am.
* Accidentally knocking a pint over on my way to the toilets and getting abused.
* Deliberately knocking a pint off the same table on the way back and wrestling with a large man.
* Getting barred but refusing to leave.
* Getting physically carried out of the pub and thrown onto the pavement.

* Running back in through the door and falling flat on my face.
* Telling the off-licence owner he's a bastard for refusing to sell me a bottle of Jameson.
* Hugging the off-licence owner for selling me a bottle of Jameson.
* Coming back to an empty house, seeing my black eye in the bathroom mirror and crying.
* Scrabbling around for Fintan's cache of coke, Aidan's stash of hash and our cornucopia of over-the-counter medications.
* Popping them all into my mouth and washing them down with Scotch.
* Sweating and palpitating wildly.
* Hearing the most beautiful female singing while floating on my back through balmy, dappled sunshine.

All flashes white, my head lands with a thud and my innards erupt.

I'm lying in a pool of bile, insanely high. I recognise the lino of our bathroom floor and Fintan's shoes. 'Jesus Christ, Donal,' he chants, over and over, fussing and flapping.

I wake in his arms on the bathroom floor. He's sobbing. I'd never seen Fintan cry before.

'You selfish bastard,' he shouts, punching me hard in the back and jamming his finger down the back of my throat. 'I thought I'd lost you,' he says, sounding crushed, betrayed.

'Don't know why you bothered,' I say. 'I'm going to die soon anyway.'

Chapter 32

St James's Park, London
Monday, June 27, 1994; 11.45

I step off the District and Circle Line distressed and dizzy. It's as if someone has spooned out my insides and replaced them with prickly, chalk-dry wood scrapings.

Every shallow breath is an invitation for my stomach to spew, making those steep steps out of St James's Park tube station a tense, tonsil-squeezing round of Russian roulette.

PC Lynch, request to attend New Scotland Yard, 12 noon. Reply to confirm.

I should be flapping after this morning's brusque text but, having spent the night turning my guts inside out, I simply don't possess the energy.

My biggest fear is that there's been some sort of complaint. I can think of several candidates; messing up the Julie Draper cash drop; illicitly sniffing around the Nathan Barry murder; failing to inform my boss at the Cold Case Unit that I'm no longer seconded to the Kidnap Squad. My career is already hanging by a thread; I'm anticipating one final, definitive snip.

What do I really care? The pay's rubbish. I keep getting overlooked for promotion. As Zoe pointed out, I simply can't handle the pressure. And being tormented by the recently whacked has somewhat lost its allure. I'm twenty-five and, in all likelihood, doomed to die young. Why not just walk away?

A flash of the warrant card, a quick frisk and I'm fetched up to the office of SO10 on the fifth floor, agonising over what that acronym stands for. Surely not *Sacking Officers?*

I step out of the lift onto blue carpet so plush that I can no longer feel the soles of my feet. I moonwalk through wooden doors, past sombre portraits of former commissioners, in search of a sign.

I knock on SO10's door. A clipped male voice tells me to come in. I open to six world-weary eyeballs leering at me through thick cigarette smoke.

'Hi,' I say, wondering if the suits balefully surveying me have ever looked anything other than decidedly unimpressed. In their own way, the three men embody the classic stereotypes of the modern British detective; Mr Smooth, Mr Rough and Mr Fast-Track.

Mr Smooth, in his forties, is rocking a postmodern Poirot look, complete with immaculate black suit with cufflinks, coiffured jet-black hair and a neatly trimmed black moustache. Oozing the pallid radiance of a 1920s movie star, he's clearly meticulous, confident and in charge.

Mr Rough is a jowly, overweight, hard-drinking street fighter and the type of roughhouse, wife-beating senior cop who, typically, takes an instant dislike to me.

Mr Fast-Track is straight out of Eton; a fresh-faced, ruddy-cheeked, Hitler Youth blonde, seemingly insouciant to the greatness being thrust upon him by the warped but enduring British class system. In short, they're the three

Ronnies: Coleman (thin and smooth), Atkinson (fat and racist) and McDonald (a clown).

'Sit down,' says the Poirot tribute act. 'You're in role now. React to what you see and hear.'

I'm so washed out, I'd struggle to react to an anally inserted cattle prod.

He points to a TV set next to his drinks cabinet. 'I'm a paedophile and I'm watching a man getting sucked off by an eight-year-old boy on a video. I've got copies for sale, if I'm happy with you.' He unzips his flies. 'I'm gonna have a wank. Aren't you going to join me?'

'I'll buy the video but please put your cock away,' I sigh. 'Grown men do nothing for me.'

Mr Fast-Track brays like a donkey. 'Bloody amazing,' he laughs.

Even Big Ron smiles.

'You'd be amazed how many people completely freeze,' says Poirot. 'Have you ever thought about working undercover?'

'I haven't to be honest, Sir.'

'As you can imagine, Donal, we're under considerable political pressure to make an arrest in relation to the Molly Parker-Rae case. Now, the ecstasy scene is very young, in terms of the users and the dealers. Our existing UCs are simply too long in the tooth to infiltrate. We've been researching candidates who we feel may be able to get into the ecstasy dealers down in Windsor and Slough. How would you feel about taking on something like this?'

I'm too stunned to speak. Am I still tripping? Haven't they heard about my history of messing things up? Maybe it's some sort of sick pre-sacking humiliation exercise. One question screams out.

'With respect, Sir, why me?'

'You're the right age. Your background is virtually non-existent. You've never been on the electoral roll or had a utility bill in your name. No wife, kids or parents in the UK. No mortgage. In fact, the only trace we could find of you outside of your employment here is one building society current account.'

'You're a living shadow, Donal,' booms Fast-Track.

Poirot toasts me with a glowing smile. 'You are one of just a handful of young officers we can easily and quickly construct a backstory around that's check-proof. Now, you won't all be suitable for this work. There's every chance none of you will be, but you just passed your first test with flying colours.'

I can't for the life of me see how that frankly risible role-play exercise suggests I'm ready to infiltrate a drugs gang. Why didn't I just call in sick?

'What we need now are volunteers for further testing,' says Poirot. 'This isn't any usual course. There's no set length, no beginning or end to your day, no assessments or exams. You'll be tested in real-world environments, in real-life situations. We need to see how you cope with the stress of uncertainty and the unexpected. That's what makes under-cover work especially taxing.'

Poirot fixes me with an intense look.

'Although this role will be short-term, it will bring with it immense day-to-day pressures. You've got to consider your loved ones and the toll it might take on them. Like I said, it's not for everybody. If you feel you can't handle it, then please say so and it will stay within these four walls.'

My eyes are already looking through those pastel plas-terboard partitions, way beyond the horizon. All I can see is an opportunity to *stop being me*, and that's exactly what I need right now. Posh boy was right; I am a living shadow.

I've got no ties. I've got no life, not now Zoe's dumped me. And I realise something else. All my life back home, Da had been ducking and diving on behalf of the IRA; he lived on the dark side and survived. In his own way, so does Fintan. Maybe that's why I've never bonded with Da; he doesn't think I'm made of the right stuff. This'll show him.

I look deep into Poirot's sparklers. 'I'd like you to sign me up for this course, Sir.'

He nods slowly, inviting me to change my mind. 'Just remember, Donal, there are no medals for this work. And it's dangerous. If you get through the training, you're likely to find yourself associating with some heavyweight gangsters. You may end up dead in a ditch, and we won't claim you. You'll take your secret with you to the grave. In the eyes of the world you'll die a drug dealer, an underworld scumbag. Are you sure you can handle that?'

So what if I die? I'll just be seeing through what I started last night, but didn't have the balls to finish. We'd all heard about 'suicide by cop'. Why not 'suicide by deranged drug dealer'? If the rest of my life will be without Zoe and Matt, then what have I got to live for? And at least Da will be impressed, for once.

'I'm absolutely certain, Sir.'

Chapter 33

St James's Park, Central London
Monday, June 27, 1994; 13.00

This pint is taking an age to drink, each sip requiring Gary Kasparov levels of focus to coax and keep down. I soldier on because I know it's the only cure for those waves of woozy nausea. What I don't have a fix for is my intense feeling of mortification. What the hell was I thinking last night? My only defence is that I genuinely don't remember either deciding to overdose or carrying out the act.

It wasn't me. I don't want to die. I just suddenly felt so tired, so lonely, so scared about the future. They say the darkest hour is before the dawn. What's just happened has given me fresh hope, a focus, a tiny degree of certainty.

The relief of finally being recognised by senior police officers – albeit for having less domestic roots than Carlos the Jackal – makes me determined to celebrate.

All I ask of you these days, alcohol, is to make me feel marginally less wretched.

Like some inveterate village gossip, Fintan's on his way 'with news'. How I wish I possessed a fraction of his whirlwind energy and chutzpah. A fraction of it would be plenty though, otherwise I'd never know any peace.

As I battle to regain full use of organs and senses, it seems an ideal time to take stock of my tangled personal life and thwarted investigations.

We're now convinced that the Nathan Barry and Julie Draper murders are connected. 'Dusko' the bug revealed dodgy private eye John Delaney and his business partner, ex-cop Phil Ware stating as much: *Someone's talking, because no one's been connecting Draper to any of this.*

The recording also reveals that both men clearly know something about how Nathan met his end, which rules out a jealous husband or a 'Nathanised' business client. Whether they commissioned his murder, or are covering up a wider conspiracy, we may never establish. Somehow, Nathan's shape-shifting workmate Danny Bremner is involved. Quite how, we've yet to figure out.

Nathan may have had a scoop to sell about police corruption, which prompted Delaney and/or a cabal of bent cops to have him whacked. Nathan's alleged accomplice in this 'scoop' had been Detective Sergeant Duncan McCall, who died four months after Nathan, in what may or may not have been suicide.

Fintan's convinced that his colleague and nemesis, Alex Pavlovic, Fleet Street's very own Prince of Darkness, had been offered this scoop. Now he's working on a strategy to make the Prince talk.

My only lead is Delaney's reference to 'Walter'. He must be referring to Walter Moore, whose wife Karen had been sleeping with both the victim and the accused when Nathan was murdered. This spells a welcome return to the subterranean records dungeon beneath Camden Town, where I can read Walter's statements to see if they shed any light on the mess. We need nothing short of smoking-gun evidence to convince police that Julie hadn't been randomly targeted by Kipper, the serial kidnapper, but by a crafty copycat. What's missing from this brain-bending theory is motive. Who wanted Julie Draper dead, and why? How can we even go about investigating this?

Now I've been selected for undercover training, I must park both the Draper and Barry cases in limbo, next to my clamped personal life. But I make a silent promise to both Nathan and Julie: if I get through this course, and learn the dark arts of undercover work, I shall apply those skills to solving their murders.

I'm 'going for it' with this undercover role for another, altogether more childish reason; to test Zoe. If she still loves me, she won't let me risk my life by deploying undercover – and that may happen in a matter of days. The prospect of possibly losing me forever will surely make her see sense and beg me to come back. Surely . . .

It's desperate, last-gasp, pathetic. She'd expect nothing less from me.

'Quadruple Jameson?' beams Fintan wickedly. 'Maybe with a Charlie and weed speedball chaser?'

'Yeah, look, I meant to say, thanks for sorting me out last night. And sorry.'

'Sorry? What the hell were you thinking? Jesus, I daren't let you out of my sight now. Are you still feeling, you know, that way?'

'I'm not feeling anything, Fintan, okay? You know what happens when I drink whiskey. I don't even remember deciding to do it. It's not like I wrote a profound farewell note and spent ages on a hangman's knot. It was a moment of madness, honestly. But thanks for, you know, helping me out there.'

'Well I was hardly going to step over you to take a leak, was I? You need to lay off the sauce for a good old while, maybe even a few months.'

'I'm not touching whiskey or wine for the time being,' I say. 'But if I don't get another pint, I may not make it through your sensational news.'

Pumped and scoop-high, he almost runs back to our table clutching drinks.

'Turns out DS Duncan McCall, Nathan Barry's pal who committed suicide a few months after Nathan's murder, was about to give evidence at an internal Met police inquiry into corruption, literally the day after he, er, died.'

He takes a long draw of his pint for dramatic effect, then waits for me to quiz him. He loves making me work for information.

'Oh come on, Fint, I haven't got the energy to play A Few Good Men. Just spit it out, will you?'

'They were investigating links between notorious underworld kingpin, Mickey Sheeran and you'll never guess who . . .'

'Did I mention my energy levels are at an all-time low?'

'Commander Neil Crossley.'

I suddenly feel much better.

'What?'

'Turns out Sheeran is a grass and guess who his handler was six years ago? Croissant Crossley!'

'Are you sure about this? From what I hear, Sheeran had a couple of guys rubbed out when he discovered they were snitches.'

'They all say they hate rats, but every major-league villain grasses. It's the perfect way for villains to take out rivals. And it's also profitable. Every time a tip leads to a seizure, they get ten per cent of the value. It all makes Crossley look good. A real win/win. Of course, the downside is Crossley had to turn a blind eye to Sheeran's scurrilous activities. If he arrests his own grass, the whole house of cards collapses. He loses his best source of intelligence. Everyone he's put away can seek grounds to appeal over the fact that the man who dobbed them in is of worse character than them.

'So, as these handlers rise up through the police ranks – Crossley went from Inspector to Detective Superintendent to Commander in record time – their snouts make dramatic, unchecked charges up the criminal ladder, virtually immune from prosecution. The collars got bigger, the rewards got bigger. What could possibly go wrong?'

Fintan devours the second third of his pint in one wallop, giving me a chance to butt in. 'I remember my old boss Shep saying the whole system is doomed because the grass has too much power. Instead of the handler running the grass, the grass starts to run the handler.'

Fintan nods. 'After a while, it's impossible to tell who's handling who . . . the games they play to get what they want. That's the allegation here, that Mickey Sheeran corrupted Crossley with cuts from his criminal spoils. Crossley's 600-grand house on a golf course, flash suits, cars and holidays were a bit of a giveaway. Duncan McCall clearly had some sort of evidence about it, otherwise the enquiry wouldn't have subpoenaed him. Which begs the question, did he really kill himself?'

'Edwina's taking a look at the pathology report for me. If she recognises anything dodgy, what then? This could be dynamite, especially if your reporter the Prince spills the beans.'

'Let's not get carried away,' says Fintan, uncharacteristically reserved. 'I need leverage before I approach that snake. I thought it best to eliminate every other journo first, so I'm working through the whole shebang, even TV current affairs shows. It's where journalism goes to die, but they do have a lot of money. Have you checked out Walter Moore's statements yet?'

'I'm going there after this. I just can't figure out what else I should be looking for in the Nathan Barry paperwork to connect it to Draper.'

Fintan's already on it, of course. 'I've sent my most ravenous and heartless cub reporter, Dennis Bradley, down to Croydon to do some digging into Julie's life, all hush-hush,' he says. 'If Julie Draper made any enemies, he'll find out. He even looks like one of those snub-nosed bloodhounds you see chasing escaped convicts in the films. I get a dreadful sense of déjà vu every time I talk to the immoral little fucker. He really is a mini-me.'

'Must be nice to know your legacy is secure, Fint. Sounds like this venal little fucker has tripped your paternal instincts.'

'He'll get my job one day, I've no doubt about that, and he'll kick me into the gutter while he's at it. But I do feel a certain fatherly pride. Speaking of which, any news from Princess Zoe?'

He lifts his pint, jaw locking to empty.

'No, but I've got news for her. I've been selected to go undercover.'

Cue his spray of lager across the table.

'What?'

'I've been hand-picked by SO10 for an undercover assignment.'

'What, to infiltrate Alcoholics Anonymous?'

'The Molly Parker-Rae case. They need young officers to get into the rave scene down there.'

He laughs. 'My God, you in a vest with a glow stick,

blowing on a whistle and screaming "acieeed". This is too funny. You hate all dance music! Tell me you're having me on, please.'

'They've put me on a course. If I get through it, then it's happening.'

'You'll never pass. Seriously, Donal, you can't even tell a white lie. But I see what you're doing here. It's the ultimate ultimatum for Zoe, right? Why don't I call her and break the news that you'll be tackling the nation's most wanted drugs gang in a matter of days? That should focus her mind.'

'That'd be just great, Fintan, because she believes every word that comes out of your mouth.'

'You can't tell her, Donal. She'll start asking questions and you'll crack like an egg and reveal it's a course, and we all know how you've fared before on courses. Look, I'll say you weren't going to let her know as you didn't want to put her under any undue pressure. How could she resist such noble, selfless sentiments?'

Fintan doesn't take no for an answer. 'I'll see you at home tonight so, tell you how she reacts?'

'You don't have to babysit me, Fintan. I'm fine.'

'I know I don't. But I'm allowed to come home occasionally, aren't I? And what happened last night kind of brought something home to me. We only really have each other now, Donal, so we need to stick together. That means no more secrets, and no more lies. Everything up front, okay? Especially if you're planning to do something rash or dangerous. Make sure someone close to you knows, preferably me.'

I nod.

'Promise? On Mam's grave? Say it!'

'Okay Fintan, I promise, on Mam's grave.'

Chapter 34

Camden Town, North London
Monday, June 27, 1994; 14.30

I spend hours leafing through thousands of statements, looking for all those taken from a 'Walter' or 'Walt'. Just one crops up; Walter Moore, cuckolded husband of Karen.

I've always favoured the theory that an apoplectic husband murdered Nathan. Fintan points out, quite rightly, that any man gripped by jealousy would've confronted Nathan, not sneaked up behind him and split his skull like a log. What if that confrontation had already taken place? Nathan could be belligerent; maybe he ignored a previous threat to back off from a woman, prompting his frenzied killing. What if that warning had come from Walter Moore?

Records show that Walter has no criminal record or history of domestic abuse. He and Karen had lived blameless lives at the better end of Crystal Palace, raising two daughters who went on to university. But this had been personal. Sometime around late 1987 or early 1988, Walter must've realised Karen was seeing another man, maybe more than one.

Her frequent nights out, the constant calls from men to

their home, the drunken lunch clubs that lingered well into the night, sometimes over to the mornings. He *must* have known. What if Walter followed his wife, saw her with Nathan, plotted his revenge?

Fintan's right, part of me hopes he did it, to teach Karen and Nathan a lesson. Then I remind myself that I don't know the circumstances. Karen may have had perfectly legitimate grounds for dumping Walter. She just chose to do so without mercy or grace. Like Zoe.

I sift out Walter's first statement, taken just four days after the murder. His alibi seems bulletproof. A professional chauffeur, he spent the evening driving a director of British Steel around various functions in west London. The list of locations and times, vouched for by his boss, proves he could never have nipped down to South London to conduct even the swiftest of axe murders. What if he paid someone else to do it, having confronted Nathan on a previous occasion?

According to his statement, Walt hadn't even heard of Nathan Barry until after the murder; a claim backed up by his then wife Karen and John Delaney. He'd been aware that Karen had a business relationship with Delaney; the calls John made to their home had always been about work – at least the ones he'd been privy to.

My guts twinge in empathy. Like me, witless Walter had no idea she'd been cheating; another unquestioning loyal mutt utterly humiliated by a woman who claims she loved him. How many more men must there be out there, doggedly enduring sexless, joyless relationships, oblivious to the fact their partners are playing away? It's always assumed men are more likely to stray, but who do they stray with? Judging by this case, other attached women.

Walter's statement provides no insight into his personal agony, though it does offer a fresh perspective on Karen's reaction to Nathan's murder: 'She said she believed it must be something to do with some sort of drugs racket at West Norwood cemetery. When I pressed her on this, she said that Nathan had got wind that the crypts at the cemetery were being used to store cocaine, and that he was in the process of doing something about it.'

I scan his second and third statements for further references to the cocaine racket. None is made, and I can't imagine why.

Dough, blow or a ho . . .

Surely, DI Lambert couldn't have been so insanely fixated with Delaney that he ignored a classic motive for murder; Nathan Barry's uncovering of a massive cocaine ring?

Chapter 35

Arsenal, North London
Monday, June 27, 1994; 18.30

I slip silently through our front door. Coast clear, I sprint upstairs and secrete both bottles of Shiraz under my bed. Right now, I'd sooner drink cat piss direct from source. But tomorrow's my first day at Undercover School. I need to get some sleep tonight and three pints of wine is my only hope.

Right on cue, Fintan creeps gingerly through the front door as if he's expecting a massacre. He looks visibly relieved to see me trotting down the stairs, rather than dangling from the landing. He's carrying a plastic bag packed with beer cans, clearly planning to dose me up on weak lager so I don't hit the hard stuff, like some Irish Betty Ford. His ritual patronising of me has officially plunged to dizzyingly new depths.

He hands me one, plucks out another and flops theatrically onto the couch. I'm dying to ask how his call to Zoe went, and he knows it, so neither of us mentions it.

Fintan flicks on the TV. The BBC's Moira Stuart sombrely

reports that the parents of Molly Parker-Rae have decided to turn off her life support machine. Molly's family is launching a 1,500-site poster campaign to warn clubbers of the perils of ecstasy. The poster, which shows a picture of Molly on life support, bears the chilling caption: 'Sorted. Just one tablet took Molly'.

'God it's such bollocks,' snarls Fintan, flicking the TV off again. 'I saw your new girlfriend's report. Edwina found that Molly didn't die from ecstasy. She died of water intoxication.'

'What?'

'After she took the tablet, she drank something like eleven pints of water in ninety minutes. It's all these government warnings about dehydration that killed her, not MDMA. You know what the worst part of it is now? The poster campaign is being funded by three advertising companies. Guess who these companies' other clients are? Energy drinks and alcohol.'

'I don't get it.'

'The alcohol industry is bricking itself because young people have replaced boozing with ecstasy. That's why they've launched all these alcopops and that's why they're desperate to demonise E. And energy drinks are trying to market themselves as a "safe and legal" option to ecstasy. The whole rave thing has been swallowed up by the corporate monster, even the bloody tragic part of it. Oh, and speaking of corporate monsters . . .'

He pulls out another brace of cans, plucks them open and passes one over. 'As requested, I've been checking out your love rival, Christopher St. John Green. Alias Christy G, as he likes to be known on the rave scene. Or Crusty E, as he was dubbed by the newspapers a few years back.'

'He's been in the papers?'

'Oh, he's quite the character. I hate to say it, Donal, but you versus this guy is like, I don't know, Baldrick versus Lord Flashheart.'

'Thanks.'

'Back then, he gained what is known as "tabloid notoriety". It all started about eight years ago when he staged these glittering "Pirate Balls" for posh public school Henrys and Henriettas. The toff kids behaved appallingly of course, and the cameras were on hand to capture Henry with his hand up some comatose Henrietta's skirt. Those balls made St. John enough green to retire, but that was only the start of it.

'Cut to 1989, he and his posh friends were organising mammoth illegal raves across Southern England, which your lot were desperately trying to stamp out. And you almost succeeded too. Until crafty Chris discovered the BT Voicebank System. This allowed him to dial in the location of a rave from a mobile phone at the very last moment. The voicebank could then be accessed instantly by thousands. So, Chris has been credited with saving the second summer of love, which made him even more popular with the tabloids.'

'I can imagine.'

'He next popped up in 1992. By then, criminals had muscled in on the rave scene and its astronomical profits. So instead of touchy-feely baggies hugging each other and bleating about peace, you had skinhead security guards with coshes and dogs, protection rackets, lorryloads of pills contaminated with shit. Legend has it that, towards the end, Christy G ghosted out of an East London rave with a massive bag of cash while a bunch of West Ham heavies were tearing the place up looking for their cut. He was never seen again.'

'That's when he did his runner.'

'Where he ran to is intriguing. He spent a few months in Ibiza. Then he moved onto Bali and ended up on the Curacao

Islands off Venezuela. Now those islands are Dutch-owned and just a three-hour speedboat hop from South America, so they're notorious for cocaine smuggling.'

I can't contain myself: 'So you're saying Chris is an international drug smuggler?'

'We can't say for certain, but I've got someone digging away who has the inside track on these toffs.'

I'm pumped. 'It's obvious he's up to no good. How can we make sure Zoe finds out?'

He leaves that hanging. Why won't he tell me what she said today? What's his game?

He takes a greedy swig and wipes his mouth.

'I had an interesting phone call with someone today,' he teases. My insides scream: *Spit it out!*

'I spoke to the auld fella. He's got a coterie of local widows pursuing him. Can you believe it?'

'Be young, be foolish, but be happy eh?'

We laugh at the memory. Ma, who possessed a rare knack for surreal humour, had The Tams' classic played at her funeral. When the priest revealed it had been Mick and Dolores's special song, we fell about laughing. Da had been well into his fifties when they'd married, and neither foolish nor happy his entire angst-ridden life. It was her song, of course, a mantra she warbled around the house all day and played full blast on the record player whenever Fintan or me felt down.

'Ma was a real romantic, wasn't she?' I say. 'Such a shame she got stuck with that joyless lummox.'

'Ah she knew him before she married him. Da is just Da, you know?'

'Why do you always defend him?'

'Why do you always stand up for Mam?'

'Well someone had to.'

That thickens the air. Although Golden Boy Fintan escaped largely unscathed, Da's whiskey rages and black moods scarred us all. Poor Mam took the brunt of it, to protect me. But tonight, like some trainee Samaritan talking a man down off a bridge, Fintan is refusing to let any of the dark stuff in.

'So, let's face it, Donal, even our Da, Mick the Grinch Lynch, an octogenarian sociopath renowned for his homicidal outbursts, bad hip and graveyard teeth, is getting his end away more often than you. How does that make you feel?'

'Do not put that image into my head, for the love of God.'

We both silently drink to that.

Fintan sniggers. 'Remember the morning after Mam died. You went off roaming the fields, all mournful and magnificent like some malnourished Heathcliff. I thought I'd try to keep things as normal as possible, so I fried the auld fella two eggs, like Mam had done for as long as I can remember.

'I put the plate in front of him and he says, "I don't like eggs". I said, "What do you mean, you don't like eggs? You've eaten two every morning your whole life." And he says, "I only did it to keep herself happy." Can you believe it?'

I shake my head. 'It must've been the only thing he ever did to keep her happy.'

'Anyway, later I got stuck with that gombeen of a priest. I couldn't think of a thing to say to him so I told him that story. At the funeral, he turns it into a big parable about how relationships are all about endurance and suffering, and how the Crucifixion shows us the unique rewards such pain brings. Do you remember?'

'I was too busy self-harming so his words wouldn't get through.'

'I was raging and I let him know afterwards that he'd taken the whole thing out of context to promote his own bullshit agenda.'

'And you'd recognise that quicker than most,' I say.

I'm now wondering what Fintan is getting at. Such observations are normally the preamble to contrition. What has he done?

'Why are you telling me all this, Fint? In fact, why are you being so . . . nice?'

'Oh, thanks a lot, Donal. Jesus, I'm working harder than Fred West's cement mixer here.'

'Just tell me what she said. I can handle it.'

He squashes his can, hurls it into the corner and plucks two more out of his Londis bag.

'The thing is, Father Gombeen's spiel at the funeral made me realise we're so brainwashed into that kind of thinking. You know, where putting up with misery for forty years is grounds for beatification. The only road to true happiness is through the valley of tears. It's all shite.'

'Fintan, can you stop riddling. You're making me epileptic.'

'All I'm saying is, you and Zoe haven't been happy for a long time. If you two get back together now, that will be it. The Matt factor means you'll be committing for the rest of your lives. If you take your male pride out of it, and your hurt at her betrayal, is this really what you want? Because you must admit, Donal, you've been flatter than a flapper's tits these past few months.'

At last, we're on point. 'Right, so she's not budging then?'

He takes a hefty swig, to help him cut to the chase. 'At first she refused to believe that you're going undercover. Then she accused you of emotional blackmail. You may as well pull out of the course, Donal. It's not going to win her back.'

'Is that it?'

'No. Not exactly.'

'Please tell me you didn't go off script, Fint?'

'She's such a controlling cow, Donal. I can't stand watching you running after her like a puppy every time she whistles. You need to win back her respect.'

'Oh God, what did you say?'

He squirms in his seat.

'What did you tell her?'

'Look, I lost it, okay? I told her you've already met someone else, her name is Tania, she's a model on the paper and I haven't seen you this happy in years.'

'Jesus, Fintan. I've got to call her, tell her you made it all up.'

'Do not call her, Donal. For God's sake, man, where's your self-respect? You don't want her coming back to you out of charity, do you? Or pity? Or guilt? You need to forget about her. It's the only way you'll find out for certain if she really loves you. Because if she doesn't truly love you, you need to get away from her.'

He slows his blinking and breathing, reining himself in.

'Don't you get why Mam loved that song so much, Donal? Why she drilled it into us? Be happy, Donal. Be foolish, but be fucking happy. That means not being a martyr for the next thirty years, like she was. That's all Mam wanted, that we don't make the same mistake she made. Do what makes you happy, Donal, if not for you then for Mam, in honour of her memory. Okay?'

Chapter 36

Whitechapel, East London
Tuesday, June 28, 1994; 09.30

A drab prefab in Whitechapel proves my unlikely Alma Mater in undercover chicanery. I'm wondering where everyone else is when the door crashes open to a tanned, balding but pony-tailed, forty-something geezer straight out of Pimp School.

'My name is Gary and I'm your course leader,' he declares in a strong cockney accent, bling jangling, Hawaiian shirt wobbling. I can't help thinking he's trying way too hard and looks like, well, an undercover cop.

'You're probably wondering why you're sat in a classroom on your own. That's because we train each of our UCs in complete isolation. This is how seriously we take your security. We need the same commitment from you.

'Golden Rule number one of undercover work is: don't do it just to get away from your missus. Golden Rule number two is: don't breathe a word about it to another soul. Loose lips sink ships. Even hinting at what you're engaged in to one individual can come back on you with horrific consequences. Is there anything you need to tell me, Donal?'

I shake my head, thinking, *Shit, I've broken both golden rules already*.

'Right. Some boring practical stuff. Believe it or not, no British policeman works full-time in an undercover role, except the handful of top dogs who run SO10. Any undercover work has to be an extension of your existing work. If we decide you're right for this job, we'll have to get your boss to release you. Don't expect your boss to like it. Now, how familiar are you with rave culture?'

'I got dragged to one once, Gary. As soon as I discovered the bar sold only water and Lucozade, I fled.'

'Man of my own heart. I can't believe some of the shit I see. Ravers sucking children's dummies to stop the E buzz wobbling their jawbones. Stripping off and smearing themselves in Vicks decongestant to clear the lungs and maximise the E experience. Some even walk around all night with an inhaler inserted in one nostril.

'Don't be fooled by the surreal pantomime. It may have been all about peace and love at the start. It's now all about profit and loss. The underworld has taken over the scene.'

I think of Chris St. John Green's flit from those East London gangsters with all that cash, and marvel at the irony that I might be infiltrating the very scene that made him.

'According to our friends at Customs – who, by the way, enjoy a fully funded, global undercover unit – ecstasy coming into the UK has increased 4,000 per cent since 1990.

'Market saturation has seen the price drop from fifteen pounds to as little as five pounds per pill. Needless to say, the quality has plummeted too. MDMA is now a brand name for a range of concoctions that contain LSD, speed and God knows what else.

'The fact you'll see St John Ambulance volunteers at many hardcore venues sums it up. You'll see ravers getting "cabbaged" and "monged", to use the charming parlance of the day. Increasing numbers are "losing it", winding up in cults, or institutions or heading off to India and Thailand and never coming back.

'The gangs that run the scene don't care. They take over venues by force. Anyone who resists is crushed. Just the other week in East London, a club owner stood up to one criminal outfit and paid the price: a couple of nights later, a bunch of grunts armed with machetes stormed in and attacked select clubbers, all black males, then cut off two of the DJ's fingers so he can never mix records again.'

I fail to stop myself wincing. I'm Cold Case Squad, after all, where the greatest threat to physical harm is dust inhalation.

'Once the criminal gang takes over, they take complete control of the scene. They import the tablets, supply them to dealers, then charge these dealers to gain entry to the marketplace, their clubs, so the profits are vast.

'These gangs follow a well-trodden route map from armed robbery to prison to overnight drugs barons. Thanks to recent developments like cheap international flights, laptops and mobile phones, integration with Europe, deregulated banking and, of course, the demand for E, at the touch of a portable phone they've been propelled into a stratospheric world of mass cash and wildly disproportionate power.

'The gang that controls the club where Molly's E was bought are typical of the breed; weight-pumping, steroid-popping, egotistical and violent cokeheads who've made money beyond their wildest dreams but still want more.'

The verbal assault ceases while he deals photos onto my desk like playing cards. Each snarling face is upstaged by a veined and monstrous neck. 'Shaun Shaw, convictions for

GBH and drug dealing. Craig Walsh, convictions for GBH and racketeering. And the boss, Pat Regan, convicted armed robber with a taste for sadism.'

Bulging out of a wife-beater vest and leering at the camera, Regan looks wide-eyed and unhinged.

'For these guys, enough is never enough. They don't just want to make more money, they want to rip off rival gangs. That's the thing with villains, they're still petty criminals at heart. They can't help themselves. It's not enough to make a packet of cash from a deal, they have to try to mug off the other party, even if doing so might cost them more money in the long run.

'And so our gang engages in what have become known as "have offs" and "tie-ups". They find out about deals, burst into rooms where they're going down, masked and armed with assault rifles, and relieve dealers of their "tackle" and tens of thousands of pounds in cash. As another little sideline, they "tax" rivals of their super profits. Anyone who resists gets kidnapped and tortured.'

He frisbees three more photos on my desk. One and two depict faces liberally carved up with a blade of some sort.

'Major drugs barons who refused to pay their tax bill. Regan has set about so many mugs with his Stanley knife that he's even developed a signature, the "Chinese Sneeze". Check out both guys' noses. He's cut their nostrils like Polanski did to Jack Nicholson in *Chinatown*, only he always slices both.

'Although both victims are heavyweight criminals, they'd only talk to me strictly off the record. They daren't stand up to this gang because Regan and co. have no code, creed or confederates. They are maniacs and they are out of control.

'Which segues neatly into the next photo. This is a guy they lifted off the street in broad daylight, tied him up, placed a plastic bag over his head with a couple of holes in it. They then sprayed a can of highly toxic, specialist aerosol paint into one of the holes, forcing him to breathe in all the nasty stuff – propane, butane, heavy metals and solvent – which then entered his bloodstream. As you can see in the photo, this man is now a drooling lump, immobile, blind and on dialysis. His crime? The four had met at Pizza Hut and he'd refused to pay the forty-pound bill. Imagine what they'd do to a cop?'

He surveys me mercilessly.

'You sure you want to get involved with animals like this? Let me tell you now, the smart guy would get up and walk away.'

I've spent my life skulking away from danger. Conversely, Da and Fintan have always flourished in their particular Twilight Zones. I've got to show them; I'm just as tough as they are. I too can hack it amongst the maddest and the baddest. How else will I ever earn their respect?

You can't have love without respect.

Fintan said so himself, so I don't even blink.

'Okay, Donal. But no one will think any less of you for changing your mind. For what it's worth I, personally, would think more of you.'

I can always just not turn up tomorrow . . .

Gary claps his hands and rubs them together. 'Right, there's a man called Daryl who drives a red Volvo 363 and deals crack around the Venue nightclub in New Cross most afternoons. Here's a hundred quid.

'Tell him Gary sent you. He'll see you're not a regular user so he'll assume you're an occasional rock star who deals small-time to fund it. A rock costs fifteen. My advice is "eight rocks or no deal". Any less than eight for a 100 and it's not worth a dealer's time. He'll smell you're a cop.'

I can't hide my alarm. 'I don't know the terminology, Gary. I barely even know what the stuff looks like.'

'Thousands of people buy illegal drugs every day. Very few of them see themselves as Tony Montana. You're just going to the sweet shop, Donal.'

I shrug, still not sold.

'I have a series of sayings that will get you through this, Donal. Number one is: Paranoia is a soul eater. Don't let it in. Just get down there, do the deal and bring it back here tomorrow morning.'

Chapter 37

The Venue, New Cross, South East London
Tuesday, June 28, 1994; 13.30

I'm on foot, making my third circuit of the Venue nightclub, alone, isolated, out of my profoundly shallow depth; The Only Living Boy in New Cross. I've never 'scored' drugs in my life. It took me six months to muster up the courage to buy a pack of johnnies from my local Boots. It's just totally out of my realm of understanding or experience. They may as well have sent me to perform some rap, or a breakdance.

A red Volvo estate is parking up outside the KFC. As I approach, I know how those chickens feel.

'Daryl?' I say to the gargantuan Caribbean man filling almost both front seats. He turns down his drum 'n' bass but the pounding beat continues, the first rumblings of my full-blown heart attack.

'Yeah?'

'Gary said you might be able to help me?' I say, sounding way more feeble and needy than I'd planned.

'Get in,' he says.

I squeeze into the passenger seat, taking a quick scan for

anything that might prompt me to hop back out again. All clear.

'How much have you got?' he says.

'100,' I say.

He starts the engine and tootles off.

'I'll have eight for that, Daryl.'

'I'll get your eight,' he says casually. 'But I don't carry that amount on me. Cops bust me with that, I'm going to jail.'

'So where are we going?'

'I know a pub where I can get it.'

Fair enough, I think, hoping to God it's not too far. My nerves can't hold much longer. He pulls up outside the Rose and Crown pub in Bermondsey.

'Give us the money and I'll get it for you in there,' he says.

'Yeah right, I'm going to just hand you a hundred quid, Daryl. You've got a mobile. Why not call and get him to bring it out?'

'Man, are you for real? I'm not asking him to come out on a busy street in broad daylight with eight biscuits. He won't do it.'

'I'll come in with you then.'

'Fine,' he says, holding out his hand.

I plant the cash in his palm, follow him across the road.

'This is one badass pub, my friend,' he says. 'My man only does business direct with me in a back room. You're gonna have to wait at the bar.'

I perch on a stool and order a half. This isn't so hard. I think suddenly of the Velvet Underground song, 'I'm Waiting for my Man'. I've just got to get used to waiting. That's what this is all about. So I wait, and wait.

'Shit!' I jump up, look out of the window. Daryl's getting into his car. By the time I shout his name from the front door, he's already gone.

Chapter 38

Arsenal, North London
Tuesday, June 28, 1994; 15.00

Unlocking the front door to our house in Arsenal, I turn to the sound of my name.

I think suddenly: if this is a Gary-inspired guerrilla attack, then I've just failed my second test today.

'Not me,' I lie to the amiable-looking man, hoping to salvage something from the exercise.

'I know you from Zoe's photos,' he brays, stepping forward and offering his hand. 'Chris St. John Green.'

My hand grasps his but doesn't feel a thing. I should be infuriated; the gall of the fucker turning up here unannounced. I've every right to sock the smug gob off him. Truth is, I'm too sideswiped to react at all.

'You may as well come in,' I say.

'That's terribly kind of you,' gushes Hugh Grant and I have to check he's not taking the piss.

He follows me down the hallway to the kitchen table.

'Drink?' I hear myself say, then baulk at my own hospitality. I should be reaching for the bread knife.

'Tea would be lovely.'

'We only have builder's. And probably no milk.'

'That's quite alright.'

I stick on the kettle and sit opposite him, just so he knows where we're at.

He's ridiculously handsome and coyly charismatic, the bastard, like some poster boy for private education. He's got that Princess Di haircut, complete with just the right amount of flop at the front to suggest vulnerability. Blue-eyed, strong-jawed, I hate the guts that are so tightly packed into that blindingly white, open-neck flannel shirt.

Worse still, he's got the imperious inner confidence to sit there and force me to think of something to say.

'So, I hear you were a major player in the rave scene?'

'Oh that,' he laughs bashfully. 'I'd read a lot of Timothy Leary. I thought I was going to change the world.'

'We're all a bit delusional at that age.'

Both eyebrows leap to his defence. He clearly feels he *did* change the world, no less.

'We were hurtling into the worst recession since the Great Depression. It felt good to be able to help people snap out of the living-death of drudgery for a few hours of euphoric release, every now and then.'

'Wow, you were almost like a social service.'

'I'll remember the last rave in 1989 until the day I die. We sold 3,000 tickets and laid on coaches to the wilds of Bucks where I'd hired an equestrian centre. Flares burned along the wooded approach, lasers flashed in the dark sky. We hired a fairground and a bouncy castle, all lit with fairy lights like one huge fantasy playground.

'At the peak of the night, the lights went off, the building filled with dry ice and, in total darkness, I dropped the needle on the opening chords of Strauss's *Also Sprach Zarathustra*.'

He snaps out of his trance now to address me directly: 'That's the theme from *2001: A Space Odyssey*.'

'I know,' I lie.

He slips back into reminisce. 'As the orchestra swelled, a green laser strafed the clouds of dry ice and hundreds of arms raised in unison, cutting through the smoke. All that was visible from my raised platform were disembodied hands, reaching outwards as if to touch the heavens, frozen in the strobe lights. And I remember thinking "I did that."'

'Was there a bar?'

'I'm sorry?'

'Was there a bar at that one? I've only been to one rave and I couldn't even get a bottle of lager.'

He glares at me in pained disbelief, as if I've just taken a dump in his weekend shoes. Time to get bad cop on his privileged arse.

'What about the people who died because of your raves?'

'None did,' he smiles smugly. 'You do know less than 100 people have died in this country from E, yet 30,000 die every year from alcohol. But the alcohol lobby ultimately won by forcing the government to licence raves. You got your bar in the end, Donal.'

'Good.'

He coughs and straightens his back.

'Look, I didn't come here to debate drug laws. I came here to tell you that I plan to marry Zoe. I want to make up for lost time. It's what she deserves.'

I'm too stunned to respond.

'I think it's best for Zoe and Matthew. Don't you?'

How do I answer that? He doesn't give me time anyway.

'We can move nearer to her folks, send Matthew to one

of the better schools in Highgate, Zoe won't have to worry about all this freelancing nonsense to make ends meet . . .'

'She wants to continue with her career. She loves it.'

'Yes of course she does. They have to say that, don't they? When they've got no option. The thing is, I feel *awful* for you, Donal.'

'Don't. She hasn't told me we're over. As far as I'm concerned, that means she hasn't made up her mind yet. She probably won't be able to bring herself to trust you, after what you did.'

'Yes, you're quite right. I'm jumping the gun. I do hope, no matter what happens, we can all remain friends or at least civilised about it. I want you to know I fully acknowledge and respect the role you've played in Matthew's life up until now.'

'Role? I wasn't acting, pal. I was the only dad he had, let's not forget, while you were off investing your ill-gotten gains in various druggie havens around the globe.'

His head wobbles indignantly.

'The bottom line, Donal, is that I can give Zoe and Matthew things you can't. You do know your drinking scares her. As does the fact you might drop dead any second from some congenital disease, which you refuse to acknowledge or seek treatment for. You're a bloody mess. I can't have her and Matthew exposed to that.'

I can't believe she's told him all this, and wish I'd grabbed that breadknife after all.

'Excuse me, but the day you abandoned your unborn baby, you lost any right to make decisions about him or Zoe.' My voice is shaking with rage: 'I know she hasn't forgiven you for that. I don't think she ever will.'

He laughs malevolently. 'If I know women – and I rather think I do – a dream home near mum, a four-by-four and a bloody good school might just atone for my sins.'

'If I know Zoe, it won't even come close. She has values, something you clearly lack. What will you do if she chooses me?'

He winces irritably, like a petulant child.

'It won't happen but, just to show you I'm a sport . . . if she picks you over me, I'll move abroad. Right, I'll be off. Good day.'

Good day indeed, I think. At least now I know he isn't gripped by some sudden and overwhelming paternal instinct. Because if I thought for one second his return would ultimately benefit Matt, I'd swallow my pride and stand aside. But the fact he's planning to flounce off abroad if he doesn't get his own way proves he isn't doing this for Matt. Or Zoe.

What the hell *has* he come back for then? And how can I find out before it's too late?

Chapter 39

Arsenal, North London
Tuesday, June 28, 1994; 16.30

I return Edwina's missed call hoping she's found something – anything – in the Nathan Barry or Duncan McCall pathology reports that might link their cases to Julie Draper. Edwina answers sharply; she clearly hasn't got long. I barely manage a 'Hi' before she unloads.

'Okay, Donal, just to give you some general background about male suicide in this country. About fifty per cent die from hanging. It used to be about twenty per cent from carbon monoxide poisoning but that's fallen dramatically in recent years with the introduction of catalytic converters. Until the 1970s, turning on the oven used to be the most common method, but then they introduced natural gas instead of coal gas so it didn't work anymore. Same thing now with cars. Drugs overdose accounts for another fifteen per cent; gravity about one in fifteen. Other methods are rare. Suicide by firearms accounts for less than 100 cases each year.'

'Out of how many?'

'In the UK, about 6,000 in total per annum. Two thirds of those are male.'

'I thought suicide by gun would be right up there. It's so quick.'

'It's by far the most common method in the US, but then everyone there has a gun. Only four per cent of British households have access to arms. Now, moving onto Duncan McCall. Just remind me, Donal, what is his connection to Nathan Barry?'

'They were friends who may have been trying to sell a story about police corruption. Four months after Nathan's murder, McCall killed himself. Somehow, it's all tied up with Julie Draper, we just don't know how.'

'Okay, well you're going to like this. Detective Sergeant Duncan McCall died of a single shot from a 12-gauge shotgun which he'd placed inside his mouth. Time of death estimated at 0200 hours on the morning of August 12, 1988.

'His wife found him in the rear garden of their family home in Croydon next morning. Burn marks around the wound are consistent with a shotgun held at close range, but here's where it gets tricky. They moved his body before forensics got to the scene.'

'What? Why?'

'Mrs McCall called the police and said her husband had killed himself. The despatcher sent officers and paramedics to the address to deal with a suicide. Everyone had decided it was a suicide before they'd even reached the scene. It's a surprisingly common occurrence.

'The body was lying at the rear of their back garden. Mrs McCall had to stop her two young sons looking out of any rear windows or doors until a friend took them away.

'Unfortunately, kids in neighbouring houses could see it. The first officers and paramedics on the scene decided it was a straightforward suicide, covered the body and the weapon with sheets from the house and carried it all into the home. From a forensic perspective, they destroyed the investigation. For example, you'd normally find traces of residue from the gun on the hand he used to pull the trigger, but it was clean. And no suicide note was found.'

'But the coroner's verdict was suicide.'

'McCall's life was a mess. He'd been secretly recorded by a colleague making claims about Commander Neil Crossley that formed the basis of the Met's corruption probe. You can bet colleagues had turned against him. They certainly did at the inquest, talking about his boozing, affairs and growing incompetence. His detective partner said he was cracking up under pressure from events outside his police work, which was dynamite but the coroner didn't pursue it. Also, the profile of the shotgun suicide is a middle-aged man with no history of mental illness or self-harm, so it fitted. You know what they say, if it looks like a duck and it swims like a duck . . .'

'Is it a duck, Edwina?'

'I'd be happy to stand up in any court of law and say that the only verdict that should ever have been delivered in this case was an open one. There isn't one shred of evidence that Duncan McCall killed himself. When I saw who the coroner and the pathologist were, well . . . I wasn't particularly surprised.'

'What do you mean?'

She sighs. 'The coroner is a Freemason and the pathologist, Tom Witheroe, has since been struck off the Home Office register. The thing is, they were also the coroner and pathologist in the Nathan Barry case.'

'Are you suggesting some sort of cover-up?'

'Quack quack. Now I really must fly.'

Chapter 40

Arsenal, North London
Tuesday, June 28, 1994; 17.30

Fintan insists we watch the big game at home and returns with his trusty old Londis bag, rammed full of piss-weak lager.

'All we need is a nil-all draw and we're in the last sixteen,' he announces, handing me alcohol's equivalent to a can of spam.

'And what do Norway need?'

'It depends on the result of the other match, which takes place at the same time, but a draw would probably do them too.'

'Right, so an incident-free, deadly-dull goalless grind is what everyone's after?'

'Correct.'

'I'm going to need something a bit stronger.'

'Well you needn't bother sneaking upstairs for a crafty Shiraz.'

'What?'

'I poured it down the sink.'

I'd be freaking out if two fresh bottles weren't nestling

in my work bag. It's the least I need after today's bruising encounters with the men who stole my drugs and woman. But I sigh disappointedly for effect.

'How did spooky school go today?'

'Well. Really well,' I say.

'Ha!' he crows, pointing at me. 'They haven't taught you how to lie yet! You're redder than a self-immolating Tibetan monk. What happened?'

I tell him about the Bermondsey Hustle and he almost passes out from hilarity.

I skip over Christy G's premature victory lap around our kitchen table a few hours ago, for fear that a second dose of tragicomic vaudeville might render him unconscious. Instead, I hit him with Walter Moore's claims that Nathan Barry had been about to unmask a cocaine racket at West Norwood cemetery.

He whistles. 'I wonder how much cocaine? Because that sounds like the first viable murder motive I've heard.'

I follow up with Edwina's headlines: there's no proof Duncan McCall killed himself, and the key people calling the deaths of McCall and Nathan were either bent or incompetent, possibly both.

His eyes bulge with possibility. 'We've got to find out what scoop Nathan and McCall were hawking about. That's got to be the key to this.'

'You still think you can get the Prince to talk?'

'I've got to find a way to *make* him talk. Especially now we're making so little headway on Julie Draper.'

'What about this Rottweiler pup of a reporter? Hasn't he managed to unmask Julie Draper's secret homicidal nemesis yet?'

'Sneer all you like. He will.'

'If this nemesis actually exists.'

'He's turning up some decent stuff. Julie wasn't quite the meek Mavis everyone has been led to believe. A good sales rep for starters, one of their best, according to her classified employment record.'

He flings me a folder marked *Human Resources: Julie C Draper: Confidential.* I daren't ask how his cunning understudy managed got hold of it.

Fintan continues: 'She was ambitious too; did night courses in Gemology and jewellery-making and regularly travelled to Antwerp to wheel and deal rare stones. She had a hell of a collection of jewellery, and an antique Rolex watch.'

'Snap! So had Nathan Barry.'

'Funnily enough, hers has gone missing too.'

'Maybe their killer is a Rolex nut? What was that slogan again?

'Men who wear a certain brand of watch guide destinies,' says Fintan. 'He's found no lovers or exes though. Her friends say she didn't seem interested in boys, or girls for that matter. Her parents are convinced she bought a mobile phone recently, which no one's been able to track down. That could tell a story. But the police weren't interested in any of this. I'm telling you, Donal, it's Nathan Barry all over again. They're so blinkered by one suspect, Kipper, that they're not properly pursuing other lines of inquiry.'

The game starts, Fintan's kicking every ball, but I'm finding it hard to engage. I dwell instead on those chilling visits from Julie Draper a couple of weeks back. I close my eyes and re-run the startling images through my brain, racking it for any connection to what we now know. What had she been trying to tell me?

'Did you ask your Rottweiler puppy man to check about her fish?'

Fintan casts off my question with an irritable shrug.

'It's a simple enough request. Her friends probably know, so we wouldn't even have to bother her mum and dad.'

He picks up his phone, jabs out a text. 'It's a good job he's junior, because if I was to ask an experienced reporter to find out the name of a murder victim's pet fish, I'd never live it down.'

His phone pings almost immediately.

'Her fish are named Ben and Jerry. Happy?'

'Crossley said they were Mutt and Jeff, or at least that's what she called them in her proof-of-life call.'

'Maybe he made a mistake.'

'Or maybe it was some sort of coded message. She was a crossword fanatic, don't forget. You know all fish tanks are supposed to have what are called hiding places for the fish, to stop them getting overstimulated? Get your man to go to Julie's home and take a root around the fish tank.'

'I'm not asking him to rummage around her fish tank. Jesus, Donal.'

'What harm can it do?' I protest. 'I'll get hold of her proof-of-life call tomorrow, work out what she did and didn't say. If I get even an inkling that she's talking in code, I'll go and tickle her fish myself. Meanwhile, why the hell aren't we trying to win this? Wouldn't that put us top of the group and get us an easier draw in the next round?'

'Hold what we have is the mantra,' says Fintan. 'We'd be stupid to take any risks at this stage.'

To avoid slipping into a coma, I grab Julie Draper's employment file. Impressively, she'd been one of Crown Estates' top five salespeople nationwide every single quarter since starting there four years ago. That's out of 2,000 employees. Yet she'd never managed to win the title, thus consistently missing out on the star prize: a fortnight in the Caribbean.

'She was the Jimmy White of real estate,' I say. 'Always choking it.'

'You'd think she could've cooked the books a little, even just once, to win one of those holidays,' says Fintan.

The final whistle finally sounds. Ireland have bored their way through to the last sixteen.

'Julie was a bit like Ireland and Norway tonight,' I sigh. 'For some reason, she didn't want to win.'

Fintan sits forward, eyes like saucers. 'My God you're right. You're a bloody genius.' He picks up his mobile. 'Dennis, I need Julie's entire list of sales since she started there . . . like yesterday would be good . . . yes all of it.'

He hangs up. 'She didn't want to win, because that would've drawn attention to her, or to someone she sold properties to. There'll be something in that list. I guarantee it.'

Chapter 41

Whitechapel, East London
Wednesday, June 29, 1994; 09.30

I decide to level with Gary about getting stiffed by Daryl. Firstly, I suspect he already knows. Chances are he'd planted Daryl with the express purpose of 'turning me over'. Secondly, I don't have eight rocks of crack or 100 quid to hand over. I dread his reaction; why do I always seem to mess up when it comes to older male authority? Why do I always feel so intimidated?

I can't face getting kicked off yet another squad. Satisfaction for Fintan, vindication for Zoe and yet more proof that she's right to trade up.

Gary remains chillingly deadpan throughout my story.

'Four out of five of our trainees fall victim to that scam,' he says. 'That's why I sent you his way first. He reads people better than he can read words.'

'Is Daryl a dealer or a cop?'

'I told you real-life situations. You can't learn from anything else. You don't need to know any more than that.'

'What did the one in five do, you know, who didn't get Darylised?'

'I'm not going to insult your intelligence, because you know you should never have handed over the cash like that. He's got to deliver the goods to the table, otherwise no deal. You're the one with the money. That's what he wants; the money has got to be the commodity that gets handed over last.'

I redden and shrink, like a boiled prawn.

'There's a broader picture here too, Donal. Daryl didn't need to rip you off. He would've made a nice packet out of this deal. He could've made thousands out of you long-term. Instead, he chose to rip you off.

'That's one of the key things I'll keep drumming into you about this world. Drug dealers tend to think only about the here and now. And they love ripping off the other parties in any deal. That's what they're always looking to do. That's their drug, their high.'

'I feel like a right eejit,' I say.

'You shouldn't see this as a fail. You should see it as your first lesson. You told me the truth. Most rookies try to edit or spin what happened, to save face. This means you've grasped the importance of trusting us completely. That's another key point I'll be constantly driving home. You've got to learn to trust your handlers with your life and tell them everything.'

His eyebrows shoot up as if to say: Anything else? I read his signal.

'I broke your first two golden rules of undercover.'

His shakes his head resignedly. What's left of my inner steel adopts the foetal position.

'I signed up for this hoping my ex-girlfriend would beg me not to do it, at which point I'd planned to pull out. Both her and my brother know about it. I should've told you first thing yesterday morning when you asked. I'm sorry I didn't, Gary. But that's the situation as it stands.'

He gives me a kilowatt stare.

'Anything else?'

I shake my head.

'Your brother's a problem we need to address anyway. Of course, we knew you'd told some people close to you. It's human nature. We were waiting to see if you'd level with us.'

I'm beginning to wonder what else these people know about me.

'Today was your last chance to tell me or I'd be failing you. Again, it shows you're learning to trust us. And I've always found the Irish to be the least trusting of authority. It's stamped in your DNA. I'm glad you did. Another one of my mantras is "never get caught in a lie".'

Good, because I'm on a confessional slide and I've let go of the sides. He'll soon see I'm simply not cut out for this role and release me back into my comfort zone of perennial under-achievement.

'The thing is, Gary, I can't lie. I never could. I probably should've flagged that up too.'

'You won't have to lie in this role, Donal. Not if your handlers do their job properly. Like I say: never get caught in a lie. Whoever you buy gear off doesn't need to know anything except how much you want to buy. So that's all you need to say and that's all you need to do. No lie necessary. In fact, it's better that you feel you can't tell a lie. That way, you won't even try to and get yourself tied up in knots. Read my lips; never get caught in a lie.'

I nod and feel my confidence clamber gingerly off its stretcher.

Gary's eyes glint. 'Just to satisfy the romantic in me, did your ex beg you not to do it?'

I laugh, a little bitterly. 'Like Daryl, she read me like a book.'

'Why are you still going through with it then?'

'Because I've never achieved anything before. I've got to show her I can do it. And my brother and father. Most importantly of all, I've got to prove it to myself.'

Gary pops a travel bag on the desk, unzips it, pulls out clothes still wrapped in polythene.

'Designer clobber,' he announces. 'You need to look the part. And this is a real Rolex, worth forty grand, so for the love of God don't break it or lose it or leave it on a sink in a public loo, as I once did.'

'I think I'd feel more comfortable with a fake, Gary.'

'These guys know their bling. You need to treat all this as your uniform. When you put it on, you get into character. More importantly, when you get home, you shed your outfit and your character for the sake of your loved one.'

He hands me a file.

'Destroy this as soon as you've digested the contents. The man in the photo is Ray Briggs, ex-armed robber, current fixer for some West Indian dope importers. He knows what you look like and is expecting to see you at the entrance to HMS Belfast today at 3pm. He's got a job for you. When it's safe, call me with the details.'

Chapter 42

Whitechapel, East London
Wednesday, June 29, 1994; 11.00

Julie Draper's abductor made a single proof-of-life phone call to her office's main number. The audio recording of that call has just been delivered to me at Spooky school.

The kidnapper speaks first. Using some sort of electronic voice changer, he sounds like a cross between a Northern bingo caller and the singer on The Bugles' 'Video Killed the Radio Star'.

'This is a recording of Julie reading three random headlines from today's *Daily Mirror* newspaper.'

After seconds of rustling, Julie's tape-recorded voice sounds feeble and frayed. "Playwright Potter dies"; "Chinook Tragedy: 29 confirmed dead"; "Blair and Brown in secret leadership pact". Tell Rex, Dino, I miss them and the fish, Mutt and Jeff.'

The tape snaps off. The phone goes dead.

'Mutt and Jeff' is a famous old US comic strip, and cockney rhyming slang for 'deaf'. What else could it mean?

I call Fintan. 'She very deliberately refers to her fish as

Mutt and Jeff. We should at least explore the idea it's a message of some sort, maybe an abstract clue?'

'Okay, I'll check with the boys down in the cuttings library. Between them, they literally know everything and would make a decent living just doing pub quizzes. You know who you should ask . . . Queen Cryptic herself.'

'I've managed not to call her for three whole days.'

'This is business, right? I promise, if you act cool and a bit detached, you'll seriously boost your chances. Especially now she thinks you've already found her replacement.'

Gary's mantra still chimes fresh in my mind; never get caught in a lie.

'I can't tell her I've met someone else, Fintan.'

'You won't have to. I've already done that. Like I said, just be cool. It's your best chance of winning her back.'

I'd already thought of Zoe. She tackles the *Guardian*'s cryptic crossword every single day, almost always finishing just two or three clues short. I dial her number in a state of excited dread, as if I'm about to ask her out for the first time.

'Hi,' I say brightly. 'I need your brilliant mind for just a couple of moments, if that's okay.'

'Umm, okay,' she says uncertainly.

'In her proof-of-life call, Julie Draper deliberately called her fish Mutt and Jeff, when their names are Ben and Jerry. If you were presented the clue "Mutt and Jeff'" in your bewilderingly abstract crossword of choice, what would your answer be?'

'I need to give that some thought. Can I call you back with the most likely candidates?'

'I'd really appreciate that. Thanks Zoe.'

Cue a cringing silence.

'How's Matt?' I blurt, finally. Infuriatingly, she says something at the same moment so neither of us hears the other. More cringe, then overlapping apologies. When did we forget how to converse?

'Call me when you can so,' I say awkwardly and hang up.

Fintan gets back seconds later.

'Mutt and Jeff were the codenames of two British double agents during the Second World War. They were Norwegian engineers sent to the UK to spy for the Nazis, but were turned and secretly worked for the Allies under the so-called Double Cross system. They basically fed the Germans false information, such as the Allies were making plans to invade Norway.'

'So Julie could be trying to tell us that whoever kidnapped her is secretly working for someone else, or has deliberately misled the investigation with misinformation.'

'I think she's letting us know that her kidnapper is not Kipper. How's Zoe? You called her right?'

'I called her but I don't know how she is. I never asked.'

'Good, man. Treat them mean, as they say. I didn't think you had it in you.'

'I don't,' I mumble, remembering that only our inability to speak in turn prevented me cracking.

I'm heading for the tube when Zoe calls.

'Okay, this is the best I can come up with,' she says, sounding disappointed. 'Mutt can mean dog, black, blackguard, smelly or stinky, junkyard or junkie. Jeff has got to be Bridges.

'The only words that make any sort of sense together are "junkyard bridges" or "black bridges". I've had a quick look at scrapyards from Croydon down to the south coast. There's one near Pease Pottage called MJ Bridges. Might be worth a visit.'

'My God that's amazing work, Zoe,' I gush, unable to contain my excitement. 'You've given me a firm lead.'

'You should take that breeze block you found at the ransom drop. That might confirm a connection. I'll drop it off at your place now, leave it in the front garden.'

I check the time: 'Damn, I can't go now. I'm on my way to see some dodgy armed robber.'

'You could let the kidnap squad know.'

'And let them take all the credit? No way.'

'Glad to hear it, Donal,' she says. 'You've let that happen way too often.'

'I know. Not anymore. No more Mister Nice Guy. How's Matt?'

She smirks.

'What?' I protest.

'He's fine thanks, Dirty Harry. Still asking about you a lot, which really winds Chris up.'

My chest goes all warm and fuzzy, like a freshly toasted marshmallow.

'See, he understands loyalty,' I declare, and immediately regret it.

'I deserve that,' she says quietly.

'I didn't mean . . . I'm not deranged about it anymore, Zoe, honestly. I get it now. You do what you have to do.'

My God, undercover school is working. I didn't mean a word of that! I just hope I'm not making it too easy for her to get me out of her life.

'Thanks,' she says quietly.

'I've got to go,' I gasp, managing to hang up before my voice cracks, just.

Chapter 43

M6 Motorway, Staffordshire
Wednesday, June 29, 1994; 17.30

I'm driving a white Ford Transit van up the motorway with both windows wound down, but that doesn't stop the sickly-sweet stench of cannabis cloying at my sinuses. Well there is half a tonne packed into the back . . .

As the memory of today's encounter with Ray Briggs creases me up again, I worry that the fumes are making me high.

I turned up near HMS Belfast bang on time when two men jumped out of the bushes. The smaller of the two – Ray, as I'd soon discover, and a ringer for Lovejoy – launched a faux boxing attack on me, complete with sharp nasal exhalations and sound effects. I recoiled more in shock than fear when he uttered the immortal words: 'Do you know who I am?'

'Ray Briggs?' I offered.

'You know how much my house in Chigwell is worth?' Before I could open my mouth, he added: '300 grand.' He nodded in satisfaction, then repeated the figure to himself in mild awe: '300 grand.'

I realised this was some sort of a challenge, so hit back, at least verbally.

'I've got a quarter of that on my arm,' I said, flashing the Rolex and forcing him to take a standing count. He stared at the flashy timepiece for several seconds in stunned silence. '75 grand to you, Raymondo. Now the time at the third stroke is 3.03pm. Unless you've got a serious business proposition, I'll be on my way.'

Chastened, Ray cut to the chase; he needed an experienced driver to take half a tonne of 'Bob Hope' from South London to Keele services off the M6. I'd get a grand in cash on arrival and a lift to the train station in Stoke-on-Trent. I made him go through the trip's logistics repeatedly, exhaustively, including where I'd park at the services and how I'd make myself known to the client.

Later, I passed all this information onto Gary, who assured me a surveillance team would be in place to witness the deal.

'Don't get in touch again until the job's complete,' were his parting words.

I'm now one junction away from the Happy Eater rendezvous point, unhappy and sick to my stomach with nerves. I keep telling myself: Just do the deal in Keele and skedaddle.

I come off the motorway and ease down into the services car park. As agreed with Ray Briggs, I drive to the rear of the restaurant, park up and get out. I stretch in the late evening sunshine, then give my replacement driver a twirl so he knows it's me.

Suddenly, a police patrol car appears. Slowly, menacingly, it crawls past me. As it disappears around the front of the Happy Eater, my mind goes into spasm. Do I run away? Hide? Drive off in the van? Go inside and scoff happily?

The patrol car reappears around the other side of the

building and, to my horror, turns and starts creeping my way again. When it stops right beside me, I almost barf up my heart.

'Is that your vehicle, sir?' asks the uniformed male passenger, nodding towards the van.

'Yes,' I smile, cockily.

'What've you got in there?'

I hesitate. The officers get out. I imagine both the drugs gang and my surveillance team watching on in horrified fascination. Surely this can't be part of the script.

Bad cop asks again: 'What's in the van?'

I shrug: 'I don't know.'

'You'd best show us then,' says the other.

I've no choice but to lead them round the back and open the double doors.

'What's in the boxes?' says bad cop.

'I dunno,' I repeat brightly and feel a sharp blow to the head.

Fucking hell, I'm one of you, I almost blurt.

'I said what's in the boxes?'

'Erm, I really don't know,' I repeat, politely this time.

Good cop produces a Swiss army knife, punctures some of the plastic and all of my spunk. The unmistakeable waft of cannabis snakes around us like a genie with bad intentions.

'Well?' he says.

For some reason, I decide to run. They read it and grab me, wrestling me to the ground. I endure another few clatters to the head, see black stars and feel my hands yanked around my back and cuffed.

Nearby, a car guns it out of the car park; I guess belonging to my client/substitute driver. Seconds later, a second car follows; my back-up.

Fuck, I think. What happens now? Surely they'll come back and vouch for me?

I'm bundled into the back of the police car. Good cop radios the police station, requesting drugs squad and forensics. Bad cop reads me my rights and predicts my future.

'I don't know why you're acting so cocky, lad. You've got half a tonne in there, street value two and a half million quid. You're looking at between five and seven years.'

My insides shrivel. Surely, they'll come back to get me, explain I'm one of the good guys. They can't just cut me loose. Can they?

Within seconds, the crime scene circus descends, clearly pumped by the scale of the seizure and the glory it promises to refract. Our car takes off, sirens blaring.

I'm not sure which is more shocking, the fact I'm about to be taken into custody, or the state of Stoke-on-Trent.

As I'm 'processed' at the front desk, I ask if I can make a phone call. I'm desperate to get in touch with Gary so he can spring me. But his final instruction had been clear; no call until it's all over. Part of me worries what qualifies as 'all over'. After I'm charged? Jailed?

After I finish my sentence?

I decide to call Fintan. He'll know what to do.

'You won't be calling anyone. This investigation is still live.'

'What about a solicitor?'

'This isn't *Hill Street Blues*, son.'

I suddenly remember my mobile phone and panic. I've left it in the van. Anyone who gets hold of it and dials a few of the numbers will realise I'm a cop. Is that good or bad?

'What about my stuff?'

'You'll get it all back when you're dealt with.'

I'm led past cells packed with wide-eyed ravers who all start cheering and banging the bars. Somehow, they know I've been nicked with half a tonne. I reward their cheers with a regal wave, only to feel another crack across the back of the head as I'm slung into a lone cell.

The scallies tell me they were busted this morning after an illegal rave. Police seized their speakers and equipment but not all of their drugs, which they'd secreted into the cells orally, anally and in piercings.

What follows is the longest night of my life.

Next morning, I'm unlocked and led along a corridor towards the interview suites. As we halt outside room three, I feel certain that Gary or some sort of emissary is on the other side of that door, ready to take me home.

Wrong.

I decide, perhaps optimistically, that this is an elaborate test of my mettle. I remember Gary's words: *You'll be tested in real-world environments, in real-life situations. We need to see how you cope with the stress of uncertainty and the unexpected.*

The one thing I mustn't do is reveal who I'm really working for. Then I'll pass with flying colours. I just need to hang in there, stay cool.

I refuse a duty solicitor or to answer any questions. They charge me with possession with intent to supply, whisk me to Stoke Crown Court where I'm remanded in custody. *Surely the test is now over . . .*

As they lead me to what looks like a bombproof prison van, I ask one of the security guards where we're headed.

'Strangeways here we come,' he smiles. I look around, expecting to see Gary's smirking face. When I don't, I start to tremble uncontrollably, like a rattling junkie.

I'm a serving police officer on my way to the country's most notorious prison. If anyone inside gets even a whisper of who I am, I'm dead. Worse than that, they'll torture me in ways that will make death welcome.

I can't face this. I just can't. Fuck Gary's test and mantras; first chance I get, I'm calling him, demanding that he gets me the hell out of this, while he still has the chance.

Chapter 44

Strangeways Prison, Manchester
Thursday, June 30, 1994; 13.00

I'm locked in a single cell on 'K' wing for vulnerable prisoners. I'm told it's a new policy for first-timers, until they consider me 'settled in'. Barely dried blood on the floor and wall suggest I'm bearing up better than the last occupant. For now.

I ask to make a call; they ignore me. I ask to speak with a solicitor; they say, you're on remand, you'll just have to wait. Now I'm scared. I'm in the belly of the beast, a Category A prison, the butt-fuck motel. Does Gary even know I'm here? Surely, I can make one call. Gary has got to come and sort this out!

When my door is unlocked at 5pm for 'chow and association', I refuse to come out. Frankly I don't care for the food or the company.

Lockdown at 8.30pm signals meltdown. At last, I can drop the front and cry.

As night falls, the screws vanish and the whole place erupts like a zoo. Shouting, banging, laughing, wailing; it's the soundtrack to drug-fuelled release and torment.

I can't sleep a wink, so constantly repeat Gary's mantra: Paranoia is a soul eater. It doesn't stop my mind straying into the darkest crevices. Courtesy of my mobile phone, police in Stoke must've figured out by now that I'm some sort of undercover officer-of-the-law. Who else is finding this out while I'm stuck in here? It takes just one bent cop, one quick call. Prison officers are notoriously corrupt. Who's to say word hasn't already reached the lifers on C wing who have nothing left to lose? I can't risk taking a single step outside of that cell door. But what's to stop them getting in here during association? Maybe I'd be safer out there, where at least the screws can keep an eye on me. All I know for certain is that I can't hack this, whatever the hell is going on.

Next morning, a prison guard tells me I've got a legal visit. Only when he reassures me that the rest of the prison is still in overnight lockdown do I follow him out of that cell.

The woman in the visiting room looks like an Asian Salma Hayek; I hope she's here to spring one Irish Desperado. She stands to reveal a short, tight-fitting charcoal-grey skirt and a clingy white blouse. She must have known she'd be coming here today when she dressed this morning. What is she trying to do, trigger another Strangeways riot?

'Hi Donal, I'm Farhana Dar, your solicitor,' she says.

'Who sent you? Who's paying you?'

'It's not unknown for prisons to bug visiting rooms. Can I just tell you where we're at with getting you out of here?'

'Please.'

'We've got another court date this afternoon where we'll reapply for bail. Representations will be made directly to the judge in chambers.'

'By who?'

She looks at me in amused disbelief.

'Hopefully you won't have to stick it out here much longer.'

'Hopefully?'

'We're doing our best, Donal.'

Chapter 45

Stoke-on-Trent, Staffordshire
Friday, July 1, 1994; 11.30

I emerge from Stoke Crown Court relieved, aggrieved and in fevered search of a drink. They must have called the nearest pub The Oak as a joke. Or maybe they knocked a few down to make room for this rancid old shack.

I'd heard how people who've spent years in prison show classic tell-tale signs on release. They wait for people to open doors for them and hate the tang of metal cutlery. My electing to drink outside in the semi-derelict pub garden shows just how poorly I'd managed to cope with a mere eighteen hours of confinement. I couldn't face months or years of it; not without getting out of my head every night on hooch, or worse. But then I need to get out of my head every night just to survive civilian life . . .

'You did good,' says a familiar voice behind me.

I turn to see Gary at the door, wearing that wryly amused look that's starting to grate.

'Can I get you another?' he says.

'Yes, you can,' I snap, moody and wounded. 'Then you can tell me what the hell that was all about.'

Gary brings out two for me, one for himself. He starts with the Keele Services bust.

'Ray Briggs had to tell his connections they lost all of their gear. They took it okay. They had their own people on the plot so they saw what happened. A random stop by motorway cops. That's just rotten luck.'

I shake my head. 'Come on, Gary, you're constantly banging on about trust and how crucial it is that I tell you everything. This has to be a two-way street. Did you set this whole thing up?'

He takes a shark-like glug of his real ale.

'Sorry you had to sit tight for a couple of days. Well done not panicking and calling me. Well done not calling anyone. The thing is, we normally have weeks or months to train up a UC. Because of all the hoopla surrounding Molly Parker-Rae, we had to find a way to fast-track candidates so we can get someone in this weekend. Look, Donal, if you're still interested, you've been selected for the role.'

I'm speechless. 'So, you did set me up then, to boost my credentials?'

He remains inscrutable. 'If you agree to take it, you can let your ex know, but no one else, especially not your brother. Are you in?'

I want to say yes, but I've just endured one of the most terrifying ordeals of my life. Throughout it all, I'd no idea what was really going on. I need assurances that I'll be protected.

'The thing is, Gary, how am I supposed to infiltrate this hardcore criminal gang, when they don't know me from Adam?'

'You're right to ask. We've got someone already on the inside, someone you know.'

I can't disguise my anxiety.

'He's just inside the door there, waiting to make his grand entrance. Come on out,' he shouts.

I turn and feel my mouth drop.

'I don't know why I'm agreeing to this, Lynch,' he laughs. 'You nearly got me killed last time.'

Bernard Moss, the people-hating, dog-loving, IRA-supporting ex-British soldier, steps out into the ramshackle garden.

'Last I heard, you were being filleted by Jimmy Reilly,' I say, reeling from his manly shoulder slaps.

Bernie is one of those complex but gifted chancers who seems to constantly straddle that blurred line between criminality and intelligence. He's got form for all sorts – GBH, threats to kill, fraud – but also a medal of commendation from the Met, awarded for our work together last year.

With no more noble a motive than saving his own ass, Bernie helped me launch a sting operation targeting his boss, notorious London villain Jimmy Reilly. The sting took down Reilly but it was Bernie who wound up at the sharp end, literally; twenty-four stab wounds delivered by his apoplectic boss on realising he'd been betrayed. I didn't know a human body could bleed that much and survive.

Bernie recovered and retired to Norfolk with a hefty Met pay-off, to write his best-selling autobiography – *Nutters!* – and consult on several dubious TV series that shamelessly glorified 'hard man' criminals.

'What brings you back from the fens or the broads or whatever they call that God-forsaken part of the world, Bernie?' I ask.

'I got bored, Donal. Missed the mischief, I suppose,' he

says in his sing-song Brummie accent. 'And I've learned that you can trust criminals a hell of lot more than anyone who works in publishing or TV.'

'I don't doubt it. So, you've got the inside track on the Slough/Windsor rave scene then?'

'It's a long story. Let's save it for the journey home.'

By the time Gary's jag roars onto the M6, Bernie's in full flow. 'What you've got to understand about the guys who run the scene down there – Shaw, Walsh and Regan – is they snort a lot of coke and take a lot of steroids. The result is known as 'roid rage' and it ain't pretty. News about Molly breaks and they're driving around to their suppliers kicking the shit out of them, saying one of them must've delivered a contaminated batch. They used lighter fluid on one poor bastard, set his hair on fire.

'A couple of days later, they learn that it wasn't the E that killed Molly. They go back around the suppliers declaring: "Business as usual". Except the suppliers have got the major hump now and claim they can't get hold of any.

'Regan and co. are in a right flap. Got four clubs running Thursday to Sunday night and fuck all E to sell to the punters.'

As ever, I'm struggling to keep up.

'Hang on, Bernie, what's your connection with this lot?'

'Like I said, I got bored and I wanted to get back into the game, so I did what anyone needs to do to fast-track into criminality. You remember the criminal Holy Trinity, Donal; Slap, Scrap and Crap. I set up a security firm to supply bouncers, a scrapyard to crush getaway cars and a waste disposal furnace to destroy evidence. Suddenly I'm indispensable. I made sure the book gave no hint as to who I was really working for when we put Jimmy Reilly away, so they see me as someone who boosts their credibility.'

I nod. 'So when they run out of E suppliers, of course you step in to save the day.'

'You're learning, Lynch. Finally. I took one of their muppets to one side. This kid's always desperate to impress them. I tell him he can save the day by saying he knows a guy on the Liverpool scene who might be able to help us out and get us a lorryload of E in a hurry.

'They ask me to check this guy out. I discover you're a mid-level player with a lab in Dublin looking to export E and weed. You already supply some major firms in Liverpool that you've got family connections with. They know I've got family up there too. Through them, I've been able to connect with you.

'You've had some bad luck lately, which means you're having to lie low and stay away from Liverpool for a few months.'

He produces a copy of today's *Liverpool Echo*, opens it at page seven, points to the left-hand column.

Busted! Cops Smash £3M Drugs Ring

A massive haul of high-grade cannabis destined for the Walton area of Liverpool has been intercepted, police revealed today.

Cops swooped on a Ford Transit van at Keele Services on the M6 and discovered drugs inside with a street value of £3 million. 'It's our biggest value haul so far this year,' said DI Gerry Macken of Liverpool drugs squad. 'We must give credit to our colleagues in Staffordshire for responding to intelligence we received and co-operating fully.'

Donal Lynch, 25, of Sandymount, Dublin was arrested at the scene and has been charged with drugs offences.

Gary registers my rage via his rear-view mirror.

'Look, Donal, I had to get that load of cannabis off the streets, but I also needed to build your cover. It was my idea to get the traffic cops to stumble across it almost by accident, so that the people you were working for wouldn't smell a rat.

'Liverpool weren't supposed to make it look like it came out of their brilliant intelligence network. That's pissed me off. On the plus side, crims don't believe a word the police say. They saw for themselves it was a bad luck thing.

'The main thing is, having been held in Strangeways and charged, there can be no doubt that you're a middleweight drugs trafficker with connections. It's there in black and white.'

I still feel like I'm only being shown what they want me to see.

'What about my phone?' I ask.

'We were able to wipe it remotely.'

'What about the drugs trafficking charge then? We can't have me getting off and local plod suspecting I'm either undercover or a grass.'

Gary smiles: 'We can make it drag on for months, Donal, without anybody knowing anything. Then we'll reveal you've skipped to Dublin. Everyone knows what a nightmare extradition is from there right now. Trust me, we're masters of inefficiency and bungling bureaucracy when we need to be. And when we don't, for that matter.'

I turn back to Bernie: 'What other ways are you checking me out, you know, for them?'

He speaks to Gary: 'I think it's time Donal here got to see his new home?'

Gary smiles. 'We can swing round there as soon as we hit north London.'

'Déjà vu,' I say as we turn into the Woodberry Housing Estate near Finsbury Park, a high-rise complex so grim that

Spielberg used it to double for the war-torn Warsaw slums in *Schindler's List*. It holds more recent history for Bernie and me.

We park in front of Wandle House, a five-storey, red-brick block, pockmarked with satellite dishes and sad-face clothes lines. I follow Bernie to the stairwell.

'Another way they might check you out is to sniff around your gaff. We've made this look like a typical dealer's lair.'

Sure enough, number 16 on the first floor looks prepped for the Apocalypse. The front door is stitched shut by five heavy-duty locks. The front window is blocked inside by a mattress.

Bernie hands me a bunch of keys and watches me take ten minutes to crack this fortress.

'You'd better work on that,' he says, chuckling to himself. 'You never know when you might need to get in here in a hurry. Or out for that matter.'

The door opens to a studio flat containing a futon and little else. We hover awkwardly in the lack of space.

'It's a bit like where I slept last night,' I say. 'But with slightly less character.'

'We'll make sure uniform come around here looking for you a couple of times a week,' says Gary. 'The neighbours will think you're Pablo Escobar. You might want to get friendly with one and ask him to make a note of the times/dates they call. Maybe slip him a twenty for the intel. It's all about building cover. But this is your home now until this job is over. You live here and nowhere else, understood? Right, I've got to run. Bernie can fill you in on the rest.'

I open the front door and stand aside to let him pass.

He stops to face me. 'You've shown you're made of the right stuff, Donal. You'll do great. Just remember; paranoia is a soul eater. Never get caught in a lie. And, where possible, never have the merchandise and the money on the same plot.'

'Got it,' I say, thinking easier said than done.

'I've agreed to act as your handler on this. So keep in touch, okay? And try not to get bounced into anything before checking in with me first.'

I return to the bedsit, find Bernie leaning against the kitchen counter.

'What do you drive?' he asks, out of the blue.

'A maroon family saloon, funnily enough, Bernie.'

'You can't use your own car for any of this. The DVLA is too vulnerable. Have you got access to a decent set of wheels that can't be traced to you?'

'Funnily enough, yes. My brother has commandeered a sporty Porsche from a work colleague.'

'Perfect. One last thing. Computers, the internet, this is the new frontier. Everyone reckons internet fraud is the promised land so all these wannabe villains have got geeks on their payroll now, covering that side of things. I'll make sure our geek provides the last, crucial part of your cover.'

'And what's that?' I ask, genuinely stumped.

'There are two search engines on the web, Yahoo and Mosaic. If Tate or any of his goons search your name, they'll come across several articles about your father.'

'What's he got to do with anything?'

'Ah come on, Donal. Why do you really think you've been picked for this? The only thing that's making anyone sit up and pay attention is your dad and his connections to the IRA. That's the part of your cover story we can use to make you untouchable.'

Chapter 46

Pease Pottage, West Sussex
Friday, July 1, 1994; 17.00

Barrelling along 'Sunset Boulevard' towards Brighton, I realise it's been over two weeks since Fintan and I discovered Julie Draper's body.

Meanwhile, I've lost a girlfriend, a job and two nights' liberty.

It had all seemed worthwhile six hours ago, when Gary told me I'd been selected for the task of infiltrating the country's most wanted drugs gang. I felt I'd finally achieved something as a police officer, purely on my own merit – even if it had required me getting busted with a load of drugs. Now, like so much in my life, this achievement feels tinged by *his* shadow.

'The only thing that's making anyone sit up and pay attention is your dad and his connections to the IRA.'

He may as well have said: *You're nothing special, Donal. You weren't even the best candidate. But who else can boast a terrorist for a dad?*

I left Ireland to get away from Da. I joined the British

police force – his sworn enemy – to drive an intractable wedge between us. He rose spectacularly to the bait, declaring that he never wanted to clap eyes on me again.

Mam got ill so we tried to rub along, for her sake. I know he loved her, in his own bloody-minded, irascible way. But the sheer scale of his moral and political hypocrisy made it impossible for me to respect him. As he made clear at Mam's funeral, the feeling is mutual.

Yes still, somehow, he guides my destiny, and he doesn't even own a fucking Rolex. Can you ever truly escape your parents and their sins?

My mind turns to Julie Draper who'd been working so hard to escape her humble roots. Her dad, Bill, had spent his entire life on the assembly line of a local forklift plant. Julie wanted more. She'd already achieved more; selling houses with such efficiency that her commission alone trebled what her dad brought home in wages. But, as Fintan's cub reporter confirmed, precious stones were her real passion. She'd topped her gemology class; her eye for uncut stones had already brought her to Antwerp's famous diamond district and earned her thousands. Had she been drawn into shady circles beyond her scope of understanding?

Maybe her reference to 'Mutt and Jeff' had been an ingenious, multi-layered clue that referred not only to the place where she'd been held against her will, but also to the motive and character of her abductors. If Zoe's cryptic crossword skills are up to scratch, then I'm about to find out.

I turn off the M23 at junction 8 in search of MJ Bridges scrapyard in Pease Pottage, trusty old silver breeze block perched on the passenger seat.

I would never have diverted home to retrieve this characterless hunk of concrete had it not featured so prominently in Julie's chilling visit to me. Sure enough, thanks to Zoe, we now know the block itself and the paint covering it are rare and specialist. So specialist, I hope, that they'll lead me to Julie Draper's killer.

I drive through the scrapyard entrance, past multi-coloured towers of crushed cars to a squat prefab office in a distant corner. I pull up and take a deep breath. Scrapyards are traditionally hostile places for police. Dealers tend to neither ask nor care where metal comes from, knowing that, once crushed, it all looks alike and fetches the same price. I don't even have a warrant, so decide to play it low-key.

I walk into the prefab, cradling my silver breeze block with a carefree air, as if it were a perfectly normal commodity to bring into any office environment. A middle-aged woman with lustrous dyed blonde hair and a tanned, wizened face looks up from a dirty great ledger. She's a ringer for Led Zep's Jimmy Page, though less feminine. Her saggy eyes drop slowly from mine to the block, darkening.

'Paint that yourself, did you?' she says in a faltering West Country accent.

'Can I speak with Mr Bridges please?'

'What about?'

'I'm just wondering if he might have more of these blocks.'

'He deals in metal, dear,' she says slowly and loudly, enunciating each word as if addressing a deaf halfwit. 'You wanna go to a concrete place for more of those.'

'I'm told he has more here. I'm willing to pay top dollar.'

She frowns, then smirks in disbelief. I can see she's thinking: This'll give the old bastard a laugh. She gets up and walks over to a CB radio.

'Gareth, can you hear me?' she says.

'Aye,' says Gareth, in an even thicker West Country lilt.

'Got a man here wants to show you his special block.'

'You what?'

'He's painted it and everything.'

'What are you on about?'

'He wants to buy concrete blocks off ya.'

'Tell him I don't sells blocks. I buys metal,' he says, sounding like Wurzel Gummidge on crystal meth.

'Oh, I never thought of that. Just get over here so I can get him out of my hair will ya?'

Now the excruciating wait. She pretends to get on with her work as I act like I have a burning interest in crushed cars.

'You're not a copper are you?' she says.

I laugh: 'What do you think?'

'Thought not.'

I hear Gareth's stomp long before I see him. He's enormous, with a face like a half-mashed turnip.

'What's all this about?' he groans.

I hold up the block to my chest. 'Have you ever seen one of these before?'

'Not painted. Who are you and why do you wanna know?'

'Can we step outside?'

He turns and I follow.

'I'm a police officer, Gareth, but I'm not interested in you or anything you're doing here.'

He stops and turns, sizing me up before squinting at my badge.

'I've got nothing to hide,' he declares. 'Follow me.'

He stomps towards another corner of his plot. I have to trot to keep up.

'It's so quiet,' I say.

'You wait,' he laughs.

He stops, finally, at a run-down old brick shed.

Poorly stacked inside, about forty concrete blocks. Although not painted, each has three flutes and is identical in design to the one that's now sucked all feeling out of my arms.

'I bought this place in 1981,' he says. 'I've never used this shed or them blocks. What use would I have for 'em? They've just been sat there.'

My heart's galloping, sensing a breakthrough. 'Are there any other buildings on this property?'

'No. Just the prefab. Can I ask what's this about?'

I take a walk around the shed. It sits inside a flimsy wire fence. On the other side is a dirt track. A sudden rumble startles me. I look around just as a massive plane screams overhead, no more than 100 feet above us.

'Gatwick's right over there. We get 'em every ten minutes now,' says Gareth.

'Where does this track come from and lead to?'

Gareth raises a beefy arm. 'That way goes to the road you came here on, which eventually takes you back to the M23. This way is just an access road to some fields.'

'Who owns the land?'

'It used to be Lord Irvine's. He died about, ooh, four years ago. It's now been bought up by some company who, I'm told, are hoping to make a killing if Gatwick airport expands.'

'Have you seen anything unusual along here in recent weeks or months?'

He shakes his head. 'Only time we had trouble here were a good few summers ago. Poor old Irvine had lost his marbles by then. Silly bugger agreed to let these bloody ravers down here. Wrecked the place, they did. Left rubbish and shit everywhere. Where are you going?'

I've climbed out through a gap in the wire fence.

'I'm going to take a walk to the end of this track, just to see what's up there.'

'I'll join you,' says Gareth.

'There's no need,' I say, but he's already through.

Christ, I think, he could waste me right here and crush me in the boot of one of his knackered cars. Who'd ever know? Yet my gut trusts him completely.

Just 100 yards along the track sits a dilapidated old shed. I go off-road in search of a way in, only to find a pair of large wooden doors chained shut.

'What are you looking for?' says Gareth.

'The place where a woman was held, before she was murdered.'

'Bloody hell. I've got something that'll bust that chain,' he says, marching back to his yard. I watch him slip through another busted section of fence. Beside the Gareth-sized hole, an old battered metal sign reads 'MJ Bridges & Co. Scrap Merchants'.

Moments later, he returns with a crowbar and sets to work. As the chain snaps off, the doors swing inwards slowly, ominously.

'Bloody hell,' I say to Gareth. 'I think we've just found it.'

Chapter 47

Pease Pottage, West Sussex
Friday, July 1, 1994; 18.00

I make sure Fintan gets here first. I owe him this scoop. But that's not why I call him before anyone else.

Fifteen days ago, we found Julie Draper's body a few miles down the road at Pyecombe cemetery. My boss, Commander Crossley, responded by sacking me and barring Fintan's newspaper from any further press briefings. Although banished, we've just made the single biggest breakthrough in his floundering investigation.

'I can't wait to see his flustered old chops,' cackles Fintan, a man ceaselessly motivated by personal grudges. 'I've got to hand it to you, Donal. That bloody fish thing . . . how did you even think of that?'

'You wouldn't believe me if I told you.'

'How did Julie know where she was? Presumably she was kept blindfolded?'

'She would've heard the crusher in the scrapyard and the planes landing at Gatwick. Maybe she knew the place from before? Or she saw one of the signs when he drove her here. There's an old one dumped literally opposite the shed.'

'The sad thing is, that might be why he had to kill her, once he got his money. So, how's undercover school?' he says.

Never get caught in a lie . . .

'Put it this way, I'm gathering lots of hilarious anecdotes about why it isn't for me,' I smile.

'Where've you been? I haven't seen you since Tuesday.'

'I got sent to Stoke. Then spent a night in Manchester.'

'Anywhere nice?'

'Pretty basic. Minimalist, I'd call it.'

'Never got on with that place. It doesn't seem to have a centre.'

'A city with strange ways, for sure.'

'Croissant' Crossley steams around the corner, pursued by a couple of senior officers from the Home Office forensic team.

'Ah Commander,' chirps Fintan.

Crossley stops so suddenly that his underlings almost crash into the back of him.

'What the hell are you doing here?' he snaps.

'Like you said a couple of weeks back, we're a latter-day Burke and O'Hare.'

He eyes us with wary contempt. Fintan's relishing every second so I sit back and let him get on with burning the Croissant.

'Now this is a very open spot, wouldn't you say, Commander? Nigh on impossible to secure. I mean, journos and snappers and film crews could get in from all angles.'

'We don't know for sure this is the place yet.'

'That won't stop the media circus descending, as you know only too well, Commander. One phone call and I could turn this into *Zulu Dawn*. And think about it, that'd be a real lose-lose for you. Because the Julie Draper case has slipped off the news agenda. This would put it right back on top, and you firmly in the spotlight. Do you really want that heat, Commander?'

Crossley can't hide his alarm. He'd never make a decent poker player.

'The alternative is we keep it nice and tight. You confirm to me and me only that this is or isn't the place Julie Draper was held. By the time I publish Sunday, you'll be done and dusted here, and gone. Nice and tidy.'

Crossley shuffles foot-to-foot, takes a quick glance at the heavens.

'Okay, you've got a deal,' he says, turning to walk off.

'Hang on a second, Commander,' says Fintan brightly.

Crossley stops and slouches, but refuses to turn around.

'Tell me, Commander, you wouldn't want it coming out that an officer you fired ended up solving your crime, alone and single-handedly, two weeks later?'

Crossley slouches some more.

'If you reinstate him as of, ooh, now, then I can make sure the Kidnap Squad gets the credit for this.'

He nods.

'That won't be necessary,' I say. 'I've got another job now.'

Crossley doesn't need a better excuse to flee.

Fintan turns to me in horror. 'My God, you've got the gig, haven't you?'

'You know I can't say. But I'm now living somewhere else.'

'You can't take it, Donal. I'm serious. Get back on this squad instead. You could get a medal for this find here.'

I shrug.

Fintan takes a step closer. 'I've been checking out those

guys in Windsor. They're complete psychos. If they get so much as a whiff that you're not who you say you are, they'll kill you without even thinking about it.'

'I appreciate your concern, Fint, I really do. But I've got some powerful people around me.'

So powerful, in fact, that they were able to get me slung into Strangeways.

'Jesus, Da will be beside himself,' he says.

'What? Why did you tell him? For Christ's sake . . .'

'He's already lost his wife this year . . .'

'Spare me, Fintan. The old emotional blackmail used to work when it was about Mam. He doesn't give a shit.'

'You don't know how wrong you are, Donal. Seriously, this'll floor him.'

'Don't tell him then. Say I flunked the course. You're not supposed to tell anyone anyway.'

Fintan blinks for the first time in what feels like minutes.

'I bet your new bosses haven't told you who's behind these thugs in Windsor?'

'They tell me what I need to know.'

'Well let me tell you what you need to know, Donal. Some years back, the main man in this Windsor outfit, Pat Regan, spent a few years in Swaleside prison in Kent, where he got very cosy with a lifer. The consensus is that this criminal is now bankrolling Regan and his henchmen. And he is none other than public enemy and villain number one, Mickey Sheeran.'

I check he's not pulling my leg.

'That's right. The gangster, cop killer and grass handled by our mutual friend Croissant Crossley. I can't believe they didn't tell you this. Ever get the feeling you're being set up?'

Chapter 48

Arsenal, North London
Saturday, July 2, 1994; 10.00

It doesn't take much to keep me up all night. Fintan's grim tidings about the people I'm about to engage with worked a treat. Sleep? I barely blinked.

My plunge into a fatalistic fug culminated in an early morning call to Zoe. Shiraz just wanted her to know that I still loved her and Matt. Of course, Shiraz couldn't leave it there. He then had to make the vainglorious proclamation that I'd chosen to risk my life to *prove* my love for her.

'There really is no need for that, Donal,' she said.

Shiraz then asked her if Chris had proposed yet.

'Proposed what?' she yawned.

'What do you think?' snapped Shiraz. At least I'd spoiled his surprise.

I wake on the couch to a pounding head and a pinging phone. *Connections want a meet. Pick you up 11am, Bernie.*

As ever, my trusty old hangover – that straightjacket of

apathy – keeps all emotions in check. I've approached every significant moment of my adult life in this state, or worse. Then I wonder why it never ends well . . .

I climb into Bernie's muscular Range Rover. 'Nice,' I say. 'Who are we meeting?'

'Pat Regan's older brother Ron.'

'Ron Regan? You're kidding me?'

'Yeah, so get it out of your system now, he's very touchy about it. Don't call him Ronnie whatever happens.'

'Or Nancy eh? Where are we meeting?'

'Heston Services.'

'Christ, it all happens at the services.'

'Well it's public enough for no one to try anything stupid, and anonymous enough for us not to get noticed. What we're proposing to Ron today is 10,000 tablets at £2.50 a pop. Here's the sexy bit.'

He takes a device off the dashboard that looks like a hand-held computer game and passes it over.

'That's called a GPS or Global Positioning System. The military have been using it for years and they're just starting to appear in hire cars. See that dot there? That's us. A satellite up there has literally put us on the map. Mental eh?'

'And the plan for this is?'

'Gary, your handler, would've explained to you that the most dangerous moment in any drugs deal is the handover, right? We're always trying to think of ways to make sure the money and the drugs aren't on the same plot, because that's when someone gets the pound signs spinning in their eyes and pulls a gun.

'The beauty of this is we can drop a package of 10,000 Es from a small plane in rural Berkshire or Surrey and they won't find out where until you give them the co-ordinates.

'Meanwhile, you're somewhere else with a mutually

agreed and trusted money man – namely me. You pass them the co-ordinates. Once they confirm the gear is up to scratch, they instruct the money man – me – to hand over the dough to you.'

'It's all a bit Tom Clancy, isn't it, Bernie? Couldn't we just leave the drugs somewhere for them? Like in a hotel room or a lock-up?'

'That'd be too easy for a police sting. They're paranoid after this Molly business that they're being set up. Using the GPS, they'll believe we're dropping 10,000 Es somewhere random, at the last moment, because who'd leave 10,000 Es lying in a field for more than a couple of hours? There's no way this could be a police sting because the logistics are too last minute. And they love all this hi-tech gubbins. At least the money man behind them does.'

'Who is?' I ask, hoping Fintan had made up the Sheeran connection to spook me.

'Mickey Sheeran, apparently. Now he's made his millions, he's become something of a Misadventure Capitalist. He funds criminal schemes that excite him. A few years back, he pours fortunes into this hole-in-the-wall bank scam where they created thousands of fake cards. It failed, just, but had it succeeded, it would've brought down the entire banking system. So he'll love this.'

'Why don't the cops try to turn Pat Regan against Sheeran?'

'No one goes against Sheeran. It'd be suicide. You need to just stick to the straightforward mission here; nail the guys who imported the E that killed Molly Parker-Rae and you're out.'

'What about you, Bernie? What's your mission?'

'Let's just say it's longer term. Though I'm beginning to wonder if I've got the stomach for it any more. I'd forgotten how these fucking so-called villains are always frittering time away on shit matters, like trying to persuade someone to drop charges. That's why most of them are skint. They've got to bounce around their patch all day like feudal lords, dishing out instant justice and being kings and all that rubbish, instead of just earning money.

'And then you've got the possessive gang members who always want to be best buds with the main man and get threatened by anyone who might supplant them. Take this lot in Windsor, Shaun Shaw and Craig Walsh are like star-struck teen girls with a major crush on Pat Regan. You feel like you've regressed to aged fourteen.

'You'll see it yourself this week. We're gonna have to hang out with them and get our hands dirty so they know we're onside.'

'What would be your top-line piece of advice, Bernie?'

'I've got two: don't ever back down, and don't ever look or act shocked about anything.'

He swings into Heston services and drives all the way to the edge of the car park, near a footbridge crossing the M4 motorway. I let him get out first.

A bear of a man whose wife-beater vest looks painted-on walks over and shakes Bernie's hand. With his thick black hair tied in a ponytail, leathery skin and blue eyes, he looks Romany, fearless and wild.

'This is Donal.'

'Hello Irishman,' he says, his blood-stopping clamp of a handshake bringing a tear to more than my eye.

'Hello Ron,' I wheeze, sounding like an amiable parish priest in a vice.

'I'm told you're tight with some of the Scousers.'

I nod.

'Which clan?'

'The Fitzgeralds are relations of mine,' I state, which is true. It's just that the Fitzgeralds I'm referring to are second cousins who own a pub in Tullamore.

'I've got a man on the other side of that bridge who knows the dance scene in Liverpool inside out,' he rasps. 'If you're a face up there, he'll know you.'

He turns, raises his mobile to his mouth and grunts. Every drop of blood in my head crashes south. My ears throb so hard they block out the motorway traffic. I glance at Bernie who's turned to stone.

Whoever's coming across this bridge won't know me . . . can't know me . . .

What then?

. . . public enough for no one to try anything stupid . . .

I take a quick look at Bernie's wheels. We've got to make a run for it. I glance again at Bernie. His eyes are wide, crazed. It's coming on top.

The man crossing the bridge wears a beanie hat and a green Peter Storm cagoule. His face is not one I know. Of course, it isn't. Every fibre of my being screams 'flight' but Bernie's not budging. I see now he's moved his hand into the pocket of his bomber jacket. What's he gripping in there? A gun?

A shoot-out? Here? In broad daylight?

. . . anonymous enough for us not to get noticed . . .

'Beanie Hat' steps off the bridge and embraces Ron Regan. He takes off his hat and shakes his blonde-highlighted locks.

'Hello Donal,' he says and my blood freezes. 'Bet you weren't expecting to see me here.'

Chapter 49

Heston Services, West London
Saturday, July 2, 1994; 11.20

'Hello stranger,' I say brightly.

'I hear you had a spot of aggro up there recently?'

'Half a tonne's worth,' I smile.

'I'm amazed you got bail,' says Chris St. John Green, my love rival and now, bizarrely, my lifesaver.

'Well I've no form over here, Chris. I think that helped.'

'That's good enough for me,' says Ron Regan. 'We'll be on our way, Chris. Thanks for coming at short notice.'

'Not a problem,' says Chris.

'I'd love to catch up, Chris,' I say. 'If you're not in a hurry. When I'm finished here, why don't I pop over your side, meet you in the Little Chef.'

'Sure,' he says, stalking off like a fleeing assassin, clearly desperate to escape me.

Bernie insists I follow Chris right now, leave him to pitch our extra-terrestrial E scheme to Ron Regan. It's all I can do not to sprint.

'What the fuck is going on?' I hiss into his ear, as soon

as I catch up. 'Does Zoe know you're a big shot drug dealer? Because if she doesn't, she soon will . . .'

'Steady on, Donal. I wasn't expecting to see you and I've just saved your bacon back there. Do you want me to give Ron a ring and tell him what I really know?'

That shuts me up for a few seconds. I'm desperately trying to see the angles. What is his game?

'Why did you just "save my bacon", as you put it?'

'I was bloody tempted to shop you, Donal. But Zoe would never thank me for taking you out of the game. And, like I said before, I want to beat you fair and square.'

'The game? Fair and square?' I almost scream in outrage. 'I know where you've been Chris. Curacao Islands, Bali, Ibiza. If you make your money importing drugs, then it's only fair Zoe knows before she marries you. My God, you'll most likely end up in jail serving life, or dead. Think what that would do to her? To Matt?'

He stops walking and turns to me.

'It's not what you think,' he snaps, earnest as a Slavic gravedigger. 'The police aren't the only agency with an interest in smashing drug dealing. We're not that different, Donal, okay?'

I frown in confusion.

He looks at me in exasperated boredom, as you might a dog failing to obey a repeated order, and sighs. 'There's a Chinese proverb that goes; "when the finger points at the moon, the idiot looks at the finger." Don't be an idiot, Donal.'

'What, so you work for Customs?'

'Oh yeah, we always had Customs recruiters sniffing around Eton and Cambridge, in their hi-vis bibs.'

Eton . . . Cambridge . . . of course, he's a proper spook. He's James fucking Bond while, in the words of Commander

Crossley, I'm the village idiot! Why did I ever delude myself into thinking I could compete with him?

He lowers his chin and gives me both sparklers. 'Listen, Donal, Zoe mustn't know anything about this because all it will do is put her and Matthew in danger. I trust you're an honourable man and would never stoop to such pettiness.'

'Well I do owe you one, I suppose, for what you just did back there. And I'm all for "may the best man win".' I grab his fancy cagoule and twist it until our noses meet. 'I just hope you're not lying to me, Chris, or stringing Zoe and Matt along. Because all your breeding and connections count for fuck all where I come from.'

Chapter 50

Fleet Street, Central London
Saturday, July 2, 1994; 20.00

I catch up with Fintan at the Cheshire Cheese pub on Fleet Street, his 'office' on Saturday nights where he waits for the first editions of rival newspapers to 'drop'. Bernie's picking me up here at 10pm and whisking me to Windsor for a 'sit down' with the Three Racketeers, Shaw, Walsh and Pat Regan. Earlier, Ron Regan dialled in our Dambusters concept and they loved it. I'm drinking fast, but the terror of what lies ahead keeps overtaking me. Thank God Bernie will be there, otherwise I couldn't face it.

Fintan produces a bail of printed paper and plants it between our pints. 'Julie Draper's sales records for the past four years. I've been through it and written down all the names and addresses. Maybe you could run them through the police computer, see if any have form.'

'Yeah if I take next week off. There's hundreds.'

'Just as well I've already done all the legwork then,' he says. 'I spoke to Tom Reynolds, Julie's colleague and the man you stunt-doubled for. He tells me Julie had been buying up property for an outfit based in the Cayman Islands. He'd mentioned it to Crossley and co. but they weren't interested.

'I couldn't find these purchases in her records, so I guessed she must have been using some sort of code to disguise them. I was struggling to crack it. Then, in her 1991 sales, two purchasers caught my eye; Edith Ashcroft and David Lean. Remember when I got busted down to obits a few years ago?'

'After you punched someone at the Christmas party.'

'After I was forced to defend myself at the Christmas party. Anyway, I remembered that Edith Ashcroft is the real name of Dame Peggy Ashcroft, who died in 1991. So did the film director David Lean. Both had connections with Croydon. Then, in March of this year, I noticed a purchase by one William Travers. Bill Travers, the TV presenter, died that month and came from Croydon. Bingo!

'I went back through each Friday's *Croydon Advertiser* over the past four years, wrote down all the names featured in obituaries, cross-referenced them with Julie's sales records and came up with nineteen fictional transactions.'

'Wow, very *Day of the Jackal*.'

'She then gave them fictional addresses that would be hard to spot. For example, Travers is listed at 76 Eldon Avenue, Shirley. The even numbers on that road only go up to 74. It all points to a money-laundering racket and, with the amount of properties involved, we're talking a major criminal organisation.'

Now I get his excitement about the 'Have What We Hold' Ireland-Norway snore draw. 'She made sure she never won salesperson of the quarter in case someone took a closer look at her work.'

Fintan nods. 'The question now is, did she conspire in the money-laundering scam or was she a stooge who got wise and threatened to blow the whistle? Either way, let's assume she confronted the brains behind it all. What would he do?'

'He'd have to kill her to shut her up,' I say. 'But he wouldn't want police snooping into her sales records so, to hoodwink them, he makes sure they connect her kidnapping to a previous case, which had been carried out purely to extort money.'

'And it worked, until now,' says Fintan. 'Though it's a little baffling to me just how easily police have been fooled.'

I'm desperate to knot these loose ends together, make sense of it all.

'So, we think Nathan Barry and Duncan McCall had uncovered some sort of racket involving bent cops that they were trying to flog to Fleet Street, you think via the Prince of Darkness.'

'I'm convinced. It had to be him.'

'And now we think Julie Draper died because she'd uncovered some sort of racket concerning the same people. If the rumours back in 1987 were true, those people are Commander Neil Crossley and the criminal he handled as an informant, Mickey Sheeran.'

'Now all we have to do is prove it,' he sighs. 'Hopefully the lair where Julie was held in Pease Pottage will throw up something. Forensics are still there.'

'Zoe can get us the inside track on that then. What about the Prince? Any joy gaining leverage on him yet?'

'I'll know in about two hours' time,' he smiles.

'What do you mean?'

'You'll see,' says Fintan.

Chapter 51

Windsor, Berkshire
Saturday, July 2, 1994; 23.45

When Bernie pulls up outside the Oasis nightclub in Windsor, a couple of security lackeys scamper over; one to park the Range Rover, the second to usher us in ahead of the kvetching queue.

We're corralled through a raving throng speeding off their tits on runaway breakbeats and bad drugs. It's hardcore hell; bony, emaciated, gurning faces flashing live and dead. Distracted, demented eyes set to explode. I see no love in this screaming Munchesque vision of hell, just restless souls trapped inside a merciless, eternal thud.

We're led up a spiral staircase to a mezzanine overlooking the dance floor; all very *Carlito's Way*.

Ron Regan leaps to his feet and makes the introductions. Pat Regan, Shaw and Walsh look swollen, sweaty and wired.

'It's Bernie and Biggles!' roars Pat, and they all fall about laughing.

At the next table, a gaggle of orange skeletons in hot

pants and war paint cackle like hens. I find myself double-taking one of the brunettes.

Shit, I know her from somewhere . . .

Ron Regan presents a flute of champagne and a seat at the captain's table.

'How long did it take you to learn how to fly?' Pat asks me.

'I don't fly, Pat. Why have a dog and bark yourself?'

He seems to like that.

A mirror lands on the table before me. I peer into a Rothko-style triptych of my red, drunken face, split into three by two fat lines of coke.

'Not for me, thanks,' I say. Then, borrowing a line from Woody Allen: 'Or I'll spend the rest of the night trying to take my trousers off over my head.'

This cracks Pat up, so the others duly follow suit, except Shaw.

'You're one funny fucker,' says Pat and Shaw's eyes burn into me like a red-hot tuning fork. I remember Bernie's words from earlier.

Shaw and Walsh are like star-struck teen girls with a major crush on Pat Regan. Shaw shifts irritably in his seat, patently unhappy that I'm bonding with his hero. He's by far the shortest of the trio – minus the elevator shoes and gelled hair, about 5 foot 4 – with the short-man syndrome to match.

'So, we're told you're some crazy Provo?' he sneers.

'As you may have heard, peace is breaking out,' I say, my face toasting. 'I'm seeking fresh business opportunities.'

'You look like a copper to me.'

My face is steaming now. I summon Bernie's words; *don't look shocked . . . don't ever back down.*

'Well we know you're not one anyway,' I smile and every face pivots my way. 'You need to be at least 5 foot 7.'

Cue gales of laughter. Shaw is apoplectic. Now comes the

post-hysterics awkward silence; Shaw's invitation to test my mettle.

'Tell me how you'd go about whacking me then, Mr IRA man,' he says.

I remember Gary Warner's chilling description that day in the Harp Bar and parrot every detail. Even Bernie looks impressed.

Ron Regan pipes up: 'Now if we can get down to business. Bernie, show Pat and the lads your satellite device. You're gonna love this.'

Bernie produces his hi-tech ace card, giving it the whole 'smile and a shoeshine' sales demo as my eyes drift back to the party girls on the other table. I suddenly remember how I know that brunette. A bead of cold sweat trickles down my raging hot back; she could blow my cover right here, right now. I've got to get away from her.

Ron Regan stands and announces the pizza delivery boy is on his way up.

He opens the door to a skinny, acne-ridden teenager holding six large pizza boxes.

'Do you need to have a pizza face to work there?' shouts Shaw and they all have a good laugh at that.

'Just leave 'em over there,' says Ron, pointing to an empty table in the corner.

Delivery boy obliges, then hovers at the door, face redder than his uniform.

'What are you hanging around for?' says Ron.

He holds out a quivering bill. 'That's fifty-three pounds ninety-four pence,' he squeaks. The room falls silent. Dread yanks at my guts. 'Please,' he adds, making a stand that impresses and appals in equal measure.

'Are you serious?' smiles Ron Regan, shaking his head at what he considers sheer bare-faced gall.

‘I’ll deal with it,’ says Shaw, getting to his feet and marching over to the kid.

‘How much did you say, son?’ Shaw asks, rummaging in his pocket.

‘Fifty is fine,’ says the kid, chewing his lip and wishing he’d fled when he had the chance.

I see the bunch of keys coming out of Shaw’s pocket in slow motion. Gripping them hard between his fingers in a well-rehearsed move, he lashes out in a flash. The lad’s cheek opens like a carp’s mouth. He turns away but Shaw follows up with stabbing blows to his ear, neck and shoulder. The lad yelps and squeals like a pig, pressing himself into the wall. Shaw delivers a sickening kick to his ribs which sends him scrabbling into the foetal position.

Shaw snorts like a horse. Suddenly he notices blood splashes on his cornflower blue and white Fred Perry polo shirt. ‘You pizza-delivering cunt,’ he screams, then kicks him hard in the face. The sound of crunching bone and helpless gurgling is too much for me. I turn away in disgust. At that very moment, I catch her eye. Tania, the model from Sandra’s photo casebook, half-frowns in recognition. My backbone free-falls through space.

‘I think he’s got the message,’ says Bernie, ushering Shaw away.

Bernie slips three twenty-pound notes into the lad’s pocket. ‘You got paid, then you fell down the stairs, got it?’ he says to the limp ragdoll whimpering in his arms.

Shaw pants and sniffs in primeval satisfaction, as if he’s just fucked Wonder Woman. Christ, I think, what is it with these guys and free pizza?

‘Wow,’ I say, champagne-sharp, ‘you enforce that thirty-minute delivery rule pretty strictly down here.’

Everyone laughs, except Shaw.

Bernie returns. 'I've just deposited him at the bottom of the stairs and called an ambulance, so the cops will turn up soon, asking questions. And all for what?'

The temperature in the room plummets.

Bernie's puce and pumped. 'We've got no fucking gear because you went around bashing people last week. Now I bring someone here who can solve our problem, first you insult him, then you do something stupid and bring cop heat down on top of us.'

'Alright, Bernie,' says Ron, arms outstretched. 'We're very interested in doing business with our new friend here. And we need to make it happen this week. I think we're all agreed on that?'

Nods all round.

'Great,' says Ron, clapping his hands. 'I'll order up some more bubbly. Now's not the time to get into the nitty-gritty. Let's relax and enjoy ourselves.'

I can't do either and want out. But Bernie isn't budging. The girls decide to hit the dance floor, except Tania. She sits next to Pat Regan. They talk quietly, seriously. She pushes her hair back with her left hand, revealing that green Rolex. It's definitely her and she's just glanced over at me. I feel sick, hot and spent. What is she telling him?

She kisses him on the cheek and leaves without looking at me. I know betrayal when I see it. Christ, I think, this can only play out one way; and may well involve my soft face repeatedly absorbing Shaw's set of jagged keys.

As they binge on coke and Moet, I choke on sweaty menace. Pat Regan takes a call on his mobile, responds angrily to news.

'That cunt Pete Twomey told us he's got no gear. Well he's at the Limelight as I speak, flogging lots of it.'

Suddenly we're all jogging down the spiral stairs.

'Jump in with me,' demands Pat, getting into his black Range Rover. Bernie takes the front seat, me the back. Ron Regan, Shaw and Walsh roar off ahead of us in another.

'I'm a bit confused,' says Pat. 'Tania knows your brother. He works on the same paper as her. He told her you work in TV.'

'Well it's a good front,' I say. 'It's the only job in the world where you need no qualifications or discernible skills.'

'So you don't work in TV?'

'I invest in TV projects, if you know what I mean, Pat. Good way of cleaning money.'

'Tania's an actress looking for a break. If you can help her get that break, I'll make sure you're looked after.'

'I'll see what I can do.'

He laughs. 'I'm not asking you, Donal. Get her that break.'

'Consider it done,' I say, silently thanking any God out there that I'm in this for just one job before I vanish. Then the gravity of what he just said hits me. I can't vanish; not so long as Tania can find Fintan. And Pat's letting me know this.

Shit.

He turns into an empty car park and skids to a halt. Shaw, Walsh and Ron Regan are already in a screaming match with a man backed against a wall.

'Come on,' says Pat and we hop out.

Pat walks right up to the guy and slashes his throat. The man reels back, eyes bulging, hand clamped to his Adam's apple, bright red blood pouring through his fingers.

Shaw turns to me, eyes like glass balls. 'Wanna be in our gang?' he spits. I look down to see he's presenting me with a knife. 'Finish the fucker off.'

My mouth falls open. I turn to Bernie. Almost imperceptibly, he shakes his head. *Don't do it . . .*

‘Fuck’s sake, get on with it,’ gasps Pat Regan as the man stumbles back against the wall and begins to slide to the ground.

‘Show us you for real,’ shouts Shaw, jabbing the knife at my hand. ‘Cos right now we’re not buying it.’

I shake my head. ‘I’m a businessman, not a thug,’ I say. ‘And I’m not interested in doing business with thugs. Good night.’

I turn and set off on foot, certain they’ll come after me, hurt me.

‘I told you, he’s a cop,’ bellows Shaw. ‘We’ve gotta sort him out now.’

‘Leave him,’ barks Bernie, rattled.

I clench my eyes shut, feel my heart pound in my mouth but refuse to speed up. What I dread most is the sound of a second set of footsteps, despatched to follow me, sort me out. The night air turns into thick, street-light-amber liquid, dragging at my limbs, reducing me to slow motion. My straining ears buzz. Those footsteps sound.

I make it around the corner and sprint for my life.

Chapter 52

Woodberry Housing Estate, North London
Sunday, July 3, 1994; 04.30

I bolt all five locks, spring open a Shiraz and pursue wine-based lobotomy with gusto.

My mobile pings. I click on the message.

We know you're a pig.

Gary's words from a briefing echo through my head: *Imagine what they'd do to a cop?*

I leap to my feet, pace about fast. Shaw must have sent that text. He already levelled the accusation once tonight. My refusal to fillet a total stranger has confirmed it in his mind. He let me escape earlier because they had a Judas drug dealer to sort out. Now they've finished with him, Shaw is on his way here to hurt and possibly kill me.

The landline's shrill ring snaps my last functioning nerve. I stare at it but don't pick up. It rings again. And again. I sneak a peek out of the window. Coast clear. Soundlessly I lift the receiver and place it to my ear. Nothing. Then, measured nasal breathing.

'We know who you are,' hisses a nasal cockney whine I don't recognise. 'I'm watching you now.'

I slam the phone down. That's it. I'm out.

Gary takes an age to answer.

'I'm done with this,' I whisper. 'Someone knows I'm a cop. I've just had a text and a phone call saying so. I've got to get away from here now.'

'Calm down, Donal,' he patronises and I'm sure the fucker's yawning. 'Take a deep breath and tell me everything that happened tonight, slowly.'

I debrief him fully, but fast; because that's how much I treasure my intact and unflapping nostrils. I wrap up with the chilling twist that Pat Regan's girlfriend Tania is a colleague of Fintan's.

'So, it's not like I can do this one job and disappear into thin air after all, is it Gary? I want out now, before I piss them off any more.'

Gary hums lowly, giving it all King Solomon. 'It'll look more suspicious if you just disappear, Donal. It's like you've failed their test. Now they can trace you, I wouldn't risk it.'

'What you're not saying, Gary, is – now they can trace me, I'm fucked. That's why I don't want to poke the three bears again. If they do track me down and ask why I've made myself scarce, I'll just repeat what I told them tonight; I don't want to work with thugs, because I don't.'

'Before the ultimatum in the car park, did they agree to do business?'

'What? You mean before they decided to dice some poor bastard for kicks? Yes. Yes, they did.'

'Then you're in, Donal! Top work. They were just coked off their tits by the end. They'll probably wake up and realise you made the right call. You know what I say, paranoia is a soul eater. They need you more than you need them right now.'

'Seriously, Gary, I'm way out of my depth here. I'm drowning. You must have someone else who can step in.'

Silence.

'Okay, let me put it another way Gary, if you don't pull me out right now, I'm doing a runner. You can't stop me.'

Gary sniffs. 'If you do that, I can't protect you. My bosses will assume you've turned, gone native. You'll have no one, Donal. You'll be running for the rest of your life. Besides, if you scarper, or I pull you out, we expose Bernie. He's vouched for you, don't forget. Now we wouldn't want to piss him off, would we?'

Dawn's breaking outside; harsh reality in here. I'm trapped, just where Gary wants me. I'm beginning to wonder how much of this he's orchestrated. The coils of my mind rewind, fast, faster, then SNAP! The case stops at Mickey Sheeran and Commander Crossley.

After a while, it's impossible to tell who's handling who . . . the games they play to get what they want . . .

'Hang in there for another day, okay?' urges Gary, adopting his most comforting bedside manner. 'Let's talk tomorrow. It'll look a lot brighter, once you've had some kip.'

'Alright,' I say, but I know I'll never sleep within these four walls again . . . at least not voluntarily.

I take a circuitous walk to Arsenal, checking behind me often. There I find Fintan at his Sunday morning news desk – the kitchen table – chain-smoking and scoop-scoping the days' papers.

He pushes an open copy of the *Sunday News* my way. 'Judge's Girl is £100-a-Night Hooker' screams the front page.

'Classic Sunday paper, pre-roast sleaze,' announces Fintan,

jabbing his finger at Alex Pavlovic's byline. 'And a classic Princes of Darkness turnover.'

I skim through, hoping not to be contaminated by its unabashed tone of relish.

Twenty-year-old 'pretty blonde' Jennifer Garrett had been educated at £30k-a-year Roedean college, worked at Lloyds of London and lived at one of her father's 'swanky properties in trendy Marylebone'. She's turned her back on all that and now 'touts herself to boozy businessmen at a sleazy Soho cabaret bar.'

The story concludes with the classic tabloid disclaimer. 'Back at the hotel room, Jennifer offered full sex for £100. Our reporter made his excuses and left.'

Fintan leads me into the sitting room, inserts a VHS tape, presses play and provides ball-by-ball commentary. 'Gerry Woods, all-round surveillance genius, inserted a camera in a bedside lamp. There's Jennifer looking smoking hot, listing out her terms. Here's the Prince making his excuses and leaving.'

Fintan turns to me and waggles his eyebrows. 'Give it a few minutes. Now who can that be knocking? Why it's the Prince. We can't hear him anymore, because he's removed his radio mic in the hallway, but my bet is he's now flush with cash and busy revoking those excuses.'

Suddenly the camera spins, flickers and blacks out. 'That's the bedside lamp getting mysteriously knocked over, not the first time the Prince has suffered such misfortune, according to Gerry.'

He whips out VHS one, slaps in a second.

'But this is the first time I've ever found a use for a Corby trouser press. Courtesy of covert camera two, that humping great sea lion is the Prince of Darkness, giving the fragrant Ms Garrett three minutes of joyless, laboured missionary I hope she manages to blank from her mind before she reaches her deathbed.

'As for the Prince, he knows that shagging the mark is a straight red card. He's too toxic for any other newspapers. So, he's got to talk to us now, or this video will find its way to our incongruously sanctimonious proprietor.'

Chapter 53

Arsenal, North London
Sunday, July 3, 1994; 12.00

Gloomy Sunday; no Mam to call, no Matt to cuddle. Tomorrow, he turns twenty-three months. I bet Zoe's marking this minor milestone today, probably at Sylvia's. I bet every penny that Chris will be there.

'So Sylvia, Patron Saint of Unshakeable Conviction, how did you find it within your righteous self to so readily forgive the moneyed, titled, upper-class lizard who abandoned your pregnant daughter?'

It's been just a week since Zoe decreed me mentally unfit for even visiting rights. If she's going to cut me out of his life completely, she needs to do better than that. Nothing left to lose, I dial her mobile.

'I've been meaning to call you,' she gabbles.

I know enough to interpret that as: 'I've made a decision but I haven't been able to bring myself to break the bad news to you, yet.'

'Work first,' she says. 'Whoever held Julie Draper at that

shed in Pease Pottage was extremely forensically aware. It's been virtually wiped clean.'

I groan. 'Virtually?'

'There's no prints or DNA, just clothes fibres, some footprints. Dumped in the scrapyard nearby, they found a couple of empty cans of cellulose paint matching that on the block.'

'Can you text me the exact make of that paint?' I say, suddenly remembering Pat Regan's artistic aerosol attack on the man who refused to pay for his spicy pepperoni.

'Of course. What's got you excited?'

'A substance like that was used in an attack on a drugs dealer last year, and I know the identity of the attackers.'

'Is it these dreadful thugs you're targeting in Windsor?' she says, and I swear she's become posher in the past week. Singed by St. John, perhaps? I let it go.

'The thing is, Zoe, if we can connect Regan and his goons to the Julie Draper kidnap scene, we know they're already connected to Mickey Sheeran. This could be massive.'

'Just to warn you, the cans came up clean. It'd be purely circumstantial.'

'Well at least it proves it to me.'

'I'm really glad to hear it. But be careful, Donal.'

'It's nice to have someone worrying about me.'

'I still care for you, Donal, so much. You know that.'

'Consolation prize alert.'

She just wants to get this over with, so sticks to her script. 'You'll always be like a brother to me, and an uncle to Matt.'

Silence. Deafening, heavily-pregnant silence. Fuck it, I'm not speaking.

'I've decided to give Chris another chance.'

Morrissey's agonised yowls fill my head. *'I know it's over, and it never really began, but in my heart, it was so real . . .'*

'Good,' I hear myself say, shocked by my composure, more shocked still by an overwhelming feeling of relief. 'Can I make one final request before I slip out of your life forever?'

'Yes, of course,' she says, clearly shocked by my indifference.

'Find out what Chris does for a living, where he gets his money from and why he came back. Oh, and ask him what he would've done had you picked me instead of him. If you're happy with his answers, then you deserve each other and I'm delighted for the three of you.'

Chapter 54

Manor House Pub, North London
Sunday, July 3, 1994; 20.00

Ron Regan turns up and heads straight to the bar. He'd called earlier, asking for a meet, assuring me he'd be coming alone.

'Bernie doesn't need to know either,' he'd said, which troubles me.

He plants four pints on the table. 'I'm sorry about last night,' he rasps. 'The boys got out of control. They're under a lot of pressure right now.'

'No disrespect to you, Ron, you seem a straight-up fella, but I can't be dealing with that. It wrecks my head.'

'I know, I know,' he says. 'Look, from now on I'll make sure we conduct business when business should be conducted, before the pubs open.'

'Listen Ron, I'm not Mary Whitehouse, okay? I don't mind mixing business with pleasure. But it all got a bit *Scarface*, wouldn't you say? I'm not going to stab some lad I don't even know.'

'They're wishing they'd made the same decision. The

victim, Twomey, is under police guard in hospital. Pizza face has already given a full statement revealing all. The walls are closing in.'

I turn to Ron. 'Maybe they wouldn't be under so much pressure if they didn't keep hurting people for kicks. They're not professional.'

Ron shifts in his seat, cheek muscles twitching. 'It's not that. They've got a monster deal going down. That's why they're on edge.'

I'm desperate to get out of this whole business. Now, I see my chance. 'Hang on a minute, Ron. If they've got another monster deal going down, then I'm wasting my time here.'

'It's not E,' whispers Ron. 'It's heroin. If the boys can make this deal happen, they can fuck off to Northern Cyprus, at least for a year or two, until the heat dies down.'

'Christ, how much are they bringing in?'

'100 kilos. But they need your help.'

I check he's not joking.

'They've got a proposition for you, Donal. If you get on board, you might be able to retire too. They want to run it by you tomorrow morning. Can you come back down to Windsor?'

'Only if it's on neutral territory, and in public.'

'There's a pub near the train station called the William the Fourth. Noon. Like I said before, not a word to Bernie.'

Chapter 55

Windsor, Berkshire
Monday, July 4, 1994; 11.00

I'm so early they could rename the pub the William the Third. But I need time to key myself up, rehearse my messages. I'm hoping they'll be the last ones I ever have to deliver to these psychos.

Pat and Ron Regan arrive friendly, Walsh and Shaw hostile. I don't care; *they* invited *me*. If it all goes to plan, they'll bin me this morning and I can walk away from this kamikaze caper unscathed, physically at least.

I decide to make my 'it's not you, it's me' speech first. 'You need to understand something, gents. The IRA are in peace talks. As you may or may not know, my father is one of the negotiators. Spooks are doing their damnedest to discredit him. News that I'm running around knifing drug dealers would get me into trouble with people who, with the greatest respect, are far heavier than you.'

They all nod. Some facts are indisputable; you don't mess with those Provo loons. Gary came up with that this morning. The next part of my speech is all mine. 'That makes me toxic right now, so if you choose not to do business with me, I understand.'

They don't nod; shit.

Gary repeatedly pressed home a second point this morning: Don't tell Bernie about the brown.

'He'll sniff a massive reward and lose interest in the E. Remember, all we care about is the E. Keep pushing the E.'

'We don't need your E,' says Pat Regan.

'Well, sorry to say I'm of no use to you, gents,' I announce, getting to my feet.

'We need guns.'

I don't remember sitting down; I just sort of fell on my arse.

'I'm sorry?'

Shaw's been itching to put it up to me: 'If you're who you say you are, you can get us guns.'

'Have I mentioned the peace process? A stack of IRA guns being used for drugs crime in Windsor, the Queen's home town . . . I don't think so.'

Pat Regan smiles that smile I now recognise as the precursor to a psychotic episode: 'You get us guns, we buy your E. And we all keep Bernie out of it, because he doesn't like guns. You don't get us guns, we send Mr Shaw here round to see your ex and your boy.'

I freeze.

Shaw plants some photos on the table. My entire body unfreezes now, and spasms out of sync. I see Zoe and Matt walking out of our flat; Zoe and Matt at the park. Where the hell is Chris? For once, I want him there. His presence would be better than no protection.

Paranoia is a soul eater. Don't ever back down . . . don't look shocked.

Fuck, I need Bernie.

I lean back, away from the photos, and eyeball Shaw. 'Peace process or not, you harm them, and I'll get every batshit crazy IRA motherfucker on planet earth to track you down and really fuck you up, you short-arse piece of shit.'

Shaw's on his feet. Ron Regan grabs hold of his shoulders. I can't feel or hear anything now, just an express train screaming between my ears

'We need guns by Thursday morning, latest,' says Pat, clearly amused.

'You don't need IRA guns, Pat,' I protest, sheer rage snuffing out all fear. 'We're talking AK-47s here, M16s, stuff designed for massacres . . .'

'The bigger the better,' Pat smiles.

'Lead to protect the lead,' adds Walsh.

'I'll see what I can do,' I tell Pat, but I've lost all sense of what's going on now, or who I'm supposed to be working for anymore. All I know is; they've got me by the balls and there's no way out.

Chapter 56

Windsor, Berkshire
Monday, July 4, 1994; 11.30

I brief Gary from the Long Walk, threatening to take a short one right off this project unless he stumps up what I need.

'Twenty-four-hour covert protection for Zoe and Matt, starting right now, do you understand? And, unless you supply me with guns by tomorrow, this E deal is over.'

'Tell them you can definitely get hold of guns,' says Gary, for once sounding alarmed. 'But you need to shift your E first.'

'I've got no leverage, Gary. If you don't get me guns, you're placing my family and me in danger, because these people are nuts.'

'We'll take care of Zoe and Matt, Donal. You have my word on that. But you've got to hang in there. Tell them you need to make the E deal happen to finance the guns, you know, oil the wheels.'

'They won't budge.'

'I can't sanction guns, Donal. Surely you understand that?'

I understand only too well. 'Then we're fucked,' I say and hang up.

Chapter 57

Highbury, North London
Monday, July 4, 1994; 15.00

Riven with suspicion, the Prince of Darkness insists on meeting Fintan and me in a public place.

'His antennae were twitching right away,' says Fintan. 'I swear the fucker has a sixth sense.'

Ever the comedian, Fintan nominated the Bank of Friendship pub halfway up Highbury Hill, where we now slouch expectantly, waiting for Machiavelli himself to waft in. I tell Fintan about Pat Regan's 'guns for E' proposition and crude threats if I don't go along with it.

'How the hell did they find out about Zoe and Matt?'

I'd been thinking about little else. 'All I keep coming back to is that chat between John Delaney and Phil Ware in the Harp Bar, you know, the one picked up by Dusko, where they agreed to get the Prince to check me out. I think I've been checked out by the Prince, who fed Delaney who then passed my personal info onto Pat Regan because they're all in this together.'

'Jesus,' gasps Fintan, for once trailing the action. 'This is getting way too heavy. If it wasn't for Tania knowing me, I'd hand you a blank cheque and say go on holiday somewhere very far away, for a very long time.'

'If it wasn't for Tania knowing you, I'd already be gone. But if I vanish, they'll come after you, Fintan. They're that mental.'

Fintan adopts that pained, brain-burners-to-the-max expression. 'How the hell can we extract you from this? At least we've got history with Bernie.'

I nod.

'He's the only one you can trust, Donal. I don't understand why they're cutting Bernie out. You need to keep him involved because he's the only one looking out for you.'

'Gary says he doesn't want Bernie knowing about the heroin deal because he'll smell a reward and forget about the E.'

Fintan looks at me in disbelief. 'Where was Gary Saturday night? You need to tell Bernie everything and insist he's involved. We know we can trust him. Otherwise whose got your back?'

He stares at me defiantly.

'Okay, okay, I'll tell Bernie everything,' I say.

Fintan drops his elbows on the table and rubs his face. 'Your only way out of this mess is to make sure Regan and his mob get arrested with a massive quantity of E. Somehow, we've got to convince them you have guns stashed somewhere . . .'

Alex Pavlovic ghosts in, spooking us into silence. As soon as he sits, Fintan turns the laptop his way and presses the space bar. The Prince squints in confusion, then stares in wide-eyed realisation. Within seconds, his face turns soft, almost mournful.

'How did you persuade Gerry Woods to stitch me up like this?' he asks quietly, ashen-faced.

'He didn't know I was targeting you,' says Fintan, pushing the laptop lid down respectfully.

'And why were you targeting me?'

'We know Nathan Barry and/or Duncan McCall came to you with a story in 1987 or 1988.'

'That's ancient history.'

'Tell us everything, and I mean everything, Alex, and I'll personally destroy all evidence of this misdemeanour.'

He sighs resignedly. 'And if I don't?'

'You will,' smiles Fintan. 'Otherwise how will you finance your myriad addictions and ex-wives?'

'Are you recording this?'

'No. And you can search us if you want.'

He takes a deep, confessional inhalation, then blows us away.

'Okay, so we know the Brink's-Mat robbery in 1983 was the crime story of the decade? Laundering twenty-six million pounds in gold basically set up every criminal outfit in London. In late 1987, Nathan Barry and Duncan McCall approached me claiming that one hundred million pounds worth of cocaine had come in from Florida, bought with Brink's-Mat money. The main mover behind it was Mickey Sheeran who, as you know, made his fortune laundering Brink's-Mat money and is handled by Commander Neil 'Croissant' Crossley.

'They said they had proof that Crossley and two other top-ranking cops helped babysit the load to ensure it got through. The coke reached somewhere in the Midlands, where it was carved up and distributed. It all sounded a bit far-fetched to me.'

Fintan is bucking in his seat. 'Far-fetched? That's the crime story of the century.'

'Yeah but how could I even begin to stand it up? Nathan

and McCall were demanding forty grand up front for the evidence. I knew the editor would never agree to that, not without knowing what this evidence was and whether it actually qualified as proof. I wasn't convinced they had evidence at all, certainly not enough to run a story of that magnitude.'

'Oh Christ,' interjects Fintan. 'Don't tell me you approached Crossley.'

The Prince shrugs resignedly. 'Nathan Barry wouldn't budge. I didn't see any option. Crossley admitted that Sheeran was now handling him. They're in the same Freemason's lodge, and Sheeran holds the more senior position. So he controls Crossley, just like his accomplices in this racket controlled their handlers. They'd amassed so much dirt on Crossley and co. that not only were these cops powerless to stop their criminal ventures, they had to actively ensure the load got through.'

'Crossley told you this?'

'Off the record. He made me strip before he talked.'

Fintan leans forward. 'So, Crossley and these other top cops were being bribed by Sheeran and his associates?'

'It's not that simple. If Sheeran and his accomplices got caught, the first thing they'd do is dish the dirt on Crossley and the other two senior officers. We're talking about three of the highest-ranking cops in London. Think about it, every prisoner they'd put away over the previous twenty years would have grounds for appeal. Because of their seniority, they're connected to thousands of prosecutions. The consequences would be catastrophic.'

Fintan's eyes almost pop out. 'My God, it could've brought down the entire criminal justice system.'

Alex nods slowly as Fintan resumes. 'So, Crossley and Sheeran got their grunts to approach Nathan to try and force him to hand over the evidence?'

Alex looks pained. 'I told them he probably didn't have any, but they wouldn't listen.'

Fintan's face creases in horror. 'But they couldn't take that chance, could they, Alex? So, they whacked him. Nathan was probably killed for no reason, but he's still dead.

'Then they approached McCall, in case he was holding the smoking gun. McCall knew something, that's why he'd been summoned to appear at that inquiry into Commander Crossley, so they whacked him too. My God, Alex, by going to Crossley, you effectively signed their death warrants. You might as well have killed them yourself.'

Alex shudders. 'Nonsense. I was naïve, Fintan, okay? I'd just landed the job and, to start with, I genuinely believed Nathan and McCall were trying to shake me down. When I didn't cough up the money, they went to Crossley and tried to shake him down.'

Fintan's in full Rottweiler mode. 'What do you mean "to start with" you believed they were trying to shake you down? What did you find out subsequently?'

Alex hesitates; he's about to yank the pin out of this pulsing grenade. 'Seven months after Nathan got killed, the drugs squad busted a cocaine racket at West Norwood cemetery. They found twelve million pounds worth, a massive haul, but they only caught the small-fry delivery boys. The thing is, Nathan had told me that some of the cocaine load was being held there, but I hadn't believed him. I realised then that Nathan and McCall hadn't been bluffing, McCall hadn't committed suicide and John Delaney didn't kill Nathan Barry.'

My brain hurts: 'Why then are the police so hell-bent on nailing Delaney, Phil Ware and the Warner brothers for Nathan's murder?'

Alex shrugs as if it should be patently obvious. 'Delaney

was told by the Warner brothers to get Nathan Barry to the pub that night, leave at nine and then keep his mouth shut. The Warners told Phil Ware to bodge the investigation and keep his mouth shut. When they saw what happened to Nathan, they didn't need any more persuading to do what they were told, otherwise they'd get the same. Delaney and Ware kept their side of the bargain by deliberately misleading and undermining the cops all these years, so that the conspiracies have now pretty much buried any chance they'll ever get to the bottom of it all.'

'My God,' gasps Fintan, his gymnastic brain devouring scenarios. 'It's like JFK, Jimmy Hoffa, Marilyn Monroe. They just sit back and let the conspiracies grow. I bet, like Lee Harvey Oswald, whoever swung the axe that killed Nathan is dead. Delaney is the Jack Ruby fall guy. Crossley is J Edgar Hoover, the shape-shifting puppeteer behind the whole conspiracy.

'We've got two perfect murders here. First McCall, because they managed to get it recorded as suicide, then Nathan Barry, because they managed to fudge it and muddy the waters so thoroughly that the truth now can never be found. Who were the other two senior cops?'

'I've only ever discovered the identity of one. DCI Frank Vaughan.'

My brain thrashes about like a netted fish and I struggle to breathe: 'The same Frank Vaughan who was the senior investigating officer in the original Nathan Barry murder enquiry?'

Alex nods without meeting my eyes.

Fintan sits back, brain still whirring. 'So, Alex, let me get this straight, you were handed the scoop of the century, but you never wrote a line about it?'

'Without evidence, what could I do?'

'And you never took your information to other contacts you have in the police?'

'What, and end up dead like Nathan and McCall? No thanks.'

'I know you, Alex, you must've figured out some way of turning this to your advantage.'

He smiles. 'Have you honestly never considered why the cops turn a blind eye to our, shall we say, less palatable activities? Those senior cops had no idea I could never run this story. They thought I'd spiked it as a favour, in return for future favours. That's why they ignore our excesses.'

Fintan shakes his head. 'Alex Pavlovic, saviour of Fleet Street. I often wondered how you always got the inside track on major crimes. Like Julie Draper, for example. You were the first to report a connection with Suzy Fairclough's abductor, Mr Kipper.'

For the first time in this exchange, Alex looks guilty.

Fintan goes in for the kill. 'But you know as well as I do that Julie wasn't abducted by Mr Kipper, was she? I think your pals Commander Crossley and Mickey Sheeran kidnapped and killed her. Crossley had the inside track on the Kipper case and used that knowledge to derail this investigation. He set Donal here up to hand over the ransom money, knowing she was already dead, and knowing they could take advantage of his lack of experience, throw him under the bus later. But someone made a mistake dumping her body and it all started to unravel . . .'

My skin prickles with indignant rage. My God, Crossley set me up to fail! I was their Fall Guy. Village idiot indeed.

Fintan slams the table hard. 'Why did they kill her, Alex?'

Pavlovic's eyes seem to lose all life now, as if he's unplugged himself. 'I don't know what you're talking about.'

'As soon as they kidnapped Julie, you agreed to help

Crossley make it look like Kipper had struck again, didn't you? To cover his and Sheeran's tracks. You helped them fool the police and, with your expert help, they then fooled the media into falling for the Kipper connection, hook, line and sinker. My God, Alex, you're their PR man! How can you live with yourself?'

Alex gets to his feet. 'You can't prove any of that and it wasn't part of our deal. You asked me to tell you what scoop Nathan and McCall had tried to sell me. Now I've told you. Deal done. If that video ever sees the light of day, I will personally call in an outstanding favour from my old pals Sheeran and Crossley. Do you understand?'

Chapter 58

North London
Monday, July 4, 1994; 13.30

'Donal, what are you doing right now?' teases Edwina down the phone, and I nearly crash the car out of erotic terror.

'Nothing too pressing,' I wheeze.

'Good. I want to see your gift.'

'I'm sorry?'

'I have to sign Julie Draper out to the undertakers in a matter of minutes. I suddenly realise this is our last chance to get you close to her. I hope you don't mind, but I'm utterly intrigued by what's been happening to you. I'd rather like to see it first-hand.'

'I'm on my way.'

I follow Edwina into what looks like a chilled locker room. She grabs a drawer handle, pulls out a light-blue Julie. I lean down and make my silent promise; *help me help you, so we can catch the bastard who did this*.

I'm struck suddenly by an eerie sense of déjà vu; I shiver and spin around. But I've never set foot in this place before.

Why do I suddenly recognise those walls of chilled drawers? The metal tables? The trolleys and the blue and white floor tiles?

'Are you alright?' asks Edwina, but her voice sounds muffled, disconnected, external.

I'm beneath that monster electricity pylon again. The centre of my eyes blur and buzz in time to that nails-on-a-chalkboard white noise soundtrack. Faces flash on and off; the bony, emaciated, decaying faces of Nathan Barry, Duncan McCall, Julie Draper and me; our distracted, demented eyes, alive and dead. I see no love in this Edvard Munch vision, just the four of us trapped inside a merciless eternal thud, Dante's second circle of hell. I know I'm on the threshold, peering into limbo, purgatory or hell, maybe death itself. *Good God*, I think, *now* this *is hardcore*.

All spins. Flashes score my sight; the deafening squeals of braking trains shatter my skull. My feet flap like tassels in a breeze. A burst of noise, light and air flushes out my tormentors. I'm on the street, Edwina's got my left arm, a porter my right.

'Donal, what happened in there?' she demands.

'Don't know,' I croak, hoping to God it hadn't been some sort of premonition. Because if it had, I'll be joining those tormented souls very soon.

Chapter 59

Clerkenwell, North London
Monday, July 4, 1994; 16.00

At 5pm, Ireland kick off against Holland for a place in the World Cup quarter finals. Not long later, Bernie Moss will kick off at me for not telling him about the Tate gang's monster and very imminent 100 kilo heroin haul.

He's agreed to meet me here at O'Hanlon's on Rosebery Avenue where, once again, I'm forced to watch Irish players wilt under midday Orlando sun like microwaved lettuce leaves. I haven't even got Fintan here, the world's most obscene cheerleader, to whip me into a conspiratorial frenzy.

By the time Bernie turns up, Ireland are two goals down, I'm five pints bolder and ready to 'fess up. I tell him about my secret rendezvous in Windsor, Pat Regan's demand for guns, the threats against Zoe and Matt and, my biggest scoop, Ron Regan's revelation yesterday that they're bringing in 100 kilos of brown.

'During the pub meeting today, Walsh said something like "lead to protect the lead", so I'm guessing that they're bringing the heroin in with a load of lead.'

'And when do they want these guns by?'

'Thursday morning, latest.'

Bernie looks grave, murderous. 'If there's a major wagon of brown coming in, we need to focus on that.'

'Gary insists we make this E deal happen. He's got the Home Secretary on his case.'

Bernie scowls. 'E doesn't kill anyone. That's all political bullshit so Gary can get his OBE and Michael Howard can look like the nation's sheriff. If we bust these pricks bringing in a major load of brown, we'll save lives and put them away for a lot longer.'

'I can't go against Gary's orders,' I protest.

He senses my discomfort.

'Yes but 100 kilos of heroin at a street value of eighty thousand per kilo . . . you're looking at an eight million quid load. You do know we can claim ten per cent of that as a reward? We could both retire.'

I give him my best 'get real' stare. 'They won't trade a football card with me until I deliver guns, let alone divulge the details of their bumper heroin deal. I don't have access to guns, Bernie. Gary won't sanction them, for obvious reasons. Right now, I can't even make this E deal happen and that's the only reason I'm doing this shit at all.'

Bernie plants his meaty hands on the table and tilts forward, a proposition to sell. 'What if I get hold of two or three shooters? You offer them up as goodwill, you know, there's plenty more where they came from.'

My expression lets him know I'm open to ideas; anything to end this horror.

He sniffs defiantly. 'But I'll only risk it for the load of brown.'

Beer-bold, I bait him: 'Gary warned me you'd do this.'

'Do what?'

‘See the pound signs and forget about what we’re supposed to be trying to achieve here.’

Bernie baulks in disgust. ‘You don’t know anything about why I’m here, dealing with these fuckwits. No idea at all.’

His homicidal glare makes me cower in conciliatory resignation. ‘You told me yourself, Bernie: you missed the mischief.’

‘Did I fuck,’ he spits. ‘That shit killed my eldest boy, Vince, last year. Now my third lad, Darren, is dealing it for the bastard that killed Vince. That’s why I came back. I want to crush every fucker that imports and peddles that shit. Heroin’s evil, truly fucking evil. I don’t give a fuck about E, Gary or Michael fucking Howard, just as they don’t give a flying fuck about us.’

He thumps the table and sends my heart rate into orbit. ‘I saved your arse Saturday night, Donal. It’s now payback time, do you understand? We target the brown and forget about the E. We forget about Gary too. We can run this operation through Customs. We have to! Mickey Sheeran’s a registered police informant which means they can’t touch him.

‘And don’t even think about double-crossing me on this, Donal. Because when it comes down to it, I’m a badder bastard than all of them put together.’

He downs his second pint and walks out just as the final whistle sounds. ‘The Irish odyssey was great while it lasted,’ laments the commentator. ‘But the party’s well and truly over now.’

Chapter 60

Arsenal, North London
Monday, July 4, 1994; 22.00

I'm slouched on the couch next to Fintan, drunkenly gouching through an episode of BBC's *Question Time.* As ever, Fintan's getting totally sucked in, his constant bickering broken only by the occasional rant. At least it's stopped him railing about Ireland's meek World Cup exit.

Michael Howard, the 'hang 'em and flog 'em' Home Secretary is in full flow, threatening life sentences 'for anyone caught selling any type of illicit drug'.

'We should be thankful he's talking only jail,' says Fintan. 'He voted for the death sentence a few years back.'

'A conviction politician eh?'

Fintan gurgles in derision. 'Oh yeah, except he's currently cutting a deal with the country's biggest drug baron. Every time this guy reveals a stash of buried weapons, Howard's knocking a few years off his sentence.'

I can't believe what I'm hearing. 'Who sanctions that?'

'He's the Home Secretary. Your ultimate boss. He can sanction what he likes.'

Fintan turns to me, wearing an expression of pure wonder that I'd only ever seen before in black-and-white science fiction B movies.

'Oh my God,' he gasps. 'You've just given me the most sensational idea.'

Chapter 61

Arsenal, North London
Tuesday, July 5, 1994; 05.00

I open a third bottle of Shiraz and my mind to Julie. I know she's coming to me because I touched her dead body today. *Let's get it on . . .*

A cold curling draught snakes around my face and chills my neck, jolting me. But my body refuses to react. I can't move, leaving the terror free to pinball about inside me, an unearthed current of doom, growing stronger, pulsing harder. I know someone's watching me, and means to do me real harm, but there's nothing I can do about it.

Julie's wild, grotesquely gurning blue face is inches above my nose, grinding against glass. Soundlessly, she's pounding the lid of my glass coffin, trying to get at me; to save me or to kill me, I can't be sure.

I start to spin slowly, not head-over-heels but as if strapped to a knife-thrower's target board. Round and round I go, faster and faster, as the case rewinds through my mind. It stops suddenly at DC Rooney in the White Horse pub.

Every Rolex has a unique serial number and a recorded service history . . .

As I spin forward again, images seep through; Matthew terrified in the dark. Zoe in a bridal gown, casting a bouquet that, mid-flight, explodes into clouds of paper money. That black silhouette turning slowly towards me. I know that profile from somewhere, because it's Matt, but a grown-up version. My God, it's Chris. He's going to harm them.

Now I'm being buried alive. I can feel soil falling over my face. Then I recognise Morrissey's morose, overblown delivery and realise I've left that bloody song on loop again.

I run into Fintan's bedroom, flip the switch and declare: 'I've seen the light!'

'Oh Jesus,' he groans. 'You're not on the whiskey again, are you?'

'Wasn't it you who uttered the words "men who wear a certain brand of watch guide destinies", Fintan?'

'It's just an ad slogan. What are you on about?'

'I now not only know who abducted and killed Julie Draper, I know how we can prove it.'

Now he sits up and listens . . .

Chapter 62

Arsenal, North London
Tuesday, July 5, 1994; 11.00

Fintan plants a fax in front of me on the kitchen table.

'What's this?' I say.

'The answer to at least one of your prayers.'

I pick up the child's drawing, inspect it closely and see it's a handwritten map.

'X marks the spot,' he smiles. 'Below the map are the exact co-ordinates, and distances in feet from fixed landmarks.'

He slaps a second fax down. It's a list, written in Da's unmistakeable 'epileptic spider' handwriting. 'And this is an itinerary of what's down there.'

I'm struggling to believe what's trembling in my hands.

Fintan's loving it. 'Some fathers buy their sons a car, some a business, others an apartment. Mick Lynch presents his second son with . . . an IRA arms dump!'

I can't even speak.

Fintan smiles. 'The best bit is, they all need servicing and the ammo is sunk somewhere else. But if you bring Ron

Regan for a walk and unearth these babies, suddenly you've got real leverage. Tell him if they buy your E, you'll take them to the ammo dump next, which, of course, you'll never have to do because, by then, they'll have been nicked with the E.'

My mind is racing. 'They say only the man who sinks an arms dump knows the location. Christ, he must have put it there himself.'

'Forget all that, Donal. Jesus, have you any idea the risk he's taking for you here? Like I've been saying, he's terrified any harm might come to you. So quit all this "he doesn't love me" shit, okay? Because he does, and this proves it. He's just never had a chance to help you before.'

'I know,' I croak, my right eye fighting back a big old fat tear.

Chapter 63

Fontwell, West Sussex
Tuesday, July 5, 1994; 16.00

Armed with Bernie's GPS and a metal detector, I lead Ron Regan into the woods behind the Little Chef restaurant. *It all happens at the services . . .*

Ron has agreed to my proposition; once he confirms the existence and location of the guns, we complete our E deal. Once they pay me for the E, the guns and ammunition, I'll lead them to the second dump containing the bullets . . . then I'm out. Of course, it will never get that far; the plan is for the Tate gang to get arrested with the E during the handover tomorrow night.

I know Bernie would refuse to let me broker this deal – he's all about the heroin haul coming in later this week – so I've cut him out. He doesn't know about this arms dump or the fact I'm using it as leverage to make the E deal happen. I feel bad but the E deal is my ticket out of all this horror, once and for all.

'Why the metal detector?' asks Ron.

'If we can't find the dump, the metal detector will find

the spade. And that'll be buried at the top edge of the dump. Also, if anyone stumbles upon us, we're just sad lonely fucks looking for Viking treasure.'

Ron nods in approval. 'Very innovative your lot, I must say.'

'By the way. Can you let Pat know I've got an audition for Tania tomorrow morning?'

'That's great,' he says. 'Though she doesn't like mornings. What's it for?'

'I've got a director who wants to try her out for a costume drama. It'll be in an office in Soho, nothing glamorous. I'll text you the time and place.'

'She'll be made up.'

I pinpoint the arms dump and we take turns digging. Eventually, Ron hits plastic seven or eight inches down.

'I thought it'd be deeper,' he says.

We both set to work now, clearing soil until we reach the edges of the heavy plastic wrapping sheet. We slice it open to find a large cool box, the lid made airtight with rubber seals, which Ron sets about butchering.

'Hang on,' I say. 'Once you get eyeballs on these, we need to put them back.'

'Oh yeah,' he says, getting to his knees and working on the seals by hand.

Eventually the lid comes free, revealing a stack of enormous guns individually wrapped in transparent plastic.

'Christ,' gasps Ron, taking the top one out and lovingly stroking it.

The risk of being spotted by some dog walker or kids is too much for me. 'I've given you the inventory of what's down here, Ron. As much as I'd like to give each one of these pieces some individual worship, I don't want to get a life sentence for digging a hole.'

That pricks his reverie. 'Christ yeah, let's fill up and get the fuck out of here.'

On the way back to the car, I remind him that if they want the guns and ammo by Thursday, then the E deal must happen tomorrow night. I also point out that Bernie is no longer involved.

'He knows nothing about this weapons dump, and I don't want him to know,' I say.

'He gets a bit funny about guns,' agrees Ron. He stops walking and turns to me. 'There's one sticking point,' he says.

'What's that, Ron?'

'We agreed that Bernie would hold the money until we're happy with the E. Now Bernie's not involved, who else do we both trust to act as middle man?'

If I could kick myself, I'd be doing so repeatedly. 'Shit, I've grown to trust you so much, Ron, I'd forgotten about the middle man.'

'It's not me you have to worry about,' he says, and he's not joking. 'Why don't we bring Bernie back in?'

I try not to look panicked. Bernie will go mental if he finds out I'm going ahead with this E deal, which will scupper his planned heroin sting. He mustn't find out. 'Let's not risk it Ron. If he gets wind that I'm doing a sideline in guns, he'll go apeshit.'

'Right,' says Ron. 'Then it'll have to be the only other man we both know.'

I can't hide my confusion. Ron laughs. 'Have you forgotten already? You're old mate from Liverpool. Chris!'

As soon as Ron gets sucked into A27 traffic, I stride to the nearest phone box and call Gary.

'The E deal is back on. Tomorrow night.'

'Fantastic! How the hell did you pull that off?'

To avoid suspicion, I decide to aim squarely for his enormous ego.

'Like you said, Gary, I told him I needed the E deal to happen to oil a few palms so I can get them guns. They really want these weapons, which makes me wonder what the hell is going down.'

He barely lets me finish. 'Forget about all that, Donal. You make sure they go and pick up the E, then you're out, okay?'

'Now Bernie's not involved, they want this Chris St. John Green to hold the dough. What do we know about him?'

At last, I have a legitimate reason to dig the dirt on this fucker. If I discover he's up to no good, I won't hesitate in letting Zoe know, and not just for noble reasons.

'I'll see what I can find out. To be honest, Donal, if he scarpers with the money, it won't matter that much. What we need to focus on is getting the E in position, and making sure Regan, Shaw and Walsh pick it up. Nothing else matters.'

That's the second time he said that and I can't hide my irritation. 'Apart from my safety, Gary,' I protest.

'Of course,' he says dismissively. 'That goes without saying.'

Chapter 64

Mayfair, Central London
Wednesday, July 6, 1994; 09.00

The nearest we could get to a studio at short notice is the upstairs of the Blue Posts pub, around the corner from the famous Ritz hotel in Mayfair. We've nicknamed it the Last Posts, in honour of the dreary old hole's curious survival amongst London's most elite private clubs and art galleries. But it holds two key advantages for us today: a separate and secure dressing room, and proximity to Old Bond Street.

Last night, Fintan buttonholed some drunken luvvie actor at the Coach and Horses into playing the role of casting director. Worried that the old soak might forget to show, Fintan's personally escorting him to the scene of this morning's bold caper. I'm driving there via Angels costumers in Islington, where I pick a selection of size 8 period costume dresses.

As soon as I unlock the upstairs space, Fintan's 'casting director' recruit bumbles in sporting a beret, a Bloody Mary, an armful of ancient papers and one of those vast, elaborately arranged scarves that seem the sole preserve of darling theatre types.

'Geoffrey Selkirk, your casting director,' he beams, oozing studied voiceover sincerity and I like him already.

Fintan makes himself scarce with the spare set of dressing room keys as I run Geoffrey through his crucial role in our elaborate plot. One: this audition must last ninety minutes, minimum. Two: he must charmingly demand Tania 'get into costume' to help her performance. Three: she must leave all modern belongings – clothes, shoes, mobile phone and, critically, her Rolex watch – locked in the dressing room for the duration.

Geoffrey smiles. 'In my experience, an actress will take the best part of half an hour slipping into a single costume, so that won't be a problem. As for her locking away all of her accoutrements, I'd insist upon it before any audition, dear boy, so it won't require much acting.' He pats me on the knee, but not in a weird, creepy way.

'I feel like I'm in an Ealing comedy,' he adds, guffawing suddenly from the pit of his rattling chest, which quickly turns into an alarming, phlegm-churning cough. Before I can ask if he's okay, his trembling hand is lighting a Gauloise cigarette, naturally, and I wonder if actors ever *stop* acting. This guy is clearly on his way out. When is he planning to start being *himself*? Or is the real him so subsumed by the character he's created, that he's lost forever? Welcome to Soho.

Fintan's safely hidden away by the time Tania breezes in, brimming with nervous energy and desperation. I feel instantly guilty. Exploiting her childhood dream seems plain wrong. As if to drive the point home, Geoffrey announces he's selected for her a monologue by Eliza Doolittle in Bernard Shaw's *Pygmalion*. Is he kindly Colonel Pickering to my hideous Henry Higgins?

Geoffrey's busy explaining the importance of 'getting into role' and 'symbolically locking away all modern distractions' when Pat Regan lumbers through the door, holding a pint of lager and a packet of crisps.

'Moral support,' says Tania.

'Don't mind me,' grunts Pat as my heart falls out of my arse.

Geoffrey almost curtsies. 'Very nice to meet you, Patrick. Though I'm not sure an audience will help Tania here this morning.'

Pat glowers and I cringe. We can't have Pat hanging around the bar downstairs for the duration; he might spot Fintan sneaking in and out and bust our ruse.

'Maybe Pat can sit against the wall over there, you know, out of Tania's eyeline,' I suggest.

'Oh very well. But take that seat in the very corner, young man, and don't even think about tackling your confectionary,' harrumphs Geoffrey, playing an absolute blinder. Pat hasn't been told what to do for years and almost enjoys it.

Geoffrey packs Tania off to the dressing room with a script and a set of keys, then sits alone and reads.

Great, I think, *half an hour to kill with Psycho Pat.*

'What's this audition for?' he demands.

'Geoffrey here is a casting director for all sorts of stage productions. He has a black book of actors and actresses that he rates. What we're trying to do today is get Tania into his little black book.'

'He better not be rude to her,' he hisses, turning my spine to jelly.

I call over to Geoffrey. 'I'd say you're a very encouraging and gentle casting director, wouldn't you, Geoffrey?'

'My role is to nurture and nourish, not cull and weed,' he thunders.

Christ, I think, *he's amazing*.

'How's plans going for tonight?' mumbles Pat.

'My man is working on a location. We don't drop until the last moment, for obvious reasons.'

He nods. 'I've been thinking, I don't want this Chris St. John Green guy getting excited and running off with the dough. I don't need the aggravation. Why don't we keep things simple and bring him and the money along with us?'

Never have the money and the merchandise on the same plot . . . someone gets the pound signs spinning in their eyes and pulls a gun . . .

I know Pat Regan asks only rhetorical questions, but I can't have him thinking I'm a complete mug. 'I don't normally agree to having the merchandise and the money on the same plot,' I say.

'Yeah, but you know you can trust us, because we still need your ammo. There's something about this Chris I don't like. He's too smooth.'

I can't help myself. 'He looks, acts and sounds like a spook to me.'

'You think?' says Pat.

I nod.

'Right then, make sure the fucker's there.'

I think back to Chris's imperious arrogance when he sat at my kitchen table and announced he'd be marrying Zoe. He deserves everything that's coming to him.

'With pleasure,' I say.

We hear the dressing room door unlock and relock out in the hallway. Tania sweeps in looking knock-out in a figure-hugging bottle green gown.

'It's got no pockets,' she says, holding the dressing room keys. It's then I spot the Rolex on her wrist.

'You look radiant, my dear,' exclaims Geoffrey. 'What is *that* on your arm?'

'It's vintage,' she whines. 'And it goes really well with the dress.'

'This is set in 1913, Tania dear. Wrist watches hadn't been invented for another decade. Now why don't you hand over the dressing room keys and watch to Donal here, so we can crack on.'

Cue a toddler-tantrum pout as I fight an urge to actually hug Geoffrey.

'What difference does it make?' argues Pat.

Geoffrey spins around.

'I really must insist you keep your counsel, sir, when inside my auditioning zone.'

Pat looks rattled. 'Alright Dickie fucking Attenborough. Don't lose your beret.'

I jump to my feet.

'Allow me Tania,' I gush, racing over. 'Give me the keys and I'll lock your watch inside the dressing room for you.'

She takes off the watch and plants it petulantly into my palm. I take her dressing room keys in my other hand and walk out to the corridor.

It's just as well I stepped up for the task. At the top of the stairs, clutching the other set of dressing room keys to his heart in shock, Fintan looks every inch the Dickensian pickpocket. I hand him the vintage green Rolex and he scarpers.

Chapter 65

Mayfair, London
Wednesday, July 6, 1994; 09.40

Watch in cupboard. Regan in trouble. Me in car on Cork Street. Fintan's text mercifully springs me mid-audition, but only after I claim that Thora Hird's had a funny turn on one of my drama shoots.

I jump in his 'borrowed' Porsche and we roar off towards Whitechapel where I'm due to meet Gary.

'It took less than five minutes,' Fintan says. 'Julie Draper got that Rolex serviced twice, most recently late last year.'

'So, the Rolex watch given to Tania by Pat Regan the day after Julie Draper died belonged to Julie and we can prove it,' I say, mostly to explain it all to myself.

'Exactly,' says Fintan.

The sheer magnitude of this breakthrough requires considerable breaking down. He lets me draw conclusion number one. 'Regan, Walsh and Shaw kidnapped and murdered Julie Draper on the orders of Mickey Sheeran and Commander Crossley.'

Other jigsaw pieces now click together. 'The day we went on that drive with Ellen and Tania, when we found Julie's body, Tania said her boyfriend had given her that watch the day before. Regan had no idea it could be traced back to Julie through its service history.'

Fintan's already found the flaw in the prosecution case. 'Of course, Regan will say he bought it off some geezer down the pub. But what it proves to us is that they're working for Sheeran and Crossley, who must be financing this load of heroin coming in later this week. It's too major league for these clowns.

'But if Regan, Shaw and Walsh were to get busted with that much heroin, they're looking at ten to fifteen years apiece. You can offer them a deal to get those sentences slashed, if they agree to give evidence against Sheeran and Crossley. It's the only way you're ever going to connect this haul to the Big Two.'

I remind him that we already have dirt on Sheeran and Crossley. 'We can connect them to Julie's money laundering. And, although he doesn't know it, we've got the Prince's confession on tape.'

Fintan shakes his head. 'It's nowhere near enough. Bernie was right. You should scrap this E deal and stay tight with Regan until the end of the week, aim for the bigger scalps. You've already established the heroin's coming in with a load of lead on either Thursday night or Friday. Surely that's enough for Customs to work on? I'm sure Gary will see it the same way, if you tell him everything.'

I tell Gary everything, almost. The only thing I leave out is that the entire E deal pivots on the fact I have my own personal arms dump. I remind him of our intel that Tate and co. are bringing in a massive load of heroin just days later, but he doesn't want to know. He still sees nothing but the E deal.

'You were brought in here to nail the men who killed Molly Parker-Rae, and you've done a hell of a job persuading them to do this deal tonight. We stick with the plan.'

I know Gary's decision is cynical, political and self-serving, but I can't help feeling an enormous sense of relief. By midnight tonight, Regan and co. will be under arrest and I'll no longer be living a lie. The constant, creeping, cancerous fear of exposure has hollowed me out and ravaged my nerves.

Gary lays a map on the table.

'Ask anything you want, suggest anything you like, speak up now about anything you aren't happy with. If we can't resolve a single difference of opinion, we abort. Anything new I need to know before we start?'

I tell him about Pat Regan's insistence today that the E, the cash and Chris St. John Green should all be on the plot tonight. 'Pat Regan doesn't seem to trust Chris,' I point out. 'In fact, I'd wager he trusts me more.'

Gary smiles. 'That's music to my ears. And you'll know why in a minute.'

He claps his hands, rubs them together; time to scrum down to business.

'So, let me tell you Regan's plan first. He'll insist that you accompany them to the load. Once they know it's good, they'll waste you right there. They'll ask Chris St. John Green if he wants the same and take their money back. That's how these guys operate and that's why they want both of you there.'

What Gary doesn't know is that I have an insurance policy; Regan needs me alive so that I can lead them to the ammo dump. I haven't told him anything about this, and I don't plan to.

Gary continues. 'Now, our plan. Firstly, not a word to anyone about any of this, understood? We're right at the sharp end now. If something goes wrong, I need to know you didn't leak.

'Secondly, as you know, having the money and the merchandise on the same plot is usually a no-no. But this is different because we'll be there, waiting to strike. Evidentially and logistically, it suits us. But it also makes this entire operation far riskier, for everyone involved.

'The thing is, Donal, we need to catch them in possession of the E. But we can't afford to have them shoot you or take you hostage. So working this out has been like that riddle about the hen, the fox and grain. But I'm convinced we've finally cracked it.

'They'll expect you to travel with them in their Range Rover to locate and inspect the load. Chris St. John Green follows in your car, where he holds the money. Before you set off, you must insist on seeing the money in your car, which we'll kit out with recording devices after this meeting.

'Here is a map of where you're taking them tonight. It's straightforward.'

He jabs a pointer at the relevant spots, military-style. 'Windsor Road, B-road across Chobham Common, track into a field. Through a gate here. The load will be waiting in the field here, though you won't be able to see it in the dark.

'Before you set off, you need to provide a walkie-talkie for each vehicle and keep another on your person. We'll give you a set of four before you leave, juiced up, tested and set to the right frequency so we can listen in. En route, you tell them that the GPS they'll need to locate the E is hidden; only you know where it is. The gate into the field is controlled by a keypad code; only you know what that code is. This way, they need you all the way to the gear. And that's when we plan to swoop.

'When the Range Rover reaches this keypad-controlled gate, you need to warn them that it opens just long enough for a single vehicle to pass through, so they must drive in and wait for you. You'll need extra time to dial in the code a second time so that Chris St. John Green can follow.

'The code is 3106. Once the Range Rover is through and the gate shuts, you need to wait ten seconds, then radio the Range Rover and say the gate won't open again. Ask Pat to come over. Show him a different code, say you can't understand why it isn't working any more. He'll see that the gate's heavy-duty, no one's bulldozing it, even with a Range Rover. There's no other way for a vehicle to get through.

'Pat may well suggest you and Chris St. John Green accompany them in the Range Rover to the load. You've got to insist you can't leave fifty grand in the middle of a field. What if it's all a set-up, organised by Chris?

'He'll realise you won't let Shaw or Walsh sit there with Chris and babysit the loot. You're not an idiot. You say you'll stay with Chris. Tell him the GPS is sitting next to a traffic cone fifty yards up the track on the right, and the load is 500 yards further on. You've programmed the GPS to beep when they've hit the spot. That's also the armed response unit's cue to move in.

'Regan's going to ask how they're supposed to get out of the field, once they've picked up the gear. Use this map to point out a second exit, way over here. They can reach it simply by following the track all the way. A green button to the right of the gate releases it. Tell Regan you'll drive there with Chris by road and wait for them. He'll see this as their chance to relieve you of the cash after they collect the E without even having to fire a bullet. What do you think?'

I'm trying to picture it all in my head. 'So, just to be clear about it, as soon as they reach the E, 500 yards from the gate, an armed unit is going to jump out of the shadows and arrest them?'

'Shoot them if necessary.'

'That seems a long way from the gate, you know, if something goes wrong while it's just me down there.'

'Bottom line is, Donal, vanish before they reach the E. Any way you can.'

I groan aloud. 'I wish Bernie was still involved. I feel safer when he's around.'

'That's exactly why they were happy to cut him out. They know he wouldn't let any harm come to you. With him out of the way, they're free to kill you and Chris.'

I feel strangely betrayed; his blunt assessment of my worthlessness to Regan and co. makes me shudder. And I'm still struggling to read how Chris fits into all of this.

'What have you found out about this St. John Green character? What's his game?'

Gary sighs resignedly; I've pinpointed the chink in his otherwise bulletproof plan.

'We've checked him out and we're pretty sure he's one of us. Though exactly which agency he works for isn't clear. What I do know is we'll be listening in to your car and tracking it throughout the operation. The way I see it, Chris is the least of your worries.'

'If only you knew, Gary,' I mumble.

Chapter 66

Berkshire/Surrey borders
Wednesday, July 6, 1994; 22.00

I'm sitting in the front passenger seat of Pat Regan's Range Rover, scared out of my wits and realising I've made a huge mistake.

They don't need my ammo! I handed Ron Regan the inventory of what's sank in that dump. I bet they've already sourced enough lead for whatever atrocity they're planning.

Pat turns left onto Chobham Common, a black, deserted scrub somewhere between Windsor and Woking. Walsh and Shaw sit in the back. Chris St. John Green tailgates in Fintan's adopted Porsche, fifty grand nestling in the boot. Ron Regan is on standby somewhere nearby. I've obeyed Gary's order not to breathe a word about this sting operation to another soul. Almost. I told Fintan it's going down but I didn't say where. I realise suddenly; no one on this earth who gives a shit about me even knows I'm here.

What we need to focus on is getting the E in position, and making sure Regan, Shaw and Walsh pick it up. Nothing else matters.

I don't matter, to Pat Regan or to Gary my handler. And if I end up dead in a ditch tonight, it won't come back on either of them.

There's no medals for this work . . . in the eyes of the world you'll die a drug dealer or an underworld scumbag.

Right now, I'm Pat Regan's prisoner, and everyone in this convoy knows it. I've already compiled a mental list of ways this operation can backfire on me.

* They could toss the walkie-talkies out of the window, cutting me adrift from all back-up.
* Shaw or Walsh could place a gun to the back of my head and take control of the entire operation.
* If so, I'll have no choice but to lead them to the E, then make one last desperate dash for safety.
* They could waste me as soon as we collect the GPS. They won't need me after that. And back-up will be 450 yards away in pitch black, blind to my plight.
* Chris St. John Green could be in cahoots. Despite his noble, Victorian posturing, he'd love to get me out of the way. Why am I putting my life in the hands of a man who has already stolen my girlfriend?

I should've told Bernie everything, right from the start. As Fintan so rightly said, he's the only one who has my back. Fintan's so good at this shit; I try to imagine what he'd do right now. I've got to somehow borrow from his quick-witted genius. My life depends upon it.

Think, think, think . . .

First, I need to establish if they plan to kill me tonight. I'll ask them what they need all those big guns for; if they tell me, they're going to waste me for sure. Why would they risk it otherwise?

Regan replies right away. 'We've got a big load of brown coming in through Felixstowe Friday morning, so big that we have to make sure no one is going to rob it off us. There's some heavy Turk and Kurd gangs in London who'll be watching, waiting for a chance. When they see the size of our shooters, they'll back off.'

My God, it's a cock-waving exercise. They don't even need ammo! I'm a dead man walking.

In a half-hearted attempt to appear in control, I tell them about the code-controlled gate into the field, and the fact I alone know the location of the GPS, which will lead us to the load.

'Fine,' snaps Shaw. 'We'll rub you out after that.'

They all laugh, way too hard. My chops are so racked with terror that they refuse to concede even a fake smile.

'You should see his face,' says Pat, in hysterics now and I realise the three of them are coked off their tits. Of course they are.

Pat suddenly turns to me, unsmiling, staring hard.

'Don't you trust us, Donal?'

'It's not that I don't trust you, lads. It's just that I've been around the track a few times.'

'What the fuck do you mean by that?'

'Remember I took Ron down to see that horse running at Fontwell the other day?' I say cryptically.

Pat nods. 'Yeah, a real thoroughbred.'

'Well that horse is no longer running down there. It's been moved to a different race track.'

I've never been any good at bluffing, so force myself to stare straight ahead and count to twenty. Their collective silence speaks volumes. They still need those enormous guns to secure their delivery later this week. Surely, they can't kill me now?

'Why the fuck did you do that?' Pat hisses, finally.

'Insurance, Pat. In the betting world, it's known as laying off.'

'Right, so you don't fucking trust us then?'

He pulls up sharply. I can hear Chris skidding to a halt behind us. Next thing, I see stars. He's hammering the side of my head.

'I should put one in you right now, you sneaky Irish cunt.'

Walsh is holding him back. 'Fuck's sake, Pat, we need those shooters.'

I expect this may prove the only time in my life when I'll enjoy taking a hammering, confirming, as it does, that I've just saved my own life.

'Arsehole,' spits Pat and we set off again.

I breathe for the first time tonight. Thank Christ Fintan and Da came up with that arms dump . . .

He turns into the track and slows to a crawl. My guts clench. Gate and flashpoint ahead. I'll be getting out of this Range Rover and refusing to get back in it again. Will Pat buy it? He knows I don't trust them one inch. Maybe he's already smelling a set-up.

The jeep stops at the gate. I open the door when Regan grabs my arm.

'Don't do anything stupid, Paddy, or I'll plug you.'

I break free and leap out. Cold gravel feels soothing beneath my trainers, but my eyes struggle to adjust to the black. I walk towards where I think the left side of the gate should be and almost stumble into a ditch. A breeze seeks out my neck. I roll my shoulders, fail to stop my teeth rattling. Why is it so damned cold?

As I reach the keypad, my heart plunges into the pit of my stomach. I realise I've left my walkie-talkie in Regan's motor. Now I can't communicate with them after they go through the gate and back-up can't hear me. Should I go back and get it?

It feels like I'm stalling, so I tap in the code and watch the gate open ceremonially inwards. The Range Rover roars through impatiently, skidding to a halt about thirty yards ahead. Chris St. John Green could've made it through too; thankfully he's obeying orders.

The gate closes. I notice now there's no birdsong. The sheep in the field aren't munching; they just stand there. They all know something's going down.

Why is it so damned quiet?

Bang!

I'm on the ground.

Bang!

I scrabble towards the gate, peer through a gap.

Two more muffled bangs. I see muzzle flashes at the open, right-hand rear door of the Range Rover. Shaw cries for his mum. The black figure ghosts to the left rear side. Two more muffled bangs.

I hear St. John Green reversing the Porsche. Bastard.

Up front, footsteps scrape the ground, scurrying about, hunting.

'Other one?' demands a clipped voice.

'Gate.'

I get up and sprint towards Chris' retreating car.

The prick turns his headlights on, exposing me. I hit the deck. Bullets ping the gate, the ground to my right and the car. He turns his lights off again and stops; bullets ping off the Porsche, making more noise than the gunfire. He's reversing again at top speed, engine screaming; the fucker's abandoning me! I roll sideways towards that ditch and keep rolling until I drop and wedge into cold, wet sludge.

I smell cordite, hear Chris spin the car around and more

clanging ricochets. I hope with all my heart they plug the treacherous bastard.

Where the hell is back-up?

Four footsteps and two flashlights hurriedly hunt me. Closer, closer comes the scraping of gravel, that merciless white beam, burning through the grass and the leaves and the insects.

White scores my eyes. I close them and hold my breath. I know this is it. Ghostly echoes of Edwina's agonised words . . .

I just can't stop thinking about their final hours, left for dead . . . knowing no one was out there looking for them, or missing them or even thinking about them. They already didn't exist . . .

No one I love even knows I'm here.

A yellow splodge floats and pulses before me, then morphs into the face I need to see most. She's here. At last. She touches my face gently. Why didn't you come before? I ask. She touches my lips to quieten me, toasts me with those smiling eyes. She's in a good place. But she's not ready for me yet. Mam's eyes tell me I'm not going to die tonight. Or anytime soon. She came to let me know I haven't inherited the dreaded family curse. I'm going to be okay! I just know it.

A motorcycle rev jolts me, roaring off in a spray of gravel as shouting sounds beyond the gate. The gunmen have fled. I clamber out of my shallow grave and sit dripping onto the gravel. I dodged a lot of bullets tonight. Thanks to Mam, I now know I've dodged the deadliest one of all.

It took a brush with death to make me realise something pretty bloody obvious. I don't need to prove myself to Da, to Fintan, to Zoe or to anyone. I just need to start living my life on my terms. Be young, be foolish, but be happy.

Chapter 67

Central London
Wednesday, July 6, 1994; 01.00

Fintan's first on the phone. I'd disobeyed Gary's orders and pre-warned him about tonight's 'sting', I just didn't tell him where it was going down. Why? If I did get killed, I wanted the people who care about me to know it was for the agents of good. Secondly, if Chris St. John Green had been conspiring with Regan and co. to stitch me up, he'd have to explain himself to Fintan.

'Are you okay?' he asks.

'Fine.'

'I've just been told about it by a source. Fucking hell! Where are you now?

'Getting driven home by the police. They've taken my statement. Now they're letting me get some sleep.'

'Sleep? You? Yeah right! Listen, you can't go to your undercover address.'

'Why not?'

'Ron Regan will be looking for you, for starters. And you can bet he has sources. When he finds out Pat's dead, he'll want to know what happened. You're the sole eyewitness to a gangland triple murder, Donal. God knows who might be waiting for you there.'

I divert the driver to Arsenal where Fintan hovers at the front door, clutching his customary Londis bag of piss-weak lager.

'I'm going to need more than that tonight, Fintan.'

He smiles. 'Fucking right, I've got four bottles of Shiraz in the boot.'

I talk him through what happened, wrapping up with Judas in the swiftly reversing German-built chariot.

'That bastard St. John Green left me for dead. He set me up.'

I ask him what he's heard.

'My deep throat in the armed response unit says they had a team in position watching the E. Because the gunman used a pistol with a silencer, they didn't hear anything until bullets started hitting the Porsche, and even that was only picked up because the Porsche was bugged.

'Edwina showed up and pretty much called it right away. It was a highly professional job. The hitman shot Walsh first in the back of the head through an open rear door. Then he shot Shaw in the mouth, punching a big old hole in his jaw. He walked around to the other rear door, opened it, finished off Walsh, then Shaw. He then invited his accomplice to kill Pat Regan, who was shot in the head and chest.

'By the time the armed unit got down to the gate, the hitmen had fled on a motorbike. Did those guys definitely try to kill you?'

My cheeks blow in disbelief. 'There were bullets pinging all around me. When I rolled into that ditch, they spent at least a minute searching for me. I thought I was a goner. Thank God the back-up had been listening in on the Porsche, because those guys had no plans to leave until they'd killed me, I know that for sure.'

Fintan holds out his beer can: 'That's one hell of a back-handed tribute to your undercover skills. Whoever was behind these murders must have thought you were one of those scumbags.'

I clink. 'Who do police think did it?'

'They're refusing to speculate, of course, but it must be Sheeran and Crossley. It was so professional. And they had the motive. Crossley must have heard about the E sting tonight through his police snouts. They couldn't risk Pat Regan and co. getting caught and offered a deal, because their only leverage would be to shop Crossley and Sheeran, so they had them wiped out.'

The door knocks angrily. Fintan has to peel me off the ceiling. He looks through the spy glass, turns back, mimes a marauding monster and mouths 'Bernie'.

I slump in tired resignation, nod.

'He looks mightily pissed off,' says Fintan.

Fintan unlocks but doesn't get a chance to open the door. Bernie sees to that.

'Fucking hell, Donal, what the fuck are you playing at?'

My hands shoot up as I stagger backwards through the sitting room.

'Gary made me do it, Bernie. And he gave me strict orders not to tell you.'

'How did you persuade Pat Regan to buy your E?'

'I got them guns.'

'What about the brown? You've just blown my fucking pension plan, you stupid prick.'

Bernie is still approaching, fists bunched, eyes wild, as the house's furthest wall greets my back.

'Now I'm gonna rip your fucking head off.'

'Ah ah, Bernie,' sing-songs Fintan.

Bernie grabs me by the throat, lifts me off the ground and spins around.

Fintan's taking snaps with the tiny stills camera he carries with him everywhere.

'I don't fucking care,' he says, casually tossing me over the back of the couch like a used beer can.

'Bernie, I know when and where the brown's coming in. And how,' I pant.

He inspects me curiously, as a baboon might an insect that's just crawled out of his hairy feet.

'You better not be bullshitting me.'

'They told me on the way to the E deal. That's when I knew they were going to whack me. I'll tell you if you stop battering me.'

He lets me live a little longer.

I gasp: 'Friday morning, Felixstowe. In lead ingots.'

'Fuck,' he says.

'What?'

'Now I have to keep you alive, you little shit.'

'What do you mean?'

'We need to go to customs with this intel. They pay £1,000 per kilo seized, but the info has to come first-hand. You agree to a 50/50 split and I won't batter you senseless.'

'Sounds more than fair, Bernie,' I squeak. 'Why don't we finalise plans over a piss-weak can of beer?'

Chapter 68

Arsenal, North London
Thursday, July 7, 1994; 01.45

I'm briefing Bernie about the brown when an incoming phone message catapults me to the front door.

'What?' say Fintan and Bernie in unison.

'That snivelling prick St. John Green is outside.'

They chase after me. 'At least hear him out,' Fintan pleads.

'Fuck that,' says Bernie. 'Give him a right-hander for me.'

Chris stands defensively behind the Porsche; both the car and his characteristic cockiness shot to pieces.

'Sorry to inform you, Chris, I'm actually still alive, despite your best efforts,' I scream, striding around the car towards him.

He lurches to the front, speaking fast.

'I was trying to get you on the walkie-talkie. Why didn't you answer?'

I make another lunge, but he's lightning on his feet. I decide not to admit leaving my walkie in the Range Rover. What's that got to do with his abandoning of me under heavy gunfire?

'Funnily enough, Chris, I was a bit tied up dodging bullets. Why did you continue reversing when I was running towards the car?'

'I didn't see you until I turned the headlights on. Then you went mental so I flicked them off again. I stopped for you, but you hit the ground and vanished. Then bullets started slamming into the car. If I'd stayed another second, I'd be dead.'

'Bullshit. You stopped for a nanosecond, then broke the backwards land speed record. You wanted me killed, so you could have Zoe and Matt all to yourself.'

'Check for yourself,' he pleads, pointing to the car.

Fintan is already inspecting the damage, almost gleefully. 'To be fair, it does now resemble a burnt-out colander,' he smiles.

Reluctantly, I peel my glare from St. John Green's pleading eyes to Fintan's weather forecaster hands. Sure enough, the car's soft top is riddled.

Bernie's inspecting the damage, intrigued. 'If any of these bullets got through, you were a dead man. I can't figure out how a soft top stopped even one of them.'

Fintan knows the answer. 'Because it's been welded shut.'

Bernie looks at us in disbelief: 'What?'

I can hardly utter the words. 'Fintan got the roof welded shut. Those welds are what's saved the life of the man who stole my fucking girlfriend.'

Oh and what a great old laugh they all had about that.

Chapter 69

Felixstowe Docks, Suffolk
Friday, July 8, 1994; 11.00

Me and Bernie sit in my car, drinking instant coffee out of polystyrene cups and waiting for our ship to come in.

'How are you going to spend your fifty grand?' I ask.

'I'm putting it into my scrap metal business so I can give my Darren a job, get him away from that crowd he's hanging around with. What about you?'

'I'm going to put down a deposit on a flat in Crouch End.'

Bernie throws me a confused look. 'I thought she was shacking up with this Chris fella?'

'I just like the area,' I smile.

'You just want to show her she should have had more faith in you. Fair enough,' says Bernie and I realise he doesn't care two hoots. I'm just his cash cow and soon I'll be milking.

Earlier, my customs 'handler' Will confirmed that search teams were 'turning over' the only load of lead due in for several days; thirty-six large ingots from Izmir in Turkey. Gary gave us his blessing to take the intel to Customs.

Although our E mission hadn't gone to plan, he could now categorically state that they'd identified the men behind the E that killed Molly Parker-Rae. Job done. He's writing a letter to my boss recommending me for promotion. That fully-fledged, non-acting Detective Constable rank that has eluded me for two years is almost mine.

Yesterday, I found out that a haulage firm has already been hired to transport this shipment of lead to a storage depot just outside Atherstone in the Midlands. The company that owns that depot is based in the Cayman Islands and, two years ago, purchased three homes from Crown Estates in Croydon, via an agent called Julie Draper.

Forensic accountants can prove that the directors of that company are Mickey Sheeran, the gangster, and his handler, Commander Neil Crossley of the Yard. In other words, the drugs stashed inside these ingots can be directly linked to Sheeran and Crossley. As soon as the lead reaches the depot, warrants will be issued for their arrests.

Meanwhile, customs placed a tap on Ron Regan's mobile phone and can already prove his key role in this heroin deal. Bernie's convinced that, facing the prospect of twelve years inside, Ron Regan will turn Queen's against Sheeran and Crossley to avenge the murder of his brother Pat in what has already been dubbed The Range Rover Killings.

'The underworld would expect that,' he explains.

According to the customs lawyer, this will be enough to charge Sheeran and Crossley with profiting from drugs trafficking, for which they'll face sentences of up to twelve years.

In short, all that's needed to trigger their downfall – and expose the nexus of crime at the heart of Scotland Yard's top brass in the mid-1980s – is for those customs search teams to locate the heroin stashed inside the lead ingots.

It's our best chance, but also our only hope of putting

Sheeran and Crossley away. The taped confession of Alex Pavlovic, crime reporter and Prince of Darkness, that Sheeran and Crossley had commissioned the murders of Nathan Barry and Duncan McCall aren't enough to charge them. And whoever eliminated Pat Regan, Shaun Shaw and Craig Walsh also wiped out any chance of charging Sheeran and Crossley with the kidnap and murder of Julie Draper.

It all comes down to these oblong hunks of lead.

My phone rings. My hearts stops.

Will from Customs says: 'We've had to let those lorries go. We didn't find a single speck of heroin, anywhere.'

'Okay, Will,' I say brightly. 'Keep me posted.'

I tell Bernie 'still no news' and suggest he fetches more coffee. As soon as he's out of sight, I say 'Sorry Bernie', start my car and speed off in the opposite direction so that he doesn't murder me with his bare hands.

'Fuck,' I scream at my clean sweep of failures. Somehow, I've managed to lose the girl, the bad guys and the dough.

Chapter 70

Arsenal, North London
Friday, July 8, 1994; 21.00

'Well at least there's some good news,' says Fintan. 'The police now have to fix Jamie Benson-Smythe's war-ravaged Porsche. You should've seen his face when I handed it back to him today.'

I sigh, going through the motions. 'Raging was he?'

'He was absolutely thrilled. He's thinking of keeping it, as a trophy. No messing, he said it would provide a great talking point for his dinner parties. Can you believe this eejit?'

'Oh yeah, another one of those eejits with a good job and loads of money. I dare say he has a knock-out girlfriend as well?'

'He also has two special assignments from me this weekend.'

'Hang on, Fint, you said you wouldn't send him out for a packet of crisps.'

'The connections these toffs have, you wouldn't believe. They're all interbred, basically, then they attend the same schools and colleges and give jobs to each other's kids, who interbreed some more. Honestly it's worse than parts of Offaly!'

'You never quit do you, Fint?'

'So, first Jamie BS casually mentions that George Field MP is an old family friend. Since we printed that story about Field and his cigar fetish, we've had a whole raft of rent boys contact us with all sorts of lurid tales, most of it unprintable. I've sent Jamie down there today to meet with George and "Total Brunt" to discuss how he can help salvage George's political career, hinting strongly that if he's willing to throw a bent Scotland Yard Commander under the bus, we'll not run any more rent boy revelations and may even commend him for taking a stand against police corruption.'

'Let's hope the Commander he referred to on that tape was Crossley.'

'It has to be. They're all in the same Mason's Lodge.' Fintan's looking at me expectantly, about to burst. 'Guess who else Jamie's great pals with?'

I struggle to hoist a single disinterested eyebrow.

'Chris St. John Green. He's known him since Eton. He's heading down to their family pile tomorrow for the weekend with a specific brief from me: find out what the hell Chris is up to and who he's working for.'

My head nods but my heart's not in it.

'I thought you'd at least be vaguely interested.'

Fintan's like a dog dropping a chewed-up ball at your feet. He won't quit until you throw. 'It's brilliant work, Fintan. It really is. I'm just sick of getting my hopes up and having them dashed again.'

This dog bites; Fintan grabs my arm and squeezes hard. 'I've been treading fucking eggshells for two weeks and I can't take another second of it. Things didn't work out for you this time, but plenty of people are bending over backwards to make sure you get another shot at it. All you need is one lucky break for everything to start changing, Donal, so, in the name of all that is holy, get your head out of your hole and start using it, okay? Otherwise they'll be no one left to give up on you, you selfish prick.'

Chapter 71

Arsenal, North London
Saturday, July 9, 1994; 09.00

The same images and phrases torment me all night, just as they have every sleep since Julie Draper last came to me Tuesday night. Matthew terrified in the dark. Zoe in her bridal gown, tossing great bundles of cash. Tania's voice: *Once you've had twenty-five, you don't want less . . .*

Chris in silhouette, turning slowly, malevolently.

Gary's pearl of wisdom: *They're still petty criminals at heart . . . they have to try to mug off the other party in any deal.*

A fresh twist this time; deafening bangs that turn out to be someone trying to hammer their way through our front door. Except those knocks are real, and furious.

The big red face gurning through the spyhole is just about the last I want to see right now, but he's not taking an unanswered door for an answer.

'Bernie, I can explain . . .'

'Yeah forget all that,' he says. 'Ron Regan's got greedy. Don't they always? Not content with making a couple of million out of the 100 kilo heroin importation, he's decided to double-cross Sheeran.'

I try not to look thick.

'Instead of leaving the lead ingots buried in the ground as ordered, he can't resist trying to fiddle an extra few quid on the side. Ron and his pal dug them up and they're touting them around as scrap.'

'So there *was* heroin in those ingots?'

Bernie nods impatiently. 'Yeah! I don't know what those Customs search teams were playing at. I offered Regan £700 for the lead. He wasn't happy with that so he's ringing round a few other dealers.'

'Jesus, Bernie, all we need is a trace of heroin inside that lead and we've got them,' I cry. 'You've got to get hold of it. £700 is peanuts. Offer him more.'

'If I suddenly offer him more, he'll smell a rat. We need to find out why customs missed the brown. Call your handler and find out.'

I ring Will and break the news; somehow, 100 kilos of heroin slipped through their search team's fingers. Minutes later, he gets back.

'They drilled into each ingot multiple times at different angles,' protests Will.

'How big was each ingot?'

'400 centimetres by 154 centimetres, or about 13 feet by 8 in old money.'

'And how long were the search team's drill bits?'

'Er let me see,' says Will, fumbling about. 'Twenty-five,' he says finally.

'Inches?'

'Er no,' Will mutters quietly. 'Twenty-five centimetres.'

Vingt-cent, I think, it's all connecting . . .

'No wonder you didn't find any of it, Will.'

'But they drilled those ingots all over. The smugglers must have known the length of our drill bits. Jesus.'

'Yeah well thanks to Bernie, we've just been presented with a second chance.'

Chapter 72

Slough, Berkshire
Saturday, July 9, 1994; 14.00

In the end, Ron Regan agreed to sell the lead ingots to Bernie, so long as Bernie turned a blind eye to one final fiddle. As customs 'search teams' butcher the ingots in Bernie's yard, he tells me how Ron Regan felt compelled to stiff his confederates until the bitter end.

'He insisted on cash for the lead, of course, and on charging VAT at 17.5 per cent, which he promptly removed from the envelope and stuck in his back pocket before ripping up the invoice and receipt.

'So, out of this scrap deal, he's split the £700 with his pal and made an extra £122.50 in VAT. In other words, for the princely sum of £472.50, he has landed himself a life sentence and sold out the nation's deadliest and most untouchable crime syndicate. And he wouldn't even let the 50p go.'

They're still petty criminals at heart . . . they have to try to mug off the other party in any deal.

Right on cue, the frenzied yelps of sniffer dogs seal the

fate of Mickey Sheeran, Commander Neil Crossley and Ron Regan. Will from Customs almost gallops over to confirm what we've just witnessed, and agrees that office-bound Fintan deserves to hear the news first.

As ever on a Saturday afternoon, he's frantic. 'You've got to get them to hold off charging anyone until tomorrow,' he says.

'I'm not sure I can do that, Fintan. And why would I?'

'Let's just say something sensational has cropped up. And you owe it to Nathan Barry's family.'

'I don't have any say in this.'

'Yes you do. Tell your handler Will that if he holds off charging anyone for twelve hours, I won't run the story about how, despite top-grade intelligence, customs allowed 100 million pounds worth of heroin into the country. Scrap that, put me straight onto him now.'

Will nods a lot, loses colour, then says: 'Off the record, you don't have to worry about *sub judice*. We'll be arresting them this evening but not charging them until much later tomorrow. But in return for this, Customs will be expecting extremely positive coverage when this case goes to trial.'

Chapter 73

Arsenal, London
Sunday, July 10, 1994; 09.00

'Where there's a gutless Will, there's a way,' smiles Fintan, presenting me with a copy of today's *Sunday News*.

Ex-Police Chief Murder Probe, screams the headline. '*Yard Commander and cop killer Sheeran "paid for murder of private eye"*. Exclusive, by Jamie Smythe-Benson and Alex Pavlovic.

'You gave Pavlovic a byline?'

'He'd nothing to do with this story, but it totally fucks his relations with Crossley. That'll teach him to threaten me.'

The scoop, based on the explosive claims of 'committed anti-corruption campaigner' George Field MP, claims to 'crack the six-year riddle of the country's most notorious unsolved murder.'

Field reveals that Nathan Barry, a constituent who'd been working on top-secret Tory projects in January 1988, handed him a sealed envelope 'containing the names of two men he claimed wanted him dead'.

According to Field: 'Nathan instructed me that, in the event of anything untoward happening to him, I should pass the envelope to a trusted senior police officer.'

After Nathan's murder, the MP for Lingfield opened the envelope, found the names of Commander Crossley and Sheeran inside, along with a list of allegations Nathan had been about to leak to an unspecified Fleet Street source.

In an extraordinary twist, Field reveals how he and Crossley belong to the same Freemason secret society lodge in Lingfield, where Mickey Sheeran holds the role of First Warden, or second-in-command.

According to Field: 'Out of courtesy, I brought the matter to Crossley's attention. He demanded to see the note and insisted it was nonsense, so I let the matter lie. However, from what I've since found out about Crossley, I feel duty-bound to follow my conscience and go public with my concerns.'

Field goes on to explain how 'several junior members of the Lodge later approached the Nathan Barry investigating team with claims to deliberately muddy and mislead the investigation, including a Detective Constable Neil Rooney and local businessman, David Bremner.'

Fintan takes a long, self-satisfied drag on his cigarette. He then surveys me, as if weighing up my mental state for further revelations.

'Spit it out then,' I say.

'This wasn't Jamie Benson-Smythe's only scoop this weekend. As you know, he spent Saturday night down in Somerset with the St. John Green clan. The champagne was flowing and it all got, as he put it, a tad lairy. First thing Chris confides is that he informs for Customs, who turn a blind eye to his own drug importations. But he's been sailing too close to the wind and is desperate to get out before he ends up either in jail or dead.

'Turns out Uncle Cyril St. John Green passed away late last year and left them all a shitload of money in trust funds. Old Cyril was a bit of a hairshirted Presbyterian moralist and attached lots of bespoke conditions to each trust and how and when certain monies are to be released. Guess what he demanded of young tearaway Chris?'

I can see what's coming. 'That he makes an honest woman of the mother of his bastard child?'

'He won't get a penny until he marries her and, better still, if they divorce, the money tap will be turned off.' Eyebrows like kites, he produces that vaguely deviant Jack Nicholson smile. 'Now, I wonder does Zoe know anything about this?'

My gaze returns to his newspaper. I flick through some more pages, allowing his game-changing newsflash to sink in.

For once, he cracks first. 'Well? She'll see right through his motives now. This will blow that smug, upper-class gobshite out of the water.'

I stop at page 44; Sandra's photo casebook. There's Tania, in a green thong and see-through bra, playing the part of a reluctant girlfriend being pressured by her boyfriend into group sex.

I turn the paper towards him. 'Ever since I got her that audition, Tania's taken a right old shine to me.'

Fintan frowns and blinks at the same time, like an owl in a headlock.

'What do you mean?' he laughs, but in a decidedly unamused way.

'I bumped into her at the police station a few days back. They needed statements from both of us about Regan and co. Anyway, we got talking and really clicked. We went for a drink last night and had a little snog at the end. She's invited me round to hers tonight.'

'You old dog. What about Zoe, Matt . . . the dirt on Chris?'

'I have to let Matt go, for everyone's sake. I've done all I can to try to be a part of his life. No one else wants it. I want him to forget about me, for his sake.'

'That's really fucking big of you pal. And noble to boot.'

'Oh it's not that,' I laugh. 'I just want Zoe to be really unhappy.' I giggle again at the sheer emotional recklessness of it all.

'Jesus,' says Fintan, shaking his head with a mixture of pride and disbelief. 'Hey, I bet Tania's found out about your fifty-grand reward money. That's what's going on here.'

'Probably,' I say. 'But what the hell? As Ma would've said, Be Young, Be Foolish but Be Happy, right?'

'Damn right.'

Epilogue

Donal Lynch was tested for Fatal Familial Insomnia, got the all-clear and promptly blew his Nathan Barry reward money taking Tania on trips to the world's best Shiraz vineyards. Days after the money ran out, he and Tania split but remain good friends.

Zoe married Chris St. John Green in one of the decade's most lavish society weddings. Donal Lynch declined an invitation to attend and severed all contact. The couple separated soon after.

Gangster Mickey Sheeran and Scotland Yard Commander Neil Crossley were sentenced to life imprisonment for trafficking heroin and the murder of Nathan Barry. Although the Julie Draper murder remains officially unsolved, Sheeran and Crossley were named as her killers in Fintan Lynch's true crime best-seller, *The Curse of Brinks-Mat*. On his wine-based world travels, Donal Lynch sent postcards to Crossley in prison from several exotic locations, always signing off 'With Love, The Village Idiot'.

Private investigator John Delaney and ex-cop Phil Ware won compensation from the Met Police for malicious prosecution, but were later jailed for phone hacking celebrities, along with crime reporter Alex Pavlovic.

Edwina Milne retired from the Home Office and dedicated herself to the investigation of unexplained phenomena and spiritualism. She is now one of the highest-paid speakers on the US paranormal lecture circuit.

Mick Lynch died on Easter Sunday 1996 with both sons by his side. His last words were a confession to his younger son Donal; he'd ordered the murders of Regan, Shaw and Walsh, but only after they'd threatened Zoe and Matt. The IRA contract killers sought out Donal after the murders that night on the specific instruction of his father, to ensure that he was okay.

'I just never had the chance to help you before,' were Mick Lynch's final words, before he grabbed and held Donal's arm with all he had left.